ONLY THE IMPOSSIBLE

If only Alix knew, Gasca, the old priest thought. If only Julian had told her. The power of the Magdalene was too powerful to be merely wished away; it had to be either rejected or embraced—yet first of all it must be faced. The fact was that Alix *did not* know. Julian *had not* told her. Now, she wore at her neck the key to a mighty power that more than one man had been willing to kill to possess.

The truth was there, plain to discern, as it had been since the day that poor foolish bastard Jacques de Molay called down the wrath of God on Philip of France through lips that were already charring black from the witchflames.

". . . Unto the thirteenth generation," the Grand Master of the Templars had cursed, as throughout all of Europe his once-proud Knights Templar were grappled down from the sanctity of their holy places and ground into the dust.

Now Alix was in the midst of a vendetta that had ripened for more than a hundred years.

"The Magdalene," Gasca whispered.

A dead man's curse and vengeance had kindled the beginning of the Maltese Star. He had no idea exactly where Alix's fate might lead her but he was almost certain it would not be to the quiet of a convent.

Gasca struggled to think. Yes, perhaps someone else—someone who had already begun to be tempted. He searched his memory and plucked out Alix's smile and the way her eyes had lighted when she spoke, though briefly, of the Knight Brigante. He compared them to the way her mother's eyes had shone when Olivier Ducci Montaldo was near, and those of Francesca—dear Francesca—when there was even the mention of Belden of Harnoncourt's name. The Maltese Star had carried bloodshed and tragedy to these women but it had also brought them love in the end. It had healed them.

But none of them had ever had to touch what lay before Alix. None of them ever had had to go that deeply—or had been so alone.

The old priest smiled as he remembered Latin words from his first year of priestly study. *Ad impossibile nemo tenetur.* No one is held to that which is impossible. He had found these words to be true many times in his own life. He prayed that they would be true for Alix as well.

BOOK YOUR PLACE ON OUR WEBSITE AND MAKE THE READING CONNECTION!

We've created a customized website just for our very special readers, where you can get the inside scoop on everything that's going on with Zebra, Pinnacle and Kensington books.

When you come online, you'll have the exciting opportunity to:

- View covers of upcoming books
- Read sample chapters
- Learn about our future publishing schedule (listed by publication month *and author*)
- Find out when your favorite authors will be visiting a city near you
- Search for and order backlist books from our online catalog
- Check out author bios and background information
- Send e-mail to your favorite authors
- Meet the Kensington staff online
- Join us in weekly chats with authors, readers and other guests
- Get writing guidelines
- AND MUCH MORE!

**Visit our website at
http://www.kensingtonbooks.com**

THE MALTESE STAR

Deborah Johns

ZEBRA BOOKS
Kensington Publishing Corp.

http://www.kensingtonbooks.com

For

MARSHA, DERRICK, JANINE, LYNN

The Kids

How seductive is war!

Sir Jean de Beuil
1415

Castle

One

It was just a dream and Alix knew it. But it was also real and she knew this as well. In her dream or out of it, the man and woman were in love. One could tell this. *She* could tell this, as she stood within her dream, standing just a little away from them and staring through her clear turquoise eyes at their shared dark beauty.

The two of them fit so well together, as if they had always been in love and always would be. Alix would have had to be blind not to see this. It was evident in the way the man took the woman's hand and tucked it around the safety of his arm, the way his soft eyes smiled down into her even softer ones, the way he reached down and gifted her with the last wildflower that remained upon their path. Alix had heard that he'd always been like this with this woman. He could not help himself. Since childhood, whatever his hand fell upon, whether a diamond or a dandelion, he had given it to Solange.

He, Robert de Mercier, one of the mightiest nobles in mighty France, wanted to give her everything that belonged to him. Even after all these years and the birth of their son, his love for this woman was palpable. Alix could feel it scintillate the air around her. She tasted it on the bile in her throat. She knew that this love was not a dream and that it would not pass with waking.

If anything, Robert's passion for Solange had grown through the years, especially after the birth of their child—his child. Any woman could see the signs of his passion, especially a woman who loved Robert as much as Alix did. Who needed him as much as she did. She watched as Solange reached to brush a wayward leaf from his cloak and smooth back a curl in his crisp, dark hair. Wifely gestures.

Except that it was she, Alix, who was this man's wife.

> *The Count de Mercier has ever but one love.*
> *His heart forever.*
> *His childhood flower, Solange.*
> *His life's one quest.*

How easily troubadours and jongleurs gossiped in their witty tunes about the passions and the sentiments of life, not thinking that what was love for one was often heartbreak and humiliation for another. Or not caring. For years musicians had earned bright silver half-livres by warbling on and on about the great love Robert, Lord de Mercier, bore his peasant mistress. Certain sensitive noblewomen, safely cocooned within the steel clauses of their own carefully arranged marriage contracts, had been known to swoon sympathetically at the mere mention of so great a passion. The scandalously impossible *liaison* between a First Peer of France and one of his serfs could only be rationalized by thinking of it as the truest of true loves.

Love was the basic gossamer intertwined within all of chivalry's most resplendent myths. It was deemed as important to life as bread, and almost as necessary as battle and conquest. Thus, everyone in France, be it the humblest Parisian glover or the king himself,

knew of Robert's passion for Solange. But unfortunately—at least for Alix—there were too many other
tales to carry in these warring days for the story to
have worked its way throughout the rest of Europe. It
would have had to be startling indeed to have traveled
as far as the Emperor Sigismund's court in Hungary.
No one knew or had time to care about the niceties
of a French love story there. Life was too real and too
rugged. It had to be seized quickly and on its own
terms. Which is why Alix's loving but unsuspecting parents, Count Olivier Ducci Montaldo and his wife the
Lady Julian, had betrothed, dowered, and married
their only child into this nightmare.

Alix herself had learned the truth soon enough. It
had been waiting in the courtyard of her husband's
castle to greet her two years ago, when she had arrived
fresh from her marriage at the Cathedral in Buda. She
had been all of sixteen years old. The truth had been
dressed in rich blue velvet and pearls. The truth had
been dark and graceful and full, not thin and light as
Alix herself was—the kind of woman who, even now
that she was wedded, could easily have passed for a
boy. The truth had taken Robert's hand and smiled at
him and led him away.

"He had no choice." For an instant, in the dream,
Solange turned to face Alix and her eyes filled with
something that might well have been compassion. "He
needed to make a noble marriage. He needed to pro-
duce a legitimate heir, or else his lands would have
been forfeit to the Duke of Burgundy. You know that
as well as I. He told you so himself. Robert did not
marry me because he could not, but he has always
loved me. He will always love me. I am the mother of
his only child."

Even in her sleep Alix felt the pain of this as she
clenched her hands, digging her fingernails deep,

deep into her own flesh. Any mention of the son
Robert had fathered upon his mistress brought out the
same shameful reaction. Alix could not help herself.
She fought against the feeling and loathed herself for
it and confessed it repeatedly to Padre Gasca, but she
hated Solange's child.

Above all else, she hated the child.

Soon after their arrival and the meeting with Solange,
her husband's visits to her chamber—never frequent or
especially ardent, even during the early weeks of their
marriage—had ceased completely. Alix had heard
chambermaids snickering behind their hands as she
passed through the cold and friendless halls of her new
home. Yet she knew that one day Robert must return to
her. He had no choice. He needed an heir—a legitimate
heir—or else his lands would be confiscated and devolved to Lancelot de Guigny—or worse, to the new upstart warrior lord, Severin Brigante Harnoncourt, who
eyed them from Angevin, Italy. It was a universal truth
that in this, the year of Our Lord 1414, a legitimate heir
could only be begotten upon a legitimate wife. The
Duke of Burgundy's threats had been enough to make
Robert marry her. Surely in the end they would be
enough to make him bed her again as well. Especially
now that Burgundy had taken the particularly risky step
of siding with the English against his own liege lord, the
King of France. Alix, never particularly prayerful in the
past, prayed each night that Robert would come to her.
She loved her husband. She had never loved anyone
before him, and in her heart she was certain that she
would never be able to love anyone else. Despite everything, she must continue to love Robert.

Yet that did not mean that she loved his son. She
fought against it; she prayed against it. She had to continue reminding herself that the pain in her life was
not the fault of a six-month-old boy. Nothing mattered;

no argument helped her. Robert's child should have been hers.

Things were different now, however. They had changed. Robert would not be able to refuse her much longer, not with the Duke of Burgundy turned traitor. Not with Guigny and that upstart Harnoncourt both threatening his lands. The very air they breathed was filled with the scent of war and usurpation. It was only a matter of time now. Robert must come to her. He must put her to bed with his heir.

Alix shivered in her sleep and snuggled more deeply into the shelter of her fox fur blankets. In her dream she watched Robert as he took his mistress's hand and crossed toward the dense, dark forest that lay beyond his castle. Alix had seen him do this a thousand times before in the reality of wakefulness, but she frowned now in her sleep. Something was wrong. Something was missing. But then Alix saw the two of them turn back and smile at the young child who gurgled and waved at them. For an instant all time stopped, and the three were framed in a golden glow of falling autumn leaves. The child giggled rapturously, and the sound of his happiness rippled upward into the sky and the clouds that were just beginning to form upon its surface. Even the ravens, flying swiftly south and away from the threat of winter, stopped to squawk and flutter, obviously wanting to be part of the pretty scene playing out below them. The beautiful, loving parents; their perfect, happy son. Alix heard the boy's laughter ring through her dream and she winced.

Then, from her place just outside the circle of their love, Alix sighted her husband's young squire rushing toward them. He ran forward with the intense, slow motion that one saw in a nightmare that was just about to deepen. But this was not what had attracted Alix's attention. Her forehead crinkled in perplexity as she stared at the running youth, as she tried to piece together what was wrong. And then she recognized his livery. Robert's squire no longer sported the crisp silvery blue of the Counts de Mercier. His tunic was a blaze of bright scarlet, and in his hand he carried the standard of a scarlet flag that rippled and undulated over his head. Alix frowned at this. What could it mean, all this red? All this running? Whose colors did he wear? Who called his allegiance now?

"Alix."

She heard Robert call her name and she turned toward his beloved voice, just as she always had and just as she doubtless always would. She thought her heart would burst with love for him.

"You must care for Yvrain now," said the man to whom Alix was married. "You must see that he is kept safe for Mercier. You must promise me that."

Alix hesitated.

"You must promise me," Robert insisted. His image had grown faint but his voice still carried. "Promise me before it is too late."

Not wanting to, the Countess de Mercier nodded.

The babe was alone now, and he was no longer laughing. His parents had moved far, far away, almost to the very edge of the forest. At the tree line, they turned to look back at him with sad, reluctant faces. But they did not come back. They did not motion for him or wait for him. They moved on.

Alix shivered again, and as she lay dreaming she automatically reached to touch the Maltese Star that hung at her throat. It was the same small golden, six-pointed charm that had belonged to both her mother and her grandmother. Alix felt the amulet grow warm and move just slightly beneath her fingers. She felt its power. For the first time in a very long time she let it call her back to Belvedere.

That is when the screaming started.

At first she thought that this, too, was part of the dream. These cries for help and mercy and the ring of clanging steel. They would fade as well with wakefulness, even as Robert and Solange were fading. And Yvrain with them. In fact, Alix could no longer see any of them, though she strained to do so. She had no wish to leave her dream. Somehow she knew that waking would be worse than any nightmare.

"Robert!" Alix did not care about Solange now; she was no longer wracked by jealousy. She and Robert could work things out—as long as he didn't leave her. As long as she was not left all alone to face what would happen next.

"Countess, wake quickly! Quickly."

Alix heard the agitated whisper. She tried to shrug it away. Just a little of the dream remained and she stood on tiptoes within it, straining to snatch her husband from the world of shadows that was rapidly enveloping him.

"Quickly."

Alix felt the shake and the cold as her fur rugs were flung aside.

" 'Tis Lancelot de Guigny, coming to kill you in your bed just as he's killed all the others."

Through the slit in her eyelids, she recognized the short, squat shape of Young Sophie, her maid.

"Guigny, here? How can that be?"

"Only the devil knows—for it was he who doubtless spawned him. But indeed he is here and set to murder all of Mercier."

Instantly Alix was wide awake. "Then we must get

to my husband. We must inform the count." Her feet were already on the cold stones of the castle floor, her eyes looking beyond Sophie to the door of her solitary chamber.

"The count is dead." Sturdy Sophie grabbed a mantle to wrap around her mistress's thin night tunic. "He was killed in his sleep and Solange with him. Lancelot de Guigny sent knights disguised as mendicants to seek hospitality within the keep. The count opened to them and they in turn opened the castle to their lord. De Guigny thinks he has killed you, the lawful wife of Mercier. Perhaps, if we are fortunate, he will think that for a few moments more. But then he will come. You must leave this place. Now. With sure haste. The Knight de Guigny will want no living witness to his treachery. He will leave alive nothing that can lay claim to Mercier."

"But the village . . ."

"The village will be left to itself once blood-lust has been spent in the castle. It is only you he will really want. It is you he will kill."

Sophie did not wait for Alix's reply. She threw a fur blanket around her and pushed her toward the door. A scream rang from the Great Hall below them.

"My husband cannot be dead. No one would dare to kill the Count de Mercier. I must get to my husband."

Sophie shook her fine, young curls. "Go to the window, my lady, and see what is left of the castle of Mercier. See if the count could still be alive in this horror."

Cold wind blasted them as Alix flung back the heavy velvet hangings. No clouds marred the winter's sky or blocked the placid, broad moon that cast its crystal light down into the courtyard upon the dead and the dying. Alix had never known the garrison at Mercier contained so many men; she had never thought the world itself capable of containing so much pain and horror.

She looked up to stare at the red and cream standard of Burgundy flying from Mercier's ramparts.

"Good God," she said and she crossed herself. Her hands chilled against her forehead and she felt the ice slither into her and chill the very beating of her heart. "Good God."

But there could be no God of Goodness in the mass of death she saw below.

The hill beyond the castle shimmered with movement and she turned to it. Men—enemies—still galloped toward Mercier. The moon's light rippled against a dark standard that heralded the approach of a force of at least fifty more. They rode fast, holding their bodies low and tight against the wind. Determined to make Mercier before first light. Desperate to make sure they played their part in this carnage of conquest.

She looked up once again at the arrogant standard of Burgundy fluttering above her head. She could see it clearly in the torchlight that ringed both the inner and outer curtains of the castle and in the glow of random fires.

Tears stung her eyes. More than anything else, this contemptuous display of colors told her that her husband was dead. Since the time of Charlemagne, when Robisart the Bold had established this fortress, no colors other than the silver and bright blue of the lords of Mercier had ever flown from its ramparts. It had never been taken.

But it was taken now.

For all of his faults, a living Robert de Mercier would never have allowed this desecration. This meant that he was surely dead. Alix knew this with dull certainty. Yet no matter whose standard graced it, the Merciers were still the traditional seneschals of this outpost and she, Alix, was still the Countess de Mercier. It was her duty to protect whomever and whatever remained within its borders.

"I must get to my pigeons. I must send for help."

"To whom?" Young Sophie's eyes were wide with terror. "Mercier is held under the banner of Burgundy. The duke is liege lord here and for a thousand leagues in any direction. The Knight de Guigny holds this place for his brother and with his brother's consent. Who can help us? We are surrounded by the duke's power on all sides. You must seek sanctuary from the monks at Haute Fleur and from there beg for mercy from the duke himself. Save yourself, and plead for the lives of your people. 'Tis only a part of the castle that is burning. He has left the village in peace thus far."

With this declaration came a wild hope. "But then perhaps Robert did manage to escape . . ."

Alix ran from the window to the chamber door. She slammed past it and into the corridor that led to the noble rooms of the Counts de Mercier. She had to get to her husband. There might still be time. If he were still alive and she saved him, they might be able to redeem everything in the past. Surely if she saved him he would love her for it.

Sophie caught at her mistress easily, yanking her arm with such force that Alix almost toppled.

"He's dead," the maid hissed. "I saw him myself. And 'tis Lancelot de Guigny who did the killing. Do you really want to see how he did it? Do you really want to see the mess he made of the man you love?"

Alix stopped and looked into the maid's eyes and saw the truth there. She shook her head. More tears slipped from her eyes but she determined they would be the last—at least for this night.

"There, there," said Sophie with a quick and clumsy hug. "But you, my lady, are alive and you must live on."

They ran then. Alix felt her body act on its own as she raced. Up these corridors, down those. Dried thyme on the castle's floor-stones bit against her bare feet as she ran through it. Near the heart of the castle, the herbs beneath her feet were matted with blood. She heard a woman scream and the sound of men laughing. The scream continued long after the laughter had stopped. But here, on this noble floor, where the carnage had begun and where it might well end, there was only silence. Which is why, as they ran nearer to the hidden donjon stairs that would take them from the castle into the safety of the hills, they heard the child's cry with such clarity.

Yvrain, Alix thought and her heart stopped as she remembered.

Alix, I beg of you, save my son. Save Mercier.

The sound halted them in their tracks. Breathing heavily, they glanced at each other. Sophie's brow furrowed.

" 'Tis the boy," said the Countess de Mercier. She had never once called Solange's child by name, pretending that she did not even know what he had been christened. But she spoke his name now. "They have not killed Yvrain. They have not killed Robert's child."

In Sophie's eyes she saw awareness of what this meant, and fear of it.

"But they *will* kill him," the maid whispered. She held tight onto her mistress's arm. "They *will* kill him—and immediately, once they realize the oversight. All know of the Count de Mercier's son. The Knight de Guigny is a bastard himself, and thus knows a bastard's determination. He will not let this child live. He is too much of a threat."

Sophie stopped and drew back. She had said what needed saying but as a member of the countess's household, she knew the hurt that the birth of this little one had caused her young mistress. She also knew the danger they faced if they stopped to take the child with them. Robert's child. If he had hopes to hold Mercier, then Lancelot de Guigny would not rest until Yvrain was dead. Sophie had risked her life to save the young countess, but she wanted no part in the choice that the countess would now have to make.

Alix felt the blood pound at her temples, bringing back the hatred. She remembered Solange's slights and her ridicule. Alix remembered her own pain. And she remembered how this child had caused it. But the baby, Robert's baby, was crying—yet not really even crying, only whimpering. He wanted his mother and his father near. He had been awakened to death, just as Alix herself had been, but he was too young to know the danger. How old was he? Dear God, only six months.

Abruptly, into that silence echoed the clang of steel. The sound soon died but not its echo. This seemed to go on and on until it became the only thing still resonating in Robert de Mercier's dark and deadly castle. It thundered up from the horror below in the Great Hall to the horror that lay all about her on this, the noble floor.

Still hesitating at the doorway, Alix shifted slightly and slipped in blood. She looked down into the dead eyes of the child Yvrain's nurse. The old woman's arms were flung wide, almost in supplication. Alix stared at the dead woman for what seemed like an eternity as the clang of steel began to ring out once again. For an instant this weapon-clashing was Alix's only reality but it was in that instant that she made her decision.

She went to the child and picked him up and snuggled him to her breast.

"There, there," she crooned to him just as Sophie had crooned to her. She touched his dark curls and smiled at him, as the screaming and the laughter started up again. "You are Yvrain of Mercier and I, Alix, plight thee guardianship. You will come with me now. I will keep you safe."

Two

Lancelot de Guigny had never felt so pleased with himself. The quest of Mercier Castle had gone much better than he could have hoped—or that his half-brother the duke could possibly have anticipated. The fortress had fallen within the few short night hours between matins and prime. His mother had called them the devil's hours because of their darkness. Lancelot shivered now at her remembrance, but he did this inwardly and only for a minute. He would deal with the devil later—right now he had enough on his hands with the upstart Angevin knight who stood before him.

He pointed an elegantly ringed finger at Severin Brigante.

"They say you are related to Belden of Harnoncourt, and that is why my brother called you here."

The other man said nothing. Slightly irritated, Guigny was forced to continue. "You don't look like him, though. I fought against him at Arrezzo with the Sire de Coucy. Harnoncourt was a dark man, not fair as you are. But he was large like you and you seem to have his eyes."

Guigny's blue eyes narrowed as he again waited for the response. It took some time in coming.

"Belden of Harnoncourt is my uncle," said the knight finally. "I am his brother's son."

"Some scandal there, I heard," replied Guigny, wrinkling his brow in feigned reflection, though of course he knew perfectly well what had brought this knight's father to disgrace. "But I hear you've reformed the Gold Company. *That* was, indeed, a great mercenary army. Made famous by your uncle, according to all accounts, and now become a heritage to you."

"Nothing of Belden of Harnoncourt belongs to me," said the knight. He fixed Guigny with his strange, deep gaze. "Not even his name. I am known as the Knight Brigante. I have taken on the Gold Company because the Duke of Burgundy called me to do so. There was nothing of heritage in it."

Guigny sighed. "Indeed. 'Tis a certainty that one must fight for one's own birthright in these wicked days. I am brother to the duke—*older* brother to him—but from the wrong side of the bed, as they say. My mother was no noblewoman. She was disgraced and burned as a witch for my birth, but the old duke brought me up along with his heir Jean, and we have always remained together. Always together. I was his bodyguard at Nicopolis when he led that disastrous campaign against the Sultan Bayezid. I was also one of the men he trusted to—do away with Louis d'Orleans, his cousin and the king's brother. For years I have toiled long for my brother but thus far to no estate. Mercier is destined to be my freehold."

Guigny heard the wistfulness in his own voice and checked himself. It was not like him to prose on before a stranger. He looked about at his men milling around the Great Hall. The smell and the insanity of blood lust were still upon them, this craving that made man do strange things. But that would fade soon and they would start to listen. He would do well to be careful. No use ruining what he had so carefully constructed—

not when he was so close to what he so desperately craved.

"Tell me of yourself," he said. "Tell me why you've come."

Guigny's gaze never wavered as the knight before him neatly skirted the first question. He recognized this in the way he so easily plunged into answering the second.

"I've told you that. The duke has called upon me with my army," replied the Knight Brigante. "He has asked me to assist you, nothing more."

"Nothing more," echoed a thoughtful Sir Lancelot.

Severin Brigante's French was good although it was heavily accented with a light lilt of the South. He had said he was an Angevin—a follower of the House of Anjou—and had received his golden spurs in the contested Kingdom of the Two Sicilies, which lay beyond holy Rome. Guigny doubted this. The knight before him certainly did not look French. His light hair and sun-darkened skin contrasted with the deep-smoke grayness of his eyes. There was something strange about him. Guigny determined to examine his background. If he found scandal—as he most probably would—it might prove useful in future.

"But as you can see, all has been attended to here." The duke's half brother waved an arm expensively clad in dark green velvet. "There is no need for further aid. You can take that word to my brother—but tomorrow. Wait here this day and rest yourself and your army. Take the refreshment that the women of Burgundy know how to offer to a weary man."

There was a titter of laughter from those nearest to the raised dais of the Counts of Mercier upon which the Knight de Guigny now sat. But Severin Brigante did not join in.

"I carry the duke's mandate," he bellowed, holding

the sealed parchment aloft. In the Great Hall all activity halted as the other knights and their men stopped to listen. "In it he commissions the Gold Company of Tuscany to help in the defense of the castle of Mercier. We will uphold our commission until the duke himself clears us of his order."

"The castle is aptly defended," snapped Guigny. "You can see that easily enough. We have no use of further aid from foreigners. The duchy of Burgundy is safe again. There will be no further seditious backing of Charles of France from within its borders. Robert de Mercier is dead and his dark-haired, vixen wife with him."

Guigny's face glowed with triumph as he said this, but then gradually clouded as he saw the dubious shake of the Knight Brigante's head.

"The Countess de Mercier is not a darkling," said Sir Severin. "The Lady is clear-eyed and fair-haired and neither is she vixen. She is as fine as down, as soft as sunshine."

Alix held Yvrain close against her breast, more to quiet than to comfort him. Poised for flight, she stood quite still so she could listen, though really there was nothing to hear. Light from the wall torches flickered against the dead body of the child's keeper. Alix deliberately held his back to it so he could not see the bloody spectacle. Not that children, especially peasant children, could really understand anything, she told herself; not that they could really see.

Still, it was no use frightening the child and making him cry.

"The battle has quieted," she whispered. "We can send to the duke or to Padre Gasca at the monastery at Haute Fleur. He is a holy man and an old friend. He will surely know what we should do."

"We need to get to the village," Sophie answered. "We can hide there until another nightfall and then make a safe-way to the monastery. Lancelot de Guigny is the duke's brother. Jean of Burgundy will not help Mercier against his own."

Alix forced herself to be quiet and to think. Her fine brow wrinkled. "Not the village. That will be the first place they would look for us. They will want to kill the child. Someone will betray us."

"But they love you in the village," Sophie insisted. Somehow the low hiss of her words made them more imperative. "You have done well for the people. They would never betray you."

Alix shook her head. "The Knight de Guigny will offer money. The village is a small place and poor, with no hidingness in it. He will offer money and someone will betray."

Without realizing it, she looked down at the corpse of the nurse, her arms thrown wide as though still pleading for life. Alix thought of herself like that, and Sophie. She thought what a man capable of doing this to an old, defenseless creature would be capable of doing to them. Young Sophie was a virgin still; Alix herself had been bedded but few times. She shuddered to think what could be done to them before the final killing. She shuddered to think what Lancelot de Guigny would do to this child.

Unless . . .

Without thinking, Alix began fingering the Maltese Star at her throat. Without knowing why, she became yet more still and she listened.

"Unless," Alix said finally, "we are able to outwit him."

"Outwit Lancelot de Guigny?" questioned Sophie.

It was obvious she thought her mistress deranged by the sudden tragedy and that she herself must prepare to take charge. "He has already killed the count. Lord Robert is dead, just as Guigny has always wanted him to be. They say Severin Brigante rides from the South to abet him. You cannot possibly expect to wrest from them what they have so securely taken. We must flee. It is our only chance. We must run from them."

In her mind's eye Alix saw again the riders she had seen from her chamber window—the men making fast and quick to Mercier. She saw again their dark banner and sensed something familiar in it.

Severin Brigante. Where had she heard that name?

"It is Guigny we must think of," said Alix. "He is the one we must outsmart."

"And how?" Just then the child Yvrain began to whimper against Alix's breast.

"What of your mother?" she asked.

A light glimmered in Sophie's eye. "Indeed, my mother will help us. One of the duke's escorts raped her when she was but a young lass. She bears no love for the House of Burgundy and even less for Guigny, who has always headed the duke's bodyguard. She also lives apart from the village and is noted for speaking her own mind. Others are frightened of her, but she is plucky and knows no fear herself. She is the Wise Woman in this place."

Alix had already started to wrap Yvrain in her own fine fur blanket. "Then take the child to hide with your mother, at least for a time. Tell her that the Countess de Mercier is grateful for this favor and that she will be rewarded well."

Sophie stiffened. "My mother will want no silver for doing but her duty. She midwifed Yvrain at his birthing. She would not now wish him dead."

"Of course she would not," said a chastened Alix.

"It is only my own fear speaking through me—a fear that has not loosed my tongue to thank you yet for risking your life this night to save mine."

Sophie blushed and bobbed her a curtsey as she took the child from her mistress.

"We should be going, lady," she said. "It will be light soon and we must be safely away."

"I stay," said Alix. She shook her head to cut the quick reply. "Go straight to the house of your mother and hide the child there, then show yourself about the village. The stray raping will be over now that Guigny thinks himself firmly in control of Robert's castle. He will want to bring peace again so as to impress the duke. You will be safe, but keep the child hidden. Keep him far from that maddened man."

"But lady . . ."

"Obey me," said Alix. Her voice was crisp, the voice of chatelaine to the great fortress of Mercier. "Run quickly down the hidden seige passage. Hide the child with your mother. Do not look back. I have things that need doing here. I will meet with you later."

Sophie hesitated and then bundled Yvrain and hurried with him into the darkness.

Alix allowed herself no time to go to the window to see that the maiden and the young child had made good their escape. She must aid them, that was all.

"I will go to Lancelot de Guigny," she told herself. "I will distract him. Perhaps he has already realized that I still live and has started the hunt. Perhaps not. But when I present myself to him I must make sure to occupy the whole of his mind so that his thought cannot wander to the child. Above all else I must make sure that he does not remember the child—or that he thinks him dead."

She waited until she was certain that Sophie and Yvrain were no longer near and then she, too, stepped into the hallway. She retraced her steps along the stone landing of the noble floor until they led her back to the chamber her husband had shared with Solange. The heavy wooden door was slightly open. The mark of a mace had shattered deeply into the polished wood. Alix hesitated only for an instant and then pushed the door aside.

Death had come quickly and it had found the two of them together. Robert had fallen at the foot of the bed; Solange still lay upon it. The Count de Mercier had had no time to round his sword but he still clutched his jeweled dagger. Alix bent down and took it from his cold hand with her equally cold ones. She reached to the floor to retrieve her husband's mantle. She wrapped it around herself but she still shivered from the chill. It did not help.

She bent down to close her husband's eyes and to whisper in his ear. "Somehow I thought it was not true, that a mistake had been made or that a miracle would happen and I would find you here alive. Instead now I must stop him from desecrating you further. I must see you decently buried, my husband, and for this I will need help."

"You are a bold piece, my lady, presenting yourself as you have, alive and requesting a noble favor. Certainly you must know that I want you dead . . ."

"But as you can well see, I am not."

". . . and the child-bastard with you."

"He, instead, is truly dead," said Alix. She forced the hauteur of a great lady into her voice. "I saw him so myself and had my maid fling his body into the stream. I want him not on any part of Mercier—not even buried upon its lands."

Guigny's eyes narrowed, though the Dame de Mercier's hatred of her husband's love child was not news to him. Everyone knew of it, and no one blamed her for it. Aside from troubadour prattlings, Mercier was generally deemed the weakest of men.

"But you would do better by your husband?" questioned Lancelot de Guigny with a slight shrug and a smile. "And yet you are noble-born, lady, and know no traitor can be buried on hallowed ground. Robert de Mercier will follow the custom. His body will be quartered and displayed upon the four ramparts of his castle as a warning to all who might think themselves powerful enough to oppose their liege lord."

"My husband was no traitor," said Alix. "He was always loyal to his liege lord."

"Then what would you call his perfidy?" Guigny fixed her with a highly interested stare.

Alix was well aware that strangers surrounded her and that the man she faced could kill her with just as much ease as he had killed her husband. De Guigny had obviously changed after battle as befitted his new position as lord of Mercier. He sat on Robert's raised dais and in Robert's chair but he was dressed much more flamboyantly than the true count would ever have dressed.

Guigny's tunic was exquisitely cut of dark red samite shot through with silver and gold threads while his mantle was set with rows of embroidered silver moons and bright suns. A scarlet cap crowned his dark head. His golden-hilt sword was girt on with a silken belt and chased with a silver scabbard. Alix judged him as a man who had looked to every detail, both in the taking of her husband's castle and in the keeping of it. Everything about him was meant to impress. Her luck with him would lie in the unexpected and the bold and she knew it, but this knowledge did not stop her being afraid. Her hands were ice, her knees knocked together so hard that they hurt.

"Then what would you call it?" replied Guigny. His face was bright with interest. "He openly boasted that should war come between England and France, Mercier would plight itself with Charles of France, even though his liege lord, Duke Jean of Burgundy, has openly professed for the English cause."

"There is no dispute," said Alix quietly. "Charles is the legitimately crowned king of this land. Henry Plantagenet of England is just an upstart. Even the duke's own brother, Philip of Burgundy, has pledged himself to the rightful king."

"I am the duke's brother," said Guigny. He framed the words in menace. There was a short laugh, immediately followed by an inquisitive silence as his men watched Sir Lancelot spar with this slight woman. Even the dogs seemed to sense the quizzing. Their ears perked expectantly.

"I meant no offense," replied the Countess de Mercier. This time she accompanied her words with the merest of reverences. "I spoke only of the duke's younger brother because he is his heir. All know that you are older brother to Duke Jean and that he relies most heavily on your discretion."

Guigny nodded his satisfaction and Alix continued.

"My husband did not traitor himself against the duke," she said. "He wished always to do his duty to his liege lord. But in this matter he differs—differed—from Duke Jean. He thought Henry of England a whelp of a king and without the strength to hold united two such independent kingdoms. The people of France would not permit this, no matter the legitimacy of Henry V's Plantagenet claim. My husband only wished to avoid civil strife."

The cat in Guigny emerged now in his smile. "And he acted totally without a trace of selfish interest . . ."

Alix, knowing what would come next, nodded.

". . . and not because my lord duke had refused permission for the traitor Mercier to marry the strumpet Solange?"

"How could he marry another?" said Alix. She raised her voice so it could carry over the laughter of the men. "My Lord of Mercier was married to me."

Guigny wagged a dismissive hand. "Noble marriages are easily forfeit to papal annulment. It is the blessing—or the curse—of the class. One has but to remember how the powerful Eleanor of Aquitaine rid herself of France's Louis VII once her fancy had settled upon young Henry of Anjou. The same Henry who, in his turn, went on to become the first Plantagenet King of England and thus laid family claim to both Paris and Westminster. What a fluke of japing history that was! This overlapping of thrones is one of the reasons our two countries are contentious to this day."

Alix cared nothing for the rivalry between France and England that had ravaged the two countries with war since the Battle of Poitiers some eighty years before. Especially now, with Robert dead and his castle held, she had no longing to look to the reasons that had brought the Mercier to this sorry turn. She opened her mouth to say just this—when her glance was drawn to the slightest of movements.

It was as though the earth around her slowed. Not stopped, she would say afterwards, but slowed so that each of its instants crystallized and grew distinct. The flick of her head, the lifting of her gaze up and beyond the Knight de Guigny, until it caught the answering gaze of the man standing just behind him.

She saw the flash of his golden hair but it was his

eyes that captured her immediate attention. How dark they are, she thought, and deep.

Alix had only space for a brief impression before Lancelot de Guigny's justifications called him to her attention once again. But even in that short sand-span of time, a forgotten memory whispered to Alix.

Severin d'Harnoncourt, who called himself the Knight Brigante, had seen her initially in Paris, at the court of the very King Charles they now discussed. He had been there, as usual, to request a grace for his father. She had stopped at the palace of the Louvre in the midst of a triumphant progress, passing through France as the wife of a powerful noble and making her reverences to the king, her husband's liege lord, before going on to take up her destiny as mother to the future heirs of Mercier.

Both of them had been so alive with their purpose and yet how dismally they had both failed in it. How many things had happened since then and few of them had been good. Now he had only to look within his soul to see the rankling of his own losses and he had but to look upon her face to see the ravages left by her own.

Ah, but she had been lovely when first he had seen her!

The Countess de Mercier had marked him with her freshness. She had brought springtime into the debauchery of a court ruled by Queen Isabeau, a woman whom even her friends routinely referred to as "that German whore." His own parentage had taught the young Knight Brigante to be very sensitive to that word and he never used it. There had been nothing whorish about the young Lady Alix. Not with the ripple of her long golden curls; not with the flash of her truly extraordinary turquoise eyes. In his mind he could still see her now as she made a deep reverence before the vacant stare of France's poor, mad king. He remembered that she had carried a small bouquet of spring violets, something which her husband had noticed late and scowled upon. Severin remembered that she had laughed and that she had been dressed in brilliant white.

She was still dressed in white—Severin glimpsed the peeking of her night tunic beneath her oversized man's mantle—but it was no longer a virgin's white. The hem of her garment was dark with blood and blood had dried upon her bare feet. Standing where he was, raised upon the dais, he could see the imprint of those feet upon the thyme as they had crossed the Great Hall's stone floor, as the Countess de Mercier had come to stand alone before the murderer of her husband.

There was nothing left of laughter about her now. And yet . . .

And yet, there was still something unique and bright about this wasted woman. Severin caught himself staring at her now, just as he had caught himself staring at her then.

A plethora of war banners, which had been seized down through the centuries by generations of Mercier warriors, hung from the Great Hall's high wooden rafters. They fluttered gently now in an unseen breeze. Alix felt them call to her. She must ensure that there would be no more desecration within these walls. Robert was dead, but she still carried the Mercier name and its duty just as so many bannerets before her had carried its flag.

"I know that you meant to kill me with my husband," she said. "But we did not sleep within the same bed. There was no love between us; he had great devotion to another, a fact with which I am sure you are familiar."

There was loud and knowledgeable guffawing at this from the men gathered around the chamber but Alix could not wait for it to end. If she let Guigny linger too long on the thought of Solange he might grow more curious about the child. He might determine to see a body and search the stream for it. He might ask which of his men remembered killing a boy. Alix could not risk this and so she plunged on.

"Therefore you must realize that 'tis not mere wifely devotion that brings me in supplication before you." She matched her words with a deep reverence. "But rather 'tis my duty as a daughter of France and vassal to the Duke of Burgundy to beg for the release of my husband's body so that it can be properly prepared for Christian burial."

Again the dogs grew silent as all laughter cut dead. Every gaze fixed on the Knight de Guigny.

He raised a dismissive hand. "You, my lady Alix, are daughter to one knight and were wife to another. You know the rules of such matters as well as do I. Robert de Mercier treasoned himself against his liege lord. The Mercier holdings are therefore forfeit. The count's dead body must now fulfill the duty that his live actions traitored. That is the custom and the law. I repeat, he will be quartered and hung upon the ramparts of his castle to serve as warning to anyone else who might take a mind to stand against the interests of his liege lord. And most especially if that liege lord happens to be Jean, Duke of Burgundy."

Around her, Alix heard clapping and sword hilts thumping against walls and wooden trestles. Quartering was normal consequence for treason and the men showed neither sympathy nor shock that this should be the fate of even so great a lord as Robert de Mercier.

It was useless for Alix to argue that no treason had been proved against her husband. Lancelot de Guigny knew this well but as its subjugator, he also knew that the freehold of Mercier now belonged to him. He needed only the Duke's parchment of confirmation and he would be the new seneschal of this great place. His was a mighty interest and Alix knew it was useless to appeal to any sentiment that did not take that interest well into account.

She opened her mouth to speak again but another voice cut smoothly into her words.

"Perhaps there has been enough bloodletting for one night," said the knight she had noticed before. He had a rich voice, she thought, though she found it pitched low. It was a commanding and beautiful voice and Alix held herself to silence whilst he spoke.

"Mercier lies safely within the duke's provenance once again. Perhaps we should not threaten the neighborhood's peace by fastening ourselves so implacably to the barbarisms of war."

All eyes turned toward this knight, including those of Lancelot de Guigny, though his smile was hardly pleasant.

"I don't think the lady has yet met her champion," he said. His eyes shone out of his slender face, dark as jet-stones. "Lady Alix, may I present the Knight Brigante. He and his men rode in well after the capture but he seems to want to take part in the division of spoils."

"I have no interest in the spoils of this fortress," replied Severin. "I and my men are paid well enough by Jean of Burgundy to help in its holding until the duke himself can come and lay his traditional claim. What I say, I say from my experience—and it is an experience that you as a knight have had as well. This is a place within the duke's own holdings; it is not just a fortress which we mean to sack and leave. As such we look to the best interests of our liege lord. Too much blood-flow could work against us with the people. It could cause them to lament the loss of the Mercier."

"Are you a Jacquerie?" asked Lancelot de Guigny. His voice had not lost its mocking tone. "Ready to teach us all the rights of low-born men? You seem such by your interests."

"I am concerned for the duke's property, as I am pledged to be," replied Severin. "His interests here will not be served by a revolution of the peasantry. You yourself mentioned the Jacquerie. You know the perturbation that their rebellion raised just a few short years ago."

"They were mere peasants and quickly crushed, as worms always are when they set themselves against lions."

Again Guigny's men guffawed and clanged their swords.

"I speak not for a peasant revolt. I only remind you, Sir Lancelot, that the Mercier have ruled this land in peace and prosperity since the time of Charlemagne. The people are doubtless loyal to them for this same peace and prosperity. Count Robert made an error in his ways and has paid the price of that error with his life. There is no gainsaying that fact, but surely the priest and his flock would look with kind consideration upon the new count-designate should he show mercy and allow the Lady Alix a Christian burial for her husband in consecrated soil."

Alix said nothing as the two men pressed their points. She could not understand why this unknown knight should so vigorously defend her husband against the rising wrath of Lancelot de Guigny. In the whole of this Great Hall, he was the only one who had spared a word to help her. She did not know from whence he came. She did not know why Sir Lancelot, known to listen to few, would even countenance his interference. Guigny had called him her champion. Perhaps, for some unknown reason, he was.

"Holy God, help him," whispered Alix. "Help me."

But God did not seem to be listening to Merciers on this most unholy night.

"It is justly decided! Do not talk to me of pleasing peasants!" roared the duke's brother. "I will have Alix of Mercier to the dungeons!"

Alix jumped, and as she did the mantle that covered her opened. She watched, puzzled, as Guigny's face lost its blood coloring and turned quite pale. For an instant he seemed entranced by her. He could not move his eyes away from her face and then she realized that his gaze held at her throat and the small amulet that twinkled there. When he spoke, his voice was like the smooth purr of a cat.

"Perhaps we can speak of this again on the morrow. The terce bells ring and dawn must be growing in the east. I will take no action against the traitor Mercier's body today, except to move it from the noble floor deep into the castle cellars. It is cooler there and the body will keep better until a decision is made. We will discuss this once our own bodies have recovered from their fatigue."

Alix, amazed, lowered herself into a deep reverence. As her forehead touched the paving stones she reached, without thinking, to touch the Maltese Star at her throat.

Guigny himself moved to raise her.

"We will speak again, my lady. Perhaps there is some way that both justice and mercy can be served in this enterprise. We will see. In the meantime, the Knight Brigante will escort you to your chambers. Please honor my men with your presence at this day's main meal."

"But I am widowed now. I would prefer to stay within my chambers and recite the prayers for my husband's soul."

"I will send nuns to wait upon you. There is a Benedictine convent filled with them within a donkey ride. I am sure they will be more than eager to help you with your prayers. They are rumored expert at litanies and rosaries," replied Guigny. "But I will have you at my table tomorrow. Much will be decided then about certain fates."

His menace was clear and Alix bowed to it.

"As you wish, my lord."

The Knight Brigante nodded to her and gave her his arm. He was dressed in black-and-gold livery, as were his men. Alix knew these colors well because her father had once proudly sported them when he commanded the Gold Company—Italy's premier mercenary army. She wondered how such a young man as the Knight Brigante had risen so quickly to general it for she assumed, from the deference shown him, that this was his post. But she asked no questions. She put her hand upon his arm as they followed behind two of his knights, who held high torches aloft. They led the way through the still-dark passageways of the castle she had once called her home.

"I thank you, Sir Severin," she said to the man beside her. "I owe this reprieve to your kind intervention."

"I played no part in what happened. If Count Robert is saved, it is you who saved him. Or perhaps it was the charm that you wear."

"The Maltese Star? But how could this help me?"

For an instant this strange man stopped and looked down at her. Alix could almost feel the force of his concentration through the flicker of torchlight as she turned to him.

"Don't you know?" he said finally. "Lady Alix, it is the only thing that can help you."

She shook her head. "I know nothing of this amulet, only that it was worn by my mother and by her mother before her. No one has ever told me what it meant." She hesitated and then asked, "Can you?"

Again the silence, as though he assessed her and carefully weighed his response. "I know something of it. Long ago my father wore it—but only for a short time. Still, it changed his life."

"Yet he no longer wears it?"

"No," was the Knight Brigante's brief response.

"Please tell me what you know of it." Alix's voice was earnest, even pleading. "I know nothing. I am eager to learn."

The honor guard had gone ahead and now waited patiently further along the corridor. Severin held his arm to her again. She reached for it, but as she did her whole body started to tremble. Her teeth chattered. Her hands clenched so tightly that her nails drew blood. She felt its sticky dampness. In horror she sensed tears spurt from her eyes. She tried to fight them back, to hold onto herself, to clutch herself together, but the more she tried the more violently she shook.

"Help me," she whispered to the man beside her. But he had already reached out to her; he was already holding her close.

"This will pass," he said. "It is but the body's reaction. I have seen it many times with even the strongest warriors after battle. Stand here with me by this window and we will pretend to be viewing the dawn.

Breathe deeply and I will try to warm you. This will pass. It always does."

And amazingly he was right. In the end it passed, though not quickly. Alix's teeth stopped their chattering and her tears dried. She became more aware of the Knight Brigante's soothing voice as he talked her through the worst of it. She became aware of his arm around her and the way he held her close.

For the first time in her life, from within the firm enclosure of this unknown knight's arms, Alix Ducci Montaldo de Mercier, one of the great peeresses of France, felt that she was safe.

Three

Never in her life had the Lady Alix been forced to dress herself. She was forced to do it now on this, the first day after her husband's death. This was to be only the first of many changes.

Waking had brought with it the immediacy of her situation and Alix had not kept her eyes shut against it. Instead she had climbed from her bed. When no maid appeared, she bathed herself with the cold water in a basin and struggled with the latchings of a simple black-and-burgundy wool tunic. She thought it best to ration her widow's mourning with a bit of the duke's colors; Guigny had still to give assurances concerning Robert's burial. She would have to approach him again and it was best to keep him in good humor by showing her loyalty. If, indeed, her husband had shown fault, she could represent repentance by flaunting the duke's colors. That she had to plan through the consequences of even the way she dressed was another indication of her changed life. She would not think of this now. She must get to the dangerous task of sending off word with her pigeons, and the equally dangerous one of arranging sanctuary for the child Yvrain.

She dressed with exceeding and unusual care. During the short years of her marriage, Alix had had few people to impress with the way she vested or the way she moded her hair. Robert had shown no interest in her and his visitors had been few. On more nights than not, she had excused herself from the Great Hall table to read through the parchment books that were her only diversion. She glanced at them now, piled high but neatly on a wax-stained trestle table near the window. Most of the manuscripts were interesting and many of them beautiful, on paper from the Italian city of Fabriano. They had been sent to her by Padre Gasca, her mother's friend who had retired to the nearby Abbey of Haute Fleur, and by other monks and learned folk. She would read anything that was presented to her—parchments on the scientific studies of the Arabs, translations of ancient works by men like Aristotle who had lived across the sea, theological treatises on how many angels could dance upon the head of a pin. She hadn't cared; she had read them all, and gratefully. Robert had not objected; he was a learned man himself. Sometimes she had thought that it was only through her reading that she had managed to live through the humiliation of loving a man who so deeply and blatantly loved another.

Now, with widowhood, she sensed that she would have little time for leisure occupations. Her own fate was fairly assured. If he had not as yet killed her, it was unlikely that the Knight de Guigny would decide to do so now. Common sense told her this. Blood lust crested and then ebbed after the first rush of victory. No, she would be convented far away, wherever and whenever the caprice of Guigny's fancy decided her end. She was safe but her husband wasn't. Not yet. Not until she saw him buried, with the prayers for the dead spoken over him and holy water sprinkled over his remains. Only then could she retreat from being the Countess de Mercier and be allowed to mourn. She knew that she must never show herself to Lancelot de Guigny as she had shown herself to Severin Brigante last night. The new holder of Mercier must never see her weak and crying.

And so she piled her golden hair high, veiling it with black lace but not a widow's customary black wimple. Severin Brigante had said that her small Maltese Star interested the Knight de Guigny. Alix pulled it from within the bodice of her tunic; she made sure that it showed well.

For an instant her mind flicked back to her childhood and to Belvedere. Before her father had come to claim them, she had lived alone with her beautiful, dark-haired mother. Julian Madrigal had been the village Wise Woman but this had left time for her to play with the golden daughter who so deeply favored Julian's own mother—the witch, Aleyne de Lione. Julian had gamed with Alix and crooned to her and told her jongleur fables—but never anything about the six-pointed amulet she had dutifully hung at her daughter's throat.

Although Alix had asked her about it.

"It is called the Maltese Star," Julian had said with some reluctance. "It has been passed down with the women in our family since before the time when tales began. More than that I cannot tell you. You must learn its secrets on your own." Alix, the child, had not insisted. Somehow she knew that Julian Madrigal spoke the truth.

Now she smiled grimly as she studied the Maltese Star in the piece of mercury glass that adorned the luxuriously tapestried walls of her chamber. She tilted first herself and then the glass in order to see better. The amulet was a strange, small thing, easy to miss. But Lancelot de Guigny had not missed it and neither had the Knight Brigante, who had promised to tell her its tale. She hoped fervently that he would do so—but later. First she must see to the pigeons and then to the child.

She had crossed to the chamber door before she remembered. Last night, before going to her lone bed, Alix had moved her prie-dieu to a far corner of the room. She had draped it with Robert's bloodied mantle and placed his jeweled knife beneath the holy crucifix of Our Lord. She had put two beeswax candles in silver holders and lit them. Then she had knelt down to pray.

She prayed now. Silently and fervently, she entreated heaven for Robert's soul and begged that, if God were so willing, the Count de Mercier would look down from wherever he now rested to the woman he had made his wife. And that he would finally approve.

In the manner of his mother, a noble lady related to the legendary Eleanor of Aquitaine, Robert of Mercier had constructed a vassalage modeled on the cultured values of the South of France. Although because of his notorious liaison with the peasant Solange, few men—and fewer women—of rank would deign to call upon him, still he filled his castle with traveling jongleurs and troubadours. He brought rose clippings and exotic plants with him from the East and with these he had designed intricate, espaliered gardens. He read fine books and set an exquisite table. His chef was rumored to be one of the finest in Burgundy and under the threat of constant enticement by the duke himself.

In fact the only thing that Robert had neglected in his castle—besides his wife—was its defense. This fatal omission was now being rectified.

On her way up the winding donjon staircase that

led to her carrier pigeons, Alix stopped to gaze through an arrow slit at the scene below. Never, in all her years at Mercier, had she seen the inner and outer curtains of such hives of activity. The day was early yet—the bell for nones at mid-morning had yet to ring—and yet the dead had been cleared and reconstruction of the breach had begun. The knights and their men-at-arms huffed under their burdens; many of them were without tunics, though the winter day still shone down coldly. The Knight de Guigny was nowhere in sight. But he was not the one whom Alix's eyes so diligently sought.

Severin Brigante worked alongside his men. He, too, had stripped to his breeches and Alix, staring closely, saw sweat glisten along his arms and his chest. Now in daylight she noted that he was much larger than she had imagined him to be last night—and she had thought him large enough then. He was much bigger than her husband, who had been small, fine-boned, and elegant. But then Robert de Mercier had been a nobleman born. He would never have been caught lifting massive stones and swabbing in wattling as the Knight Brigante was doing now. Alix could not even imagine Robert doing such demeaning work.

Yet, the knight's men did not seem to mind it. They joked and laughed alongside their young, fair-haired general with a camaraderie that Robert's garrison had never displayed. She heard them teasing and even nudging at him, and heard him laugh back. Without thinking, she leaned just a little closer into the opening to hear what they said.

It was as though the Knight Brigante saw her. In any case he stopped what he was doing and stared up at the donjon with a slight frown on his face. Alix felt the cool, clear stare of his ember-colored eyes brush against her and she started and stepped back.

"Oh, if only you had not murdered my husband."

The sound of her own words and the horror of their meaning caught her like a slap. She crossed herself and turned to hurry up the stairs. Never once in the long, lonely years of her marriage had the thought of another man crossed her mind. She must be a wanton indeed to stare so disgracefully at a half-clothed man when her husband was not yet even decently buried. When he had been dead not even one whole day.

Sending messages by pigeon was one of many things that the early crusaders had learned from Saladin's army in the East. When he heard of this, Robert de Mercier, ever keen for novelty and knowledge, had immediately constructed a large coop on his ramparts and equipped it with well-trained birds. He soon tired of his folly and had left his pigeons to their fate. Instead Alix, who read the same parchments as her husband and was left much alone, took up the interest when his slackened. She used the birds to communicate with Padre Gasca at the Abbey of Haute Fleur, which lay just a day's journey away near the important town of Vezeley. Padre Gasca had known Alix's mother well. Surely if anyone could help her now, he would be the one to do it.

The industry of the invaders had not as yet carried them up onto the far reaches of the ramparts. Alix noticed this with relief as soon as she pushed through the heavy oaken door. Her pigeons, safely hidden behind a stone pillar, cooed and fluttered against the bars of their twigged cages as she neared them. Beside them large plaice swam lazily in the donjon's food-pond.

Alix chose one of the larger, fancy rock-pigeons, bent

and kissed its smooth feathers, and then carefully tied
her message to its tail with flax string. She raised her
hands above her head and released it to the sky. Then
she reached for another pigeon and repeated her mo-
tions. She squinted up to gauge the weather. Thankfully,
the day was bright and sunny. Her pigeons had a tendency to lose themselves when the air was overcast or
clouded, though in all her reading Alix had never
learned the reason for this. Still, it was best to send forth
two rather than one on such an important mission. She
had need of someone she could trust and more than a
foreboding told her that she might need that help soon.

She had strong intuitions—as had her mother and
her grandmother before her—and she had learned to
trust them in order to survive.

After releasing the birds, Alix waited. She went back
to her apartments, expecting that Sir Lancelot would
send for her as he had promised. She practiced what
she would say to him, trying out words that might persuade him not to desecrate Robert's body and to release it to her. In her mind she spent precious little
time appealing to any higher ideals he might possibly
entertain; instead she followed the lead of the Knight
Brigante and predicted dire consequences for rash actions. But her plans did not matter. Sir Lancelot did
not call for her.

Instead, he sent two nuns who had obviously been
roused from higher occupations at the convent. Old
and ugly—this was the truth, though Alix felt guilty
thinking it—they showed little interest even in the gossip of what had happened at Mercier. They had been
called to wait upon the Lady Alix; their use of this title
and not the more exalted one of countess told her
much about where their sympathies lay in this political
encounter. They frowned when they saw Robert's knife
upon the small altar and his blooded mantle draped

over the prie-dieu. There were short mumbles about pagan ways, a sigh and a mention of "foreign upbringings." But in the end they settled beside Alix and prayed for the repose of the count's departed soul. No mention of his threatened body was made.

Well, at the least they will be of help with my lacings, thought Alix. This thought proved fruitless as well. The two women were dressed in brown Franciscan homespun. It was obvious they had not been near a lacing in years and equally obvious that they disapproved of a young widow who would let even a touch of color mar the uniformity of her mourning. With a wife such as this, they seemed to say, and a mistress like Solange, the Count de Mercier had received only the deserved end of those who made frequent bad choices.

After a while Alix tired of attempted conversations with them and she even tired of her prayers, though not without guilt. She must pray for Robert and she knew this; it was her duty as a good Christian wife to plead his soul through any Purgatorial pangs. But the freshness of his death was still too overwhelming. She remembered last night when she had fallen to shards with Severin Brigante; she was frightened that this might happen again with the more formidable Lancelot de Guigny. She still had her duty and she must look to it. She must send pigeons, she must prepare herself to plead to Guigny and to the duke himself should this prove necessary, she must look to protect Yvrain. She must think all *around* Robert but she must not think *of* him, at least not yet.

A maid brought up a round of cheese and bread and a healthy jug of Mercier's fine red wine. The nuns ate with good appetite; the food and drink seemed to soften their disposition toward Alix. One of them even moved to brush a lock of her hair from her face. But this attitude was short-lived. Before many grains had passed through the hourglass they sat softly snoring before the fire. Alix picked up one of her manuscripts—a beautifully worked treatise from the famous medical school of Salerno in Italy—and sat for a time reading and puzzling over its alarming ideas. She squinted closer to see that she had seen and understood correctly. Could her blood really be scouring through her veins with the same indolence or velocity as water through a brook bed? She doubted this. Men often reached implausible conclusions and something in this concept seemed lacking in order and even in control. Still . . .

In the end she must have dozed as well because the knock at her chamber door startled her. The manuscript fell from her lap to land with a bang on the stone floor.

"Enter," she called, standing up and smoothing her skirts in anticipation of the Knight de Guigny.

Instead it was Severin Brigante who stood inside her chamber. Alix stopped her reverence in mid-curtsey.

"Oh," she said. "I was expecting Lancelot de Guigny."

For an instant a smile played at his lips as he glanced over at the two nuns. Their arms were crossed formidably beneath their scapulars and their faces wore identical expressions of distrust. They had grown instantly alert at his entrance.

"Then you did well to have adequate chaperonage," he said. "The Knight de Guigny is known to be a potent adversary."

Alix stared at him and then completed her reverence. "The Knight de Guigny is not my enemy," she said. "He has taken Mercier but so far he has treated me with great fairness." She made sure the nuns heard every word.

She was disappointed when she arose again to see that the smile no longer even half-lit Sir Severin's face. Instead his warrior's gaze circled her chamber. She saw it light upon the rich hangings and the tapestries and the enormous dais for the raised bed. She saw it take in the improvised altar and she saw him frown. Then it lingered at the pile of manuscripts upon the trestle.

"These are yours?" he asked.

"Some are," she answered. "But many of these belonged to my husband. He let me choose from his library as I wished."

"But you *read* these," he insisted.

"Of course I read them." Alix's laugh was short and puzzled. "What other purpose would they serve? Do you think I could learn anything by merely observing their pretty illustrations?"

He colored deeply at this and then turned to face the nuns. "With your permission, I must have a word with the Countess de Mercier."

They nodded, reaching down reluctantly to gather their rosary beads.

"Alone," he added. That one word was sufficient. They looked rebellious, opening their mouths, but like most women, whether religious or lay, they had taken vows of obedience to some man and they obeyed this one now. They might go immediately to prattle to the Knight de Guigny, but they would not now go against the expressed order of the Knight Brigante.

"As you wish, my lord," the elder nun said.

"Will we not have an honor guard to take us to Sir Lancelot?" Alix asked as she trotted along beside Severin.

"Whatever made you think I was taking you to Lancelot de Guigny? He is not even in the castle. He rode off this morning with but two men-at-arms to pray at a shrine in the forest. He will not be back before morrow."

This came as a surprise. Lancelot de Guigny had not struck Alix as an especially devout man. She wanted to further question the tall knight but something in his demeanor tamped her words. He had not offered the courtesy of his arm and she found it difficult to keep up with him. No matter how hard she tried, he seemed always just one step in front of her. He did not seem to notice that she almost ran. Rather he seemed to be deep within his own thoughts and Alix followed him silently, with no idea where he was leading.

But she learned this soon enough. The two of them rounded corner after corner, going further and further from the comforts of the noble floor and nearer to the donjon steps that led to the ramparts.

He cannot know of the birds. I sent them off too long ago. 'Tis impossible that he has captured one.

She was soon to learn that it was not impossible at all.

Severin led the way up the winding stone stairwell, pausing for a moment at the arrow slit Alix had gazed from that morning.

"This is the place," he said, more to himself than to her. "This is where I saw you."

He did not turn to her or say anything more. They passed on. Alix dragged a little behind, knowing that Severin had discovered the pigeons and puzzling what she could possibly say to explain them away. Her heart bumped within her chest. He had been kind to her the night before—even foolishly kind when he defended her against Guigny—but she had no doubt where his loyalty lay.

They were at cross purposes in this; Alix must see to the burial of her husband's body and Severin to the wishes of his lord.

He reached the top of the stairs and pushed the heavy door to the parapet open before her. She did not look at him as she passed through it.

The first thing she heard was the cooing of the pigeons. It sounded like thunder. There were only ten of them, including the two she had sent out on mission.

"They seem like a thousand," she mumbled to herself. "If he had not seen them he could have *heard* them all the way to the outer curtain. Even the fish seem to be splashing about with an exceeding noise."

"Did you say something, my lady?"

Alix looked at him closely but there was no irony in Severin Brigante's voice.

She turned away from him toward the rampart and the stretch of Burgundy that lay beyond it. A light breeze ruffled the hillside but the land was still sere with winter's blight. She gazed across at the main frontal rampart toward the strange banners—the rich red of Burgundy and the strange light green of his half brother. They reminded her of the precariousness of her situation.

"Mercier Castle is the possession of the Knight de Guigny now," she reminded herself. She turned back to the Knight Brigante. "Tell me how you discovered the message pigeon."

Severin did not waste time with guile. "My men were out hunting. One of the falcons took it down. The man-at-arms brought the note to me. I assumed it was from you. I had seen you at the arrow slit this morning—just for an instant, but I had seen you. So I knew that you must have sent this bird."

He seemed ill at ease. He looked her straight eye-to-eye but his face had colored slightly. She could sense his discomfiture and it puzzled her and this puzzlement made her voice testy.

"But of course you would have known that I had sent the bird," she said. "I signed my name to the note. Do you not have it with you?"

He looked at her for an instant more before reaching into the belt of his tunic. As he lowered his head a raft of sunlight struck his short hair and gilded it. Alix found herself noticing just how bright and golden it was. And how it looked clean and full.

"Is this your note?" he asked, handing it to her. "Is this the missive that you sent?"

The tiny piece of onion paper, though crumpled and grubby now, was unmistakably hers and there was no use to lie about it. Her name was written upon it. She had finely sealed it with her crest. He knew that she had attempted treason and he would soon bring her before Lancelot de Guigny. He would have no choice.

"Of course 'tis mine," she said shortly. "That is my hand. There is my name."

"Where is your name?" Severin did not look away from her as he asked the question. Alix became aware of just how dark his eyes were and of their strange color. Neither black nor gray, they seemed some shade between; perhaps the color of a dark wood, she thought, which had been burnt slowly to ashes.

Uncomfortable with the intimacy of this idea, Alix answered him more brusquely than she otherwise would have. "It carries my name upon it. What is wrong with you, Sir Severin? Cannot you see the spelling? Cannot you read the words?"

"That is just it, my lady," he said, still never once looking away from her. "I was a pauper knight and I have no learning. I am asking you to tell me the meaning of these ciphers. I am asking you to teach me how to read your name."

Four

"But that is impossible," Alix said. "You are a nobleman and a great knight. Of course you must know how to read."

"Not so impossible," Severin replied. For the first time he looked away from her and south toward the low Burgundian hills that she had watched before him. "I come from what one might call the decadent half of an illustrious family."

Alix said nothing. She let him continue.

"I'm sure you have heard of my uncle," he said, still looking out over the same hills. "He was Belden of Harnoncourt, founder of the Gold Company, the great mercenary army that your own father once commanded."

"And that you command now," she added.

"Yes, that I command now," he said and there was heavy irony in his voice. "Though I doubt my uncle would be pleased to hear the news of it. He has no idea I even exist, nor would he acknowledge me if he did."

There was a flutter and a cooing from the pigeons but Alix did not turn to it. She kept all of her attention on the man who stood just a little away from her.

"You see, Countess, I am son to his younger brother Guy."

"I am related to the Sire d'Harnoncourt," said Alix.

"He is married to my Aunt Francesca, younger sister to my father."

"And it is because of your Aunt Francesca that the whole of this plight began." Severin said. Alix had known him but a short time, but still the bitterness in his voice surprised her.

"I cannot imagine my aunt causing any difficulty," she retorted. "My father told me that she held onto the Castle of the Ducci Montaldo and kept his family together against supreme odds. When first she came from the east, my mother lived with the Lady Francesca. She adores her. Everyone adored her."

"Including my father," replied Severin. "The Lady Francesca was betrothed to Guy d'Harnoncourt before she put him away for the Sire. But my father was the younger son. He inherited nothing outright; his total dependence lay on what his powerful older brother deigned to give him. And when his brother wanted the Lady Francesca he stopped at nothing to gain her. He stole her from my father, her rightful spouse, and then left my father penniless. Guy d'Harnoncourt was forced to join forces with the French under Louis of Anjou, who had come to reclaim the Kingdom of the Two Sicilies. They had already failed in their quest before my father reached them. Only poor stragglers remained in Apuglia. He did his best for me but his misfortunes had broken him. When he died his last words were a prayer that someday I would redeem his name so that his brother might forgive him. He blamed himself for what had happened." Severin gave a derisive snort. "My father was a saint."

"And your mother?"

Again that same cynical snort, so different from what Alix expected. "I never knew her. She deserted my father soon after my birth."

Alix wisely said nothing to this and Severin continued.

"You can help me," he said. She could feel the intensity of his dark eyes full upon her. "I have soldiered since I was five, and not for great lords but for poor ones who would have me. The knight I began my paging days with had but one horse and one mule to call his own. He owned neither castle nor manor house. I had no money for page fees or boardings, but from there I went on. I took whatever pagings and squirings were offered. By the age of ten I had picked up my first sword for battle and I have battled continually since, from the south of Italy to Outremer and the Holy Lands and back up to France and into Burgundy with Duke Jean." For a second he paused and smiled more to himself than to Alix. "I never had time to learn of reading and book subjects. I did not even need them to continue in my task. Words are not needed when one has a sword. Now," he said simply, "I feel the lack."

"But why come to me?"

"Because you will help me." The look on Severin's face did not quite match the confidence of his words. He had doubts that she would help him and Alix knew it.

"We can strike a bargain," he added.

Alix remained silent, knowing that he would continue. After an instant he did.

"You have what I want. You know to distinguish words and you can teach me that. In exchange I have my sword and I will use the influence of that sword to see that your husband—that Robert of Mercier—is not left for the ravens. I will champion his right to Christian burial with Guigny and if necessary with the Duke of Burgundy himself."

Alix sucked in her breath. "How will you do this?

'Tis Lancelot de Guigny who commands at Mercier now and he has determined to use Robert as example."

"More than anything else, Guigny wants recognition and a title. In order to have both he not only needs to take Mercier, he must also manage to keep it. And to keep it he must show mercy and bring peace. This is something he will readily understand when it is pointed out to him. Despite his threats and blusterings, his thoughts are probably already picking along this path. I will just make his way easier by allowing him to be magnanimous."

Alix could see the wisdom in this. For the first time since her husband's death she felt the smallest sliver of hope. She looked carefully at the man who stood so close beside her on the rampart. She considered his girth and the deep-golden weft of his short hair; she examined the simplicity of his black tunic and the plain link belt that girded his sword. She examined his eyes. And then she nodded her assent.

"We will do as you say," she said to him. "And I thank you for your help."

She would have curtseyed into a deep reverence before him, but Severin Brigante reached out and stopped her. His hand was firm as it took her arm.

"But you must pledge to me that you hold no other secrets," he said to her. "Just the message pigeons, nothing more. I cannot defend you unless I know the whole of the truth."

Alix opened her mouth around that truth but then she shut it once again. How could she tell this man about Yvrain? How could she tell him that she held concealed the child who might one day call an end to all the plans that had been so carefully plotted against the House of Mercier? How could she tell this stranger—this enemy—of the death promise she had made to her husband?

So instead of the true words, she heard herself saying, "No secrets. I hid only the birds," and prayed that God would look down and understand the lie.

God didn't seem quite near enough on this crisp day and on this lonely rampart but Severin Brigante was and Alix felt him study her. She grew uncomfortable under his scrutiny and quickly reached with her cold fingers to take the crumpled message from his hands.

"This is my name," she said, opening it to him. "This is Alix. A-L-I-X . . ."

She moved closer and forced his attention to the word. Behind them the pigeons cooed and fluttered in their wooden cage while a shaft of sunlight bounced against the Maltese Star at her throat.

It winked at him.

"No one followed me," Alix said. She put down her basket of dried seeds onto the packed earth in front of the Wise Woman's house. "They think I have gone to the gardens to gauge the ground for spring planting."

"The Knight de Guigny thinks the chatelaine of Mercier would attend to her own garden chores?" said Young Sophie. Her freckle-splashed face looked dubious. "He may not be noble-born but he should know better than that."

"The Knight de Guigny is no longer at Mercier," replied Alix. "He is gone on pilgrimage to a shrine within the forest. He will not be back until after vespers—at least that is what I have been told."

" 'Tis well that monster should do penance," Sophie replied. "The priest spent all the day within the meadow blessing new land to hold the dead of Mercier. The Knight de Guigny's men raped two women in the village; they called them spoils of war. One of them still bleeds from her handling."

"We should take advantage of Sir Lancelot's absence and make plans for the care of the child," said Alix anxiously. "Is your mother near?"

"She has gone down to the stream to regard the cress that grows there. It should sprout again just after the spring thawing. She left me to guard Yvrain. Would you care to see him, lady? He is just inside."

"No, no." The Countess de Mercier shook her head. "Let him rest. I will stay here in the sunshine until the Wise Woman returns. I must talk to her before I am missed."

Alix sat down on a rough wood bench and leaned her back against the stone cottage. The Wise Woman had not chosen to place her hut within the walls of the village, but this was understood. A witch's house must be near running water and it must stand free. It could not hide within the shelter that others instinctively sought. Everyone knew this, even the slowest of peasants; the knowledge of it added to a Wise Woman's allure and also to her price. Many were the things demanded of her. She must not show fear—that was the most important. Even if her knees beat together and her heart hammered in her breast she must not let men know that she feared them. Often it was only courage that stood as her barrier against the violence of brigands and roving knights of the Inquisition that the Spanish saint, Dominic de Guzman, had brought to France.

A Wise Woman must be strong.

Alix thought of this now as she looked around her at the small clearing. It was a neat and tidy space, not at all what she had expected though she realized now

that her expectations had been formed by wives' tales
and illustrated romances. The cottage edged the forest
but the earth before it was neatly smoothed and
packed and there were woven baskets hanging from
large iron nails hammered into the wattles. She
breathed deeply of the rich smells that floated out
from them. Alix guessed that they were filled with
dried herbs and roots—all the things that a witch
might need for healing work. Her nose identified one
or two: sweet borage, thistle—a few other random
scents.

Though her own mother had briefly served as one,
Alix had never encountered a Wise Woman since coming to France. The illustrious Dame de Mercier's few
illnesses had been cured by the scientific skill of monk-
physicians from Haute Fleur and, as she had never
been with child, she had never had need of a midwife.
She was curious, and a little frightened, at the idea of
meeting one now. She wondered if Sophie's mother
would be stooped and wrinkled and if she would have
warts and a hooked raven's nose. She wondered if she
was truly a witch. Alix shivered deliciously at the fearful
thought.

So deep was she within her own fantasy that she did
not hear the woman approach.

"Welcome, my lady," she said. "I am Sophie, Young
Sophie's mother, and I am the Wise Woman here."

Alix jumped to her feet, though actually she immediately realized that there was nothing frightening or
harmful about this woman. Her skin had been tinted
deep brown by years of summer sun so that even now,
winter, it still looked burnished and healthy. Small,
bright eyes peeked through the webbing of wrinkles
of her handsome face and she was dressed in a neat
flaxen cloak. Sophie carried a basket of small green
leaves—the first true green that Alix had seen since

the start of autumn—and her hands on the basket's hemp handle were strong and sturdy.

The Wise Woman smiled at her; it was a wry smile filled with sympathy and compassion. Much to her horror, Alix felt tears well and the trembling that had so embarrassed her last night with the Knight Brigante. She put a hand to her mouth to stop the sobbing but the sounds came out anyway in huge, dry clots. The storm, though fierce, passed quickly. Through it all, the Wise Woman stood nearby but did not touch her and for this Alix was grateful. She knew that she would die if she were touched.

"I've spring water," said Sophie, but only when Alix had quieted. "I will pour you out some."

She filled a wooden goblet from a leather flask and held it out to the Countess de Mercier. Alix drank it down through the last hiccuping remnants of her tears. The water tasted fresh and pure.

"I must beg pardon," she said. "I don't know from whence these spells come. I don't know what causes them."

"They are caused by the shock and the loss. You have suffered much, my lady—and not just in these days of massacre. Perhaps too much for a young one to bear. The sobbing may be your body telling you that you must rest and gain strength for what still lies ahead."

"I have no time for resting," said Alix. "Not while I still remain countess of this place. I must see to my duties. Is Yvrain safe?"

"I will bring him to you." Sophie did not wait for the Countess de Mercier's response. She moved quickly into the cottage and emerged with the child in her arms. Yvrain's clothes had been changed from the lace and fine linen of his nightdress. He was swaddled in the sturdy cottage-weave of a village child.

Without wanting to, Alix marked his shiny, dark hair and bright cheeks. Yvrain yawned sleepily and reached out. Sophie placed him into Alix's arms before she had a chance to protest.

"But I've never held a child before," cried the Countess de Mercier. She did not add that she did not want to hold this one now. She was too ashamed to tell anyone how much she hated him.

"Then 'tis high time you held one and best you start with Yvrain. He cries just as you do," said the Wise Woman. "Like yours, my lady, his tears strike up from nowhere and they flow without warning. We are lucky to be so far from the village that his weeping cannot be heard. You were wise to send him out to us."

"You were good-hearted to have him, and I am deeply in debt to you for your help," said Alix, gingerly holding the child. "But you know of course that the Knight de Guigny would have us tortured and put to death if he were to find the child here. I told him Yvrain was already dead and that his body had been tossed into the stream. I'm sure he believes that I killed him."

" 'Tis a convenient belief for him," said Sophie, "and he might persist in it because it lessens his own guilt."

Alix could sense no fear on her as the witch continued.

"I follow the old ways and not those of the new Church, but I know that if we were to allow the Knight Guigny to kill this defenseless child then there would be little of true living left in the life that remains to me. I must defend him—just as you must. But it is best he be gotten away from here and quickly. Have you a plan?"

Yvrain started to fret and without thinking, Alix rocked and soothed him. "I sent off pigeons to the

Monastery of Haute Fleur. One was captured . . ." Alix
stopped and blushed, remembering the reading pact
she had made with Severin Brigante and the lie she
had told him. ". . . but the other may have safely arrived. If so, we will know soon. My mother has a great
friend at that monastery. He is Padre Gasca de Loran
and though he is an old man now he will surely take
to his donkey and reach us once he hears news of the
danger. We can safely trust Yvrain to his keeping. The
Monastery of Haute Fleur was one of the first founded
by Bernard of Clairvaux when he began the Cistercian
Order and preached the Crusade. He is canonized now
and considered one of the greatest saints of Burgundy.
No one, not even Lancelot de Guigny, would dare to
break a sanctuary established by a saint. Yvrain will be
safe there."

"Aye," agreed the Wise Woman.

"Ali! Ali!" cried Robert's child. Surprised, Alix bent
toward him and tangled his plump fists in the loose
flow of her fair hair.

"I have been thinking," said Alix to the Knight Brigante, "that perhaps we should begin our lessons with
the simple Psalter. All children are taught their prayers
by rote. You were as well, were you not?"

Severin nodded.

"Then 'tis well to begin an unfamiliar study with
something that is already known. This is new for me
as well. I've not taught reading before."

She stopped and smiled. Severin was amazed at how
much that smile brightened and changed her.

"But I will pay first for the instruction," he said. It
bothered him to be in anyone's debt. "Lancelot de
Guigny returned from his pilgrimage this eventide at
vespers. I have arranged to meet with him just after

the main meal when he will be mellowed with wine. I will put forth my suit at that time. The Monastery at Haute Fleur has sent word that a certain Padre Gasca de Loran—a guest with them of dubious Portuguese origin but an ordained priest all the same—has taken saddle to a donkey and should be arriving this late-night. He also has requested an urgent audience with Sir Lancelot. You would undoubtedly know something of his mission?"

Alix faced him squarely. "I sent forth two pigeons and only one was caught. They both carried the same message of appeal to my mother's old friend to come and aid me in my quest of Christian burial for my husband."

They were again on the secret place of the rampart. They had decided to meet there because it was removed from the main interests of the castle. No one would bother them here. Winter's dark had settled early and a cold wind blew, but Alix could see Severin's face clearly in the light of the torches that shimmered below them in the castle keep.

" 'Tis good that you did that for we will need all the persuasive help we can get," said Severin. "But the lessons are important to me and I have given my word. The Knight de Guigny will allow Christian burial for your husband. He will not maim him; he will not leave his body to the ravens."

Alix would have curtseyed an obeisance but once again he stopped her.

"No reverences," he said. "I am but fulfilling my part of our pact. It is nothing to me personally if Robert de Mercier and the whole of his garrison rot forever on top of God's earth."

"But the dead of the garrison are already decently buried on newly blessed land and the few injured who were left alive have been medicined and cared for," replied Alix, looking straight upon the Knight Brigante. "They say you are the one who arranged these things but surely the Knight de Guigny will not approve them. Did you do this as well only for the lessons in reading?"

Severin looked away from her. "These lessons are important to me," he repeated.

Certainly he had not wanted to become involved with this. He had not planned it; he did not want it. The taking of Mercier's castle had been just a labor for him. The duke had sent word to Tuscany, hiring the Gold Company. His terms had been more than handsome and Severin had responded. It had seemed a wise idea then, now his golden spurs jingled irritably as he strode to join the Knight de Guigny in the Great Hall. But what else could he have done? He was the mercenary general of a mercenary army. That he should command *this* particular army—the Gold Company, which had been led successively first by his uncle and then by Alix's father—was a jest of the gods and best left to be understood by them. All he knew was that when the chance to learn reading had presented itself, no tumbler could have leaped for it as quickly as he had. He had, as usual, craved the opportunity to push on, to distinguish his name, to amend . . .

But amend what? What had *he* done?

Severin shook his head as the noise of his spurs rang out even more angrily. He was a warrior, and not given to introspection. One day he would be able to demand that Belden of Harnoncourt acknowledge his brother and take responsibility for the great mischief that had been done to him. He would reach that goal and he knew it. He had lived for nothing else since Guy d'Harnoncourt had died begging that what had been cast wrong be set right. And Severin knew he would do this; he knew he was close.

Still, there was the little question of the Countess de Mercier.

"I'll not think about her," he pledged aloud, "I haven't the time."

But time was exactly what they would be spending together.

He had no idea what had possessed him to ask her for the lessons in reading. The fact that he had no parchment-learning was a secret that he had held closely to himself for most of his life. He had early on learned ways to hide and counterbalance his inadequacy by working sums in his head, studying other people's movements, letting them speak first. So what led him to confess all to a chit of a woman who looked on him with loathing?

It was *because* of her look, he decided, forgetting that he had just vowed to stop thinking about the Lady Alix.

He knew that more than one night's tragedy had changed her from the girl he had glimpsed in Paris to the chatelaine of Mercier Castle. Despite himself he kept remembering how she had smiled then—and the way she didn't smile now. He suspected that her sadness predated her husband's death, horrific and unexpected as that death had been. He had seen death before; he knew the emotions it brought forth. Anger, grief, disbelief—but not this deep sadness.

He wondered what her life had been.

"God's tooth," he swore.

Well, there was nothing for it. She would teach him reading and he would champion her cause. They had made that pact. Soon spring would come and it would find him across the mountains and in Rome, on mission for the duke. Or at least Jean of Burgundy had intimated as much when last they met. Severin found, again to his surprise, that he missed his own country and would be grateful to be in Italy once again. One day soon there would also be the reckoning with his uncle. He would meet Belden of Harnoncourt on equal terms. Severin smiled. A sweet life lay before him.

There was just one small matter to be settled first.

"She's right, you know," Severin said.

Theirs was a solitary meal but a fine one, in acknowledgment of the fact that the Knight de Guigny had fasted all day. The Hall sat empty around them. Sir Lancelot had brought his own chef with him from the Burgundian capital of Dijon. He had made sure the man was placed in the first caravan of provision wagons that had entered the castle after its capture. Indeed, a great deal of effort had been lavished upon the safety of this one man. Guigny thought him worth it. The night meal was an extravagance of roasted doves and dressed greens, spiced fruits and wines. Severin ate what the liveried servants put before him but he did not share Sir Lancelot's taste for culinary refinements. He looked with aversion at a poor peacock that had been plucked, roasted, and then made to suffer the final indignity of having his plumes stuck back into his marinated body. Severin sighed. He would have much preferred a simply roasted joint.

Besides, peacocks brought bad luck.

"Have some of this raisin sauce," said Guigny. He seemed to ignore Severin's remark as he handed over a small but exquisite beaten silver bowl. Severin wondered at its provenance. Although he had held Mercier in possession for only a short time, Sir Lancelot already moved through the castle with such propriety that one had trouble discerning if what he offered was his own or if the blood of Robert de Mercier still glistened upon it. As usual, Lancelot de Guigny was superbly outfitted in a dark velvet tunic whose sleeves were edged in miniver. The very English Severin Harnoncourt marveled at the French knight's fastidiousness and watched as he helped himself to a pretty slice of cloved orange.

"I take it you mean the Countess de Mercier," Guigny said at last. "A most interesting woman that— and a pretty one as well. One wonders at Robert's taste in choosing a peasant over her."

Severin, the victor of more battles than he cared to name, was not about to let himself be led into a blind that centered round the prettiness of a grieving widow. " 'Tis better to bury Robert de Mercier," he said. " 'Tis better not to stir up controversy when you are so new in the possession. A simple transition is always best—one that does not give cause for counteraction."

"What counteraction could there be?" Lancelot's bored voice belied the glint of interest that Severin could see in the depths of his cold eyes. "Jean of Burgundy is liege lord here. Acting through us, he has merely shown his sovereignty. Robert de Mercier's body upon the battlements will serve as a warning to all the other nobles of Burgundy that the duke will countenance no traitoring within his realm. That is the warning given. It will be the warning taken."

"But many hereabout hold loyalty to King Charles to be as important as their fealty to the duke. They see Jean of Burgundy as the betrayer to his own liege lord," said Severin mildly. He had taken adroit charge of the conversation and forged on into it before Guigny could clear his mouth to speak. "The taking of Mercier Castle is enough. If, in this Christian land, the Count of the Mercier is not offered a

Christian burial, it might stir up the tides of revolt. 'Tis already shocking enough that such a powerful man died unshriven, especially when he was surprised within his own abode by false monks to whom he had offered hospitality. You could easily have the Church itself and all its prelates upon you for that. Already, hearing rumor, the Abbot of Haute Fleur has sent one of his priests to bear witness to what has happened here. If you do not show compassion, you will turn Robert de Mercier from a debauched adulterer into a saint."

Lancelot stared at him from behind hooded dark eyes. He no longer pretended to be entranced by the marzipan monkey that lay upon his silver plate. "But I have shown the Widow Mercier great mercy. Both her life and her honor have been spared—at least so far." Guigny's voice grew petulant. "Surely she cannot be pleading mercy for a husband who was slain while he slept with another? Instead she should be offering *te deums* in thanksgiving that she has been liberated from the farce of her marriage. Through her father's blood she is a de Montfort of France. You know how proud that house is. Living a situation like this cannot have been pleasant for her."

Severin shrugged in the universal way that all men shrug when they discuss the vagaries of women.

"I can offer no reason for her actions," he said. "All I know is that she begs for her husband's body."

"What is your advice in this matter?"

"That you should let her have it." That was what Severin meant to say and he said it, but then for some reason he heard himself add, "It might be good to hold the Lady Alix in friendship. It is she who wears the Maltese Star."

* * *

She was sleeping when the knock sounded, but the priest did not wait for her reply. He entered her room before she could even open her eyes. After all, his were the hands that had brought her into this world.

Alix sensed him all around her. She smelled his warm apple smell that so reminded her of childhood's happy times in Italy at Belvedere. Once awakened, she was not at all surprised that the priest had come. Or that he had managed to enter the besieged place that Mercier Castle had become.

"Padre Gasca," she said. She struggled up from beneath her fox rugs and smiled at him through the chilly light that his torch threw around them. Her fire had died and she shivered in her bed. "I knew that the messenger pigeon would reach you. I prayed to the Madonna. I knew that it would be so."

" 'Tis always good to pray, but you knew I would. I had already dray-packed my donkey and was begging leave of the Prior when your message arrived."

He chuckled and the whole of his nut-brown face seemed to dissolve into the brightness of a smile. His smile reminded her of something, of someone, and she frowned, trying to remember; but the priest was speaking again and the shred of thought left her.

"I traveled in upon my donkey. Have you ever known me to take any other means? Why, even when I accompanied the Lady Francesca to England and when I went with your mother to Hungary did I not . . ."

But Alix, who knew this man well, would not let herself be sidetracked by this prattle. He had received her message; that much was clear. The Monastery of Haute Fleur was not far but it passed through roads that neither the duke's nor Robert's troops had managed to totally free from brigands. Even a person as other-

worldly as Gasca de Loran would not have set out upon
them without preparation.

She reached for her black velvet shawl and wrapped
herself in it, then moved to sit upon a stool that
flanked the remnants of her chamber's fire. She motioned the priest to the ornate chair beside her.

"How did you hear?" she asked him.

"Priests are always the first to hear of disaster. Word
reached us at Haute Fleur whilst we recited our matins.
It was still the dead of night. I imagine the dying had
not even finished their last agonies when we began the
prayers for their immortal souls."

"Twenty dead," said Alix, staring into the fire.
"Mostly from the garrison but two women as well. I
could have been among them. The Knight Brigante
saw them all buried. He did this today whilst Lancelot
de Guigny went to pray and do penance at a forest
shrine instituted by Bernard of Clairvaux. He sought
the intercession of the saint."

"A saint who has been in heaven for these two hundred years," mused Gasca, "seems a most unlikely
source of pardon for a living man."

"Guigny has taken a position that has stood impreg-
nable for hundreds of years. He is at the height of his
powers. The only man standing between him and divine destiny is his half brother the Duke of Burgundy."
Alix paused. "You have heard what he plans for
Robert's body?"

The priest did not need to answer. Instead he
reached over and patted Alix's shoulder. Unbidden
tears welled up in her eyes at his touch, just as they
had with Severin Brigante and just as they had with
the witch in the woods.

*Don't touch me, she wanted to shriek at her friend. Don't
touch me or else I'll shatter into shards.*

But of course she, the Countess de Mercier, could

not scream. She could not allow herself to shatter. She must never allow her feelings to break through and prevent her from doing her duty. Never. So instead she jumped up and began to cram wood onto the dying fire. Behind her the stool she had sat upon clattered to the floor stones.

"We heard everything," she heard the priest say. "It is rumored that after his days of prayer and penance, Lancelot de Guigny will present himself before the Abbot of Haute Fleur to seek the pardon of his sins. These are feckless times and one would not want to have upon one's conscience the murder of a sleeping man—especially a sleeping man of higher rank than oneself. The ancient Greeks believed that rash actions such as these often return to haunt."

"Sir Lancelot was never vassal to Robert," Alix said shortly. "Guigny serves only one overlord and that is the duke himself."

"Indeed?" said the priest.

Alix righted her stool and sat upon it once again. Her hands had got dirty from the wood and she wiped them on the rich fabric of her cloak.

"Strange they took your maid away," said Gasca from behind her. "Does she not sleep with you in this room? Most do, I am told—on small pallets."

Alix kept her eyes dutifully on the fireplace as she said, "She was frightened. She knew the Knight de Guigny had made a mistake in killing Solange—in not killing me with my husband. She was afraid that he would rectify it and might take her as well. She ran away."

Forgive me, Sophie. But I cannot let even this kind man know that we hide Yvrain. At least not until Robert is Christianly buried.

With a whoosh the kindling burst into flames.

"Lancelot de Guigny makes no mistakes," said

Gasca mildly. "If you live still, my little one, it is because he sees benefit for himself in that fact. Have you spoken to him?"

"Last night. I went to plead with him for Robert's body. The customs in this case are barbaric and he has proven himself to be a barbaric man. He said that Robert must serve as an example. He will be quartered, the Knight de Guigny assures me, and his body put upon the four posts of his castle. He said that Robert was a traitor against the Duke of Burgundy, his liege lord, and that he must meet a traitor's end. But of course you know that."

"It is but our duty to know the happenings in the parish," replied Gasca, but he had the grace to blush.

"Robert did only what he saw as right," said Alix. "Even Duke Jean's own brother Philip has turned against him in this. He thinks it akin to regicide to traitor a legitimate king—and regicide is something that happens in England, not in France."

"Charles of France is mad, and his periods of lucidity grow far between. France is no longer ruled by him but by his wanton wife, Queen Isabeau." Gasca had wrapped himself so deeply in a fox rug that only the grizzled top of his tonsured head stuck out. "We don't even need to whisper this fact anymore. The world knows it."

They sat for a moment in silence, watching the fire dance and crackle before them.

"It was all only an excuse," Alix said finally. "Guigny has always wanted Mercier Castle, since he has no fortress of his own, and for that he needed my husband dead. Robert was a kind and good man who was always taken advantage of by those who loved him most. In his heart he was ever loyal to the duke. He would never have seriously planned open revolt."

A lift of the eyebrow was all the response Gasca made to this. Not for the first time he marveled at the tendency in human beings to hold tightest to that which hurt them most. Robert de Mercier was a weak and selfish man who had tortured his innocent wife— and yet rather than be relieved his death had freed her, Alix clung to the memory of a man who had never existed. Indeed, she seemed quite intent on embellishing him, making him into the perfect husband. One glance at the makeshift altar she had constructed in his memory told him this. The priest sighed. Human nature was what is was and there was no gainsaying this. Gasca looked up, and the Maltese Star that Alix carried at her throat captured his gaze. He wondered how much Julian had told her of its origin—or how much the Knight Brigante would. He had a feeling that Sir Severin knew a great deal about its history, as well he should, considering how low his father had been brought by it.

At least Alix has the power to break free—if she chooses to.

As if reading his thoughts, Alix raised her hand to touch the talisman. She stroked it idly as she began to speak again, probably without realizing that she did so. The gesture was not lost on the priest.

"Burgundy sees an advantage at this time," Alix was saying, "what with the king weakened and the queen involved in her own debaucheries. He saw this same advantage once before when he had Louis d'Orleans, the king's brother—who also just happened to be the queen's lover—murdered. Duke Jean, of course, said that he was doing this for the good of France. However, being the king's cousin, he also benefited from the elimination of a rival. It perched him closer to the throne."

Gasca wondered why she was telling him this now. Doubtless she had heard the gist of the story from her father, Olivier Ducci Montaldo, who had fought beside Jean of Burgundy at that debacle of a battle against the Sultan Bayezid at Nicopolis. But why would she give this history lesson when surely she must know why he had come? She *must* know. Alix was the Magdalene's daughter, and if legend were to be believed she would one day be the Magdalene herself. Surely she would know what was about to happen. She had all the instincts of a great Wise Woman.

He edged forward just a little in his seat, and strained to hear the terce bell.

Yet when he spoke, it was in his usual calm and mild way. "That is human nature and makes him no worse than the mass of men. The best of us can rarely admit our own wrongs, and Burgundy can hardly be numbered among the saints. Duke John is a spoiled and proud man—and an ugly one. He was jealous of his more graced cousin and had him hacked to death by ruffians on a Parisian street. Naturally he lied to one and all—himself included—that he did this for the honor and glory of both France and its king. Thus are the ways of men. I doubt that even Genghis Khan thought himself a monster."

"Yet monsters live," said Alix quietly. "But I will not have that demon Lancelot de Guigny hack my husband's body."

The terce bell ceased its ringing. Gasca, though old and arthritic now, got readily to his feet and reached out to Alix.

"Your cause has been championed," he said, taking her iced hand. "Lancelot de Guigny has agreed to Christian interment for my lord of Mercier. We go to bury him now."

It had been decided that Robert's body would find its final, simple rest in the churchyard of the castle keep, and not within the church itself. Not even Alix had expected more than this. Burial was a particularly delicate issue because besides Mercier ancestors, the church housed the bones of St. Christophe. No one actually knew very much about this particularly blessed person but in life he was reputed to have visions where he viewed and conversed with the Three Wise Men and in death he was deemed a miracle worker. Visits to his shrine were steadfastly encouraged because tolls and pilgrimages were lucrative for the village coffers. This was especially true during winter months when participation at fairs and markets might slacken but when miracles, at least monetary ones, were needed just as much as they were in summer.

Robert could not be buried in the same church as a holy man. There was no question of this.

Lancelot de Guigny wanted no chance left that the dead count might come back to haunt him from the grave. Times changed and notions with them. Guigny, a bastard, was well used to looking at life through reality's prism. He knew that what was looked upon as treachery today could easily be seen as heroism tomorrow should the King prevail in the end, against his cousin, Burgundy. A shift in that story could change the role that Robert had played in it as well. Sir Lancelot, hedging his betting, would allow the man burial, but he thought it best to keep him as far removed as possible from the saint so there could be no mistake in identity.

He, himself, would not attend.

"An adulterer," Lancelot had said to Alix in the brief moment that she had been ushered into his presence and he had given permission for this hushed, secret burial. Even though it was deep night and the castle slept around him, his eyes had been as alert and predatory as a cat's. Alix had felt his heat surround her.

The Knight de Guigny referred to Robert's infidelity and the Countess de Mercier had made a low reverence to him as if in acquiescence. But they both had known it was not the adultery that kept the late Count de Mercier from taking his last place with the remnant of his industrious family.

So Robert was to be secretly buried near the castle, and not in the village. He, from such an ancient family, would be buried in ground blessed only that day. Alix stood shivering as she held the rush torch for Padre Gasca. She had wanted him to wear something more substantial, a fur cloak or blanket, against the bitter cold, but he had said no. The burial of a body and the blessing of a soul were sacred duties that behooved a certain humility on the part of God's chosen emissary. He wore the simple homespun of his Franciscan order. Alix wore her mourning black. Her only jewelry was the Maltese Star her mother had passed on to her.

Alix had also decided that Solange should be buried beside Robert. As she explained to the priest, the plot chosen and blessed was necessarily small and far removed. If she were not buried here, Solange would have been put in unholy ground. Alix was not prepared to do this; nor was she prepared to leave her husband's mistress without being prayed over. It was bad enough that they had both died unshriven and without being able to confess their sins to a priest and ask forgiveness.

Although she did not say this to Padre Gasca, she was certain that her burying of Solange beside Robert was a weakness on her part and that a stronger woman would not have done it. She had visions of this stronger woman taking her revenge, and making sure that the lovers were separated at long last and for eternity. Alix was not this strong woman. She was too weak, she decided, too frail.

And feeling too much grief.

All around her, wind whipped just enough to force her attention to Padre Gasca as he intoned the ancient Latin words of the *Dies Irae* and the other prayers for the repose of Robert's soul and for that of Solange as well. Above her head the moon was full and silvery, floating on the shadows of the winter sky. Sometimes, when it peeked out through the scudding clouds, she could clearly see the priest beside her but even when she could not see him she could hear his words.

"That day of wrath, that dreadful day
When heaven and earth in ashes lay."

The verse was so harsh, too harsh to give Alix a comfortable knowledge that in the end Robert's soul would find repose. Her mind wandered to the times without number when she had looked out of her chamber window to see the only man she loved—the only man she was quite sure that she would ever love—as he loved another woman. As he picked flowers for his mistress and gently pulled a leaf from the dark curtain of her hair.

How often she had wanted Solange dead and, if she were truthful, how often she had wanted Robert to suffer as well.

But not like this, she whispered. *Never like this*.

She had never wanted him startled from sleep to face a death that was so quick and so unjust. She had wanted him to suffer, but only so that in the end he might love her and talk to her and pick flowers for her the way that he had picked them for Solange. She had wanted what Solange had and she had wanted what her own mother, Julian Madrigal, had, and even what the village slop woman had. Someone to love her. Was it so wrong to want her own husband to love her? Was it her desperate longing for Robert that had brought down such disaster?

For just an instant, guilt wracked Alix so strongly that she thought she would lose her balance. But there was no change around her. Padre Gasca continued his serene recitation of prayers meant to guide Robert's soul and that of Solange on their way to heaven.

There was a footstep and Alix turned to face Severin Brigante. He was alone. He had come without knights, and in the company of only two men-at-arms. Alix could think of no reason for his being there; he had not even known her husband and had arrived at Mercier after the killings. But she decided that the Knight de Guigny had sent him as emissary to make sure that the stipulations for the burial had been justly carried out. They would not want the myth of martyrdom to enshroud the Count of Mercier. She felt the heaviness of the Maltese Star around her neck warm her, as though it had taken added heat from the torch which Severin Brigante held. She heard his voice fuse with hers as they gave proper response to the priest's prayers.

Something swished above their heads and Alix looked up to see Lancelot de Guigny's strangely shaped banners fluttering from the ramparts. Night had leeched all the color from them and they floated black against the black sky. Her glance caught movement as a man's shadow hastened to blend into the shade.

She wondered who that dark man might be but then assumed it must be the Knight de Guigny. Who else would have interest in such a simple task? Padre Gasca finished with his Psalter and then sprinkled incense and blessed water over the oak caskets. The men-at-

arms slowly lowered them on sturdy hemp ropes and
began to tamp earth into the open graves.

Alix crossed herself and hurried off, not daring to
look again at the Knight Brigante lest his quick mind
read her thoughts.

At last Robert was safely buried.

But there still remained the question of his son.

Five

They began their reading lessons late on the next day but one after Robert's small funeral. They agreed to meet on the hidden rampart where they had first pledged to help each other and they continued to meet there—weather permitting—as the end of winter turned gradually into the beginning of spring.

Alix decided upon a beautiful Psalter from the monastery at Cluny for the subject of her tutoring.

"Though it is in Latin and I would have preferred something in Italian, which is the native language for us both."

"And I would have preferred learning something more interesting than my prayers."

"Perhaps later," replied Alix, "but in these risky times a knight cannot be too well-versed in words of intercession. Not when he may find himself, from one instant to the next, compelled to recite them before heaven's throne." She smiled.

Severin would have recited anything—a host of prayers or Caesar's speeches—just to keep that brief light upon her face. He loved it when she smiled.

But, "We will start with the prayers," was all that he said.

She ordered the Psalter from the monk who cared for Robert's library. This was not in any way thought amiss. The Countess de Mercier had often been known to amuse herself with her husband's valuable parchments and manuscripts. Many of them still lay about her own chambers, as though their actual place was there. Robert had never objected to this diversion for her; the monk saw no reason why he himself should object now.

The manuscript was duly procured and sent to the Lady Alix.

It was actually quite a lovely object, though less for its bright illustrations than for its careful bindings. Robert de Mercier, priding himself on a book collection that could match that of the King of England, had taken special pride in his copy of the Cluny Psalter, because he knew the king, his rival in this, did not as yet possess one. It was that rarity—a bound book. Its covers were of softest, dark deerskin and its hinges and nails of beaten silver.

"We will begin with this psalm," she said, pointing to the first symbols on the ivory-colored parchment. She read the words aloud in their written Latin. "Now please repeat."

Severin pointed to the words as she had done. But as she began the next phrase he shook his head and placed his fingers upon hers so that their two hands moved together.

" 'Tis easier this way for me," he said, "if I touch the words with you as you speak them."

Alix hesitated, but then she complied. The warmth of Severin's hands made her realize how terribly cold her own fingers were. On the few times Robert had come to her it had been for a serious purpose—the planting of seed—and he had treated his task and her body with the detached and deliberate respect a farmer might show for well-harrowed ground.

There was nothing planned about the way Severin

touched her, however; when his hand brushed against her it seemed the most natural thing in the world.

On sun-filled days and clouded ones, the large knight and his tutor sat huddled together on their small wooden bench, as their hands and their eyes traced a pathway through the Psalter, and its jumble of symbols gradually arranged themselves into recognizable words.

"How goes the child?" Alix murmured. She was seated in the small lady's balcony that overlooked the Great Hall. Both she and Sophie were bent over mending that the Knight de Guigny had sent up for their attention. They spoke in whispers, heads bent close together. "Has anyone heard him cry? Has anyone come near?"

Young Sophie glanced quickly around, although they were the only two in this small space. Only then did she shake her head. It had been four weeks since the massacre. Already the castle was beginning to function—and function well—under its new lord. Sophie, loyal though she was to the memory of Count Robert, could still see the improvements that his successor had made.

De Mercier's talents had lain in directions far removed from the traditional ones of a knight-warrior. List fields that for years had lain fallow and deserted now stood spruced and ready for action. More importantly, the castle's deteriorated battlements had been improved and watches set throughout the night. War was coming, everyone realized this, and the common folk knew that there was nothing they could do to deter it. The only thing for them was to pray that they would find the fortress snug and fit when they were forced to run to its shelter.

Lancelot de Guigny had given them this.

The village was rife with rumors about the castle. The peasants of Mercier had seen violence aplenty and had suffered under the yoke of the dukes since time beyond mind, but no one could remember a time when the castle itself had passed from the lax hand of the regional knight-count to the iron one of his liege lord. This was truly a wonder and had caused no end of fervent speculation and gossip, especially now in winter when there was less work to do in the fields. No one could make a clear decision about what had happened but thought it best to take an attitude of patience and let events play out.

Even the village priest counseled this. "With the world in such a state of rampant sinfulness," he admonished his congregation one day amidst the reading of the psalms. " 'Tis perhaps best not to make a hasty alliance until the lights of fate point out the true victor. We are but fallen men and mightily prone to the commission of error and poor people pay most when they err."

Even the least man in the village knew the scandalous fact that the Duke of Burgundy had not as yet confirmed his half brother in the lordship of Mercier.

Young Sophie saw the strain of these events on her young mistress and she remarked upon them to her own mother, the witch. Alix's hands were chalk-white against the black stuff of her mourning. Her face, too, had drawn in tightly upon itself—even more so than in the last days of her marriage to Count Robert—and sometimes her body trembled. The only time she seemed to relax her guard was when the Knight Brigante was near. Otherwise she was wan and silent.

Sophie remarked upon this to her mother.

"Have they made no provisions for her?" Sophie the Elder had asked one day as she dandled Yvrain at her knee. "Has the Knight de Guigny taken no decision?"

"None." Her daughter's face glowed fervently. "The Lady Alix expects to be convented. When she speaks of it, which is rarely, she says that this is surely what will happen. She does not believe that the Knight de Guigny will repay her dowry from the storage chests of Mercier and without it she will not return to her father's house. She wishes not to beggar herself, even to her own family. For her this is a matter of honor. Still it is the Duke of Burgundy who will decide this matter. He is titular lord of Mercier; the castle was taken in his name, although the Knight de Guigny holds its expectations. The duke is expected at the castle from day to day, but as yet no time has been settled upon for his arrival. But my Lady Alix says it does not matter to her when he comes. She has determined to spend the rest of her life in silent prayer and devotion."

Sophie the Elder had nodded but said nothing.

"No one comes near my mother's hut," Young Sophie now said to her mistress. "They are superstitious as to what will happen. His parents flaunted him and so Yvrain is well known at Mercier village. But the few who realize he has found refuge with my mother will not risk a witch's wrath by betraying her to Sir Lancelot—especially as they know my mother and they do not yet know the Knight de Guigny. These are mightily uncertain times. No one wants to put himself under the protection of a lord not yet confirmed in his title."

Alix nodded. Below them there was a great burst of laughter from the Knight de Guigny's table and then the braying of dogs. Alix took advantage of the noise and the mirth to further question her young maid.

"You are certain that no one has made inquiries?"

Sophie shook her head, the mop of her curls wagging forcefully.

"That child will be the death of me," Alix whispered. Sophie saw her shiver. Almost, she thought, as though a goose had crossed her grave. "From the day of his birth he has brought me nothing but misery. Yet I must see him safely settled. I have no choice in this. Padre Gasca has gone back to Haute Fleur to beg sanctuary there for Robert's child. If this is granted then he will be safe. No one would dare the wrath of heaven by violating the sanctity of that sacred monastery."

Peasant common sense made Sophie forget that she spoke to the rightful Countess de Mercier. "And how would you do that? Lancelot de Guigny flaunted all the rules of chivalry by surprising Count Robert in his sleep. Do you think he would not dare to murder his son—especially when this son is illegitimate and friendless? Yvrain has no champion."

"I am his champion," said Alix with some vehemence, "and I have promised to see him safely settled."

Sophie lowered her head and attended more closely to her mending. Her peasant's common sense told her that the Countess de Mercier would be much better off if she tore out her hair and threatened self-poisoning. Sophie thought it dreadful the way her mistress insisted upon this duty to Yvrain.

Yet that was not the worst of it.

There was also the small altar within the Lady Alix's chamber. Two low beeswax candles were always kept burning on the trestle where Count Robert's bloodied mantle had been placed and on which his sheathed dagger lay. Sophie had caught her mistress crying there more than once.

Sophie also had begun to entertain the thought that her mistress might have developed the fey habit of reading minds, though perhaps she did not realize that she did this.

As if in response, Alix said, "Father Gasca has promised to send an emissary once he receives the Abbot's pledge to succor Yvrain. Then I have but to deliver the child and I will be free."

Sophie nodded, then carefully removed the Lady Alix and Yvrain from her thought. She no longer knew just what her mistress might pick up.

Beside her, Alix looked over the ornate railing and down past Sir Lancelot and the rowdy men. She became aware that Severin Brigante was watching them.

She smiled at him.

Severin was not expecting that smile, nor was he expecting the effect it had on him. It took his breath away—though normally he would have been embarrassed to use such an overworked jongleur-phrase. Still, how else could he describe what had happened to him? He had stopped breathing, and then found that this essential function could only be started again by a conscious effort of his will.

"No," he whispered aloud. "I will not allow this. I am too close to my ends to let a woman handicap me now."

He had known since childhood to be wary of women. His father's disastrous life had taught him this; his own life as a warrior had instructed him still further. Women were a luxury that few men could afford, especially men who had to chart their own way in life. Severin, determined to prove himself to his father's brother and the rest of the aristocratic Harnoncourts, knew that he could ill afford to lose himself in the

intricate webbing of the Countess de Mercier's plight.
He had seen that her husband was decently buried; in
exchange she was teaching him his letters. Severin had
always been at great pains to ensure that his relation-
ships with women were like this—paid for and bal-
anced. These were concepts he well understood.

And yet . . .

And yet he felt dazzled by Alix de Mercier—dazzled
and out of his depth. For an instant he let memory
transport him back to the Palace of the Louvre where
he had first seen her looking so fresh and untouched
amidst the indulgent overripeness of King Charles's
court. He had glimpsed her only in passing; the fact
that he could remember it with such facility was, in
itself, quite shocking.

No, not the Countess de Mercier.

He fumbled his throw at dice and his squire giggled
gleefully at the unexpected windfall.

As he handed over silver half-coins to the winner,
Severin took this as another sign that he had best attend to his business and put the Lady Alix far from
his mind. Her days at Mercier were numbered now.
The Knight de Guigny, possessed of her castle for some
weeks now and back from another of his frequent pilgrimages to the woodland shrine of St. Bernard, had
confided to him that the Countess de Mercier would
soon be convented.

Though there were many points with which he
found himself in disagreement with Sir Lancelot,
Severin heartily concurred with this new development.

"Indeed," he had said to Sir Lancelot as they
preened their falcons after the morning's hunt. "I
think this best for everyone as long, of course, as she
is comfortably situated. The Lady Alix is but newly widowed and comely and nuns can sometimes be drearily
in envy of a pretty face. She has suffered greatly. I

would not like to think that suffering would continue in another form."

This was a long speech, coming as it did from the Knight Brigante. He enjoyed the fame of being taciturn, if not misogynistic, where women were concerned. The Knight de Guigny spared him a sharp glance.

A soft "Indeed, I will see that she is well serviced," was all he said.

He preened his bird before handing it over to the falcon's keeper.

"Is not my Beauty well named?" he said to the Knight Brigante. "She is the most perfect bird I have ever trained."

Severin nodded, not hearing.

He worried that the lady Alix was too thin. As the weeks went by he did not see her gaining, although he watched for this. Instead she seemed to close more and more in upon herself, her skin becoming so transparent that Severin was sure he could see the small, throbbing heartbeat at her throat. Secretly he watched its pacing while he followed her words with his voice and then gradually began to copy them with ink on vellum. The heartbeat skittered sometimes—he was certain of this. At night, he would recall the beating of her heart beneath her skin as he lay on his lone bed. He would try to tell from this if she were getting better; if the days were already providing the healing that, in the end, they must. The gentle beating at her throat was the only indication she would give him of her feelings and Severin knew this. The Lady Alix was always very polite to him and very restrained. Once she had even told him that she knew he had not participated in the killings at Mercier. She also thanked him for seeing to her husband's burial. But it would have taken a potshead not to notice that her daily trips to the castle ramparts were the fulfillment of a duty, nothing more.

Severin Brigante Harnoncourt was no potshead.

When rationality predominated—and it prevailed, thanks be to St. Cuthbert, most of the time—he quite readily understood the way she must feel. The Lady Alix was in the most delicate position of having to remain the chatelaine of a castle to which she now bore a dubious title and to serve men whom she must surely hate. But she could not leave, at least until the duke's official visit. She, no less than her husband, was a vassal of Burgundy, and she must await either the explicit or implicit directives of its lord. Severin knew all of this. When his mind was rationally set, he would nod his head in silent agreement with his magnanimous thoughts.

The trouble was that his mind was not always rationally set. When it was not, he was far less tolerant of the Lady Alix's attitude.

"You would think Mercier was killed defending *her* rather than her rival," Severin would grumble to himself as he tossed upon his soldier's cot. "You would think him a saint."

Since the early days of his knighthood he had always slept upon the same bed. Indeed, so comfortable was his cot that he always rolled and transported it with him no matter his mission or his quest. But at times like this he found its packed husks rough and comfortless. He marveled at how small it now seemed.

All women confounded him—perhaps his mother most of all. He wondered why he had suddenly thought of the Lady Chiara. He had not thought of her for years.

One thing was certain—he could not allow himself

to sit day after day beside a woman as self-contained
as the Lady Alix, a woman whose life fairly vibrated
against the dark and simple stuff of her mourning
clothes. Who needed to put on something that was
fine and spring-like so that the life within her could
begin anew. The convent would come soon enough,
barring some miracle. That would be her fate and she
had accepted it. She had told him so herself. But
Severin, his brow furrowed, thought it a little soon to
consign her to such an austere future. God obviously
thought so as well because it had been nearly two
months now since the castle taking and the Duke of
Burgundy had yet to appear. Still, he was bound to
come and when he did he would remove this vexing
question of the Lady Alix.

To a man of Severin's stern temperament, the
thought that time would soon rid him of the troubling
Countess de Mercier was bound to be a consolation.
Like a fool, he allowed himself to be consoled. No
longer did he control himself quite so rigidly when
they met for their late-afternoon sessions upon the secret rampart. What was the point to it? She would soon
enough be convented; he could allow himself to study
her for the few weeks that remained to them together.
What harm could come of that?

So study her he did, just as he studied his letters.

The first thing he noticed was that her mourning
clothes hung like bags around her. She had obviously
lost weight since her husband's death. Severin practiced
his nouns and verbs, dutifully following her finger and
her pronunciation with his own. The translucency of
her skin secretly appalled him. She obviously needed a
fattening up. All the time the sound of her voice took
them deeper into the Psaltery, Severin's quick mind was
making its plan.

"Two frails of figs should do it," he thought. He

sent to Dijon for these and on impulse added ginger, pressed grapes, lampreys, almonds, rice, cinnamon, and spiced cake to his order. He would have added marzipan and confections to his list as well but decided that the days were growing much too warm for such heavy stuff. He did not want the Lady Alix to sicken, just to fatten. Two good knights, abashed at being given common work to do, were nevertheless dispatched upon this errand. One more was sent galloping after them to add a length of good velvet to the list. A deep forest green was the color of the Counts of Nevers—Jean of Burgundy's title before his ascent to the dukedom—and it was in plentiful supply throughout the country. Severin, in his close but secret scrutiny, decided that this would make a perfect dress for Alix. It would bring out the sea color in her eyes. He liked the idea of being party to that. Just as he liked the idea of draping her in cerulean-dyed silk. Severin did not at all think it strange that he should personally write a certain famous Lombard dyer concerning this matter, even though he knew that by rights the Lady Alix should still dress in mourning cloth for at least the next six months.

He presented his purchases as a gift from the duke—even though Jean of Burgundy knew nothing of their provenance—because he knew that she could not refuse them under such a presentation. He settled down again beside her on the weathered bench, careful to watch for signs that her cheeks were filling and that the hunted, hurt look was leaving her magnificent eyes. He did this under cover of the words she was teaching him—the distinguishing of all the little symbols, that for so long had remained meaningless to him, into so many parts of a tale.

He thought she began to look better.

One day, as they were both deep into the enfolding

of the March month, Severin was startled by a hint of rose upon the air. He thought this strange. The year was yet new and not even green leaves shone upon the hills, and yet he smelled the ripe perfume of summer. He sniffed, this time deliberately. The fragrance wafted from the Lady Alix; the Knight Brigante was certain of this. This caused him to study her more carefully and he smiled secretly at how his small tutor had changed in these few weeks. She still covered herself in strict mourning, but her cheeks had bloomed and the fingers he covered with his sturdy hands were no longer cold and thin. And now she wore the lush scent of roses.

For the first time in his life, Severin Brigante Harnoncourt did not probe and ponder to discover why this happiness existed. He did not tensely try to estimate where it would lead; he did not try to envision how it would end. He did not question himself in any way. He just lived these pleasant spring afternoons as he learned to read under the tutelage of his pretty teacher.

"No, no, Sir Severin," she said. Her lips and her eyes smiled at him even as she lightly shook her head. "That is not the meaning of the words. You know this. You have correctly read them before."

Severin, a great knight and keen warrior, had known little of gentleness in his life. But he found that he did not mind it now. He smiled back, corrected himself, and began the reading of the passage once again.

In that instant, and for many such instants, the comforting thought that the Countess de Mercier would soon be convented was the furthest thing from his mind.

"Have you a wife?" she asked him.

It was a warm day and for the first time they had

removed their cloaks and sat upon them. Below, on the hills, a shepherd walked leisurely beside his flock. They had taken to lingering together after their lessons and this day Severin had brought the treat of a small ginger cake and a flask of cider. He was in the midst of a healthy bite but he managed to shake his head.

"Why?" she questioned with the full intensity of her turquoise eyes upon his face. "You are a large man but not uncomely. Your face is stern but your regard is just. Furthermore, you are general of a great army. I cannot imagine that, as yet, you have not permanently mated yourself."

Severin turned his 'just regard' fully upon her. He was always suspicious of women, and especially so when one of them took him by surprise. "I am a poor man, and poor men do not often have the privilege of taking on a good wife."

"That is not the true reason," she told him levelly, "though I am sure it is one that you have used often and to good effect. Does your lack of a wife have basis in your quest to salvage your father's name?"

Severin, stunned by Alix's frankness, might have lied to her—but he didn't.

"I have no time for a wife," he said. "And I have no castle in which to maintain one. I have plighted myself to revenge my father's slighting. To do this I must use all the resources that come to my hand. I have no time for a wife."

He hated himself for this lame repetition.

"And no inclination for one, either?"

He colored at this. "Are you suggesting that I have no interest in women? I assure you, my lady, that my interest is quite keen."

Now it was Alix's turn to blush, but she held her ground and her gaze did not waver. "Yet, Sir Severin, you are the type of man that many women would choose. And not just poor women, either. You could well have married a fortune and been much further along your road of vindication. I wonder why you have not chosen to do so."

For the life of him, Severin could not force his eyes away from her.

"I saw enough of marriage when I was young. I did not know my mother but I could readily see how marriage to her had marked my father. How it had destroyed him, with the help of his brother—and of that Maltese Star you wear."

He had meant this last to be a catch-bone, a lure that would divert her attention to less threatening topics—at least topics in which he felt himself to be less threatened. Indeed, he saw interest flicker deep within her eyes and warm them. But she did not reach out for the bone he offered.

"And after that, as you grew, was there no woman who appealed to you?"

"Oh, there were many that I wanted to make my own, and I did this." His boasting sounded hollow even to his own ears. "But a wife would necessarily call me to other duties and other concerns than those which I have chosen for myself."

"Or that your father chose for you," replied the Countess de Mercier. "But marriage is not just a wife—it is children as well. Do you not miss them?"

"Do you?"

"Of course." She looked away for the first time, up to the budding green of the hills before her, to the setting sun, and to the curl of night-birds that swept high into the sky from the safety of their daylight hiding. "Of course I do. I loved my husband. I wanted his son—fiercely wanted it."

Severin was surprised to hear his voice break the

silence. "*Why* did you love Robert de Mercier? It was quite obvious that he did not love you."

Immediately he wanted to apologize, to beg this woman's pardon for the hurt he knew he had inflicted. But she was already answering his question. It was too late to stop her.

"I loved Robert," she said as she once again turned to Severin, "because he was my husband. My own mother and father love each other with such a passion that I thought this passion was a gift one naturally received at marriage. Just as the Emperor Sigismund gave me a set of gold plate at my wedding, I believed that God, in like manner, would give me my husband's love. I was wrong."

"You were also young." Severin forced his voice low. "God's tooth! How old were you when you married him?"

"Sixteen."

"And he a man of more than thirty and with a peasant mistress following his scent like a lapdog."

Alix's face turned red with rage. "Sir Severin, when you speak of my husband you should keep a civil tongue within your head."

"A civil tongue?" Severin was decently angry now, all pretense gone. "You ask me to keep a civil tongue when we speak of a man who cuckolded you and kept his mistress in *your* rightful place within *his* bed. Who died defending this same mistress?"

"I think it best we leave this place," she said, her eyes chilling to a cobalt blue. "And that we never come to it again. I part soon for a convent in Picardy—Sir Lancelot informed me so today. I have asked only for a few days more—there still remains something to which I must attend. After it is completed I will leave Mercier for good."

This only stoked Severin's anger. He lashed out at her before she could turn away.

"I suppose it will make no difference to you," he said with great sarcasm, "changing one nun's bed for another."

If he had not been a trained warrior, she would have managed the slap. Both of them knew it, and neither of them cared. As it was, Severin was just a little too quick for her, just a little too skilled. He had grabbed her small hand into his large one before she had finished her arc and then used the leverage of her body's motion to pull her snugly close.

He was bent on kissing her even before he realized that that was what he wanted to do. He had never been so determined to kiss a woman in his life. He even wrapped his arms around her shoulders, not around her waist, so that he could bring his weight to bear upon her and give her no room for escape.

But at the last instant he hesitated—hesitated while his mouth hovered only a finger's span above hers. He had no idea why he did this. He could have been spellbound. He only knew that he hesitated. He waited. He wanted her to come to him.

In the end she did just that. She crossed that finger's chasm that separated them and drew him close. Severin felt the soft circle of her arms enfold him, felt the beckoning closeness of her mouth.

He took his time in kissing her. He did not want to push this moment away and so he kissed her mouth with exquisite tenderness, determined not to frighten her. He took his time.

Gradually she opened to him and he drew her nearer. He could easily have spent the rest of his life just kissing this woman, but there was a commotion at the wicket gate. A drunken beggar called out for traveler's sanctuary; a drunken sentry shouted no. The ensuing argument quickly turned into a pitched battle. The cries and blows strained upward and broke the spell.

When he opened his eyes, the Countess de Mercier stared back at him. Shock had widened her eyes and blanched her cheeks.

"I'm sorry," she whispered. "Oh, God, what have I done?"

"You've kissed me," he answered quite calmly. "Where is the harm in that?"

"Where is the harm in that?" The Countess de Mercier was anything but calm. "I am a fresh widow, Sir Severin, and I love my husband. Now I have sullied his name with my wantonness. He was a proud man from a proud family—fine and cultivated and good. He was everything that you are not."

Her words stung Severin back into the icy part of himself where he lived. He felt his lips stretch into a smile. "Indeed, my lady, your husband the count may have been good in many things but I doubt his manners and cultivation got the response from you that I just did. I doubt he cared to get it."

He watched the color drain from her face and thought for a second that she might try to strike him again. He sincerely wished that she would. But she did nothing. She said nothing. Instead she turned from him and walked away. The only sound on that late afternoon was the echo of her pattened feet rushing into the body of this huge castle that had never been her home.

You kissed me.

You came to me.

She might hate and despise him but Severin realized that this had not stopped her reaching out to him. It had not stopped her kissing him.

And he exulted in the thought.

Six

During her years at Mercier, Alix had had little use for mirrors. In fact, she avoided looking at herself as much as possible. In his vague way, Robert had tended to pretend she wasn't there and after a while she had followed his lead and disappeared into herself. It had been many months—well before her husband's death—since she had seriously looked at herself in a mirror.

She looked now.

What she saw was decidedly strange. Her cheeks were flushed, her eyes bright, her skin glowing. As much as she might want to, she could not believe that all of this had been brought about by the hasty retreat to her room. She knew Severin's kiss was behind this heightening of her coloring—the kiss and the fact that she had wanted it so much. When he hesitated, she had reached for him, reached for him and held him shockingly close.

Alix stood for a moment transfixed, carefully examining all the changes one kiss could make. Beside her, the beeswax candles on the small altar touched light to Robert's jeweled knife and his bloody mantle. Guilt welled up so sharply within her that she wanted to cry or run. She could do neither. Her future was not in her own hands and neither were her actions. She had promised Robert to see his son to safety.

But now that she had kissed another man—and worse, had enjoyed kissing him—this promise had become onerous to her. She wanted her duty over and done with. She wanted the convent. At least there she would be safe from herself.

It had been more than two months since Padre Gasca had left them. He had promised to send word when she could come and insisted that she not send messages to Haute Fleur before he told her the moment was ripe.

"These are trying times," he had whispered, mounting his donkey for the short journey to Sophie's cottage. "The duke may bluster and Lancelot de Guigny may think himself titular of this castle—but they both know they risk a traitor's death in arming themselves against their king. The lines are firmly drawn. Henry V may have legitimate right to France's throne but it is Charles VI who sits upon it. They may win much by allying themselves with Henry of England, or they may lose everything. This makes for interesting choices amidst interesting times."

Alix remembered these words now. She knelt down at her chamber altar, careful not to look upon the possessions of her husband. She crossed herself and asked for forgiveness and then prayed, with great fervor, that the priest would soon arrive with word for her and that she would be freed to leave Mercier for good.

Although Gasca de Loran did not himself come, he managed within the next week to send a most able emissary in his stead. Late one day, just before the castle portcullis was due to close, the Knight de Guigny received word that the Lombard merchant Dino Rispoli had arrived with a shipment of the household spices that had been ordered by the countess back in the waning months of summer.

"You know this man?" Sir Lancelot asked Alix. They had just finished an especially excruciating evening meal, over which she had been called to preside. She opened her mouth to deny the order when she remembered that Dino Rispoli was a good friend both to her father and to Padre Gasca. They thought him intelligently capable and admirably discreet. She remembered that her father had used Dino Rispoli when he needed something done quietly, and with a certain élan. Only the Italians could manage to be both cunning and elegant at the same time.

Dino Rispoli swept in when he was summoned. He did not glance at the Countess de Mercier.

It would be known all through Christendom that Mercier Castle, recently taken by force, might be in need of many new things. The vanquisher would want to put his own stamp upon his possession as speedily as he could. Of course, now that the castle had changed hands the merchant thought it best to consult with the Knight de Guigny. They would no longer ask directly for the Countess de Mercier, at least without his consent.

Alix had thought of this as well. She kept her eyes demurely lowered but she watched the scene through the curtain of her lashes, her heart pounding. Her small hands were white against the black stuff of her mourning cloth. She saw fretfulness flit across Sir Lancelot's face and then watched this harden into shrewdness.

"I have no interest in matters of the kitchen," he said, "but a keen one in your travels. You have been to Westminster?"

The merchant nodded.

"And to Dijon?"

Again the nod.

Alix realized it was of utmost importance that she demonstrate exactly the appropriate amount of interest, nothing more nor less. Yet it was hard to do this in a room so closely packed with drinking men and barking dogs. She was frightened that she might miss something and she knew that she must not.

Rispoli was at his obsequious best. "Indeed, my lord count, I have been to both courts." He easily gave Guigny the title that the duke had yet to confer.

Guigny's small, dark eyes were bright with interest. "Speak up then, man, and tell us what you've learned. 'Tis plain enough you've not made so long a journey just to sell new spice and cheese. I'm sure you've brought other goods that are priced well for selling."

Again the small Lombardian smiled, but this time he did not bow. His silk tunic was every bit as richly formed and bordered as Guigny's and both men knew this. Sir Lancelot, taking the inference, offered his guest a seat very near his own. For an instant anxiety rippled through Alix. The chair indicated was on Guigny's far side. She was frightened she might not hear what they spoke. But she needn't have worried. Dino Rispoli was there for the benefit of the Countess de Mercier. He deftly placed himself near her and the Knight de Guigny either did not notice or did not object.

"Which first?" said the merchant.

"Why, this, of course." Guigny reached to his jeweled belt and pulled forth a velvet bag of coins. They jingled as he dropped them onto the trestle table.

Rispoli smiled but did not reach out. "I meant which kingdom, my lord Lancelot. Do you wish to hear first of Westminster or of Dijon?"

"England," said the Knight de Guigny sharply. "My

brother keeps me well apprised of his movements. I need no news of Burgundy."

His features tensed around the lie.

Rispoli nodded, as did the rest of Guigny's men who stood nearby. Though everyone knew that this was not so.

"In England all is as it was before," said Rispoli, declining wine but settling more deeply into his seat. "Young Henry does not share many of his late father's interests but he shares the quest for France. These Lancashire Plantagenets think the throne rightfully theirs. They accept no compromise on this subject. It comes to them, they believe, through Philip the Fair's daughter who married England's Edward II. Isabella was the daughter of one king and sister to three others, though not allowed the throne because she was a woman. Instead it went to Philip the Fair's nephew, who became Philip VI and thus started the Valois line. The Plantagenets have never accepted his right to kingship."

Guigny smiled. "And there were many in France who agreed with their assessment. Powerful French nobles placed him upon the throne but he was known throughout his realm as *le roi trouvé*, the found king.

"They say Philip VI had difficulty with his own position," added Rispoli, his dark eyes dancing. "He had not been raised for the crown and he seemed to find some difficulty in accepting it. In the end, of course, the choice of king meant war between France and England."

"And profit to you." Guigny's smile matched the merchant's in its brightness. "Now tell me what you know of the Maltese Star—the amulet that my Lady de Mercier so prominently wears."

If Rispoli were surprised by this turn in the conversation he did not show it. Instead he peered with sudden interest at Alix, as though observing the amulet for the first time.

"Interesting," he said.

"But hardly unique."

No one had noticed Severin Brigante but he had moved from the shadows and stood close behind the Countess de Mercier. Rispoli did not miss this, and glanced quickly at them both. Alix felt her cheeks burn.

"Indeed, hardly unique," agreed the merchant. "It was said to be much dispersed in both Italy and France, especially at the end of the last century. You, sir, are Severin Brigante Harnoncourt, are you not?"

Severin nodded. His face remained impassive.

"Your father wore that amulet," said Rispoli, "though your uncle never did. Interesting. It is said to mark the remnant of the Knights Templar."

"Were they not all killed by Philip the Fair?" Guigny's voice was mild with interest. "And more importantly still, theirs was a celibate warrior order. What place would a woman hold with them? Why would she wear their symbol?"

"Because she *is* their symbol," Rispoli answered. "The woman who wears the Maltese Star is the Magdalene—she is the warlock's witch."

There was a gasp from the others and then a snicker. Alix, hearing all of this for the first time, kept her face still. She didn't know if Rispoli spoke the truth, or if the whole of what he said was meant only to hide the true reason for his presence. She would discover this soon enough. The Maltese Star, and what it implied, did not interest her now. She had her mission.

"My lord," said the merchant Rispoli, fixing Lancelot de Guigny with a smile that was studied in its weariness, "I am here with choice merchandise. We have brought spices with us that not even the king as yet possesses. For example, coriander, which comes especially from the East and is sweet when dried but quite tart and tasty while still fresh. It should grow well in this part of France, just as it does in the lands beyond the Silk Route."

"I care nothing about spices," replied Guigny. " 'Tis the Lady Alix who still runs the household here. Take your information to her in private—after all, is that not what you came to do?"

The Knight de Guigny's smile remained quite pleasant, even as his eyes grew cold.

"A very astute man," said Rispoli when he and the Lady Alix were alone in the castle's spice cellar. The air surrounding them was cool and pungent, the light dim. The room was also far removed from the castle main. Alix had thought it the obvious place in which to meet with the emissary.

"As well he might be," she replied. "He, like Philip VI, finds himself wearied by a title that is not, perhaps, without contenders."

"At least Philip did not kill for his throne," said Rispoli, running his fingers through a hemp sack of dried thyme. Its scent prickled the air. "Instead, the Knight de Guigny has. However he was not the man of whom I spoke. I made mention of Sir Severin."

"Sir Severin interesting?" scoffed Alix, though her cheeks flamed. She had tried very hard not to think about Severin Brigante since she'd kissed him. It angered her that he came or was brought so continually to her mind.

"But of course you do not wish to speak of the Knight Brigante," Rispoli said, as though reading her mind. "Instead you are interested in news I bring from Haute Fleur and Padre Gasca."

"And how you came to bring it," Alix said.

"That can be simply answered." Rispoli no longer amused himself by playing with the herbs. "It is natural for me to pass by the monastery on my way from the fortress of Dijon. Abbot Suger is always interested in hearing current tidings so that he and his monks can be prepared. As men of peace they want no war, but they realize with the rest of us the imminence of the approaching fight. France will be divided with Henry of England's coming."

Alix, captive in a castle that buzzed with men restless and anxious to be off about their war business, shook her head impatiently at this. She had her own duties and must be about them before many days passed. The first peasants were already venturing toward their fields in preparation for spring planting. She could see them each morning through the leaded prisms of her chamber window: small, indistinct shapes heading off industriously toward the valley's fields—and toward the witch's hut that housed Yvrain. There were more of them each day.

"What did Padre Gasca tell you?" she asked, trying to keep the impatience from her voice. "I am sure he must have told you something."

"He said that Count Robert's child is under your protection and you wish to see him safe within the monastery," replied Rispoli. Outside they heard drunken laughter but it seemed to come from far away. "He said that the way is cleared and that you may bring the boy to sanctuary at Haute Fleur."

"Thank you," said Alix, though she could not have said who exactly she was thanking or for what. "Oh, thank you so much."

Seven

Severin smelled her perfume, though he knew this to be impossible. The Hall was large and still closed down for winter. Even this early into the day, there were at least twenty knights and men-at-arms milling about. Not to mention the dogs, and the smell of last night's scraps and bones.

Yet, still Severin smelled her and the sure, warm touch of spring roses. It was the same scent that had enveloped him since their kiss.

He knew she was in danger.

"She wants to make a retreat," Lancelot de Guigny said. They were alone with the maps of Burgundy and France and the eastern part of Britain stretched out on the trestle before them, each chart with variously colored banners indicating individual feudal fiefs and the dragons that reared up from the far lands that no man had seen. Severin glanced at them before raising his gaze again to Lancelot. "A religious retreat at Haute Fleur."

"But the weather threatens." Severin gestured toward the fogged leaded windows of the Hall. "Could she not wait until true thaw to have her religious conversion?"

"She wants it now," replied Lancelot. "She feels the need to pray."

He reached over and took a tankard of spiced wine.

The jewels on his finger rings gleamed in the firelight. It was obvious that, at least for him, the discussion was finished. But it wasn't for Severin.

"She may very well need the rest and the time away. It would also help you solve your own problems."

Lancelot looked over at him, amused as though there were no way at all that the Countess de Mercier could help him. But he had stopped fidgeting with the maps.

Severin met his dark gaze with his own lighter one. "You have already built up a good feeling by sparing her life."

Guigny nodded at this, although they both understood the reason that this had been done. It had nothing to do with his chivalric oath and everything to do with what best served his interests in the present situation. It was certainly also true that he would want nothing to happen to the daughter of Olivier Ducci Montaldo, a man who had been instrumental in saving the Duke of Burgundy's life on the battlefields of Nicopolis.

"The Abbot of Haute Fleur is staunchly for the Burgundian cause," said Severin. "He calls the Court at Paris a scandal—the king a madman and the queen a common whore. He thinks the Duke of Burgundy a saint."

Guigny smiled at this, a smile that did not quite illumine his eyes. "That he should think well of my dear brother has probably more to do with the rankness of these times than it does with the odor of sanctity emitted from Dijon."

"It is not what I forget," Severin answered in a carefully modulated voice, "but what the Abbot seems to have forgotten that is important here. The Dukes of Burgundy are known to be great supporters of the monks at Haute Fleur. They endow perpetual masses for their souls and then, as assurance, sweeten the gift by donating beaten gold chalices studded with jewels so that the priest, as he lifts his hands in prayer, will not forget how richly the monastery has been treated."

"True enough," said Lancelot, and he chuckled. By making him bastard son of a duke and yet heir to nothing, nature had formed the Knight de Guigny to plot and plan.

"It might be a good idea," he said finally.

"And she would be away." Severin carefully looked down toward the parchment maps, as though he had no idea of the import of what he said. "She would not know what went on at the castle in her absence."

The only sound now was the crackle of the fire and the distant crash of steel against steel as two knights played at battle on the list fields.

"Indeed, it might not be a bad idea that the Lady Alix be allowed to go to Haute Fleur to spend some time in reflection and devotion. Indeed, she might include the new Count of Mercier in her prayers. You may tell her that she has my permission to depart. She must only tell me what she needs and I will put it at her disposition."

"I will tell her," replied the Knight Brigante.

Guigny speared an apple with a great show of nonchalance.

They continued on the subject at the next morning's hunt.

Formal permission was asked of the Knight de Guigny that the Lady Alix de Mercier—she no longer referred to herself as countess, especially in her dealings with Sir Lancelot—be allowed time for pilgrimage to the great shrine at Haute Fleur. Discreetly couched within the parchment's message was reference to the comfort that the Knight undoubtedly took from his own frequent journeys to the woodland shrine of St. Bernard. The Lady Alix said that she, too, needed the succor that only the saints could afford, especially now that her life would so soon take a different direction. She did not specifically mention the convent but Guigny read its inference between the lines, as he had been meant to do. She did not mention the horror of her husband's death but he understood this inference as well.

The Knight de Guigny would have much preferred to keep the lady firmly captive in his castle, but he could not—at least without admitting that she was, indeed, being held as prisoner. This fact was clear to the lowest scullery at Mercier, but it could not be openly acknowledged. Guigny was not as yet entitled at Mercier and so by right of fact the title of the castle still belonged to the Lady Alix. Under French liege-law he was her guest and not she his. Therefore, when she made her reasonable request, Alix knew that Sir Lancelot would be forced to give it a reasonable reply.

"Prayer is necessary at time of transition," he said, after calling her into his presence. "Therefore I will grant your request to go on pilgrimage to the holy places. In fact, you must allow me to aid you in your endeavor by lending you my good knight Aimery de Foix as escort and champion."

Short, squat, ugly—Aimery de Foix was Guigny's trusted henchman. He would report her every movement to Sir Lancelot and Alix knew this. There would be no chance of secreting Yvrain to safety if she were under this knight's care. But she said nothing as she sank into a deep reverence.

The next day, which was the day of departure, Sir Aimery was taken grievously ill with stomach cramps and vomiting after having gorged himself on a marzipan apple that the Lady Alix had prepared for him with her own hands. This happened just as they were leaving—and after the Knight de Guigny had departed for his day's hunt, taking the Knight Brigante with him.

"It makes no matter," Alix said, taking the bridle to her palfrey from Huguet le Févre, another of Guigny's knights. "The Merchant Rispoli will escort me. His business necessitates the availability of gold florins and so he is always most adequately manned. I will only ride to say good-bye to my maid. She has asked that candles be lit for her father at the shrine and I go to assure her of my intention to do this."

Alix knew her story to be flawed but, as Severin Brigante had pointed out to her, many of Guigny's knights were not educated and thus had grown used to taking directions. She counted upon this fact now and was not disappointed. Sir Huguet looked confused for an instant, but eventually he bowed to her wishes. He went so far as to settle her upon her palfrey.

The Widow de Mercier had been granted a three-day prayer retreat at a monastery that was but one half day's ride away, he reasoned. Guigny had said to watch her carefully but what damage could this small and defeated woman do to them bound, as she was, on such a pious mission?

The Knight le Févre actually waved to her as she rode away toward the Pilgrim Road.

As soon as she was out of his sight, the "pious" Widow de Mercier spurred her horse deep into the forest. Sophie and her mother were waiting for her near the stream, the mother carrying a lightly swaddled Yvrain and the daughter with a woven hemp sumter filled with provisions for the journey. Alix smiled at them and reached for the child. She hurried on. Padre Gasca would be waiting for her at the crossroads.

* * *

Severin had been anxious to reach Alix but she had eluded him. He was determined, however, to claim an audience with her as soon as he could safely rid himself of the Knight de Guigny.

"It is the least I can do," Sir Lancelot said, and shrugged. His aping of certain blasé manners of the French aristocracy—to which he was only bastard-born—always irritated Brigante, but never as much as on this day. "I cannot keep the countess from her religious devotions. It would be heartless of me."

"You have done worse to her," Severin said. He was edgy and nervous as the men cantered noisily over the drawbridge and reached the open road. "And you would do worse to her now if you thought it to your advantage. You want her because of the charm that she wears. That six-pointed amulet they call the Maltese Star."

One of the hunting dogs barked furiously and snapped at Guigny's soft boot in its golden stirrup. Sir Lancelot furiously whirled his whip upon the animal and sent it crying away from the pack. Severin knew that this was only a distraction, a way for Guigny to collect his thoughts and hide his playing hand. The Knight Brigante still patiently awaited his attention as the new lord of Mercier turned back.

"But it will do you no good," said Severin. He could feel the oppression of Guigny's eyes upon him. "None whatsoever. My father wore that amulet and friends of his did as well. He could not part with it—even when he knew it carried him to his grave. It had that much of a hold."

"Without meaning to be offensive," Guigny said, although it was obvious that this was exactly what he meant to be, "I've heard it was other substances, not a silver amulet, that led to your father's extinction."

"But the gold amulet was behind it," Severin said. "It was behind everything that happened to him. I wouldn't be too curious about it if I were you. It is said to have brought a curse on all the men who craved it and wore it—to the men who *had* to have it."

"And not the women?" Severin knew they were both thinking of the Lady Alix. "It seems that there are women who choose the Maltese Star as well. What was it Rispoli said yesterday—something about the Magdalene being the warlock's witch? Odd that the Lady Alix would choose to visit Vezeley as well as Haute Fleur—Vezeley where the bones of Mary Magdalene are said to be interred."

Again Severin smelled a clean, soft hint of spring roses in the air but this time his mind grasped the meaning behind the scent. Alix was in danger—its presence surrounded her just as the scent of her perfume surrounded him. It was his warrior's intuition that told Severin this and so he wasted no time in doubting himself. Nor, now that his instincts had spoken, did he waste time in doubting Guigny's ultimate intention. He might toy with the idea of the Maltese Star and learning its secret, but in the end he would need the Lady Alix dead. The child Yvrain was dead, or someone would have come forth with proof by now of his existence. But the Widow de Mercier still lived and, though he could not now overtly murder her as he had done her husband, still Lancelot de Guigny could not long let the situation continue. Even firmly convented, she would always be a threat to him whilst she lived.

But Severin allowed none of these thoughts to show upon his face as his horse cantered along beside that of the Knight de Guigny. Instead he smiled and called

out merry answers. All the while his eyes looked to the
forest and toward the road to Vezeley, as he planned
his moves with care. It was but a quarter sand-span
later that he managed to make a creditable excuse,
nod his head to the Knight de Guigny, and gallop into
the forest.

The priest was waiting just where he said he would
be, at the crossroads that guided the pilgrim toward
Haute Fleur. He doffed his cowl at Alix's approach and
smiled. She handed the babe to him, then scampered
down from her horse and curtseyed her thanks.

"So this is Yvrain," said Gasca de Loran. Delicacy
prevented him giving the child his father's surname,
though one quick glance showed that this was Robert's
son. Even though the babe was less than a year old,
he already carried the silky dark hair and fine features
of the last Count de Mercier. Padre Gasca crossed himself and silently prayed that the resemblance between
them, which was marked, would not extend to the shar-
ing of a violent death. "You did well to save him," the
priest said to Alix. "You have acted with great courage."

"I prom . . ." But Alix changed her mind in mid-
thought. "I did nothing. He was kept with the mother
of my dressing maid. She is something of a hermit and
blessed—or cursed—with the witch-rumor that often
accompanies a woman who makes her way inde-
pendently. The village folk stay clear of her, especially
in the winter months. But with the coming of spring
when there is need of love potions, and crop
charms . . ."

She let her voice trail off. Perhaps it was not best to
talk about the ways of a Wise Woman to a sacramented
priest.

"It is now time to take him to a safer place," the priest finished for her. "I have spoken to the Abbot and although most of his sympathies lie with the Duke of Burgundy—mad King Charles is known for the licentiousness of his court in Paris, not to mention the scandals of the Queen—Father Suger can neither countenance nor condone Lancelot de Guigny's actions in this matter. To kill a sleeping man when you have been given hospitality in his house . . ."

Now it was Gasca's turn to let his voice trail off. His small squirrel's face wrinkled in disapproval and it was only after a moment that he continued. "The Abbot agreed with me. The Church, as you know, forms its own estate and is under no jurisdiction except that of God Himself. Despite the confusion of these times— what with one pope in Rome and another in Avignon—this fact still holds true. The Abbot, a most enlightened man, took advantage of this mass befuddlement in order to offer sanctuary to this innocent child."

The word "innocent" stung Alix, though she could not have said why.

She turned back to her horse. Helping each other with the child, they remounted and headed toward Haute Fleur.

"Then we should hurry him to sacred ground," she whispered. "There is no way that even someone as ruthless as Lancelot de Guigny will hunt him down if he is known to be under the protection of the Abbot of Haute Fleur."

"Indeed. But there are many miles between here and the ancient monastery. Lancelot de Guigny might have guessed the secret and means to have us killed upon the road. It is not well to underestimate him—as Robert de Mercier must have realized to his chagrin." The priest shivered and then hastily added, "Not that

I have any compunction about the spilling of my blood. I have always stood prepared to shed it in the service of Our Lord and for the edification of His Church. But to have it wrenched from my veins in service to Lancelot de Guigny's monumental ambition is not something I believe that God is calling me to do—unless, of course, I wrongly discern His will."

Alix smiled sadly. "I doubt there is danger of that. Lancelot de Guigny has never pressed for word of the child. I said on the first day that Yvrain was dead. I swore his body had been cast into the stream. Sir Lancelot probably believes that I killed him."

"And why would he think that?"

"Because I hate Yvrain," Alix said, turning away. "I have but done my duty."

"Duty?" questioned the priest and then said nothing else. He could not look at how protectively Alix still hid the child—how protectively she *had* hidden him these two dangerous months—and not think that something more profound than duty stoked her actions. He was wise enough to understand that she must be left to assess her own actions and in her own way. But he thought what a marvelous mother she might have made and silently shook his head for the fool Robert de Mercier had been and for the botch he'd made of so many lives.

From the first instant he'd set eyes upon him, Gasca de Loran had realized that the Count de Mercier was a weak man—not only weak but also blind to his own faults, hiding his common venality beneath the guise of romance and thwarted love. Too lacking in character to give up the pleasures of his peasant mistress and yet too weak to openly oppose Burgundy and publicly plight his troth to her as wife. Instead, he had followed the path of subterfuge, choosing a suitable public wife and hiding an unsuitable private mistress. In the end he had served neither woman well.

It was Alix who was the strong one, little Alix whom Gasca had helped to birth. But Alix was making a myth of Robert de Mercier, surrounding him with the stuff of undeserved legend, and she had the power to make this false legend real.

A sunbeam pierced the forest cover, striking against the Maltese Star at Alix's throat. Gasca was sure it winked at him. Though a scientist, and therefore not a particularly superstitious man, the Portuguese priest had the strongest inclination to cross himself. He would light a candle for her at Haute Fleur, he decided. And he would say his prayers.

"I hate him," Alix repeated, reaching down from her horse's ornate saddle to gather the child Yvrain back into her arms. "I hate him and that will never change. You should save your prayers for those who will benefit from them."

That she had read his mind did not disconcert Padre Gasca. Alix was, after all, the Magdalene's daughter. More power than this lay within her grasp—if she but chose to use it.

Severin spotted them about midday. The old priest sitting tranquilly upon his donkey, munching at an apple, and the young woman with a hand loosely upon her horse's bridle and an arm wrapped around a small bundle, holding it near. Instantly his trained eye glimpsed all the ways they were in danger. The road stretched wide but was wintertime deserted. The forest gave good cover for attack. They were far from the nearest village. His list went on and on. Their obvious innocence of the danger infuriated him. Never in anger had he laid hands on a woman but he would have

cheerfully throttled the Countess de Mercier had he
been given the chance.

"I know that I am looking upon a vision. This cannot possibly be the Countess de Mercier and her good
confessor that I see."

The Knight Brigante had whirled from nowhere on
his warhorse to block their path. Severin was just angry
enough with Alix de Mercier to use the menace of his
bulk to frighten her.

He realized, in the second before he firmly reined
his horse before her, that he quite enjoyed the thought
of frightening this particular woman. Relished it even.
He wanted, once again, to see emotion play against
the passive piety of her features, just as it had when
he'd kissed her.

"I . . ." he thundered, but then he stopped. What
could he say? How could he say it?

He had the strangest sensation that they were the
only two people left upon the earth, even though from
the corner of his eye he could see the old priest beam-
ing curiously and he could hear the gentle cooing of
the child. Still he felt himself to be alone with her.
And he felt recognized—as though by looking into her
clear turquoise eyes he could look into his own
clouded dark ones. As though in seeing her small and
slender frame he was seeing his own great bulk.

As though by coming to her, he had come home.

This strange recognition lasted only an instant,
which was good because Severin found it highly dis-
concerting. He swung from his saddle with the profound conviction that the powers of fright, which had
stood him in such good stead in battle, must somehow
be deserting him. The baby had not stopped his playful
cooing and neither of the ridiculously defenseless
adults seemed particularly frightened of him, either.
Moreover, no one made a move to whisk the child away

and try to hide him. Both the priest and the young
woman stared at him as though they had been expecting him for quite some time. Severin, who had the
happy capacity of being able to laugh at his own ex-
pense, would have found the scene amusing had he
not already found it so amazing.

"Robert's boy," the priest said shortly, pointing to
Alix's bundle. "The heir."

"My husband's son," agreed the Countess de Mercier.

She turned toward him and now that he was close
beside her, Severin could see the ticking of a small muscle at the very corner of her mouth. She was frightened
after all. He did not blame her. There would have been
hell to pay had the Knight de Guigny discovered that
the child still lived and, worse yet, lived and thrived practically beneath his very nose. Because, of course, this
much was obvious. Severin wanted to laugh out loud;
he wanted to howl with laughter. All the searching and
the bribing and the assurances that the child could not
be found. That he must be dead. And through it all this
little slip of a woman had outfoxed them. What a grand
revenge! One day, when they were safely out of this, he
would be genuinely interested to hear the telling of this
tale.

"So our good Padre Gasca has not come only to
console the bereaved widow," he said. He watched her
deep, clear eyes turn to stones. For Severin, the others
might as well not have been in the room.

"He's come to take Robert's son to the Abbey at
Haute Fleur," said Alix. Instinctively, she held the baby
closer. Severin wondered if she even knew she did it.
He thought she looked enchanting. He knew she
smelled of roses.

"And how do you propose to see that he arrives?"
Severin asked. He edged his horse a little closer.

"There will be rich rewards from Sir Lancelot for the one who brings this child to him—back from the dead, as it were."

"We are in the process of arriving," she said, "as you can plainly see. Now, Sir Severin, you must decide if you will help us or if you will not."

It was as simple as that.

The priest, on his much-slower donkey, lagged on the road behind them. Gasca kept the child with him, saying he knew more about children than did the Lady Alix. He was, after all, the eldest of ten. Both Severin and Alix heard Yvrain's giggles floating up to them on the wind. The afternoon was cool and crisp, colder than the last few days and with just enough of a breeze to pull at the simple black silk veiling Alix wore. She was wrapped well in furs, Severin noted with approval. A few days of good weather did not mean full spring-time and he was pleased that she was prepared for any storm. Her horse was skirted in simple black. Lance-lot's largesse had not extended to letting her flaunt the colors of the Counts of Mercier in areas where the memory of the brutal killing of Robert might still be fresh. Guigny had gifted the nearby villages with wine from the Mercier cellars and prudent quintals of grain. But one never knew with peasants. Sometimes they could not be bought as easily as could the nobles. Sometimes they could have quite a keen sense of wrong and right.

Alix determined not to be seduced again by the Knight Brigante. The first time had been bad enough. The memory of his kiss, and of her disgraceful behavior, still burned. She often thought of it. There had been times when she wondered if she should apologize for wanton behavior. Alix had no idea what other women did in situations like that, if reaching out for a man automatically made her a whore. Certainly, she had never dared reach for Robert. He had made it quite clear from the beginning that it was he who controlled their sexual couplings. Now, riding through the spring-bound countryside with Severin beside her, she wondered if this were true with this man. He had not seemed particularly shocked at her behavior. She slipped him a sly look from beneath her lashes. She wondered what he thought.

Alix watched his mouth as he talked. She was starting to think him less ugly. His lips were nicely formed, his eyes bright, his face well chiseled.

'Tis well for me that I am convent bound.

"What was it like to live with Robert?" Severin asked. He spoke so softly that she could barely hear his words.

She could barely hear her own when she answered him.

"Lovely in some ways, and so painful in others," she said. The words surprised her. "He was so perfect—with his name and his elegance and his wealth. I was in awe of the fact that he looked at me and wanted me. I was pleased that other women were jealous of his attentions. He was all I could ever have hoped for or wanted. It made me feel that I was special because I considered him to be so and he had chosen me. This was at the beginning."

"And afterwards?"

"Afterwards came the pain."

They rode in silence for a while as sunlight dappled through the gray clouds up ahead. Together they tried to understand what Alix had just said.

"But why did you not turn to the Maltese Star?"

said Severin finally. "Surely its power would have helped you."

"I know nothing of its power," Alix replied with a shrug. "But I know there was no power that could have helped me. Robert truly loved Solange—and there is no force or might effective against that."

"Are you sure?"

Alix looked at him. She had been straining for months under the twin burdens of responsibility and loss and she was very tired. Deep within her something wakened. She felt it reach out to her with tentative fingers. The feeling, though strange and new, was not altogether unpleasant.

"No," she answered truthfully, "I am not."

Their eyes met, light to dark. In the end Severin was the first to look away. "There is Haute Fleur," he said, pointing to the impressive mass of stone buildings that rose up on the hill before them. "Is it not interesting how the arches of its cathedral rise up with the majesty of hands in prayer?"

Eight

It was night now and chilly. Alix suspected they would have a few last cold days before the warmth of spring truly settled. Padre Gasca had ventured outside the walls to see how she managed. By rights the priest should have been in bed long ago, but he had lingered. He had come directly after her lone meal and established himself quite firmly before the waning fire. Alix, fed and then left to her own devices, had been glad of his company. She had not seen Severin Brigante since their arrival and did not expect to see him again until they left in two days' time. According to the Rule of this Cistercian monastery, men did not mingle freely with women and they did so only when necessary. She imagined that the priest must have something of importance to tell her, or else even he would not have come.

They had put the baby in her care, something she should have conjectured a monastery filled with celibate men would do. But she hadn't.

"I know nothing about children," Alix cried as she looked about the small cell Abbot Suger had given to her as hospice. It was well beyond the main monastery walls. There seemed no help at all for her within its plain interior. She had been placed in the small stone guesthouse that was saved for the noblewomen who visited the powerful abbey either as wayfarers or to pray at the shrine of St. Yvrain, which was housed within the main church. One of the reasons they had brought the child here was that he was named for the saint who formed an important part of the abbey's fame, a hermit known during his life for great rectitude and piety, and, after his death, for miracles.

Alix's gaze moved quickly from the plain wood furnishings, to the small nun's bed, and then to the somber fresco of the Madonna and her Child who smiled down at her from the whitewashed walls.

"I have no idea what to do with a child," she said to Padre Gasca. Yvrain slept peacefully in his makeshift cradle, which had been formed by the long half of a new wine cask. Alix considered this sleep as a miracle wrought by the saint. "I have no idea how to dress or change him. He will need bathing—Good Lord! And what will he eat? What food is there? I have no . . ."

"He is well weaned," the monk said equitably. He reached out a socked and sandaled foot to set the small cradle in motion. "Sophie is past childbearing age and dared not hire wet-nursing for him. He is used to sucking his milk from a clean hemp-cloth—or even now from a wooden cup. At Mercier she told me that now he sleeps uncommonly well."

Under the Rule of their community, only the Abbot among all the monks was allowed to speak with women, but a certain laxness was allowed for Padre Gasca. He was, in fact, a visitor himself and not a member of their Order.

" 'Tis good you thought to question the Wise Woman about this," Alix said, "because I did not."

"You did enough," replied the priest. "Without you, Yvrain would surely have been found and killed."

Alix said nothing but she knew the truth. It was a truth she could not share with the priest she had known from birth—but there was someone, perhaps, who understood her. One person who could listen and not judge.

"Even the Knight Brigante must know more about swaddling children than do I."

The priest smiled over at her in his wizened, questing way. "I think the Knight Brigante may know a great deal about many things."

Alix let her mind flex around this thought.

"Did you know him before?" she asked finally. "Had you met him?"

"I knew his father." The priest looked over at her with clear eyes.

"Sir Severin told me that his father was once betrothed to his brother's wife," Alix said. "Is that true?"

"Indeed he was," said Padre Gasca. "But they were both children then. It was not serious—though for many years your Aunt Francesca thought it to be—until she met Belden of Harnoncourt."

"But their love was not honorable. It led to a ruinous life for the Sire d'Harnoncourt's brother."

"Guy ruined his own life," said Gasca. "As well as many others."

Alix grew thoughtful. " 'Tis rumored that the Knight Brigante did not have coin enough even for a warhorse when he started his way in life—nor for a sword or a suit of armor. Worst yet, he had had to fight his way free from his name. He told me this much himself. He said he had started his paging days by the time he had six years."

"And lucky he was to find a knight who would take him in," said Padre Gasca. "Guy d'Harnoncourt left him little in the way of heritage—and that little was severely tainted."

Again Alix grew thoughtful. It was some time before she spoke again.

"Father," she said, "may I ask you something?"

She kept her own gaze down but she could feel his upon her.

"Of course you may, my dear." She didn't have to look at him to know he faced her kindly.

"When you were younger," she began, "before you became a priest . . . Years ago . . . Did you ever want . . . Did you ever feel . . . ?"

She let her voice trail off, conscious of his eyes upon her. Only now she wished for a distraction. She wanted Abbot Suger to come and chastise Padre Gasca to his bed or hear a bell start ringing. She wanted the cry of brigands at the gate. But nothing happened; no one came.

"Did you think carnal thoughts?" The words rushed from her mouth. "Illicit thoughts," she finished.

"Such as making love to a woman?"

Alix nodded, and forced herself to face him squarely in the fire's glow. "A woman you shouldn't have wanted, perhaps because of your priesthood. A woman it was unnatural for you to want."

"It is *natural* for me to want a woman," said the little priest. He waited an instant after Alix's sharp intake of breath before he continued. "But there are other things that come naturally to me as well and that I consider more important. I love my vocation as a priest and I have always cherished it."

Alix nodded at this. Knowing his vows and the dedicated life he had lived, she could see the logic in what he said. Still, his answer skirted her question.

"But I mean really wanted—specifically. Did you ever want a certain woman? Did you ever think specifically about what you would do with that woman if you could?" She brightened. "Or did you just pray one day and the whole idea of 'wanting' simply vanished?"

"No, it wasn't that easy," said Gasca with a chuckle and then grew silent as he thought back. He was getting older. It had all happened long ago—and really to another man. But he knew what Alix was asking him and he was determined to answer her truthfully.

"Yes," he said. "One woman."

She looked up then, and over at him. "And did you think of kissing her? Did you think of her carnally?"

"Oh, yes, quite carnally," the priest said. "I was not a child when I fell in love; in fact, it happened right before I took my final vows. I was very attracted to her. And I had always thought that the strong, physical pull—and I assure you it was both strong and physical—could only accompany an equally strong spiritual bonding."

"You mean you thought you were destined to mate with this woman?"

"That is what I thought," he said.

"Soul to soul?"

"More than soul to soul, if that be possible," said the priest. "It was the moment in which I felt myself most strongly tempted—and not because the woman was a temptress. One cannot be tempted by something he does not truly desire. Luisa would never have tempted me against my will. She could not have done this and she would never have tried. Our bond was not like that at all. Rather, she was the pretty younger daughter of a lesser noble who held title near my father's demesne. The two of us had spent many happy times in each other's company during the years and there was the possibility—the distinct possibility—that we could have grown old happily together. We were well suited in many ways. We both liked the countryside near our home in Portugal. We loved children and young animals. She was sympathetic to my interest in alchemy, though she put little faith in my elixirs.

"We had not seen each other in years when I received permission from my bishop to return to Lorca to visit my mother's grave. I was a man but still a novice and not as yet a professed priest. I had yet to take my final vows. Still in principle free, I could certainly have married had I wanted. My family had never wanted the priesthood for me. It was looked upon as something for younger sons and paupers—not the vocation that it was for me."

"Why didn't you?"

"Because I didn't want it," he said simply. "I did not love her enough to sacrifice my true vocation for her. It was selfishness on my part."

It was surprising how easily the words came. At the time he had thought his decision painful and momentous, and perhaps it had been both. But it had been *right*. At least right for him. He had felt the weight of its pain for months afterwards and thought he would never be free from it. It amazed him now that, after almost fifty years, the blister of its ending had been replaced by a warmth.

It was the *rightness* of this choice that Gasca knew must be conveyed now. Or else Alix, innocent of her powers, might take an exceedingly wrong path. It was an instant before he spoke again, but this time the words were forceful.

"No, I did not want it. It was not my destiny to be a married man. I could have done it, and perhaps I could have done it well, at least to appearances—but inside I would have known the difference. I would have known that I was not doing what had been given me to do. For me, marriage was only a diversion that came at the last moment to tempt me from my course. I had already found my true calling in life—my true vocation."

Alix leaped at these hopeful words.

"A temptation comes," she said, "when one has important work to do ahead."

She found it a relief to discard her feelings for Severin Brigante with such neat tidiness.

"Have you ever felt that way, Lady Alix?" asked the priest, very quietly. "Tempted?"

She felt her cheeks grow hot again but she could not bring herself to lie to someone who had just spoken such a deep truth.

"Once," she answered. "And for only one man. I kissed him. I wanted to kiss him. But I see now that it was only a temptation—just as it was only a temptation for you. It was an enticement to keep me from doing my duty to my husband."

"But your husband is dead . . ."

"To his memory, then."

". . . and you are still alive."

His last word seemed to echo into the embers of the dying fire.

Alix pushed away and walked to the darkened window. She stared for a long time at the world that lay beyond it.

"I think 'tis awfully chill for springtime," she said at last. "Perhaps there is still a trace of winter yet to come."

Her last words were a whisper and Gasca just barely caught them.

"Kissing isn't enough," she said.

Gasca listened to the sounds of comfortable snores and grumblings that surrounded him and wished that his own sleep could be as peaceful. The monks, tired from the simple but strenuous day of prayer and labor, had settled in for the few hours sleep that divided the night between their prayer times. Gasca would be rising with them before the pre-dawn reciting of the Psalms for terce. He tried to wiggle more comfortably into his husk mattress but the sprigs that formed it poked through and dug at his arthritic bones.

He felt his age. And worse, he felt useless and even slightly afraid. It had been a long time since he'd felt frightened and at first he had not even recognized the emotion. He felt afraid.

At first the thought was just absurd. His experiments in alchemy had cost him many friends and put enemies in their place. He had the distinction of being put under interdict by both popes in this unholy schism—by the one at Avignon for what he had taught at Paris and by the one in Rome for what he had taught at Oxford. He had tried to tell himself the reason for this was the habit he wore. Unlike the Benedictines or the Cistercians, whose guest he was at this abbey, his fellow Franciscans were noted more for their piety than for their scholarship. Like their sainted founder, Francis, they were more at home speaking with birds and trees than they were defending their own before the Inquisition. When his mathematical studies at Oxford had resulted in the unheard-of apostasy of a round earth, his own religious order had sorrowfully shrugged its collective shoulder and left him to his undoing. This came in the form of the Dominicans, who were busy organizing the Inquisition, and who had not welcomed his tainted presence at Oxford—the great university which their own congregation had been instrumental in founding. The memory of this still smote.

He had faced his share of troubles in the past, and he thought himself quite through with them. He had pictured ending his days here in the peace and beauty of Haute Fleur in manual labor and meditation and doing just enough laboratory experiments to keep his mind agile for his prayers. It seemed he had been wrong. There was work still ahead of him and he had the unwelcome certainty that it would be fearsome work indeed.

If only Alix knew. If only Julian had told her. The power of the Magdalene was too powerful to be merely wished away; it had to be either rejected or embraced—yet first of all, it must be faced. Julian should have told Alix of her heritage. But the old priest was too much of a realist to waste much time in the unhappy land of what-might-have-been. The fact was that Alix *did not* know. Julian *had not* told her. Robert de Mercier's widow innocently wore the key to a mighty power that more than one man had been willing to kill to possess. Simon Malville, Guy d'Harnoncourt, for example, and the list went on and on. Gasca, a simple priest, still shuddered when he thought of Archangelo Conti, a cardinal of the Church—and what this man had known and done.

And Lancelot de Guigny was no fool. He had shown great intelligence in not wreaking havoc upon the peasantry of Mercier, as most other knights would have done. The general plan of warfare was to weaken one's noble rival first by killing or maiming as many of his peasants as fell within sword range. But this was weakening for the conqueror as well as for the conquered. Guigny was cunning enough to know this. What else might he realize as well? He had kept the Countess de Mercier near him for almost three months now when his first instinct must surely have been to convent her as soon as her husband was fresh in his grave. Why had he not released her?

Guigny would have heard the rumors and once he had heard them, been at pains to discover their truth. And the truth was there, plain to discern, as it had been since the day that poor foolish bastard Jacques de Molay had called down the wrath of God on Philip of France through lips already charring black from the witch-flames.

". . . Unto the thirteenth generation," the Grand Master of the Templars had cursed, as throughout all of Europe his once-proud Knights Templar were grappled down from the sanctity of their holy places and ground into the dust.

Of them all, only Peter of Bologna had escaped to be the instrument of vengeance. And his revenge had grown fearsome indeed.

Now Alix was in the midst of a vendetta that had ripened for more than a hundred years.

"The Magdalene," Gasca whispered. His voice sliced like a knife through the sounds of peaceful slumber that surrounded him. One or two of the monks mumbled darkly in their sleep.

A dead man's curse and vengeance had kindled the beginning of the Maltese Star. He had no idea exactly where Alix's fate might lead her but he was almost certain it would not be to the quiet of a convent in Picardy.

Gasca found himself an old, tired man who must once again confront its evil and this time with but the aid of one young widow, one helpless child—and perhaps someone else.

On his dark bed, Gasca's body stiffened as he strained at thought. Yes, perhaps someone else—someone who had already begun to be tempted. He looked within his memory and plucked out Alix's smile and the way her eyes had lighted when she spoke, though briefly, of the Knight Brigante. He compared them with the way her mother's eyes had shone when Olivier Ducci Montaldo was near and those of Francesca— dear Francesca's—when there was even the mention of Belden of Harnoncourt's name. The Maltese Star had carried bloodshed and tragedy to these women but it had also brought them love in the end. It had healed them.

But none of them had ever had to touch what lay before Alix. None of them ever had had to go that deeply—or had been so alone.

The old priest smiled as he remembered Latin words from his first year of priestly study. *Ad impossibile nemo tenetur.* No one is held to that which is impossible. He had found this to be true many times in his own life. He prayed that they would be true for Alix as well.

City

Nine

Alix had thought there would be someone to help with the child. In her life there had always been someone to help with everything: a maid to arrange her tunics and her hair, another to light fires in winter and open windows in summer. The first time she had ever dressed herself had been the morning after her husband's death. The pinning up of her own curls had heralded the beginning of a new life.

But while she may have been able to arrange her own hair and clothing during an emergency, she really had no experience of children. An only daughter herself, she was too young to remember the years in Italy when her mother had been Wise Woman of the village of Sant'Urbano and she had romped with the other children. She had forgotten what it was to play.

It was not that her needs were totally overlooked by the good monks. Alix was a countess, after all, and from a very powerful Burgundian house. Even they, in their piety, knew that allowances must be made. The trouble was, they had no way of knowing who would make a good nurse and who would not. Suger de Montbard, an Abbot both pious and crafty, chose someone to help her but as most of the women were already in the fields turning the ground for planting, he had to select a helper from the few souls who were not already occupied at the field.

He chose a devout spinster who reluctantly agreed to help the Lady Alix in her plight. The woman was full of good will and obedience, and the monks were assured that these virtues would be enough to guide her through any emergency. That she had no knowledge of babies, or even how they were made, was deemed a minor matter that the workings of heavenly grace could easily overcome.

"I am Marie," the woman said in presenting herself to Alix at the cottage door early the next morning. "I am competent."

She dropped an enormous flax bundle onto the dried thyme that the monks had scattered through the cottage to absorb the winter moisture and then looked over at Alix and smiled a very wide, very snaggle-toothed smile.

Alix smiled back. But the beginnings of serious doubts already niggled as to Marie's actual competence. For one thing, she blushed and shook her head when Alix inquired as to her husband; then she blushed even more deeply when mention was made of possible children.

"How could there be children with no husband?"

Alix sighed. A question was then made as to brothers and sisters. This discreet inquiry occasioned a prolonged coughing fit.

Yvrain, who had slept peacefully through the night, began to howl as soon as the door closed Marie inside. The woman looked over at the small cask where he lay, then back at Alix, then back to the cask once again.

"The child cries," said Marie. She made not the slightest move toward it.

"Well," said Alix, "I imagine children cry when first they awaken."

Marie nodded in agreement.

"It means they want something," Alix continued gamely. "I imagine he might be hungry."

Both women looked down at the hemp basket Marie had brought; the look upon both their faces suggested they had found the Holy Grail.

If not the Holy Grail, the sumter contained at least a container with milk inside. Alix's hands encircled the earthenware bowl and found it warm. The milk must have come from one of the goats that she had glimpsed yesterday on the hills around the monastery. She silently thanked the monk who had thought to send such a blessing to them.

"But there's no cup," she said. "How will he take his milk without a cup?"

At this Marie looked lively. "Perhaps he is too young for a cup," she said. "Not all of them can handle one from birth."

Alix thought it doubtful that any child could actually handle a cup from birth but she decided not to comment upon this. She looked deeper within the flax basket and rooted among the apples and cheeses and bottles of water and wine, but she could find nothing that seemed of any help. In the meantime, Yvrain continued to voice his discontent. His face had grown quite purple from howling.

"Perhaps we should see to him first," Alix shouted. Marie readily agreed to this. The Countess de Mercier had the distinct impression that, at that instant, Marie would have agreed to the existence of unicorns had these been proposed to her. But she said nothing; she was afraid that if she did the woman would take offense and leave her alone with this screaming child. Even the thought of this terrified Alix and brightened her smile to the maid.

The two of them approached the cask and gazed down at the lustily crying child.

"Mon Dieu," said Marie, crossing herself at the incredible clamor. Alix felt like crossing herself as well— or cursing the fact that she had not thought to bring Sophie or Young Sophie with her.

"I know nothing of babes," Alix wailed, forgetting for an instant that she was the Dame de Mercier, "and I surely will kill this one if I try to handle it."

There now appeared the added question of a certain particular odor.

"He has gone upon himself," said Marie.

The maid hid within the safety of her lowly rank and looked hopefully toward her new mistress.

At least this was a thing Alix knew a bit about. She instructed Marie to search for linen in the sumter. When none was found she pointed to her own under-tunic upon the stool and motioned the maid to tear it. While she did this, Alix removed the offending garment from a kicking Yvrain and cleansed him with water from the stone bottle. Then she patted his bottom with the orange-clove water she had brought within her pack. Yvrain seemed to like this and actually held quite still while she wrapped and then tied the stripped linen around his round, soft little body. But his cooperation proved short-lived. He was crying lustily again before Alix fit the stopper again into its bottle.

Still, Alix had been buoyed by her success as a changing maid. She moved on with confidence to the feeding. She had triumphed in her first-ever attentions to a child—the covering upon Yvrain's bottom stayed in place, though now he was kicking furiously and had turned purple again—and she could move on with confidence to the next step.

"Bring my own cup," she said to an admiring Marie. " 'Tis in that sumter over near the corner. My own is silver, not wood, but I don't think that will make a difference to the child."

She was not absolutely sure of this, however. She imagined that there were many rules and regulations concerning the care and feeding of children and she had always seen them fed—even the most royal of them—from little wooden bowls. She thought there must be a reason for this and that the reason might have something to do with the alchemy of silver against their small mouths. There were so many things she did not know and she was so ignorant of children and their particular needs that she could easily do harm where she meant well. But she could not worry to stop her action now.

"Now bring the milk," she instructed. Marie scurried to comply.

Alix settled into the chair that Gasca had occupied the night before and found that Yvrain fit right within the crook of her arm. When she held the cup to his lips he drank thirstily. Beside her, Marie sighed with relief. The baby drained the cup and continued lapping at it once the milk was finished so that Alix, more comfortable now with her babying skills, confidently asked the maid to bring more.

"He will need bathing," she said with authority. "I will see to that as soon as he has finished with his morning meal. If you will, Marie, please bring water to be heated."

The maid had bobbed a curtsey and disappeared from the cottage even before the words had finished echoing upon the air.

Now that his initial hunger had been satisfied, the child drank more quietly. He snuggled closer and even reached one little hand up to cup it around Alix's upon the delicate silver tankard. Without thinking, Alix ran her nose through Yvrain's downy hair and drew him near. He drank his milk to the last and before much time had passed both the child and the countess who cared for him had fallen into an exhausted sleep.

The Dame de Mercier dreamed, as she often now did, of the Knight Brigante.

Severin Brigante Harnoncourt, justly famed for his self-discipline and determination, could not force Alix de Mercier from his mind. In fact, he thought of her so much that sometimes he feared for his sanity. Rationality had always formed the basis of his life and of his mission. Rationally he knew that she had lied to him about the child and that he should leave her to get out of the lie as best she could. He had not done this. Instead he had meekly escorted her little band to the monastery. He had not asked her the reason for her actions; he had not confronted her with her lie.

A lovesick page could have acted with more command.

Never in his life had he been so affected by a kiss. He was horrified by the fact that when he closed his eyes he remembered it and could actually still taste the sweetness of her tongue as it brushed against his. He could still feel the exact texture of her body and the weft of it within his arms. She came fully to his mind at the most unexpected moments.

Without the goading power of that kiss, Severin knew he would never have left Mercier so completely in the hands of Lancelot de Guigny. The duke would not like it. He had instructed Severin to keep a keen eye. That the Knight de Guigny went for frequent prayers to the shrine of St. Bernard was something that not even a cloistered nun could credit. Guigny slipped away to do mischief—but against whom and why were puzzle pieces that Severin had as yet been unable to explain.

But he knew he would in the end. And he was sure that the Knight de Guigny knew this as well.

"But certainly he would not plot against his brother," whispered Severin to himself as he strode to pay respects to the Abbot Suger. "He would not dare to do so."

The Abbot was waiting for him in a small room to one side of the massive refectory where the monks took their silent meals. He was a small, spry man, well known for learning and for a certain interest in intrigue. Unlike many of his religious contemporaries, he had achieved an august position while maintaining a decidedly liberal bent. He had been one of the first men to try the new phenomenon of ground-glass lenses in steel frames in order to aid a vision that he considered a trifle shortsighted. These sat perched upon his head as he smiled and heaved his rounded form to a standing position as Severin entered. The Knight Brigante was unprepared for the enormous hug with which he was greeted.

"What a grand surprise it is to have you here, my son," said the priest.

"And you, too, Abbot Suger," replied Severin, dislodging himself to do reverence and kiss the prelate's iron ring. "It has been a long time."

"More years have passed than I care to remember," replied Suger, motioning to a leather chair that matched his own. "But they seem to have gone well with you. I've heard you have accomplished exceeding wonders since last we met at King Charles's court."

"I head the Gold Company," replied Severin.

"Ah, your uncle's company." Suger tented his hands on the trestle before him. "How fitting."

Severin glanced about him at the simplicity of the

highly polished floor and the whitewashed walls and measured it against the elaborately painted tile floors and manteled chimneys and intricately bordered and painted walls at Mercier.

"A knight's life is very much like that of a monk," said Suger. "Is that not what you were thinking?"

Severin smiled. "*Ruefully* thinking would be more to the fact. They are simple things, both of our lives— made up of hard and lonely beds and many weary years away from home. You are right. In many ways our lives are alike."

"And each style of life has its own particular battles that must be fought," said the Abbot. "Now tell me what is happening with this war that Burgundy is foisting upon us."

"Henry of England sends word that he crosses the channel with the coming of the spring winds," Severin replied. He knew he would only be giving this crafty Abbot information he already had. "Jean of Burgundy has yet to visit and retake Mercier as its liege lord, but this must happen soon enough. He cannot continue to ignore the stronghold that his half brother has presented him."

The Abbot's normally benign face hardened at the mention of the Knight de Guigny but when he spoke his voice remained low and pleasant. "The duke owes much to his older half brother—and not alone for what he won at Mercier. Did Sir Lancelot not save Duke Jean's life at the battle of Nicopolis?"

"The Knight de Guigny formed part of his brother's bodyguard. The present duke's father, Philip the Bold, pressed that crusade upon France and his son led it, although he was not yet knighted. Jean of Burgundy only received his golden spurs some weeks after the crusade had begun. The Knight de Guigny was said to have brought about whatever glory resulted from that shambled affair. On the battlefield, when his victory was already certain, the Sultan Bayezid would have killed Duke Jean had not Lancelot de Guigny persuaded him otherwise."

"And his reward for that great feat was—nothing?"

The Knight Brigante remained silent. The two men could hear the sound of monks singing their psalms as they worked in the fields. "They were both young men at the battle," he said at last. "Probably it was thought that something would be done for the Knight de Guigny later, at a more opportune time. Already Burgundy was ravaged to pay the ransom that Bayezid demanded for Jean's life. There were no rich freeholds to give him. Then the old duke died and Jean ruled the kingdom in his stead. He is a strange man; they call him Jean the Fearless. A man who is neither good nor bad—but totally without fear and secure in the exaltation of his noble and legitimate position. Lancelot de Guigny may be his half brother. He may have also saved his life. But the duke feels no obligation to him. He believes that what is his he rules by divine right."

Abbot Suger considered this. "Perhaps he does not wish to draw attention to an inconvenient connection."

"Perhaps," said Severin, though he doubted this.

"But they are plighted to the same side in this arriving war?"

"Ostensibly so," replied Severin and then he deftly moved away from the delicate subject of the Duke of Burgundy toward one which he knew would interest the Abbot just as much. "Is the abbey ready with reserves on hand in case battle should play nearby?"

Suger smiled to show he realized the deft handling, but would not allow himself to be maneuvered away from a subject that was undoubtedly delicate for a man so intimately involved with Duke Jean's mission. "The Abbey is as ready as it can be. We've started the first plantings, though slowly. Something tells me that the bad weather is not quite over yet. It would not be the first time that the good Lord has surprised us with frost after the passing of the Spring Equinox. But we are hoping and praying for a good harvest. If Henry of England comes—or perhaps 'tis already better to say *when* he comes—we would not want either the abbey or its village to be in want. We will plant well and hope that the war bypasses us at least until after harvest."

"It might be best to prepare," said Severin. "Haute Fleur lies on the road that leads from Calais to Paris."

"Padre Gasca tells me that you will be heading in that direction within a few weeks' time," said Abbot Suger.

Severin did not bother to ask how the Portuguese priest had come by this information. "I go to Rome when Jean of Burgundy releases me from my present task. Italy is my home country."

"More so than England?"

"I have never been to England. I know nothing of it," replied Severin. "But since Burgundy has allied himself with England in this quest for the throne, he thinks it best to seek support from the English pope."

"Ah, the one in Rome, as opposed to the pontiff who sits in Avignon."

". . . And who is known as the French pope because he guards souls who take their command from the King of France."

"As well he might. Avignon is more accessible to Paris than is Rome. It also rests upon French soil."

"The French must have their share of saints as well," said Severin.

"There is nothing of sainthood in this coil," replied

the Abbot, unconsciously rubbing an arthritic elbow. "And very much of evil. Jacques de Molay, the last of the Templar Grand Masters, cursed King Philip the Fair of France and his henchman Clement VI as he stood roasting on his pyre. Do you recall the story?"

"Who could not remember it? That cursing is the basis for the war we now fight."

"And have fought for close unto one hundred years," the old Abbot said. "When Philip took it into his mind to pounce upon the Templars and hound them from this earth, it was said that he would have spared the Grand Master if he could. Jacques de Molay was, after all, the godfather of the king's only daughter, Isabel. The two men had been friends. But the Grand Master refused to save himself at the cost of his Order and, while the flames licked bright about him, he cursed pope and then king down unto the thirteenth generation. He called both the king and the pope to meet him before God's judgment seat within the year."

Severin picked up the thread of the abbot's tale. "Witchcraft was the charge against the Templars and torture was the method used to extract confession. My father read a parchment scribed by Padre Gasca's master at the University of Paris. Have you ever seen it?"

"Once, long ago, Padre Gasca was kind enough to share it with me. But I have examined it again just recently. I have grown uneasy lately. There have been signs." The Abbot's voice grew uncharacteristically vague.

"Signs?"

"It is a ferocious legend," said Suger slowly. "Within one month of Molay's death Pope Clement was dead. Six months later the king had followed him. He fell from his horse, took chill and died—though before this he had spent not a day sick in his life."

"But leaving three sons," prompted Severin, "who each took his turn upon the throne."

"And promptly died," finished Suger. "Following one right after the other as Louis X, Philip V, and Charles IV. The longest-lived of them reigned but six years and they each died—aged twenty-seven, twenty-eight, and thirty-three respectively."

"Only the daughter, Isabel, remained. She was Jacques de Molay's godchild and roundly rumored to be a witch and enchantress."

Suger felt a draft and shuddered. He grimaced at the pain that had begun to shoot up from his elbow. "She *was* a witch," he said.

This Severin had never heard, but the Abbot's words were designed to prick his attention. His own family had more than once been haunted by accusations of witchcraft and Templarism.

"Isabel of France?"

The Abbot smiled. "She was Isabel of England when the curse took. She had married Edward II of England when she was quite young and then schemed with her lover in his murder. She was a woman generally feared and hated and was thought to hold a malignant influence over her son, who ascended the throne of England as Edward III. It was through him that Isabel pushed her claim to the French throne but the peers and princes of France did not agree with her pretensions—nor did the University of Paris, which annulled the pretense of female lineage to the throne—and the title was given to Philip of Valois. The people hated her."

"But Edward III doggedly pursued his interests," said Severin, "as have his Plantagenet descendants after him. This is the reason for the steadfast war between these two countries. It is an ancient story now, begun with the turning of the last millennium and continuing down its bloody way into this new one."

"Which young Henry is only too pleased to pursue," said Suger. "No previous English king has taken such a determined interest in the conquest of this throne."

"No English king before this could count upon the Duke of Burgundy's support."

"Indeed," replied Suger, as his fingers worked along his arm. "These old bones are wretched. I imagine there is more to winter than we yet suspect."

All in all, Severin was happy with his afternoon within the abbey walls. He had enjoyed his talk with Abbot Suger and had managed, though dealing with a notoriously wily prelate, to learn more than he had disclosed. That alone would give him cause to rejoice. But there were other reasons. Because war—and most especially this coming war—was his lifeblood he had managed to focus his mind upon it as they spoke. He had not thought of Alix. Her scent had not enfolded him.

Once his father, drunk as usual, had whispered to him that the woman who wore the Maltese Star was the Magdalene—the Templar's goddess, the warlock's witch. She could enthrall an unwary man.

Severin had never credited his father's prattles.

Now he wondered if, indeed, he had not been bewitched.

Ten

" 'Tis a mystic place," cried Alix. She would have clapped her hands with joy had she not been holding tightly to Yvrain. "I've never seen such wonderful snow in my life."

" 'Tis normal here," said Marie. "We are so blessed that even nature's laws do not apply to us. 'Tis not the first time we've had snow in April—nor, for that matter, flowers in December."

"Flowers?" Alix looked dubiously at her over Yvrain's head.

"Beneath the snow," repeated the maid. "Small purple ones. You can see them yourself if you want. They come up at the brook bank. I have seen them once or twice, but they only bloom with the spring snow."

Alix dearly loved both flowers and legends.

"But they won't be there now," she said. It was obvious she wished to be persuaded.

"Yesterday, who would have believed that snow would bed the ground in April? Go to the brook bank, if you don't believe me. I'm sure you will find the flowers yourself."

Alix was sorely tempted. Her life within the indulgent confines of Mercier had not allowed for the adventure of discovery. If Robert had noticed her at all it was to comment upon the quality of her reading or her ability at rondele or tableau; to win his affection she had endeavored to perfect herself in ways he would approve. He had no interest in hidden winter flowers—at least he had not shared this interest with her—and so she had never cultivated this pursuit.

Now she felt it flourishing.

"Violet flowers?" she said to Marie. "Under the snow?"

The woman nodded.

Alix quickly handed Yvrain to Marie and bundled herself into her long velvet cloak. It stood out starkly against the bright-white day.

The snowfall had been quick and fierce. It had blanketed the birch and pine trees with enormous wet flakes that shimmered in the brilliant sunlight. They would be lucky if the snowfall lasted through the day.

"When it disappears it will take the flowers with it," whispered Alix. Marie had given her vague directions and after snuggling the hood around her loosened hair, Alix trudged out into the purity of this new and silent world.

Though he did not come to her hospice himself, Abbot Suger sent word through Padre Gasca of the fine letter he had scripted to the king, requesting succor for Robert's child. He had thought it best to seek help directly from Paris rather than the Burgundian capital of Dijon, especially when one considered the circumstances at Mercier. No one had heard from the duke, but everyone assumed that the thought of Count Robert immediately conjured treason to his mind and so appeal might best be made to a more sympathetic ear.

In these warring times, what was disloyalty to one lord was deemed fidelity to the other. In order to offset the duke's plans, the king would be compelled to give over Yvrain's guardianship to a strong noble—and preferably a strong peer of the south not under the sway of Burgundy. Bastard or not, Count Robert's child carried Mercier blood and could prove useful at some point. The king might need him if ever he wished to wrest control of the castle from Lancelot de Guigny. Alix smiled as she trudged through the snow. She had done her duty to her husband. She had maintained her promise and brought Yvrain to safety.

"Now I have only to wait," she said aloud. Her whispered words caught upon the morning. The stillness changed and echoed them back to her.

But wait for what?

Certainly not for Mercier. No matter what was decided, she would no longer have a home there. She knew this clearly enough; the Knight de Guigny had said it. She was an inconvenient woman and an inconvenient woman's fate lay, more often than not, within the convent walls. This fact was as irrefutable, as basic to common knowledge, as the flatness of the earth. Soon—and probably quite soon—she would be leaving the magnificence of Mercier. She would be leaving her home.

As though it had never been my home.

She looked down at the fine black cloth of her mantle as her footsteps billowed it out against the whiteness of the snow. She was in mourning still and would be so for the rest of her life. But was it a true mourning? That she no longer knew. In the short time since Robert's killing so much of life had changed for her and in ways that she never could have expected. It was true that she kept her husband's memory alive. She prayed daily at the altar she had constructed for him. She wore black to honor him. She made sure that his memory and the memory of his end would not easily be forgotten within his family's lands.

But she had kissed another man.

What's more, she had loved kissing him.

She would do it again, if given the chance. And she would do more.

A rush of snow floated down just before her. Alix looked up to see a flock of robins clinging to birch branches that already showed the budding of new life beneath their white covering. She smiled at them. Then she squinted into the sunlight toward the place where the brook should be, and she listened. There were few sounds and no trace of human life; the monks and their peasants had obviously decided to use the excuse of the snow for a free day's *congé*. Alix saw only the birds and the occasional track of some small animal that had hurried before her across the snow. She could have been the last person upon the earth— or the first.

She set off again toward the brook, certain now of the way, though she could not have told why. She let her mind dwell upon that kiss she had shared with Severin Brigante. She did not push the thought of him away—and would not have done this had she been able. She tasted him again and felt him and smelled him. She heard his voice.

"You will be but exchanging one nun's bed for another."

But not quite yet, not this instant.

She still had the Magdalene to show her the way.

Alix still had no clear idea of the Magdalene and its power—if, indeed, there was power in this unknown myth—but she was coming to have a certain idea of her own self.

She had kissed Severin Brigante and she had loved the kiss. Loved it even before his lips had touched hers. She had been the one to reach for him. When he hesitated, she had pulled him close. Severin was not like Robert de Mercier. He had nothing of that suave sophistication that had so entranced her when she had seen her future husband wend his way through the

Emperor Sigismund's crowded court. Severin Brigante was big of bone and small of learning. There was nothing of the gemstone about him. His hair reminded her of golden wheat not spun gold; his eyes were more the color of good ground than of onyx. But this did not bother Alix, at least anymore. Jewels could be cold. They could be brittle. Marriage to Robert de Mercier had taught her this.

Severin was different. Alix remembered the feeling of safety on that first, terrible night when he had seen her shivering and wrapped his own cloak around her as they walked through the stricken castle. She remembered the circle of his hand at her wrist and the feel of his fingers over hers as, together, they traced the words he was so determined to learn.

Again, she remembered his kiss.

Severin was of the earth, she realized. And like the earth he possessed deep and hidden riches—though he actually possessed very little. He owned no lands, no fine castle, no great and envied library, no title like the one of Mercier that Alix now bore. The only thing Severin fully owned was his mission. Everything he had was given over to that.

When he spoke of his uncle, Belden of Harnoncourt, Severin's face hardened and changed. She had seen this happen time and time again. He would never rest until he had righted what he saw as the great wrong that had been done to his father. A voice whispered on the air:

You are falling in love with a man who cannot love you. He may look and act differently from your husband, but beneath the surface differences he is the same man. Wedded to something that does not include you. Married to something you cannot share. Beware.

A rabbit hopped out from the tree cover, unaccountably stopping upon the path to regard her silently. Alix shook her head at him and smiled.

"I cannot live through that again. I cannot go back to that pain," she whispered to him. "I am better off convented than to live in desolation, wanting another man who cannot want me in return."

The rabbit shook himself vigorously, knocked the snow from his fur, and bumped off.

Alix, too, started up again. Snow wedged into her thin boots and she felt its cold wetness but she also heard the faint ripple that told her she was near the brook. She walked on toward the promise of snow flowers.

It was not too late, she thought. She was not dead, although Robert was and the life she had lived with him was over as well. But *she*—Alix Ducci Montaldo de Mercier—still had her life. Perhaps there might be good to come from it. She had chosen her own fate. When offered the chance, she had refused to go back to the certainty of her parents. Even though she knew they loved her, their love for each other had always been so great that she had felt excluded. She no longer wished to be excluded and thus, rather than return to Hungary, she had chosen the convent. But the convent was not the grave.

And there is always Belvedere, the Magdalene whispered. Somehow, someway—there is always Belvedere.

Belvedere is your home.

But she was a lone woman and Belvedere lay far away. And soon there would be battle between them in that endless war that had engulfed England and France and pockets of Italy since before her mother's time and her grandmother's as well. She didn't know why, but she realized suddenly that there had always been war since the Magdalene's coming. She could never make it back home alone, not with two armies massing. Best not to dream in that direction. Best to resign her life to the convent without a fight. Surely she could be useful there.

Both the brook and the two animals that drank from it came, simultaneously, to her view.

She stood transfixed and stared at the young doe and her fawn.

"Don't speak," Severin whispered. "Don't move."

His voice, coming unexpectedly from behind, should have startled her. It didn't. Alix did not move; she hardly breathed. She knew that what was happening was an enchantment and that it was the Magdalene's doing.

Alix watched as the doe and her young dipped their delicate noses into the brook. She watched the fawn lift his head and shake shards of bright water into the air. She watched his mother as she nosed him affectionately. Behind her she could hear soft footfalls moving closer. Alix lifted her head and turned just slightly toward the soft sounds, just as a blind person might.

"Don't speak."

He was right behind her. The plume of his breath clouded on the morning air and Alix felt its warmth brush against her cheek. He was so very close. Alix smelled his clean maleness just beneath the scent of pine and burning wood that topped the freshness of the morning. She sniffed the air with little sniffles with her eyes closed; she held her body very still and did not think. There would be plenty of time for thinking when she was alone in the convent. She would have the rest of her life to think. Plenty and plenty of time for thinking then, and occasions enough also for remorse and penance.

But this was not the convent.

This was now. This was Severin.

And *now* included this brilliant, pure world, these

two strangely tame wild animals, and the brushing whisper of this man behind her. She, a married woman, had never before felt a man brush this close unless he had been thoroughly primed beforehand by wine and a stern sense of duty.

But that was Robert and Robert was yesterday. Like the convent of tomorrow, he was not now. *Now* was another man and another place—far enough from Mercier. *Now* was someone who could teach her things that perhaps it was time that she learned.

If you have the courage to learn.

The sun glinted onto the Maltese Star that hung loosely at her throat and threw its light onto the snow. The fawn and its mother glanced down at the sparkling snow; then the young deer cocked his head and looked at Alix with his wide, deep eyes. It showed no fear. Alix stood, encircled by enchantment. All that was around her, all that she felt. She had been warned to cross herself and pray to the archangel St. Michael should she suspect a wayward trick. But she did neither of those things now. If this were an enchantment, then she preferred its soft magic to the harsh reality of her own life.

Besides, it had brought Severin near.

"Look, they come near us," she whispered to him.

The fawn raised his nose and sniffed the air.

"He's sniffing this. 'Tis why he came," Severin whispered against her cheek. "Remove your glove so you may give it to him."

Alix did as she was told, very gently and slowly peeling the soft leather from her fingers. She hesitated, but only for an instant, before holding it out close to her side. Severin's fingers were warm, hot even, as he pressed something gritty into her outstretched hand. A small sprinkle of it drifted down through her fingers to melt a fine passage into the snow.

" 'Tis salt," whispered Severin, still behind her. "They come for it here."

The deer moved closer, their noses sniffing the air.

Very slowly and with infinite care, the Countess de Mercier, now freed from the confines of her great castle, held out a bared hand to them.

"Did you follow me?" Alix asked, some two days later as the palfreys that she and Severin rode picked their way along the winding path that would take them back to Mercier. "Is that how you came to be in the forest?"

She did not look at him as she said the words. Instead she kept her attention on the reins in her hand, on the snow that was rapidly turning to slush beneath the hooves of their horses. She tried to calculate how much farther they must go before this isolated path joined the main pilgrim road that led northward.

She tried not to think how little time remained for her with this man, but she thought of it anyway.

"Were you following me?" she repeated when he said nothing. "How did you come to be in the woods?"

He laughed then, while above his head a startled flock of starlings scattered from their tree limb into the sky. His breath plumed out and the sight of it called Alix back to the forest and the brook and the time of magic. It brought back the lush rasp of a young deer's tongue against the nakedness of her palm. Alix blushed at the memory. She squirmed just a bit on her ornate gold-and-leather saddle.

"I wasn't thinking to find you there," Severin said. "But then neither was I surprised when I saw you."

"Not surprised?" She sniffed. "It was the middle of the forest. How could you not have been surprised to find me there?"

"Were you surprised to find me?"

"No," she said.

They did not look at each other.

"The monks do not allow hunting on Haute Fleur," said Severin. "They believe that the lands should be a sanctuary for all of God's creatures. The animals have never known malice and so they do not expect it. The deer came to you because they expect to find kindness. It is all they have ever known."

All they have ever known.

She thought of the fawn and then, suddenly, she thought how magnificent it would be should Severin run his tongue along her palm just as the deer had done. The idea flashed in and out of her mind without warning. But its power left her shaken. It left her breathless.

"Oh, God," she muttered, blushing deeply. "I am lost indeed."

"Lost?" he said beside her. "Indeed, my lady, I am sure we are upon the right road. We should have you at the castle this eventide, long before the vesper bell finishes its peal."

She quickly changed the subject. "What will you do once we have returned to Mercier?"

"The duke has already slated me for Rome, on mission to the pope. I only await his orders and then I will return home."

"You think of Italy as home?"

"It is my home." And then he added. "It is yours as well."

"I imagine that it is," she said after a while. "I have a castle there. My father gave it to me when I was dowered. But the gift was to me and not to the estate of Mercier. I think of that Castle of Belvedere as my home. I don't know that I think of Italy as such."

"Yet it is your homeland," responded Severin. "Just as it is mine."

Alix thought of this silently. "We are related, you and I," she said. "My father's sister is married to Belden of Harnoncourt. She is your aunt by marriage as well."

Severin looked straight ahead. "I know that," he said.

"They have four strapping sons," she continued.

"I know that as well." He matched the softness of her voice with his own, though he still did not look over at her. But, then, neither did Alix look at him. "I have heard often of Belden of Harnoncourt and of his doings. He is a famous man: counselor to Henry of England and to his father before him. I have heard of his family. I thought of his sons—my cousins—often. I thought what it must be like to have a family, to be surrounded by it. I was the only child of my parents."

"I as well," said Lady Alix.

"Yet we two are related. We are, in a way, family to each other," said Severin.

"But no blood binds us. There was nothing tainted in our kiss."

So immediate was Alix's response that she blushed quite crimson as soon as its words had passed her lips.

Severin laughed heartily at the sight of her confusion.

"No, there is no chance of consanguinity," he said. "You are not at all related to me."

"I was not speaking in snobbish terms," replied Alix. "You misunderstand me, Sir Severin. But you do not think so. You only wish to provoke me."

His laugh boomed even harder. "No, 'tis you who misunderstand, my lady of Mercier. I had no thought about either your rank or mine. My thoughts were all on kissing and where such foolishness could lead."

"Could lead?" she replied, her gaze narrowing upon him.

"You were a married woman," he said and he did not look away from her. Laughter twinkled in his dark eyes and lightened them. "You know about such things."

She did, she thought, but perhaps not in all the ways he meant. She looked at him closely and then deftly guided both her horse and the conversation toward a wider path.

"Belden of Harnoncourt is nothing to me. I am only distantly related to him and he has always lived in a land far from my own. I know little of him." Alix shrugged.

"And yet he saved your mother's life."

She felt herself enveloped by stillness, the same stillness that had engulfed her near the brook and had been in her dream the long-ago night when Robert was killed. A stillness that could tell her something—if she would but allow it to do so. But she remembered the warning she'd heard in the forest: the whisper that this man was merely Robert in another form and that he could never love her. Sometimes the things that emerged from this great silence were not things that she especially wanted to hear.

Yet she felt herself compelled to listen to it—and to him.

"Belden of Harnoncourt went to the east, to a fortress city named Nicopolis in search of his wife's brother, Olivier Ducci Montaldo. A great crusade was afterwards fought there. But at the time the place had just come under the suzerainty of the Turks," said Severin. "The Sire d'Harnoncourt went in search of your father, but in the end it was your mother who saw them both free."

"She's never spoken of it," said Alix, looking down

to her horse's hooves as they delicately picked their way. "Neither has my father."

"There was your grandmother as well, your mother's mother. Her name was Aalyne de Lione. She was known as the Magdalene." Severin hesitated. "Have you never heard of her? I could tell you more."

But Alix shook her head still without looking over at him. She was not ready to learn more about the Magdalene. Somehow she knew that once the vague stories and the legends of the Magdalene took shape for her, her life would change. Much more so even than it had changed with her marriage and with Robert's death. And she was not ready for that change. The thought of what her heritage might include filled her with dread.

"Sometime later, not now," she said quickly. "I am not yet ready to hear more now."

Severin immediately bowed to her wishes.

"Then we will stop our chatter and race each other to that patch of green at the next hillock."

Alix nodded. She spurred her horse and the two of them galloped over the plain.

They paused at midday for the light meal of bread and goat cheese that the kitchen monk had packed for them. They stood beside each other as they ate, gazing out from their small rise toward where Mercier stood. Alix could sense the castle, though she could not as yet see it. There were still three good hours before they would cross its bridge and hear the clang of its portcullis shutting them in. She imagined its great gray stones, its list fields, the small, dark village that nestled beneath it. But she did not do this with the pleasant sensation that coming home should give.

Mercier was no longer her home.

Belvedere was.

Home waited for her there, and the answer to secrets.

Alix had no idea how she realized this, but she knew that it was so.

She was no longer hungry. She wrapped the last crumbs of her bread and cheese and replaced them in her sumter. She put her heavy silver cup with its ornate heralding of the House of Mercier into its deerskin pouch.

Severin, too, put his food away, stropped crumbs from his cloak and tunic, and handed Alix once again into the ornate saddle of her palfrey. They pointed their horses toward the setting sun and soon the vast, stone fortress of Mercier came into view.

Eleven

It was full night by the time they reached the castle moat. Under Lancelot de Guigny's suzerainty the fortress was now kept very well lighted but still Alix was unprepared for its brilliance. It seemed that torchlight gleamed from every leaded and paned window that fronted the inner curtain. Handing her reins to a page, Alix paused to examine the structure. The light that spilled from it flickered more than it gleamed. It reminded Alix of flames upon a witch's pyre—though she had never seen a witch's burning—or of hellfire.

She dreaded going in there.

Severin walked beside her up the stairs, the golden spurs of his earned knighthood jingled against the stone steps.

Only low ranked pages seemed to be milling about but as soon as they had passed the enormous oaken door of the castle proper, other knights gathered around them—knights who were tunicked in Guigny's silvery green. Some milled about, some played at dice or backgammon, some threw scraps to frisking dogs— but all of them watched. All of them were strangely silent. Though not warrior-trained, even Alix realized that there was far too much activity for so late upon a working-night. Mercier, though taken, was as yet not secured and would not be until the Duke of Burgundy bestowed its liege. Lancelot de Guigny was too intelligent a knight not to realize that what he had so recently seized could be seized, in turn, from him. His soldiers would be given wine rations and good food to eat—that was expected. But they would also be sent to bed early because each new day would bring with it a goodly share of jousting and list field practice and the other activities necessary to keep them in fighting trim. Alix had noted, on the few occasions in which she had spent time in his presence, that Guigny was loud in his defense of his half brother Burgundy and quick to talk badly of the king. That could well prove a problem. Charles VI's madness was quixotic; it came and went without warning. One never knew when he might be capable of leading an expedition to retake the fortress of a loyal subject. One never knew when he might strike. Until the air had settled, and settled well, Guigny would have to hold his men in readiness for any contingency. Which was why so many seemingly idle soldiers milling about so late at night was most troubling. Unless . . .

The space around her was so tense that it scintillated; the air itself seemed dense enough to splinter and spin.

"Severin," Alix whispered.

He shook his head and she fell silent, following his gaze with her own to see what he had already seen.

There were no men of the Gold Company about them. The famous black tunics were most conspicuous by their absence.

Something has most certainly happened. But at least Yvrain is safe.

She had no thought but that any change in routine at Mercier in these days did not bode well.

Her seneschal came and bowed deeply. He was an old man who had been with the Merciers since Robert's childhood. He had been the first to greet Alix on her original arrival at the castle. He would be there, she knew, to see her out of it as well.

"My lady," he said, "the Count de Mercier begs an audience."

Alix saw consternation in his rheumy eyes when he rose to look at her again. She stopped, blinked.

Robert? Had Robert come back to her from the grave? But that was impossible. She knew that now. That life was over and done.

Then she realized exactly what was happening.

"Has the Duke of Burgundy passed here since my departure for Haute Fleur?"

The seneschal shook his head.

"Then you may tell the Knight de Guigny that the Countess de Mercier will attend him as soon as she has refreshed herself," she said. "Sir Severin, will you do me the courtesy of escorting me to my chambers?"

"How dare you joke with me!" Lancelot de Guigny kept his voice low. His lack of status and position within the notorious snobbery of the French elite had made of him a man well used to holding in his anger and he was doing his best to make an admirable job of it now. He was not quite succeeding. Once, many years ago in Hungary, Alix and her parents had chanced upon the remains of a war-horse that had been dead for some time. Its body had exploded in the relentless heat of summer. But before turning away in disgust, Alix had chanced to see all the putrefaction that had been contained within that carcass; she had seen the strange mixing of bright and decay that heralded death and she had glimpsed the small, scurrying life that fed upon them. She remembered that lifeless carcass now as she gazed across the trestle at the elegant, carefully manicured form of the man who now called himself the Count of the Merciers.

"I had no idea we were playing at toys." Severin stood close beside Alix as he spoke. "I thought we were discussing Haute Fleur and what had happened there. I thought you might be interested in the spring snow or at the very least in the Abbot's hope. He has sent emissaries on mission to verify the authenticity of a relic from the head of John the Baptist. He is readying himself to petition for funds with which to construct a new shrine."

"I have no interest in monk-gossip, and well you know this." Guigny almost spat out the words. "The only significance for me of this whole adventure is the amount of treachery contained within it. I know perfectly the real reason for your sudden interest in Haute Fleur. You think to have saved Yvrain le Bastarde. How foolish of you."

What he said was dismissive. His face and tone were not.

Severin Brigante did not appear to notice. "I think not," he said. "I think you could find much of interest in the cloister."

Guigny turned an arched eyebrow toward him. "You dare to disagree with me?"

"Actually, I think it is you, Sir Lancelot, who in the end will come to agree with me."

In that crowded hall, the two men became a spectacle, complete with an audience of attentive knights. One of whom snickered.

"Indeed," Severin said. He did not move nor did he take his gaze from Guigny's. His eyes narrowed. "But perhaps you are right and we should halt this foolishness. It is obvious that an accusation of some sort is hidden in this midnight's entertainment. Otherwise my own men would not have been so rudely excluded from it. May I know exactly of what I stand accused?"

Guigny slammed his tankard down onto the trestle. The hearth dogs barked and yelped, the soldiers whistled. It took some few trickles of the sand-clock before order was once again restored. In the meantime, Guigny managed to clutch a bit more tightly at the rags of his temper. He descended the dais to stand before the Lady Alix and the Knight Brigante.

He smelled of stale wine, Alix thought, and of an even staler frustration.

"You know that I wanted the child," he said. He never let his eyes leave Severin's face. "I told you that from the beginning. I took you into my confidence. We agreed that it was essential that the child be killed."

"We agreed that it was essential that the child be done away with," Severin corrected. "He must not be here if you were to keep this liege. And he is no longer here, nor will he ever again be. He is at Haute Fleur. Of course petition has been made for his keeping under a great lord's sponsorship and protection, but Robert's child will never leave the monastery. He will be made to take vows. The Abbot gave me his word."

"Abbots lie," said Guigny softly. "Allies lie."

"We are hardly allies," said Severin, just as softly, "when you have closeted my men somewhere that I know not. When you throw unmerited accusations at me. When you hold me here against my will and the Lady Alix with me. When you treat us as though we were common criminals. You've enough blood on your hands with this castle taking. It was useless and dangerous to think to kill an innocent child. Robert de Mercier allied himself against his liege lord. He was a knight, as we are, and thus knew the consequences of his actions. His child knew nothing. To put his blood upon your hands would have wrought only evil."

"The decision was mine!" roared Guigny. "You had no right to make it for me. She told me the child was dead. She told me that she had thrown his body into the stream."

"The Knight Brigante did not know that the child lived," said Alix. It was obvious that the others had forgotten her. "He found out only at the last. He did not know what I had said to you. He did not know that the child still lived until he saw me with him."

"It is well of you to defend a warrior knight, Lady Alix. Perhaps you should spare a thought for your own well-being. You are not yet safely convented and the road to Picardy can be both long and dark."

Guigny arched an elegant eyebrow. Alix saw his hand ease softly toward his jeweled dagger. Severin's moved, as well, toward the hilt of his sword. The two men seemed caught in some webbing that Alix did not understand. She only knew that she had to divert Guigny's attention. She could not bear to have more bloodshed.

" 'Tis I who am at fault," she insisted. "Sir Severin had no idea that I harbored the child. He came upon me as I left for Haute Fleur. I am the only one culpable."

The Knight Brigante, tense with his knowledge of Guigny's will and ambition, glanced at Alix with amazement. He wanted her to stop. He wanted her to leave response to him. He was capable here. He knew Guigny well.

But Alix would not stop.

" 'Twas my fault and no one else's. I found the child the night of the castle-taking. I kept him to me. I hid him within my own chambers," she lied, thinking quickly to save Sophie and Young Sophie from harm. "It was easy enough. No one comes near the rooms given to me. No one ever has."

"Except the Knight Brigante." Guigny appeared to have calmed himself once again. "Did you think I did not know about your trysts upon the castle ramparts? Of course you did not. But I would remind you that I am now lord of this place and I see it as my duty to know all that happens within its dominance."

His brow furrowed in exaggerated concentration. "But tell me, Lady Alix, did you indeed care for the child without help and by yourself? How difficult for you—for anyone! Alone, you changed and swaddled him? You wet-nursed him?"

"I did not nurse him," said Alix calmly. "He was cup-trained when I took him. And I fed him from the Mercier tankard. The rest I did of my own account and alone. No one helped me."

"Lady," said Severin in the voice that made blood-soaked warriors tremble. But it seemed to have no effect whatsoever upon her. She chattered on.

"By myself. No one helped me," she repeated. She stared first at Guigny and then at Severin, as though challenging him to discount her words.

"No help? No aid?" Guigny's question emerged enclosed within a deep sigh.

"No help. No aid."

The Countess de Mercier turned to face the Knight de Guigny once again. She stared at him fully and did not lower her gaze.

"Alix," Severin whispered. He saw the ambush clearly now, but it was already too late.

"You lie," said Guigny sweetly. "You had a great deal of help."

He waved a careless hand toward his nearest page. "Bring in the witch," he said.

They must have gotten to the cottage just after she herself had left, Alix realized. They would have needed the full week to inflict so much damage upon a human being: they could not have done it in a sand-span less. Sophie—because of course it must be dear Sophie, though it was hard to recognize her features within the mask of pain they had become—shuffled into the room on bare feet. The chain that bound them rattled loudly as she moved. Fresh bruises, a livid red and blue, circled her eyes and stood out lividly upon her cheeks. One arm hung loosely and at odd angle to her side. Her homespun garment, which had always smelled so sweetly of herbs and fresh earth, now hung in stained tatters from her weakened form.

Alix glanced quickly down at the Wise Woman's hands and then just as quickly away. Guigny had ordered them destroyed. It was like him to ruin anything of strength or true beauty. Alix had noticed this before. This will to devastation formed a most vital part of him; it clung to him with the tenacity of fate.

The Wise Woman stumbled and some of the knights tittered. Alix would have rushed to her had not Severin restrained her with his gentle hand.

"Charming," said Guigny as he looked at them, "if a bit late. You should have thought to check her before. Certainly you spent time enough with her. But then even servants display noble sentiments here at Mercier. I had the devil's own time convincing this witch to give me the information I sought. Only Count Robert himself seems to have lacked scruples—and perhaps the Lady Solange with him. But they are safely buried now and in heaven—at least one would hope so after the effort that the Lady Alix extended on their behalf."

"I told him nothing." Sophie's voice was reduced to the harshness of a deep croak but her words rang clearly. "He did not get what he wanted from me."

Guigny shrugged. "Luckily she was not the only one privy to the secret. It seems that most of the village

knew or suspected—but it was hard to get one of them
to tell. A few others were reduced to what she is reduced; others were offered money. In the end I heard
what I needed about the child. But it was too late. You
had already left for Haute Fleur. It became necessary
for me to rein my plans to another direction. Yvrain
le Bastarde is not the only one who still carries the
name Mercier."

"No," said Severin.

"What, you know the content of my mind? You think
yourself aware of my thoughts?" Guigny stepped back
and regarded the Knight Brigante with dispassion.
"But of course that is possible. Your own family is quite
familiar with that way. Your father wore the Maltese
Star. Your uncle, the great Belden of Harnoncourt, was
tried as a Templar Warlock before the Inquisition at
Rome."

"You'll not have her," said Severin.

Guigny giggled. "Oh, but I think I will—and I think
the lady will have me as well." He turned toward Alix.
"You see my dear Alix, in your absence I have given
careful thought to both of our sad situations. You
might say that I have seen the common thread that
binds them tight. You possess a title but no castle and
I a castle but not yet the title to it. I think by putting
our two needs together—by *marrying* them together,
in a manner of speaking—we might come to an agree-
able solution to both our plights."

Alix turned to Severin before whipping around to
face Guigny. "You cannot mean what you are saying.
I am a new-made widow. I cannot marry. I am to be
convented. You said so yourself."

"I have been about a careful research," said Guigny,
"that concerns many things, including that amulet you
wear, the Maltese Star."

"It is nothing—a family relic—it has no power."

But no one paid attention to her. She no longer seemed important to what played out between the two men. Theirs was a personal battle.

Guigny looked at Severin and smiled. "So more went on upon the parapet than even I suspected. Our Knight Brigante finds himself in love. He is ready to sacrifice the sanctity of his father's mission in order to win the Lady Alix's fair hand—or is it, perhaps, the Maltese Star and its power that beckons him?"

Severin said nothing but Alix, watching him closely, saw his fingers fist.

"Because of its power," said Guigny sweetly. "Because of what he saw it do."

Silence hung upon the air with the weight of tapestry. There was no sound; even the fire no longer crackled behind the grate.

"Or if not that, then perhaps it is the castle of Mercier that you crave. You mean to take what I have captured."

"I have no desire for this holding. Indeed, I am offering you a way to legitimize your claim to it. No one will deny a man what he has won upon the field of chivalry. Not even the duke himself would dare to do so."

Guigny remained silent and impassive. He was far too much the cunning-man to show an unwarranted interest.

"Tomorrow at morning light," whispered Severin, "unless you are too much the bastard to dare against a man awake and armed. A live man challenges you— not one you kill whilst he is lying naked and defenseless upon his bed."

The walls themselves seemed to gasp at this outrage and hold their breath to hear Guigny's reply. Sir Lancelot's men shuffled about him. From the back there the sound of a muted snigger—just one, but it was enough.

"Tomorrow then it is," the Knight de Guigny said. "At morning light. The best man will take the Dame de Mercier as prize. The other man will die."

Twelve

The knock sounded as Severin lay naked upon his narrow soldier's bed. His hands were clasped behind his head; his eyes were opened. It was very late. Beside him, the beeswax candle had almost gutted on its pewter plate. He was deep in thought and did not really hear the knock at first; when he did, he thought that perhaps it was sounded by his page. He had seen to his men before quitting the Great Hall. Once the joust had been called, Guigny could no longer hold them. Sir Lancelot would have released his men from wherever they had been secreted.

The careful mention of his bastardom had been telling. It had controlled him, just as Severin knew that it would. Now that the decision had been made to settle this match upon the field of chivalry he would be at pains to ensure that the fight appeared at least fair. Guigny would not much fear the outcome. Though seemingly slight, he was actually quite powerful and had held the lists for three days once in Paris. That one event had made a legend of him. It had not given him a freehold but it had given him a name.

Guigny would not want that name to be compromised.

The knock sounded once again.

"Enter," Severin said. He pulled the linen sheeting up around him. He wondered which of his pages would settle in for the night. It was usual that at least one slept upon a pallet at the foot of the bed. He missed this company, he found, and he was glad that one of his men had come to take up the place.

But it was no page or squire who entered and quietly closed his door.

"I do not wish you fighting over me," Alix said from across the room. "I will put my faith in the bishop. He will never read banns of marriage for a woman just newly widowed. He will not acquiesce to this travesty and I know it. But should he, I would rather marry the Knight de Guigny than to see you fight over me. I would prefer it to . . ."

"To what?" asked Severin. Alix wore a dark mantle over her night tunic. Her hair, unbound, cascaded like gold onto it. He smelled her and felt the air around him sparkle with her presence. She would easily have taken his breath away—if he had allowed it.

"You would prefer being plighted to the Knight de Guigny, rather than to me?" Severin sat upon his bed so that the sheet covered him more. Desire was upon him and he wanted to hide it—and himself. "You think that he would keep you well at Mercier? You have no idea how he would use you. You think his treatment of Sophie an isolated thing? It is his passion to wrest the life from small things, to kill the beauty in them. I saw you look upon the Wise Woman's hands. Do you think the man who destroyed her would hesitate to harm you once you were legally his?"

"I will not have you killed," said Alix. She took three more steps into his chamber. "Especially because you have brought yourself to danger helping me. You must desist from this battle. The bishop will not give this union his consent."

"You may rest assured, my lady," said Severin, "if

Lancelot de Guigny has mentioned union with you, he has already sought and received approbation for it. He is not the sort of man to propose anything that cannot be brought to pass. He is horrified of looking the fool. You are to marry, that much is certain. It is but the choice of groom that remains in question."

"They say he held the lists for three consecutive days." Alix moved a little closer. She still remained halfway across his chamber but she was near enough to him now that he could see the color of her extraordinary eyes even in the dimness of the room. They seemed to see right into him—right through him. He knew she could tell the truth in what he said.

"Is it for this?" she said, raising one small hand to the Maltese Star at her neck. She edged still closer. "Is it true what Sir Lancelot said—that it is this you want, and not me? And that you want this amulet for the power that you think it brings? Certainly that must be the reason."

"I want nothing to do with that amulet."

"But why else would you risk yourself to save me?"

"Why, indeed?" echoed a rueful Severin. "But if I win you I will wed you. I am determined on that."

"Why?" repeated Alix, moving closer. Her mantle fell from her shoulders. Through the gloom of his chamber Severin saw a richness of white lace beneath it.

Ah, so her black mourning extends only to what is seen by others. I wonder if she realizes that.

He took a certain pleasure from the thought. As though he possessed a secret about the Countess de Mercier to which no one else was privy. He doubted that the Lady Alix realized it herself.

"You said you would never wed until you were able to look upon the Sire of Harnoncourt from an equal height," she whispered. She was close enough now that her whisper carried easily to him. "What has changed you? Certainly you are not saying that you love—that you could love—me?"

"I do not love you," Severin said flatly but then he hesitated. He thought perhaps that this was not completely so but he did not wish to explore this sensation now, at this moment. With this woman so vulnerable before him. With him so vulnerable as well. It would be too easy to lie.

"But I cannot leave you unsafe and unprotected," he continued. "Once Guigny decided upon you, there was no chance that he would see you safely convented. He wants what you have—this castle surely, and perhaps the Maltese Star as well."

"No, no, no," said Alix. Her voice rang out through the darkness in what had once been her castle. Fury had fueled her with more energy than she'd felt since Robert's death. "I won't do it. I'll have nothing to do with this. It is ridiculous to think that there is a bishop on earth who would force me to marry my husband's murderer."

"I did not murder Robert de Mercier," said Severin. "I have killed no one in the fortress—and you will marry me. Permission has most assuredly been given. Have you forgotten that the bishop is a younger cousin of the Duke of Burgundy's and that the Duke of Burgundy is liege lord here? It would be well for you to remember both of these facts. Your husband forgot them. I am sure that this was one of the things he most bitterly regretted as he looked up to see Lancelot de Guigny's sword poised at his head."

She thought about this. He could see the idea that she would be forced to marry Guigny flutter like a bird within her mind and then nest there. She tried hiding the dismay of this, but did not quite succeed. He was still upon his bed and she beside it, though very near now, so near that Severin could have easily reached out and drawn her down to him. He had known many women, perhaps too many, and he could sense the need upon her. It scented the room. It weighted the air. Stoked as it was by her great aversion to Lancelot de Guigny, it was nonetheless there.

Made her vulnerable.

She may not know what she was experiencing but Severin did. Perhaps, he thought, if he reached for her now she might resist him, but only at the beginning and then not very much. She had pulled him to her once already and now, if he wanted her he had only to reach up.

"I would rather be with you," she said, "if the Knight de Guigny is my only alternative."

He smiled ruefully at the compliment, not quite sure that it was not a veiled insult.

"I would rather be with you now."

"Now?" he asked.

She did not seem to notice. "He killed my husband. I could not bear his hands upon me. I would see Robert's blood surrounding me for the rest of my life. And Sir Lancelot would not honor this feeling. He would not leave me alone!"

Once, while hunting, Severin had seen Guigny plunge his dagger into the heart of a wounded falcon. It had been one of his favorites and could easily have been saved. A splint and lacing would have sent it soaring into the sky again, had not Guigny destroyed it. He had commented upon its beauty and then had jerked its life away.

"No," said Severin quietly. "He would not leave you alone."

He hesitated. He wanted to tell her about the falcon, wanted to explain to her how much this useless cruelty had affected him. He opened his mouth to do this but then he found the words—those words—would not come. He seemed already simple enough and un-learned before her. If she knew how much this useless killing of a bird had affected him, he would feel un-manned and naked as well. He could not trust a woman with this information. Women had hurt him too much in the past.

"Then 'tis better that I have you," said Alix, her head cocked slightly and speculatively to one side. "I won't marry you. I can't. But I can bed you." Again she paused. "I think I want that. I came for it."

"Do you love me?"

"No," she said too quickly. Just as he had done.

She stopped then, did not inch closer. Instead she remained perfectly still. Severin saw the flush upon her cheek and could almost but not quite see the shaking of her hand. He knew what she was offering and he was tempted—sorely so. His whole body had stiffened toward her. But he realized he did not want a make-shift coupling with this woman. He would not take her on his small cot in this bare room.

He would not take her until she was really his to take. For some reason this was important to him.

She must be his. He wanted her free, with no ghost of yesterday's Robert clinging to her and no threat of tomorrow's Guigny. He sat more squarely upon his bed.

"Yours is a kind offer, my lady, but forgive me if I do not rise to it." His tone was ironic and in the dim candlelight he saw the flicker of her amusement. "I will wait. When next you come to me, you will come as wife."

"You are sure of your prowess then, Sir Severin?"

He thought this through for an instant. The room was so silent he could almost hear sand sifting through the time-glass on the trestle beside his bed.

"No, I am not at all certain," he said finally, "about anything."

The Dame de Mercier curtseyed into a reverence before the Knight Brigante, so low that her mantle— now once again hiding that peeking of lace—brushed against the floor and swept the odor of its thyme leaves into the air. For once he did not stop her. The scent she had aroused remained crystallized within the chamber, even after the heavy door had closed behind her. It mingled with the light perfume of roses that she always wore and that would always, he knew, remind him of her.

He may once have happened upon her as she searched for snow flowers, but he would forever know and remember her by the hint of spring that she wore.

Thirteen

The day of the joust dawned sullen and gray. No sun peeked through the clouds. Alix had slept little during the night, thinking of Severin Brigante and wondering how a man who would risk his life for her would still find her so offensive he would not wish to take her to his bed when she offered herself to him. Because that is what she had done. Even though the remembrance flamed color into her cheeks, she could not deny that this was true. She told herself that she wanted to see—*needed* to see—him so that she could persuade him from the path he had chosen. She told herself she wanted no fighting—that was why she went to him. Deep inside she knew this was not true.

Severin did not fight Lancelot de Guigny for her alone and therefore she alone could not dissuade him. She had expected this. What she had not expected was the hurt that flashed back when Severin rejected her. Just as Robert had rejected her so many times in the past. Pain burned her mind and her heart with Severin Brigante's swift dismissal. Alix was sure she would never be able to face him again and even thought perhaps that it was right she be fated to Lancelot de Guigny. At least she had something that he wanted. She would not have to fear rejection at his hands.

She was up before dawn. Before the knock sounded at her bedroom door, she had washed herself and combed her hair back and applied the rose scent from its precious wooden bottle.

"The lord says you must hurry," a strange voice said. Alix recognized neither the voice nor the accent. She only knew that neither belonged to Young Sophie. Without conscious thought she armed herself against what the opened door would reveal. She glanced around the security of her bedroom—at the tapestries and silver, at the enormous bed filled with laces and satin and silk embroideries. She hesitated, but determined not to show even a hint of this hesitation to the serving woman who had been sent to ferret it out.

"And where is my own maid?" she asked once the door had opened.

"I am your maid," said the woman, placing a saucy hand to an ample hip. "Sent to you by the lord of this castle."

She was small and dark, though young. A riot of curls spilled forth from her dirty wimple.

Alix still did not move but her eyes hardened. "I am chatelaine of this castle and have asked you a civil question. I request a civil response to it, if you please."

"She is in the village," came the reluctant reply.

"Is she harmed?"

"You mean has she been questioned like her mother?" The woman smirked. "This is a Christian state and no one can be questioned by the Inquisition if there is no cause and no proof of wrongdoing. The witch, Young Sophie's mother, would not have been tortured had she but named either her familiars or her band."

"Perhaps she had neither," replied the Lady Alix.

" 'Twas always said of her that she was a witch."

"Though not proven," rejoined Alix, standing up from her place at the fire. "That is the main importance of this jumble. Tell me your name."

The woman pinched her face together, wondering if this were absolutely necessary and if the Lord de Guigny would approve.

"Your name," repeated Alix.

"Annette," the woman said at length.

"Annette," echoed Alix. "But you are not from Mercier. That is clear from your accent."

"I am from the last village upon the road to the Shrine of St. Bernard."

"That would be St. Denis, would it not?"

"Yes."

"Yes, what?" inquired a pleasant Alix.

"Yes, my lady."

"Sir Lancelot hired and brought you here. 'Tis a fair distance. Did he bring others as well?"

Defiance once again flared in the woman's eyes. "Aye—many of us. At least eight in all."

"Because he got no loyalty in this his conquered village," said Alix, "though he has done everything rightly so far. Extra rations of ale, no bloodshed after the taking. And yet the village shows him no fealty. You might ask yourself the why of that if you mean to plight your loyalties to him rather than to your rightful lord."

"The lord Lancelot . . ." began the woman.

Alix interrupted her. "Lancelot de Guigny is not yet lord of this place, nor may he ever be. But I am its mistress. I have dressed myself, as you can see, but fetch my outdoor mantle, if you please. There is a tournament at Mercier today and I must attend it punctually."

The woman perked at this. What Alix had said obviously formed part of her task. "Lord de Guigny bids you be at the list fields by the early prayer bell," said the woman. "He says you are to wear black mourning, but he instructs that it be of rich stuff. He said that you are to leave your hair loose and good-looking."

"I would never leave my hair loose before an assembly of men."

This time Annette's smile was sly. "He said you would say this. I am to remind you that the Witch Sophie is still within the castle dungeons. She passed a peaceful night—but this could change."

The maid bobbed an exaggerated curtsey. The sound of hammering and industry echoed up from the courtyard below. Alix waited until her cloak had been brought and Annette had quitted the chamber. Then she walked to the window and stared down into the inner curtain.

Guigny must have released Severin's men during the night. She saw some of them that she recognized—Old Cristiano from the Kingdom of the Two Sicilies, and Severin's young Burgundian squire, Philip de Guienne. The list field was being tamped down and readied as soldiers from both the Gold Company and Guigny's army prepared themselves for the unexpected challenge. If once they had put on a thin veneer of camaraderie this farce had obviously played itself out. Both groups worked grimly, each man within his own camp and turning a wary eye toward the other. Alix noted that weapons were piled nearby and that the knights had swords within arm's reach.

It was strange for Alix to look out upon the unfamiliar repair of the list fields. Guigny had wrought so many changes. She thought of the chests of books that she had seen last night so carelessly scattered around the Great Hall. Those books had been Robert's pride; he had built his life around them. Now it seemed that all Robert cared about was being dismantled, and what he had despised was being built up. She knew that as soon as he had entitlement, Guigny would sell Robert's

carefully gathered library for profit. She thought of
the reverence with which Severin had always touched
the parchment books.

"It was good Robert did not live to see this," she
murmured. But she knew she did not care about the
books as he had. She loved them—that was true. They
had occupied her days and filled her nights since she'd
come to the loneliness of Mercier Castle. She could
never have survived without them. But that part of her
life was over. More and more she felt this now. Though
her husband had been dead for but a few months, she
realized that he had died to her long before this. And
perhaps had never lived for her at all.

For the first time since they had married she felt a
peace about Robert and with this peace came the beginnings of forgiveness. It was strange that on this day,
where nightfall would probably find her wed to another, she would finally be able to think of her husband with understanding and release.

Alix had never liked jousts. Of course, there had
been none of them when she and her mother had
lived alone at Belvedere before her father's return.
With the Count of the Ducci Montaldo so removed
from it, the castle had fallen into disrepair. There had
been no thought of tournaments.

Then in the vast lands of the Holy Roman Empire,
where her father generaled the armies of his friend
the Roman Emperor Sigismund, there had been little
time for faked battles. Real ones—against the Turks,
against the recalcitrant German princes, against the
members of the Emperor's own household—had been
plentiful enough. So in fact Alix had seen few of what
one prince called "these civilized approaches to the
matters of blooding." And she had never been im-

pressed with them, even at Paris where they were played out with the opulent pageantry that only Charles of France could afford. During them all, she had continually stifled yawns.

This joust would be different and Alix knew this. It would be personal. It would be hers. It would settle, if not her life, then at least her fate. Nothing would be the same again, no matter which man triumphed. The result of this day's battling would seal her fate more clearly than even the death of her husband which, in reality, had brought with it only the promise of change. What happened here would be different.

Alix sensed this as soon as she left the castle dressed in black silk with her hair loose. For one thing, this would be a deadly affair. Alix knew this well enough; she was daughter to one knight and had been married to another. Neither man had intention to leave the field with the other living. She recognized the whiff of death when it lay heavy on the air. There was no sign of the frivolity and merrymaking that usually accompanied the laying out of the lists. No bright banners flew, heralding the presence of the neighboring nobles. Despite the way he had conquered the fortress, Alix knew that no peer or knight would dare to refuse an invitation from Lancelot de Guigny—a man widely, though belatedly, deemed to be the new Count of Mercier. Especially since this prospective count had such close ties of blood to the Duke of Burgundy, liege lord to them all. In troubled times such as these it was generally thought best to strive toward giving universal pleasure. The local nobles would never have stayed home, had they been invited to Mercier.

They had not been invited.

As Alix walked from the castle steps into the inner curtain of the fortress, she realized that she was the only highborn lady in sight.

"I am to escort you, my lady," said Annette, coming up beside her.

Alix regarded the woman steadily. Normally she was not at all snobbish, but this woman and this place demanded a firm attitude.

"I am the Countess de Mercier," she said finally, "and as such I must be escorted to the list field by someone of my own rank."

"Not today," retorted Annette. "You will come with me as has been said."

"Yes, today," repeated Alix. "You may tell the Knight de Guigny that I will not take the place assigned to me unless I am properly escorted. He cannot force me to do so against my will—and he will not force me with so many others present."

It was not lost upon Alix how much the discreet and obedient Dame de Mercier had changed in the short time since her husband's death. She was not certain that she wholly liked the person she had become.

They stood like that for some time, their breath clouding upon cold air. Finally Annette abruptly turned and tramped off toward the list fields. When she returned she brought with her a new-made knight. He was young enough to still have youth blemishes upon his face; his golden spurs were so shiny new they barely jingled as he walked. But he was both a knight and a noble. Alix had made her point.

She placed her hand upon his arm and set off toward the waiting dais. As they neared the fields, Alix searched for Severin but did not see him. Instead the Knight de Guigny, surrounded by his legion of pages, smiled to her. Because her position forced her to do so, Alix made him a deep reverence. But she kept her head low.

"Come, come," said Sir Lancelot, striding toward her. "Such prostration hardly suits you. You could have

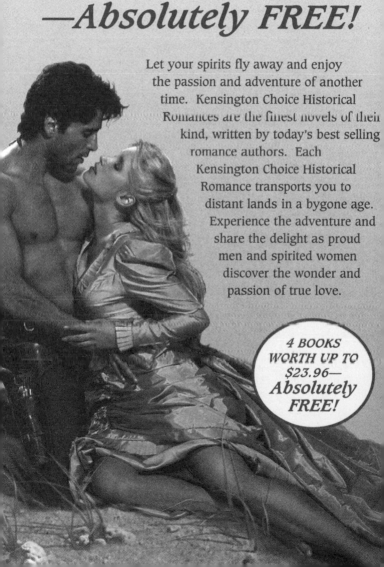

Take 4 FREE Books!

We created our convenient Home Subscription Service so you'll be sure to have the hottest new romances delivered each month right to your doorstep — usually before they are available in book stores. Just to show you how convenient Zebra Home Subscription Service is, we would like to send you 4 Kensington Choice Historical Romances as a FREE gift. You receive a gift worth up to $23.96 — absolutely FREE. There's no extra charge for shipping and handling. There's no obligation to buy anything - ever!

Save Up To 30% On Home Delivery!

Accept your FREE gift and each month we'll deliver 4 brand new titles as soon as they are published. They'll be yours to examine FREE for 10 days. Then if you decide to keep the books, you'll pay the preferred subscriber's price. That's all 4 books for a savings of up to 30% off the cover price! Just add the cost of shipping and handling. Remember, you are under no obligation to buy any of these books at any time! If you are not delighted with them, simply return them and owe nothing. But if you enjoy Kensington Choice Historical Romances as much as we think you will, pay the special preferred subscriber rate and save over $7.00 off the bookstore price!

We have 4 FREE BOOKS for you as your introduction to
KENSINGTON CHOICE!

**To get your FREE BOOKS,
worth up to $23.96, mail the card below
or call TOLL-FREE 1-800-770-1963
Visit our website at www.kensingtonbooks.com.**

Take 4 Kensington Choice Historical Romances FREE!

YES! Please send me my 4 FREE KENSINGTON CHOICE HISTORICAL ROMANCES (without obligation to purchase other books). Unless you hear from me after I receive my 4 FREE BOOKS, you may send me 4 new novels - as soon as they are published - to preview each month FREE for 10 days. If I am not satisfied, I may return them and owe nothing. Otherwise, I will pay the money-saving preferred subscriber's price plus shipping and handling. That's a savings of over $7.00 each month. I may return any shipment within 10 days and owe nothing, and I may cancel any time I wish. In any case the 4 FREE books will be mine to keep.

Name _____

Address _____ Apt No _____

City _____ State _____ Zip _____

Telephone ( ) _____ Signature _____

(If under 18, parent or guardian must sign)

Terms, offer, and prices subject to change. Orders subject to acceptance by Kensington Choice Book Club. Offer valid in the U.S. only.

KN022A

avoided all this fuss had you but accepted me when I offered. Now you will cost the Knight Brigante his life."

She rose, but still kept her eyes lowered. His words chilled her, as they had been meant to do.

Guigny busied himself by pulling chain mail gloves onto his hands. He chuckled. "Have you not seen him? Have you no kind words for him? He is your champion, after all, and one who intends to best me and take your fair hand in marriage this very day."

But Alix could not face Severin. She did not want to, not after going to his chamber and being rejected. She took the young knight's arm again and moved toward the makeshift stands ranked along the listing field. They teemed with people. It was obvious that the Knight de Guigny had demanded that the peasants of Mercier be present to witness his great triumph over the Knight Brigante. They were proving themselves to be recalcitrant and it would strike fear into their hearts. "Three untipped lances between them," whispered the young knight as he handed Alix onto the dais. "They say both men are evenly matched, though the Knight de Guigny is favored. He is more cunning than the Knight Brigante and more suited to this play. There are few to match Sir Lancelot at the lists. He held them for three straight days once in Paris."

Guigny paid troubadours to assure that his legend was circulated.

The young knight's face shone with the unmistakable excitement of bloodlust. Alix shivered.

"They know you are the cause of this," said Annette from beside her. She moved a bit closer as though wanting everyone to know that she was already on intimate terms with her new mistress and had the situation well in hand. "They know that it is over you that Sir Severin and the Count de Mercier fight."

"Lancelot de Guigny is not the Count de Mercier," repeated Alix mechanically.

"Time will see to that," replied the woman.

Annette turned to someone near her. They spoke together in the strong accent that grated upon Alix's nerves. Lancelot de Guigny had been busy since his capture of the castle, both inside and out. During his many visits to the shrine of St. Bernard he had obviously made friends along the byways. Many of them seemed to have come back with him to Mercier, just as Annette had said. Alix hardly recognized the servants who now peopled the castle, hardly recognized the soldiers who guarded it. She had to remind herself whose banner flew above the castle turrets. The pale silver and green that Guigny had chosen contrasted with the dark green of Mercier that had graced it for generations.

In its colors, Sir Lancelot's banner was more closely allied to that of the Kings of France than it was to those of the Knights of Burgundy. It was a strange choice, coming as it did from such a strange man.

A man who might win her and wed her. Alix found herself shivering in the drizzle of the day.

But at least Severin is here.

The words whispered quickly through her soul. He had rejected her. She knew no reason why he fought for her—or even that she mattered to the blood feud that now existed between the Knight Brigante and the Knight de Guigny.

Severin is here.

The rest would come later. This was all that mattered now.

Once she was safely settled, Alix strained to see Severin but could not. She saw his men, though, and that at least was a relief. They had been nowhere in evidence last night during the dark interview with Lancelot de Guigny. She had thought them imprisoned, or worse. But now, as she allowed her glance to filter slowly over the mass of men before her, she could pick out familiar faces and place names to them. There was old Cristiano who, Severin told her, had been lieutenant of the Gold Company's *condottiero* since Belden of Harnoncourt had first founded the army. And there was Young Stefano and Fife from Gloucester and Roger de Malincourt and others she had come to know. She caught Cristiano's eye, but there was no reading his expression. He held her gaze for a moment and then turned away.

Even Alix's untrained eye could see how the list field had been gouged further into the woods and enlarged. It was huge now, larger than the village. She thought it a dangerous place—one of the many dangerous places that Lancelot de Guigny had been able to create in the few short months since he had taken the castle. While she had been mourning.

The tournament horses had been set loose; they galloped and charged on the field, their movements followed by the watchful eyes of the squires and the peasantry. Pennants rippled in the air along the list fields and atop makeshift silk tents that clutched at the field. Squires, dressed either in the black of the Gold Company or the pale green of Guigny, scurried past them carrying armor and saddles and lances. One young boy, a page by his size, struggled beneath a breastplate that seemed larger than he was. As Alix watched it fell to the ground with a bang, she jumped.

Everything was so different now. Her life with Robert was over but she still held his name and the possibility of his castle. She was a weight to the new inhabitant—not wealthy enough to make a profitable marriage to someone with Guigny's pretensions but someone he might settle upon now to further his own plans. Or so he could have the Maltese Star, though she had yet to understand its significance.

And if he lost . . .

If he lost she would be wedded to Severin Brigante, a man who had no use for a wife and had rejected her when she came to him. With marriage, her name would change. If Guigny lost but managed to survive, she would be removed as a threat to him. She would no longer be the Countess de Mercier. Not that she cared. No matter what happened, the murderer of her husband would win and she would lose. It was foolish to have thought it would ever turn out otherwise, just because she had managed to secrete a child away.

Still, she wanted Severin to win her—desperately wanted this. She could not help herself. But she knew the odds against it. She saw ruthlessness in Guigny that she knew Severin did not share. She remembered their day in the forest. She remembered the doe licking the salt that he offered her and the fawn's tongue on her hand.

No, Severin was so different from Guigny.

It was then that the Magdalene whispered.

You are just the pretext for what is to come. He will kill him. Using fair means or foul, the Knight de Guigny has every intention of killing Severin Brigante today and he will succeed unless you do something.

But what could she do, standing alone on this raised dais, distanced both from the spectators and from the men who fought? What could she do, securely battened between a knight and a burly maidservant who owed their new livery and livelihood to the Knight de Guigny? Where was her hope?

"My lady."

She hadn't noticed Cristiano draw near. He had paid no attention to her when she nodded at him and had barely nodded back. But she was grateful that he had come for her now.

"My lord Severin has sent me to stand with you," he said. He was a massive man and Annette, though displeased, was forced aside by his bulk. However, once he stood next to Alix he stared down at her with stern neutrality. Alix did not care. She felt her heart leap at the thought that she would not be alone and that it was Severin who had seen to her accompanying.

"Is he ready?" she asked. "Is he well?"

"He is dressed," said Cristiano. "I imagine he is ready. He did not say."

Trumpets flourished onto the wind and the men emerged from their respective tents. From the distance Alix heard the clank of their chain mail as they crossed the sodden ground to the tournament ring. They had not yet pulled on their helmets and she leaned forward for just the briefest of seconds, willing Severin to turn to her.

He did. She could not see his eyes but the brightness of his fair hair was unmistakable. As she stared at him a ray of sunlight broke the clouds and for an instant sparkled brightly against it. But he was moving swiftly and with purpose. If he saw the Lady Alix leaning out toward him from her raised dais, he did not acknowledge this fact.

The horses, enormous destriers, were covered in armor and skirted in the colors of the two knights. They were high spirited, jerking and biting at reins expertly held by the chief pages. Their hot breath plumed out onto the air. Even this far away Alix could feel the earth shaking as their enormous hooves pawed the frozen ground. She even heard the creak of their wooden saddles.

Severin grasped the pommel, put his foot into the

stirrup, and pulled himself up. At the other end of the tournament run, Guigny did the same thing.

The trumpets sounded several long notes.

"That is the first call to arms," said Cristiano beside her. "Whatever is to happen, will happen quickly now."

Fourteen

Severin looked out through the narrow slit of his visor. All around him people were shouting for the tournament to begin. It had been a long winter and now that spring was upon them, the peasants had come from the fields and the village to have their first real look at their new count. They seemed pleased enough by him, though they had been pleased by Count Robert as well, and even loyal to him. But though they were loyal to Mercier they had not understood his gentle ways and intellectual manners, his love for music and illumined manuscripts. Delicate mannerisms would offer them no security in these warring days. Once the shock of battle had dimmed and Count Robert had been decently buried, it was known throughout the village how much they preferred the ways of a knight like Guigny, who could be counted upon to fight and marry well. He would not disgrace and puzzle them by becoming the tool of a woman who had been one of their own. He would not betray their faith by doing so openly something that their simple clerics assured them was a sin.

They might mourn Count Robert for a season but in the end they would give their allegiance to Lancelot de Guigny if he played his dice well. Instinctively they knew what they could expect from him. They were used to bloodthirsty rulers.

Severin saw Sir Lancelot at the far end of the field, watching him, and holding his horse perfectly still. He reached down and took the striped lance that his page held up to him.

The last trumpet pealed and the two knights hurled themselves toward each other. Alix felt the echo of their hoofbeats in her heart. Without thinking, she leaned forward, matching her movement to Severin's as he leaned low in his saddle. He edged his lance just slightly up and out from the crook of his arm. And then Lancelot de Guigny was upon him.

"Match!" roared the crowd.

Severin heard their bellow and simultaneously felt the sharp pain stab at his shoulder. The wood of his lance splintered as his horse raced forward to the end of the field. His shoulder ached furiously from the blow.

"A lucky hit," said Cristiano. "Guigny moves quickly. He is a warrior born, though an unscrupulous one. He will use any trick to win."

"Severin is hurt! Sir Lancelot's lance made a direct hit. He is bleeding. He needs help."

"He is assured of help," said Cristiano, laying a restraining hand upon her. "Leave him to his pages and do not distract him. You have done enough of that already."

He smiled darkly, certain that he had made himself quite clear.

The pain in his arm was bearable. Severin knew it would not kill him; in fact, the worst of it would be over by tomorrow. He had an experience of wounding and he knew this discomfort would pass quickly enough. But it would have been better, he thought dispassionately, had the wound been to his chest. As it was, he would have but one more chance to make good on his challenge before the strength of his arm gave way. Or else . . .

There was no "or else." He *must* unseat Lancelot de Guigny; he had no alternative.

His squire rushed up with clean cloths and vinegared water. Severin reached to take a fresh lance from his page as the trumpets sounded the second charge.

The rules of chivalry were strict when it came to the joust. The task was not so much to aim the lance or to carry it well. Though normally eighteen feet in length and stout, the lance figured less in the joust than it might appear. The task within the challenge was to hold to the charge and not falter from the line of its impact. Severin forced himself to concentrate and to aim his lance toward Guigny. The blow to his arm had been telling and the tip of his lance thrashed up and down as he charged. But then something happened; for no discernible reason he felt himself steady and felt power flow through his body once again. This same thing had happened to him before in battle, but he had never felt its magic or its impact as he felt them now.

He braced the lance in the crook of his arm and raised it.

Alix felt the power rush out of her heated body. Once it had gone, she felt deathly cold as whatever had caused such reaction settled and became quiescent once again. The force of its passing astounded her;

she was certain that everyone near her had felt it leave her and were staring about them in fear. Or that they stared at her in horror. The feeling had surged so powerfully through her that she was astounded it had not leveled Mercier Castle in its wake.

It had not. Nor was there particular fright on the faces of the people standing near. Their eyes were on the field where the Knight Brigante gathered strength at the last moment and dealt the Knight de Guigny a crucial blow. Sir Lancelot managed to hold his saddle, but just barely. The crowd roared its astonished approval. Alix did not join them. She did not hear them. She was thinking of the force that had used her body to launch itself into the world. She had no doubt that what had passed through her was part of her. Perhaps it was an essential part of her as well. Once her astonishment passed she realized that she *knew* this power, and that she had always known it even when it lay waiting, even when she had no way to identify what she had felt. Her mother, Julian Madrigal, had wanted to protect her. She had not told her what it was and so Alix Ducci Montaldo de Mercier had had no way of knowing that the women in her family had felt this sudden flash since time immemorial—or at least since the coming of the Templars and the Great Witch.

Trust it, whispered the Magdalene, trust what you possess.

Alix, frightened now, shook the voice away. She had no idea what was happening; she had no idea where the power that had escaped from her had gone.

The third trumpet sounded and the two men closed, their steaming horses driving hard. Severin saw Lancelot de Guigny shift his lance and angle it lower toward the heart. He wondered if that would be his ultimate goal—to run his weapon right through the heart. Would it end that way? Sir Lancelot would know the armor. He would know just where to thrust—if that was what he wanted.

Severin couched his own lance and leaned forward in his saddle, tight against the bit. The pain in his arm had grown excruciating—strangely so—but he held his course. He saw Guigny's dark eyes glitter beneath his visor just as they connected once again. The snap of wood resounded only for an instant before the roar of the crowd drowned it out. The pain was overwhelming. Severin felt its blackness and it was with some wonder that he realized he was still horsed, that he had not been thrown from his saddle. All around him spectators—his own men, Guigny's men, the peasants from the village— beat against the railing and howled out.

"Down! Down!"

It was only then that Severin realized what had caused him such excruciating pain. His lance had connected. He had unseated Lancelot de Guigny. Beneath his helmet, Severin's hair was soaked with sweat. He felt it dribble down into his face and mar his eyesight. He reached up to swipe it away, then turned to help Sir Lancelot up from the field. Now that the fight was over, the laws of chivalry demanded this.

Lancelot de Guigny had been unhorsed. Severin Brigante had won.

"It is over," cried Alix. She turned to Cristiano and would have thrown her arms around his neck had he not stepped back. She didn't care. Damn discretion and her place as a first noble of the realm. She was happy, joyous even. Severin Brigante might not love her and she might not want to marry him but at least his victory had saved her from an impossible situation. Now she would never be forced to marry Lancelot de Guigny. She would never be forced to endure the touch of hands that had blooded her husband.

"And Severin will not force me into marriage," she thought amid the clatter and whoop of triumph. "He will allow me to go quietly to my convent."

Though the words "my convent" no longer sounded the sanctuary they once had seemed.

The Magdalene whispered.

Something is wrong.

Alix whirled around toward Cristiano's astonished face.

"He is up! The Count de Mercier has not relinquished the fight."

Severin reached his hand out to Lancelot de Guigny and the next thing he knew, Guigny was pulling him into the mud. He sprawled. Severin lay there for an instant, his wounded arm inflamed, too stunned and in too much pain to move. Instantly the Knight de Guigny was on his feet again, his sword at hand.

"Knave! Knave!" bellowed the spectators.

Alix felt her heart scud, but the man who had dared custom and the chivalric code in order to murder a sleeping Robert de Mercier would not care what others called him.

It was a miracle that Guigny's first thrust did not kill him, and Severin knew this. A miracle that he had managed to scramble to his feet and pull his sword out before he was gutted. Lancelot was a strong opponent, able and sure despite his seeming delicacy, and fighting without the disadvantage of Severin's wound.

The two men parried and thrust, parried and thrust, circling and moving in toward each other and then back again. Neither was able to deliver the killing blow.

Severin felt the blood-lust cover him. It exploded as it always had in battle—coming from nowhere, riding on fury. His wounded arm stung like the devil, but it did not stop his circling Lancelot de Guigny, determined on the kill. The clang of steel against steel rang out into the early morning. There was no other sound. The spectators watched, not daring to shout. Almost not daring to breathe.

Alix, transfixed, stared at the battle. Gone was the sense that she was watching one of the intricate tableaux that mendicant troubadours presented during Pascal Tide; gone was the farce of chivalry at play. What she was seeing was something primitive.

What clashed and clawed before her now was basic hatred.

Severin realized that Lancelot de Guigny had determined to kill him. He could tell this from his opponent's first thrust of the sword. De Guigny aimed his blows directly for the head, the most vulnerable part of any knight's armor. One, two; parry, thrust. He seemed unstoppable, undefeatable. And each time Severin thrust, the wound in his shoulder flamed in agony. He shook his head to clear the sweat from his vision but no amount of sight could help him. The only thing before his eyes was a helmeted monster determined to devour him. It was the same dark something that had come to him in nightmares when he was a child and the monster had snuggled in to sleep beside his drunken father. Severin remembered him now.

And he was afraid—very, very afraid. As he had been then. But he lifted his wrecked arm and fought through the fear, just as he had always done and as he did, as he moved and thrust closer to the monster before him, Severin started to see the very faintest gleaming of a ray of hope. Through the crash and the clatter he had heard something—something faint but unmistakable. Something he was certain that the Knight de Guigny had not heard.

Lancelot still swung his sword with practiced rhythm, swinging over and over again with no sign of tiredness. Instead, Severin let his own tiredness show. He purposely slowed his thrusting and stumbled—but not much, just a little bit. He let a confident Guigny inch closer. He waited until he was just a quarter lance away.

It was then that the Knight Brigante threw down his sword.

Watching from her place upon the dais, Alix knew what Severin was going to do just seconds before he actually did it. She looked as Lancelot circled closer, coming in for the kill; confident now in his ability to make it. She saw the slick of blood that oozed through the polished steel of Severin's armor, and she knew that the Knight de Guigny saw it as well. She prayed that Severin knew what he was doing.

It was then that the Countess de Mercier closed her eyes.

"My lord!"
The clear voice of the page rang out through the silence and caught the Knight de Guigny unawares.

Severin saw him hesitate and turn his head—just a little but this little was enough to see and to realize.

The one young, blond page was not alone. There were three of them coming, running down the list field, the golden threads on their red-and-green silk liveries shimmering boldly against the gray day. Their appearance could only mean one thing. Now Lancelot de Guigny joined Severin Brigante in this realization and thrust aside his own sword. Two trumpet players, dressed just as splendidly, took position along the field and sounded three loud blasts upon their instruments. It was still echoing as the beautiful young page cried out in one voice.

"Clear way for his grace, Jean, Duke of Burgundy."

Both heaving, sweating men pulled their helmets off and threw them upon the ground. But Severin, grateful to be alive, did not gaze toward the great drawbridge of Mercier Castle where the first of the duke's train was just lumbering into vision. He barely glimpsed the duke himself, who rode in the avant-garde, just behind the flourished red-and-green banners of Burgundy and of Nevers.

Instead, Severin looked up and over the heads of the crowd to the stands. During the very thickest part of the joust, when Guigny had borne down on him with his poisoned lance, Severin had looked where he looked now and gazed fleetingly into the turquoise eyes that his own eyes now sought.

He had felt power; it had jolted him. It had saved him.

He turned now in the direction of that heat and of that light.

Fifteen

"Nature itself fashioned Jean, Duke of Burgundy, to hate his cousin Louis, Duke of Orleans," a wag had whispered in the Castle of Mercier one night over an exquisite dinner of quilled partridge. "And not merely to hate him but to kill him as well."

Now Alix, sweltering in fur-rimmed black velvet and sitting beside Duke Jean at the main table, could understand the why of this. She had met the murdered Duke Louis once when she passed with Robert through Paris on their progression to Mercier. She had thought Louis d'Orleans splendidly handsome. He was also quite charming and a favorite of his brother Charles—at least in the mad king's moments of lucidity—as well as lover to his sister-in-law, the queen.

According to Alix's father, Olivier Ducci Montaldo—who was a Montfort on his mother's side and thus related to the royal house of Valois—taking the queen as mistress had been the most costly of the many mistakes Orleans had made in his short life. And not merely because Isabeau of France was both a wanton and a harridan. This was a misfortune that could happen to any man and as long as the woman in question remained mistress and not wife, he could easily escape from his want of discretion to a tranquil home. But for Louis of Orleans his connection to Queen Isabeau contained within it the key element to the two driving forces of his life—lust and ambition.

"A devoted servant of Venus," he had been called. Seeing him once, long ago—and being dazzled by him—young Alix had believed this to be so.

Just as the slightly older Alix could see why this same dazzle would have stung jealously into the bosom of the powerful man who sat beside her. For Jean of Burgundy—called Jean the Fearless by those who feared him—was not a man to dazzle at first sight. Stooped and dark, he bent over his food with methodical industry. He applied himself with this same diligence to the wine, which he had had the foresight to carry with him from his own fortress at Dijon.

The powerful Duke of Burgundy was anything but trusting.

Like his equally ruthless father, Philip the Bold, Duke Jean was short of stature and indifferently, though expensively, dressed. He wore the deep red of his house but he did not have that taste in mixing color and fabric that had so characterized his cousin or had marked the extravagances of Robert de Mercier. Alix saw the duke glance up at the painted garlands that circled the Great Hall, she saw his eyes flicker to the conceit of Mercier banners that fluttered from the ceiling, and she saw him look with little interest at the ornate gold plate from which he ate.

This plate had been Robert's great passion; Alix remembered this now as though her husband had been dead years, instead of only months and days. The duke had come before a joust champion could be called. Surely he would annul the effects of that fighting and send her on to be convented as had originally been planned. This was the normal thing to do in the circumstance. For no reason, Alix thought of the shrine she had erected to her husband. She thought of the fragment of his blooded mantle and his jeweled dagger and the candle that brought their attention to the image of the Madonna on the wall.

Tis time to put that aside, she thought. Time to dismantle the mourning. Robert was at rest and his son safe. He would be at peace now.

Perhaps it was time she secured a small portion of that peace for herself.

But Jean the Fearless was a man little used to concord. Indeed, he neither sought nor wanted it. He craved power, and power was often a byproduct of war. And Burgundy, like most of the other men Alix knew, including her father, had devoted himself to battling. He had fought almost every single day of his life.

"A loyal garrison is necessary in these treacherous times," Jean of Burgundy said to his brother, who was honorably seated on his left side. "Do not you agree, Lancelot?"

Lancelot de Guigny nodded sullenly. He sat beside Jean, resplendent in a miniver-edged red samite tunic that was just a shade's breath lighter than the banner-colors of Burgundy, which he was forbidden to wear. Burgundy smiled at the knight's agreement. If he noticed anything amiss in Guigny's demeanor he pretended, at least, not to see it. Instead he treated his older half brother with great respect, complimenting him on his choice of chef and marking the well-ordered garrison. Even now, sitting amid the splendors of Mercier, only the sight of the men-at-arms who surrounded him sparked life into the duke's dark eyes.

"I knew your father," he said to Alix. She barely suppressed a start at the fervor of his unexpected words. "We fought together at Nicopolis."

"And at Rachowa and Vilna. He mentioned your name often, Grace, when he spoke of those times," said Alix. She fervently hoped the great duke would not be too curious as to just what exactly her father—a renowned warrior—had said. It had not been approving.

The duke was not curious.

"I earned my golden spurs at Rachowa," he said as though she had not spoken. "It was a noble battle. My great friend the Knight de la Marche was wounded there as well. You have heard of him?"

"He was a great friend of my mother," answered Alix, "and of my father. They say he is happy now."

"Quite happy." The duke shrugged. "His wound was a grievous one to his sword arm but he recovered from it. He has his wife and his children. They tell me he is happy—though how a knight could be happy doing anything but battling is a puzzle to me. I should contact him. He is a son of Burgundy and one of the first knights of France. We will have use of him in the days to come."

"Because of King Henry of England?"

"Because of King Henry of France," the duke corrected her. "The Plantagenets, being the last of the Capetian dynasty, have a stronger claim to the throne at Paris than do the Valois. But of course you would know that. You must. You are connected to the Templar Knights."

"I?" The word prickled along Alix's spine.

"Through your mother," Duke Jean said, but without looking over at Alix's pale face. "I knew her. She was at Nicopolis with your father. She had come from there, as had he—at least in a manner of speaking. She was quite a learned woman, your mother. We talked of many things. But she would never speak of what I most wanted to learn of her. She never spoke of the legend. She was a Magdalene, as are you. And the Magdalene is either a Wise Woman or a witch—

depending on who is doing the talking and what they want."

Alix kept herself very still. She barely breathed. She willed this cunning man to tell her the things that Julian Madrigal, her mother, never had.

"The warlock's witch," he said. He looked over at her then and smiled. She had the strangest sensation that he had read her thoughts and decided to comply with them. "That is what they called the Magdalene. They say that the Templar Knights worshipped the original Mary Magdalene and that each of the Magdalenes that followed, daughter after mother, was her direct descendant. The Knights Templar are central to the tale of why there should be a Henri upon the throne of France rather than a Charles."

"Because of the burnings?" Alix cast a quick glance over at Lancelot de Guigny, who sat beside his brother, but not too near. He was engaged in what seemed to be animated conversation with one of the brightly dressed ladies who had accompanied Duke Jean to Mercier. But Alix saw his eyes narrow. She saw him slice a glance at her.

"Yes, the burnings," the duke said and then expansively waved the drumstick upon which he was gnawing. "The whole suppression. 'Twas the beginning of this great mess."

Glancing up, Alix caught the full force of Severin's dark gaze upon them. Not for the first time she wished that she could fathom the secret she knew was hidden in the full depth of his eyes. She wished that she could know what he knew.

Instead, Lancelot de Guigny hunched closer.

"They were cursed," he said.

"Indeed," said his half brother, Burgundy, used to an audience and obviously enjoying this one. Even his cousin, the bishop, froze as he reached for a marzipan ball.

"Both Philip the Fair and the Pope Clement V," Guigny whispered but he was still heard. "Both cursed. By that time the pope had chosen to leave Rome and was firmly ensconced at Avignon in the very shadow of his king. As the witch-fires licked him, Jacques de Molay, the Grand Knight of the Temple and godfather of the king's own daughter, called down the wrath of God upon Philip and his house unto the thirteenth generation. He vowed to confront both the king and the pope before God's judgment seat before the passing of a year."

"A curse that held," said Sir Lancelot, quickly crossing himself. "One has only to see what happened next to his house. They say the curse of a dying man is always heeded."

"Not necessarily," replied Duke Jean reflectively. "I am still alive and healthy and there have been many dying men who took my name in vain as they passed from this world to the next. You yourself, Lancelot, might likewise hope for a gentler fate. One prays that your own actions, even within this castle, do not return as hauntings."

Burgundy turned back to the Countess de Mercier. "The king, a hale young man of forty-six, had never known a day's illness. Yet he took a chill while out boar hunting and was dead within the year that de Molay had stipulated. He joined Pope Clement, who had died one month to the day after the curse was pronounced."

"But it got worse," whispered Alix. She remembered the story. It was the one that Severin had first told her.

"Oh, yes, much worse," replied the duke. No practiced troubadour could have told a better tale. "Because the curse seeped down to destroy Philip's progeny. He had strapping sons—an unprecedented wealth of heirs—and each of them as hearty as their sire. But as each man took his turn at the throne of France—well, something happened. They each followed the other as Louis X, Philip V, and Charles IV, all to die young. The longest-lived ruled for but six years. And despite having had six wives amongst them, they left no legitimate male heir. Of course, illegitimate heirs do not count . . ."

He paused for the expected titters. Burgundy glanced at his half brother. Sir Lancelot met his gaze without blanching, a half-smile on his face.

". . . Which left only Philip the Fair's daughter, Jeanne," continued Alix, surprising herself with the particulars of the story. "She was Jacques de Molay's goddaughter and the only Capetian heir who remained."

"But the fact that she was goddaughter to the witch did not save her from the general damnation," said the duke as he continued with his tale. "Because she was a woman. The question of heredity had actually not been confronted before. There was no need for it. The Capetian line had never lacked for male heirs—at least until the cursing. A hastily called assembly confirmed the Salic Law and said a woman could not succeed to the throne of France. At least this was the rationale for her defeat. Her name was Isabeau, the name of our present queen, but she became Isabel of England when she married Edward II. Many people in both countries hated her. She was generally thought to have conspired with her lover in the murder of her husband the king."

"Had I but been alive, their deaths would most naturally have been placed at my doorstep," said Duke Jean with a weary sigh. Again the expected twitters rustled forth. Everyone remembered Louis d'Orleans, and the others.

"In any event there was the eventual reckoning," continued Burgundy.

The duke stopped his tale long enough to hail a passing servant and seize a rissole, biting into the crescent-shaped tartlet with his small, sharp teeth. "Indeed, these are marvelous pastries. The veal was some of the best I've ever tasted—and the plaice before it simply marvelous. It is a great inconvenience that the Count de Mercier—the real count, that is, the one who is no longer among us—is not here so that he can be complimented on the capabilities of his cook."

Guigny flushed darkly scarlet and a muscle began to work at the corner of his mouth. The tone had mysteriously changed. Something dark and dangerous was playing its way between the two brothers; Alix knew this, though she could not guess its cause.

I'll ask Severin about it. Severin knows them both well.

The thought was barely formed in her mind before she realized the futility of it. There'd be no more asking of questions to Severin, no more telling of secrets to him, either. The duke had ridden in with his cousin the bishop in train. Alix could hardly bear to look upon the holy man as he busied himself with wiping mutton grease from his fat face with an expanse of Venice lace. The bishop looked benignly content, which did not bode well for her future, she realized. Contentment on a bishop's face, at least in these perilous times, usually signified that promises or money had changed hands. Usually both. Though the air crackled with tension, Alix knew that Lancelot de Guigny was a power here. He was the duke's half brother; he had saved his grace's life. Though ostensibly she was saved from marriage to him by her mourning privileges, if he wanted her he would have her. And with the bought blessing of the Church.

But she could refuse him. Robert had not loved her

and Severin had refused her. Still, she would not take Lancelot de Guigny in their place.

She would convent herself first. She would run away.

"Your grace," she began, but the duke silenced her with a wave of his jeweled hand. He turned abruptly to the bishop.

"Then 'tis settled, is it not, Giscard? I've always thought it best to tend to matters as soon as they present themselves. The bride was won. She will be given. Is there any more need of dispensation from the Church?"

The bishop looked up from a dish of spiced oranges, obviously loath to be parted from such a good meal even for so noble a reason as a peer's request. "The dispensation was already granted. Naturally it concerns only the Lady Alix. She is the widow here, the one in need. 'Twas but the groom-choice in doubt," he replied through lips heavily coated with sweet syrup. "But mayhap she still needs time to prepare herself for a new life."

"Nonsense," said the duke, dismissing the matter. "She's had time enough and plenty to ready herself for this. Why should an expected wedding be put off even until the morrow? The Countess de Mercier must only accustom herself to a change in groom—and of course of title."

Alix stood slowly, rising without permission, and turned to gaze upon the duke through two cold, turquoise gemstones. "I will not wed him," she said. "It is impossible that I take the Knight de Guigny."

"My half brother is no longer Guigny," said the duke, mildly but with the air of one enjoying a great joke. "He is now the possessor of what he most wanted in the world—a title. A *legitimate* title. He will be known now throughout all of Christendom as the Count de Mercier—a noble name and with a long history to it.

That he shares nothing in this account is a fact that will soon enough be lost within the mists of time. He has risen in rank. You, on the other hand, my lady, are to come down."

"Come down?" Alix felt her legs weaken and sank into her seat—again without seeking the duke's approval.

"That is, unless our servant Brigante ascends to the peerage and takes you with him. This is always possible; I have found him to be a knight of most extraordinary talent in pursuit." Jean of Burgundy chuckled, enjoying himself immensely. "Because, by rights, now that my brother was foolish enough to have you championed you must go to the winner of that joust. Brigante fought for you—now he must have you. May God show mercy to his soul."

The crowded assembly erupted once more into laughter as the bishop nodded his agreement and clapped loudly for more wine.

Alix did not laugh. She did not clap. Through the length of the very great distance between them, Alix Ducci Montaldo de Mercier turned to face her groom.

As the duke did not wish to miss a day of hawking on the fowl-rich lands of Mercier, the wedding time was set for sexte bell on the morrow. She had been sent early to her bed, but Alix could not sleep. The arguing stopped her. She could not have slept anyway, of this she was certain, but because her own chamber was situated over the main body of the hall she was an unwilling privy to the heated words the Duke of Burgundy was having with his half brother.

"You are the proof against ruttings with a peasant." Jean of Burgundy's voice carried easily up and around the stone passages. "You see only the immediate circumstances. You have no idea how to sound the true depth of what it is you want."

Lancelot de Guigny pitched his voice low. His words were unintelligible but not the anger that laced them.

When he had finished, Burgundy laughed. The sound of it was not altogether pleasant. "That is the first true thing you have spoken. I am liege-lord here and I have decided. The Countess de Mercier goes to the Knight Brigante."

"But she is mine. She belongs to Mercier and Mercier belongs to me. You have promised it. You have declared this before the assembly."

This time Alix distinctly heard Sir Lancelot's angry voice.

"Mine," he repeated.

"Nothing is yours," said his half brother, "except that which is given you by me."

He paused before continuing and within her mind Alix saw him as he savored his wine. "You took Mercier, that is true, but you've made a rubbish of it. The planting is late, your men unruly. Rumors have reached as far as Dijon that rapes have been reported. Even killings. The people remember Count Robert with regret. You are foolish, indeed, to have spit so thoroughly into the plate from which you must eat." The duke's tone grew conciliatory. "I am forced into this and with your own actions. By now half of Mercier knows that you spiked your lance with salt to wound the Knight Brigante. What a fool you are, Lancelot—but then you always were so."

Guigny's response was unintelligible, but Alix heard the duke laugh.

"Oh yes, the child," he said. "That was your doing and no one else's. Do not try to blame the consequences upon either Severin Brigante or the Countess de Mercier. You should have sought out the child before. You should have known she would lie. What woman would give a defenseless boy over to slaughter?"

Burgundy's laugh was short and mean.

"Is this the thanks I have for saving your life?" Guigny's voice cut through the laughter. Even from a distance Alix thought she heard pain in it and bewilderment as well. "Is this the end our kinship brings us?"

"You served your own purposes in serving mine," replied the great duke. "How would it have helped you to let me die at Nicopolis? You had no lands and no title—you needed me for everything. It would not have been in your own interests to let me die."

"But brother . . ."

"Not in your interests at all," repeated the duke. His tone was one of obvious dismissal. "But now you have Mercier—if not its countess. That at least is something. And 'tis March already. Henry of England will soon embark to claim his throne. If you fight well, who knows the spoils his reign will bring to you? But one thing only—never again address me as your brother. Unless, of course, I have first addressed that title to you."

Even after the conversation had died and the castle lay slumbering about her, Alix still could not sleep. She tossed and turned upon her enormous bed, jumbling her linen and lace pillows, bunching her silk coverings beneath her body and then pulling and straightening them out again.

The change before her was enormous and she could not pretend that it was not. Going from being countess of a great castle and a rich land to a simple convented life would have been one thing. Many inconvenient widows were forced to make this transition; generally they were placed in pleasant surroundings where life was retired but not too arduous. In the end, most of them lived out their days with more freedom than that enjoyed by the majority of women. During the day they read or walked in their gardens; at night they held quiet discussion over plentiful food and fine plate. They accomplished good works. They prayed. Most monasteries were richly endowed and a wealthy widow might live well in them.

But Alix was no longer wealthy. The Knight de Guigny had taken her lands and now he held the title to them. But the move from the beneficence of the vast wealth of Mercier to being the wife of a simple knight was something else again. It daunted her. She could not imagine what her life would be like with Severin Brigante. Living first with her father's riches and then with those of her husband, she had no way of imagining what would be expected of her now.

Life had taught the Lady Alix that change was not always a pleasant experience, and she knew that marriage to Severin Brigante would bring great changes to her life. She had no way of knowing what these changes would be. She only knew that she could not say no to them.

Severin had rejected her but she still loved him. Or thought she did. She seemed fated to love men who rejected her. It seemed to be her curse.

"And I've been poor before," she said aloud, "before my father came. When my mother and I lived alone at Belvedere."

She smiled at the memory and slowly drifted off to sleep.

Marriage.
Severin had no idea how he'd gotten himself into

this mess—how he'd said yes to the idea of taking a wife and a penniless wife at that.

Naturally he had sometimes thought of marrying; it was the accepted thing. When he saw himself taking a wife, it was always sometime very far in the distant future, after he had won his fortune and proven himself to his father's kin. Then he would choose a woman from among the high nobility, someone who would bring him fortune and good name to add to what he had already achieved.

He would choose someone whom his uncle would look upon with respect.

He had serious doubts that Belden of Harnoncourt would look upon the Dame de Mercier with respect—especially when she would no longer be the Dame de Mercier but a simple Lady Alix. She was penniless now and she would be even more penniless when she married him. His own money had gone to outfitting and building up his army. He had kept very little for himself.

They had not even a home between them except her ruined castle of Belvedere. But, worse yet, Alix would not only be a poor woman—she would be a poor woman who had grown used to something better. Infinitely better.

" 'Tis a dreadful mistake," Severin groaned aloud. "A pitiful mess."

He lay alone in his chamber because he wanted none of the usual fuss of bridegrooming. He did not want the drinking and the sly stories and the knowing winks. There would have been plenty of these had he allowed them. The marriage of a never-wed man to a widow was looked upon as an occasion for ribaldry. But Severin did not want bawdiness before such a stupefying occasion as that of his own marriage. He wanted to be alone.

Perhaps the most enjoyable advantage of being without company was that he could talk to himself without arousing suspicions as to his sanity. He definitely wished to talk to himself now. He needed his own solace more than he needed comfort from anyone else. Only he knew what a mess his life would become if he married this woman. And yet he was determined to marry her. He refused to give her up to Lancelot de Guigny.

"I've no idea how this happened."

But of course, deep down, he knew just exactly how it had happened. He had seen her as she stood before Lancelot de Guigny and he had wanted her. Just as he had seen her, years before, when she stood, newly married, before Charles VI in Paris and had wanted her then.

This thought jolted him wide awake and he realized there was no use trying to sleep. Birds already chattered outside his chamber window. It was well that they could chatter. They had no idea the mess-up he'd made.

"It was the devil in me and nothing more," Severin said angrily. He repeated this over and over again as he called his pages for bathing water. He muttered it as he stropped his hair into place and yanked on a black tunic. "Or perhaps it was that damned Maltese Star."

It soothed him to blame his situation on witchcraft. It calmed him down considerably and made the turning of events all Alix's fault. But Severin's good humor soon faded. He noted that he had chosen his best tunic to wear upon his wedding day, one that he had scrupulously held apart for months. It was lightly embroidered with the fair and costly threads of the Gold Company and he had planned to wear it only when he met Belden of Harnoncourt face-to-face. He had thought it would be more than fitting. He had dreamed of the meeting, looking forward to it on many a long night. That he had automatically chosen to wear this tunic now made him angry indeed. He kicked at the pile of discarded tunics that lay beside his bed.

Unfortunately this called his attention to that bed. Small and comfortless, it might have miserably held a virgin page. Yet it had held him—alone—for years. Indeed, he carried it with him.

Now it suddenly occurred to him that he should have called for another. He would have a wife soon and it was much too small for both. Good enough for him, but not good enough for someone as fine as the Lady Alix. He should have thought. This caused him to look with a trenchant eye around the whole of his room. He found it stark, not at all fitting. The furniture was sparse and threadbare, the windows still paned in bleached linen and with no fine drapings covering them. He would have to find another place to bed his wife. But where? He, the general of one of the largest mercenary armies in Europe, found himself perplexed at the thought. He was to wed her, but where could he bed her? The problem had never come up before.

Not that he had shied away from his share of women. He had known a great many of them and intimately. Nor had he ever had to force his attentions, though everyone knew that for a knight raping and brigandage were universally considered as spoils of war. Though true he had never coerced a woman, he still had never lacked willing bodies with which to share his bed. Some of them had even stayed for more than one night, at least when he had allowed this. More times than not he was the one to say them nay. But he did not always say this. Indeed, there was a noble widow in Bari, an older woman, to whom he had returned again and again. Her touch besotted him. The welcoming softness of her body and the way it opened to him was a source of never-ending intoxication. Yet there were times when he wanted more to hold her and talk to her than to take her.

She had known his parents. She had known his life. And she had accepted him anyway.

If ever he had thought of marriage—at least before now—it had been to her, but he had returned from three years service in Jerusalem to find that, in his absence, she had wed a simple merchant. She seemed happy with her choice and she had wished Severin well.

He had not blamed her. In fact, if anything he was more than a little relieved. God must not have wanted him to marry. God must have wanted him to seek vengeance instead. He had always been quite sure of God's intentions for his life—at least until now.

It was strange that he should think about that woman of Bari now as he prepared himself to wed. He had not thought of her for years.

Since then he had spent more nights alone than he cared to remember. His life had been busy enough and productive. He had moved from the south of Italy on to Tuscany to take over the leadership of the Gold Company. He had been successful at his task. He had come to the attention of the duke, who had commissioned the army to his service now that battle between France and England seemed once again imminent. Severin felt that fate had given him the chance to redeem his name and that of his father. The thought had been invigorating and women had been the farthest thing from his mind. Or so he had thought.

" 'Twas my lust that did me in with the Lady Alix," he muttered. "That and the smell of her damned rose perfume."

At that precise moment he forgot the witchcraft reason but if someone had remembered to remind him he would have nodded a vigorous assent.

But actually, if he were being honest with himself— and he might as well be, he was about to marry her— the real reason he had determined to fight for her was because he could not bear the thought of Alix with Guigny. He could not have lived knowing that Sir Lancelot's overly refined hands were touching her or that his thin lips were pressing down upon her mouth.

He could not have borne the thought of her growing great with Lancelot de Guigny's child.

Grimacing, Severin moved quickly away from this thought. He pulled on boots that had been stropped to a high sheen, then fastened on his burnished golden spurs. Again he brushed his hair. He tried occupying his mind with all the details that surrounded the enormous change of life he faced, knowing that he did this in order not to think about the enormous change itself.

Marriage.

He had no idea what it meant. The only marriage he knew intimately was that of his parents and he had been so young when his mother left them. He could not remember her at all. He was not even certain that his spoiled and selfish parents had taken the time to actually wed. His father was quite vague upon this point. Severin did not know if they had held a proper marriage, a ceremony performed by a priest and witnessed by those around them. A sacrament. The kind of marriage he was about to have now.

Unlike his father and mother, Severin had every intention of remaining faithful to the woman he wed. This meant not only that the wedding be proper, but that the marriage that came after it be so as well. He had refused to take Alix when she offered herself to him last night because she had not yet been his to take. But soon she would be. And *this* meant that within less than a day's time he would carry the Lady Alix to his bed.

"But not this bed," he thought with something of panic.

Certainly there would be no going to Guigny for help. Severin laughed aloud at the very idea. The argument between the duke and his brother had rung out through the night. Guigny had been humiliated once again by Burgundy and would only come to the wedding if he were forced. As he probably would be. But Sir Lancelot would offer no cooperation. He was the true master of Mercier now. The sop had finally been given him. And though bastard-born, he still shared kinship with the duke. Burgundy might humiliate his half brother in order to further his own ends but not to further anyone else's.

He would have to find a place in this vastly overpopulated castle to bed his wife. Or else he would have to do without her.

Then he thought of the soft line of Alix's throat and the way he could just barely see the heartbeat in it when something had excited her. He saw the fawn's tongue against her hand on that day when all the world around them had been kissed by white. He smelled again the richness of her rose perfume.

"Got to find a bed," he thought as he hurried to his chamber door. His feet crushed against the dried thyme beneath them; his golden spurs jingled him along his way.

Alix stared at herself in the small piece of silvered glass that served as her chamber mirror. She was not exactly pleased with what she saw. She had dressed in a simple gown of black samite that had neither beading nor fur trimming. She had pulled on simple, not overly pointed, pattens that peaked only occasionally from beneath the modest sweep of her skirt. She had left her golden hair loose but only to hide it beneath the lace of a black veil.

No cloistered nun would have faulted the propriety of what she wore. But Alix did. She knew the truth of it. The gown was decorous enough in the way it hugged high at her bosom and billowed forth beneath her waist but the samite, though black enough, could hardly be called somber. This particular fabric was special indeed, having been woven of silks from Como and tinted by the expert hand of a master Lombard dyer. Even in the faint light of earliest morning, Alix saw colors dancing about in its depth. It sparkled with dark blue and rich red and even bark brown, depending upon the turn of the cloth. By being none, the gown became all colors. Alix loved this. But most important of all to her—though she did not dwell upon the implications of this—her parents had gifted her with this dress. Robert de Mercier's money had played no part in its purchase.

Nor had he chosen her small, golden-hued pattens. She had chosen and paid for these herself when they had stopped in Venice to pay homage to the ruling *Doge* on their way from the east. Her mother had told her of certain shops that hugged the many bridges that knit the city together. Once settled in Venice, Alix, a shopper born, had rushed to them as soon as she decently could. Like her mother she had spent a great deal of money purchasing far more fripperies than she had intended. She had returned in great remorse to the palazzo that Robert had rented. But she had had these shoes in hand. She had searched diligently within her chests until she found them. They had yet to be worn. She would wear them today.

"They are not adorned," she told herself, surprised that she had said the words out loud. " 'Tis only the color that is not in real keeping with true mourning."

Still, it was a bright color—not even she could deny that. Not even she could find some way that these pattens fitted within the wardrobe of a grieving widow—a woman being forced into marriage with a man who took her as a tourney prize.

Alix was not being forced into marriage and she knew it.

"I would not have worn these clothes for Lancelot de Guigny," she said, still carrying on her solitary conversation. "I would not have married him had he won me."

She turned to the veil.

Alix moved the small looking glass closer to one of the torches so she could see herself better.

Yes, the veil . . .

It too had been bought in Venice at the same fine stalls that had ruined her finances, just as they had ruined those of her mother before her. Alix wrinkled her brow. The veil's dark color expressed mourning—at least that. But it was a coquette's mourning; the pretense at grieving of a born flirt. Alix's hair shimmered through its skillful inwrought netting, golden and free. She thought, with a blush, that it made her look slightly provocative, perhaps even wanton. The effect did not displease her and she did not replace the veil with another more chaste. Instead, she took one last but thorough look into the piece of silvered glass, tilting first herself and then it in order to see better. The Maltese Star at her throat caught the light and sparkled, but Alix hardly found this reassuring.

From below she heard the village bells begin their

toll of the prayer hour. In the distance, first one monastery and then another took up the sound.

"Unhappy the bride who weds before first light," Alix repeated to herself. "And unhappier is she still when she is wed in black."

But morning had broken. First light had come. It was no longer night, and perhaps there was some hope in that.

The perfume of the flowers floated out through the chapel window. It greeted Alix as she walked the pebbled inner curtain amid pages, gorgeously dressed in their lord's livery, yawning from such an early snatch from sleep. Spring flowers. Spring violets and early rosebuds that somehow had been spared the winter's frost. They were encircled in dark green clover. She smelled them long before someone thrust the bouquet into her hands. They were so freshly picked that dew, like diamonds, still glistened upon them.

"Trust the women to think of this," said the duke beside her.

But Alix doubted the women had thought of this. She had grown used to small presents—to pieces of ribbon and dried figs and marzipan which had arrived to her with the duke's compliments—but which he had never sent. She had grown used to carved and stuffed toys and goat milk sent from the main monastery building for Yvrain with a greeting from the abbot— but which the abbot knew nothing about. Now she held spring flowers from someone who had seen her search for winter ones.

Alix knew just who had picked these roses and violets and who had formed this simple bouquet. She shook her head but said nothing to the nobleman beside her. No lady of the peerage had thought to bring her these flowers. Alix no longer gave credit where it was not due.

"I'll have no glum faces," the duke said to Alix as they waited. She did not think her face grim. It was obviously a speech that he had carefully prepared. "No crying about. And no playing the grieving widow. No matter the mistakes my brother Guigny made in taking this castle—and he made many, I will give you that—still he paid you a service, madam. He freed you from a husband who did not value you and never could. Once Robert had done his duty by you and delivered you of an heir, he would have sent you packing back to Hungary. Make no mistake about that. You think your Church and your vows would have saved you but they would not have. Many a noblewoman has thought herself safe within marriage vows one day and woken convented the next. One has only to remember what the king's brother Orleans did to his wife Valentina—and she daughter to Gian Galeazzo Visconti, probably the most unscrupulous man alive. Or at least the most powerful. Mercier loved that peasant and he would not have been gainsaid of her. If I hadn't forced him to it, he would never have married you in the first place. Certainly he could not have kept you once you had accomplished your purpose. And your purpose—your *only* purpose—was to breed him a legitimate heir."

Alix opened her mouth automatically to defend Robert, as she had done so many times in the past, even when he was killing her with his neglect and his obvious love for another. She wanted to convince this arrogant duke that in the end her husband would have grown to love her. He would have eventually come to her because she, Alix, was noble and his equal, and Solange was not. He could not have helped loving her once he saw—really saw—how hard she worked to earn this love. But then she stopped herself. Did it really matter anymore? Robert was dead.

In the end all she said was, "My husband was a good man." Words she had used many times before. This time they had finality that even she heard.

"He was not the man for you." The duke had done his duty and now appeared bored by the topic. "This time you have chosen better."

That she had chosen at all was the question. But Alix knew it was no use to argue this point. She had chosen a perfect Robert for herself the first time and she had had to live with the pain. Now this Knight Brigante had chosen her, had literally won her in a joust, and she could live with the pain of this decision as well. She knew she could.

"We should be on with this," Burgundy continued. "Don't want to ruin a whole day's hunt. I'll need your bridegroom with me, lady. The weather's cleared and there will be good falconing today. Severin Brigante's a man you want near when there's skilled sport about. Got a firm hand, he has."

The duke had brought his own birds with him and they had been given pride of place in the castle's crowded aviaries.

Alix stood for a moment with the duke beside her just outside the peaked gray stones of Mercier chapel. A robin, alone but not frightened, stared at her from the espaliered trees that were already greening along the small church's new façade. He continued to watch as Alix slipped away from the resplendent duke who stood beside her and walked over to him. He cocked his head thoughtfully as she eased the ring that symbolized marriage to Robert de Mercier from her finger. It came off easily; it had always been just a little too large. The bird seemed a conspirator as he quietly watched her wedge the heavy gold band into a place where the stones of the chapel did not quite meet. Alix smiled at the little robin then and it was a bright smile; perhaps there was a little fear edging it but it was radiant nonetheless. Then she turned back to the duke. He had not even had time to become impatient.

"I am ready," she said.

Sixteen

When she married Count Robert de Mercier she was dressed in white samite encrusted with pearls and lace. The tunic was heavy. The pearls on it kept popping off and falling to the ground. She carried a rosary as she walked down the aisle of the Cathedral at Buda between her father and the Emperor Sigismund to be presented to her new husband. The rosary had been her husband's wedding gift to her. Constructed of fifty-three glittering diamonds, six enormous rubies, a gold-and-ruby crucifix and gold linking—it had been made to impress. Alix remembered now that her mother, Julian Madrigal, had looked upon it with disapproval, although she said nothing. Alix also remembered how cold that rosary felt in her hands and how it, too, seemed heavy.

Today, though she walked through a chapel every bit as packed as had been the Cathedral at Buda, she carried spring's first flowers and wore black as she walked slowly up the aisle to take a new husband. There was nothing on her that weighted her down.

The Duke of Burgundy was partial to the flute and so music played as the Countess de Mercier was presented to her new bridegroom, the Knight Brigante. Alix tried to identify the instruments—the soft flute, the mandolin, the tight drum—as Severin took her hand and led her before the resplendent bishop. For some reason she was overcome with shyness and she did not dare look at her husband-to-be. The bishop's words rang out clearly, though, and she answered them.

No, there was no impediment to her marriage. Yes, she was a widow made. Even when she heard Severin's responses she did not look at him. No, he had never been married. No, there was no impediment to his entering into union with the Countess de Mercier, who had been born Alix Ducci Montaldo.

No, they were in no way related.

Instead, Alix kept her eyes straight ahead. There was only one fresco in this stark chapel. She had never paid attention to it before, but she studied it well now. It was of the Madonna holding her child. This was usual enough. Even in her young life, Alix had seen hundreds of these portraits smiling down serenely at her from as many churches. But this one was slightly different and Alix, as she took Severin Brigante to be her husband, noticed this difference for the very first time.

There was another woman in the fresco—a lone woman who stood just behind Mary and her baby, hovering near. A woman who hid in shadows and behind dim shadings of paint. Even staring, Alix could not make out her features; she could not see if she were old or young, fair or dark. She saw only that her clothing was unremarkable, even somber. Instead, the Virgin was dressed in bright blues and gold etched the edges of her garments. There was no brightness to the other woman's garments, and really even no shape to them. Yet her presence in the icon seemed to bring peace. Briefly, Alix wondered who this other woman might be and why the artist had seen fit to paint but not reveal her.

"You may kiss your bride."

Alix suddenly became aware of the bishop's booming voice, and just as suddenly of the fact that Severin drew near.

She was not aware of her quick "No." Only when she turned to the disapproving frown of the duke and heard Lancelot de Guigny's snicker did she realize what she had done. She wanted to tell them all that they were wrong. She would do her duty. She would be a full wife to the Knight Brigante. She was starting to appreciate what he had done by fighting for her and winning her.

But kissing him—their first kiss as husband and wife—was something private, something personal and special. Something she did not want to share with these gaudy members of the duke's court who saw this marriage as only an attempt at political gaming.

Alix had already kissed Severin. She knew that kissing him was something that was secret to her and sacred.

"Later," she whispered drawing back from him but the duke heard her and roared with laughter.

"A true woman," he said, turning to Severin with a consoling grin. "Goodwifing you already and the spousal words barely past your lips!"

Again Burgundy roared and his court roared with him. But Severin was not laughing. Alix looked quickly across at her new husband and saw the grim set of his jaw.

I will have to explain this to him later. When we are to ourselves and alone.

The words brought her some comfort though the set look upon her husband's face alarmed her. Once she talked to him he would understand. She would make him understand, just as she had with other bothersome problems in the past. She would talk to him.

It never occurred to the new Lady Brigante that the time for talking was past.

The duke immediately whisked the new groom away from his bride for a celebratory day's hawking on the dove-rich lands of Mercier. The Knight de Guigny begged leave to go on religious retreat to the shrine of St. Bernard de Clairvaux in the deep forest. If the duke thought anything amiss in this he did not say so. It was noted that Sir Lancelot had spent a great deal of time in prayer lately. This seemed natural enough. There were many things both in Guigny's past and in his present circumstance that could do with the touch of divine intervention. He had murdered to obtain a title and castle that had yet to be formally deemed his. And if this were not enough his future also held its share of uncertainties. Henry of England would be coming soon—everyone knew this, but what his arrival would herald for the duke and for France itself was anybody's conjecture. There was also the fact that the Knight de Guigny had been humiliated by the discovery that he had salted his lances when he fought against the Knight Brigante. This was a grave breach of chivalry, which had, of course, been laid to the circumstances of his birth. His mother had been a witch; she had spelled the Old Duke into her bed. What could be expected from such a union?

The duke, his benefactor, had sighed with relief as his brother rode off.

The new Lady Brigante did not ask the duke's permission to absent herself from the day's festivities. While her husband hunted, she remained in her chamber. Alix had seen the ladies of Burgundy's train and had met his formidable mother, the dowager duchess.

She had no intention of hearing their speculation and questions about the turn her life had taken.

It was pleasant enough, her wedding day. She spent it, as she would have spent most others, with her pigeons and going through the bound books that she should read. They were Robert's books and she would leave them here at Mercier. But she would miss them. She fingered through parchments and thought of passages she would like to share with Severin. He had come late to reading but he tackled it with great enthusiasm and care. She thought that this was something they could share in the future just as they had shared it in the past.

At one point, in the late afternoon, she looked across her chamber and saw the candles still burning before the altar she had constructed to Robert de Mercier. She thought it time to remove it. She was no longer Robert's countess; instead she had become Severin's wife. But the day was pleasant—her wedding day!—and she determined to enjoy it. There would be time enough tomorrow to see to the duties and the dismantling of her old life.

Severin followed the hunt with grim determination. His shoulder smarted and ached from its wound but he welcomed the pain. He sat his horse longer and soared his hawk higher even than did the duke himself. When the day's sun peaked and then began its descent, he would have urged a lingering had he not been afraid the others would laugh at him again. Their laughter, though good-natured, had been enough to bear this morning when his noble wife had refused to kiss a new husband whose station was decidedly lower than her own. There would be much speculation on the night to come and Severin knew it.

Later Severin hoped he showed a contented face,

as the duke and his minstrels led the young newlyweds to their place of honor on the dais. He remembered to smile at Alix, though he was furious with her for what she had done at their wedding, and to speak and not bark at the dowager duchess. He ate his meal and commended Burgundy on his foresight in bringing such an excellent chef in his train. Duke Jean responded handsomely and made a slight joke about hoping that Severin had not overtaxed himself with the day's activities. It was important to be fresh on one's wedding night. First impressions counted.

He would also have need of much energy soon; he would presently be sent to Rome to negotiate alliances with the pope and with the sinister Gian Galeazzo Visconti. He must conserve his strength for that. Severin managed to smile at this witticism. He was on his best behavior. When the duke's aging mother nudged and winked at him, he did not tell her how ridiculous she looked with her newly dyed orange-yellow hair nor did he ask his new bride for an immediate annulment of their marriage vows. The Knight Brigante was quite proud of himself for both these examples of his excellent forbearance and chivalry.

The Knight Brigante spoke briskly to his honor guard.

"We will be spending the night in the chamber of the Countess de—of my wife," he said. Only that small mistake, but at least he had put his meaning across. Because, indeed, Alix was no longer the Countess de Mercier. She was plain Lady Brigante now—and his wife.

Remembering his humiliation that morning when she had refused to kiss him, Severin resolved to fix that obviously unpleasant notion firmly within her head. She would be kissing him, make no mistake about it. He could not keep marriage vows if he were encased within a "white marriage" and he knew this.

There was also the matter that he had forgotten to ask the duke for a more decorous chamber. He had looked about his own this afternoon after the day's hunting and had decided that, indeed, it would never do. The Lady Alix despised him enough already; she would despise him even more once she saw how he lived.

"Yes," he said, firmly fixing her cold hand within the crook of his arm. "In your chamber, madam. Mine is that of a bachelor. I think it best you remain where you have lain in the past."

How thoughtful of him, Alix thought, as they neared her bedchamber. Only the presence of his honor guard kept her from standing on tiptoe to plant a kiss of gratitude right upon his cheek. He must have known how humiliated she would be facing him again in a place where he had once rejected her.

Yet he might decide to reject me again and within my own chamber.

Oddly there was some comfort in this thought. She suddenly realized that, though she had been married, she had no idea how to react in a true situation of marriage. She had no idea what she should do. Without actually trying, she could number the times that Robert de Mercier had found his reluctant way to her bed. And once there, rarely had he spent more than an hour's span with her and never had he spent the whole night. She had thought this normal before, or at least something that might change once he miraculously came to love her. Now she wondered. Would

Severin want more from her? Would he be disappointed with her just as Robert had been?

Severin, who had every right to expect a woman experienced in the seductions of wifedom, was in many ways to find himself with a virgin upon his hands.

Alix's heart sank at the thought of what he would think of her. He might quickly form the same opinion as had Robert—that she was useless and cold and that there were warmer places where he could spend his nights.

There were so many little things to think of and she thought of them now as she walked silently beside the man she soon would bed. Should she braid her hair or allow it to tumble? It was long when freed and its unbound length fell to the deep reaches of her spine. She should bundle it up, she knew. It was so thick that letting it lie free only tangled it during the night. It would save time on the morrow should she braid it tonight. Especially the way she tossed and turned upon her pillow. She had not slept well since coming to Mercier. She never braided or ribboned her hair in the past, even though she had defied Robert in leaving it loosened. He had found her hair distracting, he said.

One, two, over and done.

He had wanted no distractions from a duty's task.

They were at her chamber's door and he was opening it for her.

"I shall leave you alone for some minutes, while I see to the needs of my men," said her husband. Grace and chivalry laced his words. Alix curtseyed into a reverence more because she was flustered than because it was needed. He was her husband, she reminded herself, and now her lord. She bid him Godspeed back to her and heard the tittering of his honor guard.

Her chamber door closed shut behind her and Alix was alone. There was no maid to help her. She had sent Young Sophie to nurse her mother, whom the duke had immediately ordered released from the onus of confinement and inquisition once Alix had appealed to him. Alix would have gone herself to visit the Wise Woman but there had been no time and she was also frightened to call the Knight de Guigny's attention to the two women. Now that she knew he was once again at the forest shrine she would go at first light to see them. When the guards had led her out the Wise Woman had managed to turn to Alix and whisper.

"I see something," she had said. "Something—someone—dark and ambiguous. A silver man."

Yes, tomorrow she must visit the Wise Woman. Sophie would tell her what she should do.

Alix pulled off her wedding finery. She washed herself in the small tub of lavender water that sat on the trestle and watched drops of water glisten on her body and nestle down between the hollow of her breasts. She patted them dry with linen toweling and then pulled on a white shift edged in simple white lace. The shift had formed part of the vast trousseau she had brought to her marriage to Robert de Mercier but she had never worn it. On the night of her wedding to her first husband she had chosen something very intricately wrought, with gold lacings and costly embroideries.

Little good it had done her.

Strangely, tonight she felt like a new-made wife. Well, indeed she was that, though not a virgin. Robert had come to her some days after the wedding, when they were well upon the road to Mercier. One night he was just there, beside her. Alix could not remember now if she had had time to smile up at him or not.

He had lifted her night tunic to her breasts and entered her. There had been pain and the stickiness of blood and then it had been over. The whole event had taken less than a quarter sand-span. She had been left with only the foulness of stale wine that had surrounded him and the mess of her own blood that she had to clean. From the first time they were together, Robert had never stayed in his wife's bed long enough to warm his spot. On more than one occasion Alix had reached toward the place that her husband had left beside her to find the linen still cold.

She had not become pregnant by him; his seed had never taken. But it had taken with Solange.

Funny she should be thinking these thoughts now, with a new husband and a new life before her.

How different her first marriage had been. An enormous affair, it had been marked by great public trapping and a total lack of intimacy. She had not known half of the people invited. Ribald jokes had been told and much wine drunk. There had been the usual scamper as the honored guests carried her to her marriage bed. It had been Robert who insisted upon such a grandiose and collective occasion but as soon as the last reveler had left them, he had disappeared behind a door, leaving her quite alone. Alix had sat stiffly on her marriage bed wondering what she had done wrong. Why on earth would her husband not want her? She had been humiliated by the very question. And in the end, so shamed that she had not shared the secret of her marriage night even with her mother, Julian Madrigal.

How could she tell her mother something so terrible? Julian's own husband so worshipped her that Alix had always felt just a little outside the charmed circle of her parents' love. How could she tell her mother that she had already done something so wrong that her wedded husband could not love her? She must discover her fault and rectify it by herself.

She and Robert had left early the next morning for Mercier. But even when Alix discovered the cause of her pain, even when she saw Solange standing bold and beautiful in the courtyard to greet her lord, Alix had not shared her secret with her mother. The pain that she carried was not something one could send home entrusted beneath a pigeon's tail.

Now, a bride once again, Alix glanced over at the altar she had erected to her first husband. She studied the torn and bloody piece of his tunic; she gazed at his jeweled knife and his sword and his golden spurs. The only thing she had not included in this careful composition of his life was any mention of Solange— and yet Solange had *been* his life.

Tears stung Alix's eyes at this thought—a thought that she had fought against and denied and tried to obliterate for so long a time. But she cried now. Not with mourning and she knew it, but with release and acceptance. Solange had been Robert's life and he had died defending her. Yet she, Alix, could have her own life now and with someone who might love her. There was always that hope, she thought, as she heard the knock of her new husband and turned to open the door to him and to her new life.

There was always that hope.

The shrine to Robert de Mercier was the first thing Severin Brigante saw as he entered the chamber of his new wife. Alix noticed his glance at it. She opened her mouth to explain that she had meant to take it down earlier that day and that she wanted to, but he did not seek an explanation. At least he did not ask her for one. Instead he crossed the room and took her icy hands in his warm ones. Alix thought his touch exceedingly fine and something in his gesture made her think again about the deer at Haute Fleur and how they had licked salt from her outstretched fingers as, from behind her, the Knight Brigante whispered exactly what she should do. She hoped he would talk to her again tonight. She hoped he would tell her what to do, as he had then.

"Alix," he began.

She felt his hands upon her shoulders, but they were disquieting, those hands. She took two small steps back.

"You're moving away from me," he said.

Noting it, but letting her do it anyway.

Unfortunately her movements had brought her directly to the side of her enormous bed. It lay serenely before her. A woman's bed, she thought now, filled with lace pillows, and with its linen covers and fur shawls drawn back. Waiting. Inviting. She blushed again as she gazed upon it. Her eyes flew up and caught his steady eyes upon her.

"You've no reason to fear me," he said. "I'll not hurt you. I'll do nothing to you that you do not want."

But what, exactly, did she want?

One, two. Over and done.

It would be exactly as it had been with Robert. Hadn't it always been that way? Wasn't that what lovemaking was?

She climbed in amidst the linen and the lace and sat quite calmly waiting for him. She had been trained this way. She knew what to expect. It would hurt intensely for a moment and then with a dull ache that eventually faded. She wondered if he would want her to raise her gown by herself or if he would do this. Robert had always left this slight chore to her discretion.

She kept her eyes lowered as Severin, without speaking, removed his own clothes and lay in the bed beside her. He was quite naked and this came as somewhat of a shock. She could feel the heat of his body through the crispness of the sheeting. Already she knew he had warmed her bed considerably. He could go even now, and he would still leave behind linen warm to the touch. But he did not touch her and they sat side by side for a moment in silence—a silence that Severin broke.

"Do you always plait your hair at night?" he asked.

She shook her head. "Not when I sleep alone. Robert asked me to plait it. He wanted it that way. I thought you would as well."

"Very different in what we want. Very different," he said. "Do you mind if I loosen it?"

She shook her head. What could she say? No, to this man whom she had promised only that morning to obey forever before both God and man? He could do what he liked with her. Obediently, she turned her back to him and felt his fingers as they gently entangled themselves in the braid she had made. It did not take him long to unravel it. He had loosened it in an instant. She felt the weight of it curtain swiftly down her back. But Severin did not turn her around. Instead, his fingers massaged into the tenseness at her shoulders, kneading with his light touch. Alix felt her muscles loosen swiftly, as her hair had done.

"That's better," he said.

He turned her about then and looked at her curiously. Alix did not like being the object of his scrutiny; she was deathly frightened he would find something about her that was wrong. She would do anything to stop his staring and so, once again, it was she who reached out for the final drawing near.

Soon over, she thought. Soon over and then he will leave me.

But Severin did not seem so intent on quick endings. He reached out with his hands and his mouth to touch her tentatively, to stroke her softly. But this was new to Alix and she did not understand.

She found him aroused. As she had been taught to do, she moved him inside her. He tried but could not stop her. She was determined. She wanted the pain quickly over and done.

Without thinking, Alix found herself matching Severin's rhythm as she took in deep, sharp breaths. The breathing helped, but perhaps not as much as it could have. Sometimes it would catch in her throat. Sometimes it would sigh out of her.

One, two. One, two.

But Severin was not proving to be like anything she had experienced in the past. He did not seem to want things to be over quickly. In fact, instead of pressing quickly toward his release, he slowed his rhythm . . .

. . . And then he kissed her.

But not quickly or brutally. In fact, his kiss seemed much too gentle to come from the lips of a man his size. His lips barely brushed her. The whisper of his breath against her cheek seemed the most violent of his actions upon her body and it fell with a feather's softness. Alix felt her eyes close. She felt herself slipping out of control—and she must not do that. What would happen to her if she once lost control?

She wanted this moment over. It was too much for her, this climb to an unknown precipice too rare. She might die from it, it so overwhelmed her. She could not stand it and so with a woman's movement she reached down to touch him and force him onward. But he was having none of it. He brushed her hand away.

"Not now," he said. "Not yet."

"But when?"

The question wrenched from her, as she heard herself moan. He finished kissing her along her neck and was deep within the folds of her nightdress. He lifted it around her so that it billowed around her face, lightly touching it. She smelt the beauty of her own rose perfume. She felt its lightness all around her fevered face. She was so hot now that even the amulet of her Maltese Star felt warm at her neck. It felt fertile. Alix took in deep, sharp breaths. She could feel the contortions of her face as his lips slid down and down, tracing dampness along her nipples and the sides of her breasts.

He moved within her again and called sounds from her body that were wet and sticky. Loud sounds that embarrassed her and that she had never heard before. She struggled to keep her hands from him, to keep them lying calmly at her side as Robert had always instructed her to do. And there was his wound. She did not want to open it and hurt him again.

But she could not keep her hands quiet, she could not keep them splayed and open. Instead they clutched frantically at the sheet and bunched it within her fingers as once again the movement of her husband's body within her took her to that strange precipice in a faraway land.

"Severin," she moaned, as the first roiling began. It was all she could do—it took all of her efforts—to keep her hands from this man who was doing this to her. To keep them at her side, where her first husband had told her they should be.

The morning's light glimmered against the transparency of her eyelids and Alix marveled at it. It had been

months and months—years even—since she had slept
through a night. But she had slept through this one
and she felt awake and alive. And not at all bruised or
sore.

She did not feel at all as she had ever felt before.

She reached tentatively for Severin but he was not
there. Obviously she had displeased him—or else why
would he have slipped away in the night? She could
remember falling asleep in his arms, she could remember laying her head against the beat of his heart. But
she could not remember his leaving.

Just as well, she told herself. There will be enough
time to see him later. Still . . .

She had expected to awaken with him, to share the
new day's meal together as husband and wife, to plan
together what they would do on this their last day at
Mercier. She realized now that she had expected all of
this. There had been the strangest feeling within her
that this time things were different.

"Silly," she said aloud but even the sound of her
own voice did not reassure her. It sounded too deso-
late, too lonely. She had expected—what exactly had
she expected?

It had been the same thing with Robert.

She remembered last night. She remembered the
way she had moaned, the way she could barely keep
her hands from touching him. Severin had obviously
expected that she act like the well-brought-up noblewoman he had fought for and taken to his bed. She
had not done this, but she must in the future. It was
true that Severin was not Robert, but he had a right
to a chaste wife and it was her duty to be this woman.
She would never let him see her like this again. There
was always that place within her, that place she always
had where she could go to hide. She would see to
Severin's comfort, just as she had always seen to

Robert's. And she would go to this place inside herself to hide—just as she had always done with Robert.

The Knight Brigante was baffled and surly. So much so, that even the powerful Duke of Burgundy stopped his ribald inquiries into the wedding night of the newlyweds and instead gave brisk orders for Sir Severin's departure. He had made it his point to seek him out. Despite his excesses, the duke was in many ways a serious man, determined on his own course and against all others. The business that he had in Italy was serious indeed and for it he needed someone who could be trusted—someone whom *he* trusted.

He found Severin stripped to the waist in the brisk March wind, furiously and repeatedly striking his lance at the quatrain whilst his pages stood huddled in their capes about him. He did this even though he grimaced with the pain from his wounded shoulder.

"Ah," thought the duke. "Not the best of wedding nights. Of course, it never is with a widow. They've had earlier excursions to the fair and they know what they want and how to make comparisons. Indeed, for all her delicacy and youth I think the Lady Alix will one day grow into her own powers. Then poor Brigante will have to ride this pony well if he hopes to make a champion of her."

The duke chuckled to himself at his own witticism but he had seen enough of Severin's grim thrusts to know that the new bridegroom would not appreciate his jollity. Jean of Burgundy had pressing matters to discuss and had no inclination, with war so near, to disrupt his relations with one of the few men in whom he had faith. He settled his face into a serious mien.

"I send you to Italy when I leave and I think it best you take your bride with you," he said, almost as an aside to the Knight Brigante, though it was something he had thought through during the night. "Best to take her from Lancelot's attentions. I owe my half brother much—as he himself constantly reminds me. He saved my life; he did the bloody business of taking Mercier for me. But he has no love for the Lady Alix, especially because she managed to outwit and humiliate him in public by secreting away the Mercier heir. Lancelot does not take well to humiliation. Certainly circumstance has forced him to endure enough of it at my family's hands. Eventually he will get over the loss of the Lady Alix's hand. It will be more difficult for him to get over the blow to his pride. We must give him time to lick his wounds again. You will take your wife into Italy—she will like that. All wives like Italy, either for religious pilgrimage or for the opportunity to buy fine silks. My wife likes it for both."

"It is her home," said Severin shortly. "She was born there. Her father is Count Olivier Ducci Montaldo. He serves the Emperor Sigismund now. Theirs is a great family, going back to Roman times. He is, however, the last of his race. The last of its warrior lords. Or rather, my lady wife is the last of the family—but then, of course, she is no warrior."

"I would not wager upon that," said the duke. He noticed that Severin Brigante was covered with sweat and that it glistened. It was still gray for springtime, gusty and overcast. Jean found himself shivering even beneath his fine cloak and thick boots. He thought the Knight Brigante strong indeed to be so oblivious to the cold. Or perhaps he wasn't and that was the problem. "Your wife seems capable enough of battling her way through threatening situations."

There was no response for this and Jean of Burgundy, his keen eyes narrowing, decided it best to sally down another controversial byway. Severin Brigante had proved himself an able man and loyal—so much so that instinct told Burgundy he could trust him with a very delicate matter indeed.

"Put something on and take a turn with me through the lists. Mercier had let them languish but I see my brother has quickly brought them back in line."

Severin shrugged into a light tunic and fell into step beside the duke. Neither man said anything at first but the silence they shared was a contented one, marred only by the distant shout of one of their men-at-arms and by the high-pitched laughter of a noblewoman in the duke's train. Lancelot de Guigny was nowhere in sight. Nor had he been all morning.

"Gone first to the shrine and then to settle some disturbance amongst the serfs," said the page who had brought word of this to the great duke.

The boy was young and inexperienced—from Gascony, by his accent—the lie did not come easily to him. He blushed. But Burgundy had said nothing to him; indeed, he had rewarded the boy's service with a half coin. The page bowed his thanks and ran off laughing. He would remember this kindness. Jean knew, and his good will might come in handy some day.

"What with war coming," he said aloud.

Severin, who had been lost in his own thoughts, now turned politely toward him. "Did you say something, Lord Jean?"

"Only that this trip to Rome is of the utmost importance," replied the Duke of Burgundy. He kept a pleasant smile upon his face and nodded toward the hills. He did this for the benefit of anyone who might be looking on. The two strolling knights could well have been talking about the weather. "With Henry planning to embark soon at Calais it is of the utmost importance that he receive the pope's blessing in his mission. The King of England's claim to the throne of France is by far the most legitimate. But that will not be enough to guarantee support. There will be firm opposition to the thought of an Englishman— even if he is more Norman French than Anglo-Saxon—sitting upon the throne of such a proud country as our own."

"As *your* own," replied Severin. "I am English."

"But an Englishman born in Italy. Son of an aristocratic father who has as much Norman blood as does Henry V himself, and of a full-Italian mother."

Severin, who rarely spoke of his parents, did not speak of them now.

"And a native Italian speaker is exactly what I have need for in this harrow-time," continued the duke. "An accent—whether it be French or English—will be suspect now. If you ask the questions you must ask, cunning men will carefully sift through them for clues as to your intent."

"But all of Christendom knows that the Gold Company is in thrall to your grace," said Severin. The sweat had completely dried from his face and he looked cool and inscrutable once again. "They will know that you will have directed whatever question I ask."

"Will they?" said the duke. "But you have a wife now, and as you say, the Lady Alix has great interests in Italy. It is her native land. I had thought at first to offer her refuge at my fortress of Dijon but I think differently of it now. She should go with you. She will be a perfect accompaniment. Her visit to her castle at Belvedere might serve as the perfect dodge."

Above them a flock of bright geese flew in strict formation from the south. They were clearly visible below the day's storm clouds.

"Now let us return to our men," said the duke as he laid an amiable hand upon Severin's arm. "How charming that your wife observes us."

* * *

Alix stared at her husband from the secrecy of her chamber window without, she hoped, his knowing she was doing so. His body fascinated her. Amazed by her own brazenness, she watched him as he fought against the quatrain, first stabbing at it with his sword and then drawing back again. He must have been at it for the greater part of a completed sand's run, but she did not stop looking at him in all that time. A thousand things called to her attention. Never before had she allowed herself to spend time merely gazing from a window. She did that now. For the longest time she stared at the linen bandage that swathed his wound. She longed to examine it and wrap it again. She longed to help him.

He had come to her with his wound already skillfully bandaged. He had not asked for her help.

"Lady."

Alix had not heard Young Sophie enter. She jumped away from the window at the sound of the maid's voice and her cheeks flamed.

"We've brought your bath." The girl made a light reverence. "We only waited because we thought . . . because my mother said . . ." Young Sophie blushed. "But she said it had been some time for you and that you would be needing to bathe for the soreness."

"The Knight Brigante left early on. He had much to do to make his men and himself ready." She lowered her voice. "How is your mother?"

Sophie's voice was hushed. "Well, but it is not good to talk about her now—at least not aloud—and not until the way of things has returned to itself. She wants to see you, though. Today if it is possible. She asks that you come to the cottage."

"I was already coming," Alix whispered back, "this afternoon when the castle rests."

They quieted as servants entered with copper pots and steaming tubs of water. The maids at Mercier were well trained and very little was spilled or splashed about as they filled one from the other. Alix sat upon a trestle stool as Sophie went to the chamber chests. She watched as the maid picked through the dried flowers and herbs and strewed them about the steaming water. She realized that her body did ache and that she could still feel Severin upon it. She could feel him in it—in her. Furtively, she raised her wrist to her nose and turned the delicate skin to see if she could still smell him as well. She could.

Sophie, watching her, stifled a giggle. "My mother said it would be a good thing to make your water hot. She said you might need it."

"As indeed I do," replied Alix, lowering herself into it with a burst of secret gratitude. "I have much to talk about with the knight—with my husband. He will be leaving for Italy today with the duke and I know he will want to give instructions as to where I should be placed in his absence. Perhaps to Picardy—there is rumored to be quite a good convent there. My mother once knew a noble lady of Venice who was imprisoned in it."

"To a convent?" Sophie stopped arranging Alix's tunic and turned to face her mistress. "Have you not heard?"

"Heard what?" questioned Alix, genuinely perplexed. In the last two days it seemed that she had heard nothing that was not destined to drastically change her destiny. She wondered if all of life with Severin would be like that. For what seemed years and years—an eternity, really—nothing had happened to change the placid pace of her life. And now she was almost wearied with novelty. "Do not tell me that Lancelot de Guigny has decided to accompany my husband into Italy."

This had been the last piece of gossip she heard from the duke's ladies last night just before hearing the more startling revelation of her own imminent wedding to the Knight Brigante.

"But don't you know?" Sophie seemed both appalled and delighted by this fact. Her face turned quite red with the import of fresh news. "Have they not told you?"

She had displeased Severin. He was sending her away now, not just for the duration of his absence but for good.

Alix's mind whirled with the obviousness of it. Had he not left her during the night just as Robert had always done?

But she was calm when she questioned Sophie once again. "Tell me what gossip you have heard in the kitchens."

"Not in the kitchens." There was a note of triumph in Sophie's voice as she replied. "The Knight Brigante came to our cottage this morning himself. Himself—he did even mandate one of his men. He asked my mother if she would agree to go to Haute Fleur. He thinks it best for her there—and perhaps not safe at all for her to remain here. No one knows how that monster Guigny will act once the duke is no longer around to hold him tame." Sophie grew even more conspiratorial. "But he asked my mother if she could spare me . . ."

"Spare *you?*"

". . . to go to Italy."

"My husband wants to take you with him into Italy?" Alix was amazed at the quick tide of jealousy that roiled through her. "But of course he must need help in the journey for his cooking, for his . . ."

"He is taking me for you."

"For me?"

"Because you are to accompany him to Italy. He is taking you to your first home at Belvedere."

The new Lady Brigante did not see her husband for the rest of the day, nor did he send word to her of her changed circumstances. She heard nothing more either of him or from him. The list field below her chamber window was quite empty of him as well. She knew this because she looked.

Once her bathing was finished, she was summoned to join the other first ladies of Burgundy as they worked together on a tapestry that was eventually to belong to the dowager duchess, who had accompanied her favorite son. It was an enormous affair, an elaborate bucolic scene of unicorns and flute players and flowering trees, which the duchess was heavily working in silvers and golds. The tapestry pattern had been copied from a similar work at Cluny, a monastery that had been heavily endowed by her husband, the late duke. Philip the Bold, father of Jean the Fearless, wanted Masses prayed every day *in perpetua* for the salvation of his soul. Considering the crimes that were most assuredly upon it, many considered this a wise investment of gold florins. A merciful God might indeed be persuaded to show compassion to one who was known to have committed more than his share of grave sins—but it was deemed best to have constant prayers said instead. After all, Philip was not called "The Bold" for no reason. The old duke had been as notorious and blood-thirsting in his day as his son was now in his. Philip the Bold had left it to his widow to ensure that the purchased prayers were said by keeping one of the Cluny monks beside her continually—as rather a hostage, or so the gossip went.

Now that she had married "away," Alix was no longer chatelaine of Mercier and would have duties only if Lancelot de Guigny—she still could not think of him as the Count de Mercier, although she determined to be scrupulous in addressing him as such—should ask for her assistance. He did not do so, leaving Alix with no excuse to absent herself from the dowager duchess and her ladies. For this reason, she spent her first full day of married life with the ladies, pulling precious threads through flax under the watchful eye of the dowager.

Alix, who had a genuine fondness for needlework, found herself bored to distraction. She was also quite nervous. Every time there was a movement at the tapestry that divided this small room from the others—when a servant entered with the refreshment of mint water or a page came in with a message for his powerful mistress—she jumped and whirled in that direction. Not even the sly nudgings and whispers of the other women proved strong enough to serve as a deterrent.

But no word came from her new husband and he did not appear.

"No, my dear, the silver is run here, not there. A strand through green grace hardly makes sense, now does it?"

The dowager's voice was serene and the others giggled. Her daughter-in-law said, "I, too, was like this on the days after my wedding. I could barely sit still and wiggled about much of the day even after the pine-pin bath my nurse prescribed. I had my nurse with me because I was barely out of swaddling when I found myself wed."

"God's tooth—a century ago!" one of her friends said to the general merriment.

"I married a good ten years after your own wedding

date," replied the duchess sweetly and then continued, "but the herbal bath could not heal me. I could barely sit—but still could not wait for nightfall . . ."

She paused delicately for the general hilarity before she continued.

"I've heard 'tis different at a second briding—the woman being more knowledgeable and therefore less carried away by the pleasure—but judging from the new Lady Brigante I should think that not the case."

"Perhaps because the lady has finally been mounted by a man known to be an expert in the saddle?" A voice came from the far reaches of their charmed circle. There were the expected gasps and giggles and a gentle tut-tut from the formidable dowager—who was known to still harbor a colt's tooth within her own carefully dyed head. No groom was safe near her, and few pages.

Alix said nothing. She kept her eyes suitably on her tapestry work very careful by now to work the green places with green silks. But the fact that she was silent only inflamed the teasing more.

"Indeed," joined in another voice. "But no one seems to know of his expertise. The Knight Brigante appears a serious man, with little interest in the distractions that we women know so well how to afford. There are few rumors concerning him, and no gossip. Which is remarkable when one thinks how truly attractive he is."

"Such broad shoulders!"

"Such lovely hands!"

"Eyes that make one want to smolder and die!"

"Not to mention . . ."

The chorus of women stopped in anticipation that perhaps the new Lady Brigante might enlighten them on her new husband's other, more intimate, attractions.

She would not.

Soon another log was tossed upon the conversational fire.

"Much has been rumored," said a bright voice with the strong accent of Normandy, "and perhaps more anticipated. But I hear, my Lady Brigante, that your husband is the only noble without a harelip and hunchback who has not found his way into the queen's bedchamber."

" 'Twould be easier to discover a live unicorn in a mudland," another chimed, "than to find a noble who has not slept with the queen."

The dowager raised a carefully arched eyebrow. Her heavily be-ringed fingers did not pause at their task as she captured Alix within the cunning of her gaze. Her thin lips were heavily rouged in vermilion. She drew them back into a cat's smile. "We should not tease the Lady Alix. But then, after Robert de Mercier . . ."

The dowager let her voice trail for the length of two pulls of silk through canvas, in obvious hope that Alix would take up the subject of the man who had so publicly shunned her and who now lay dead. But still Alix did not speak, though she flushed slightly. Once again the dowager duchess was forced to conversational ferreting.

"Robert de Mercier was cold fire indeed, if you ask me—much romance but perhaps not quite enough actual passion. What is it our friends in Lombardy say—a great deal of smoke but not very much heat. I was never one to believe the troubadour fantasies that made his dalliance with Solange into a *grand romance*. One has only to look at our host to see the errors of *those* ways. It is an easy path indeed to satisfy a woman who looks upon you as a god and whose whole family and future are dependent upon the power of your caprices. 'Tis much harder indeed to make a woman love you when you are that woman's equal."

"Or if that woman is your better and can exercise her powers for your advancement," added the brisk voice of an attractive red-haired lady. "As the queen has so often done. And perhaps has even done with the Knight Brigante. There was no whiff of scandal about him, but certainly his swift advancement to generalship of the Gold Company was noted. He is still a young man."

Alix jumped to her feet. The fine threads that the dowager duchess had so carefully apportioned to her fell in a jumble to her feet.

"Severin obtained his position because of diligence and hard work. My husband did not sleep with the queen in order to advance himself. He would not bed a lady who has taken vows of any kind. He is not that type of man!" Alix was surprised by her own indignation.

"Well answered!" called out the frisky Countess of Cahors. "The Lady Brigante well defends her sword-bought husband. His must have been a good ride indeed!"

The others roared with laughter, and there were giggles from the serving girls who lined the walls waiting for instructions from their mistresses. Even the good monk from Cluny, who was deeply involved in calculations for the dowager's astrological chart, could not quite stifle a giggle. Alix felt no doubt about the redness of her face. The heat of it actually burned her eyebrows.

"Now, now," said the duchess as the last of the hilarity died away. "We must not tease the new bride. These are ribald French ways that the young Lady Alix may not understand—though how she could have grown up at the Emperor Sigismund's court and not be familiar with every known salacious custom is beyond me. I knew him in his youth and he was an excellent mountsman. You can take my experienced word in the matter."

Again there was a general outburst of female merriment. The dowager reached over to pat Alix's hand.

"But at least we must give credit where it is due. The Lady Brigante defends the right husband. She held on stoically whilst we talked of Robert and Solange. But when we said a word against the Knight Brigante she was fast upon her feet and that's a surety."

"Here! Here!" called out a bright female voice. "The Lady has found her true rider at last!"

This time even the monk laughed outright. Alix wished fervently that she could die.

But was it true? Had she made such a swift change in loyalty from one husband to the next? Had she lost all sense of loyalty to Robert de Mercier, who had married her and gifted her with one of the grandest names in Christendom—as he had repeatedly told her himself? Could Severin's kiss and his touch have so quickly robbed her of a lifetime's way of thinking?

And who, indeed, was her new husband? Who was the man who had wrought these great changes?

Alix asked herself this as she tramped back and forth through the small garden that lay within the castle keep. The day had warmed considerably and the espaliered trees that lined the gray walls had felt its gentle message. She could not be still. She walked back and forth, her feet beating a path through the thawing earth.

"I saw something."

Without conscious thought she remembered the Wise Woman's words.

Alix glanced quickly around, then walked purposefully to the portcullis and the path beyond it that led to the village. Her husband may not have thought to tell her his plans for her, but there was one who would know them—and who would tell.

"It might still be dangerous for you to be here, Lady," whispered Young Sophie as she looked around.

" 'Tis more dangerous for you that I am here than for me," replied Alix. She took her hand. "But I wanted to come before your mother left for Haute Fleur. Is that not where you said she was going? Am I arrived in time?"

Sophie nodded. "She is going but is still here and doing better. I know this because it has become impossible to keep her within the cottage walls—she insists on being at the brook or in the garden. Maybe the monks will do better with her; they are used to dealing with recalcitrant souls."

"At the brook?" repeated an astonished Alix, remembering to what extent Sophie had been reduced by the tortures of Lancelot de Guigny.

"She does better," said Sophie. "Follow this pathway through the trees and it will lead you to her."

Only a few small willows bordered the brook but they were in full green, casting sweet shadows as the spring sunlight dappled through their leaves. It fell upon Sophie the Wise Woman, who sat on an old flax bag with her feet dangling into the icy water. Without looking up, she motioned Alix to join her.

Alix fully believed that she had been expected.

"You are looking better," she said, wiggling down onto the brook bank. She looked at the inviting and rippling water but did not have the courage to pull off her own pattens and swing her feet.

"I am better," said Sophie. Already her voice had lost its hoarse grate. "He had me but a few days and so he could not do much damage. They kept the Templars years and years within the prisons before they were broken."

"I hear you are going to Haute Fleur."

Sophie nodded. Although the Wise Woman did indeed look better—she had even taken on a bit of suncolor in the day since her release—still Alix could see the effort that this nodding caused her. Looking closely, she glimpsed the rough mark of a pulled noose upon the other woman's neck. It was rumored that a woman innocent of witchcraft could not be hanged by a rope so this was a torture sanctioned by the Inquisition and thus able to be used by any man for any purpose. She could only imagine what Sophie had suffered at Guigny's hands.

"You will be safe with the monks," Alix said.

Sophie smiled and for a second the old radiance glowed from her face. "They made a place for Yvrain so perhaps there will be one for me as well—at least for a time. Although by all that is holy those monking men know more what to do with a small boy baby than they will with a full-grown and sufficient female.."

Both women laughed at the truth of this.

"They will pester me for the good of my soul," said Sophie, "but I will be kept safe with them. And with war coming there is need for all of us to be safe. Henry of England will assuredly land at Calais; the English have held it for almost a hundred years. He will embark there, but only to move on Paris. Mercier lies on his path, either as help or hindrance. He will need to take it. It was a kind thought on the part of the Knight Brigante to move me to a safe place. An escort of his men will take me there tomorrow. He is a kind man, Sir Severin—perhaps too kind for his own good."

A soft wind rustled the leaves overhead. Sophie looked up at them and frowned.

"Your husband is taking you with him into Italy."

Now it was Alix's turn to frown. "This is the news that Young Sophie brings me. He has asked her to accompany us but he has said no word of his plans to me."

"You do not talk," said the Wise Woman, "and this is not good. But at least you have the Power. It is growing strong in you and you must listen to its guidance."

Alix touched the amulet at her throat. "Is it this?" she questioned. "Is it this that gives me the Power?"

"A little," said the Wise Woman. "Some small part of it—though certainly not all. You must trust that it does not give you all."

The leaves above their heads rustled once again and Sophie leaned closer. She gripped Alix tightly upon the arm with her disfigured hands.

"You must go with your husband to Rome. Make no mistake about that," said Sophie with new urgency. "You will be safe with the Knight Brigante—or at least safe enough. In Rome you will meet a Silver Man. I have seen him, and this much I know. Though whether he is good or bad for you—that I cannot tell. You will know. But one thing is certain, you must hold tight to your husband. He is your protection. And you are his."

Alix did not see her husband at all on the first full day of her marriage. Nor did he join the duke's company for the evening's feast.

" 'Tis I who have made a day's widow out of you," said a complacent Burgundy as he sat beside her. "I have sent him to his army. He leaves for Rome in but two days, and you go with him. But of course you know that. He must have told you so himself. He insists that you accompany him, though I have offered you the succor within the safety of my own fortress at Dijon. At least now that you can no longer call Mercier your home."

From across the table, Lancelot de Guigny smiled. He had returned that afternoon from his mission and was dressed with exceptional elegance: his tunic of light, fine wool and bright, new rings at his fingers. In dress at least, he made a resplendent Count de Mercier. His smile brightened as his gaze shifted directly to his half brother. The two men seemed to have repaired any damage left from their quarrel.

"The Lady Brigante will always have a bed and a warm welcome here at Mercier," he said now with great affability. "We will let bygones be bygones. In the end we have both got what we wanted. She is free of me—and I have freehold to Mercier."

"Will have," said his brother, leaning across to spear a piece of roasted pork with his knife. "As soon as our cousin comes from England and we are assured of victory."

Alix, watching the Knight de Guigny beneath the shelter of her lashes, saw his jaw tighten, but when he spoke again his voice was just as pleasant and affable as it had been before.

"Indeed," he called loudly. "Then that means I shall take title to Mercier mightily quick!"

Guigny's words called forth a thunder of knives and pewter mugs pounding against the table as the knights and the ladies of Burgundy beat out their approbation of Henry's coming. Their duke looked around with his quick, dark eyes and he smiled.

Alix could not wait to get away and she asked for an escort to her chamber as soon as this was decently possible. No one was allowed to leave before the duke, who seemed set to make a long night of it, but Alix demurely fell back on her newlywed status and he excused her with a wink and a hand pat.

"Your husband is busy with his army now," he assured her. "But he will come back with the night. He is quite besotted with you."

Alix said nothing, but she doubted this.

The first thing she saw as the chamber door closed behind her was the altar to Robert de Mercier. She had forgotten it during her busy day but cleaning maids had not. They had been instructed by the Dame de Mercier to care for it and they continued to obey her instructions. The trestle was clean of dust, as was the mantle that had lain beside Robert at his desk and still had the dried stains of his blood upon it. The heft of his jeweled dagger gleamed, and the candles were lit.

Alix, gazing upon it, was appalled. She remembered the strange look on Severin's face last night when he had come to her. She remembered how he had hesitated. Now she understood the reason for this. What man could sleep next to his new bride with a dead man's relics looking on? Alix stepped swiftly across her chamber to blow its candles out, throw open storage chests, and pack the knife and the mantle and the candleholders away.

Robert de Mercier was no longer her husband; Severin Brigante was.

Alix called a young maid and, with this help, bathed herself and put on her night tunic. She settled on a trestle to await the husband she knew would appear. She had no doubt but that he would come to her. He did not want a white marriage; he had told her this himself. She imagined he wanted to breed her, just as Robert had done. Though she had to admit loving was different with Severin. It did not hurt, as it had with Robert. In fact, parts of it had been quite pleasurable. Alix remembered Severin's hands as they explored her. She remembered his tongue on her breasts and running along the skin of her neck and she blushed.

It had been all she could do to act the lady he had married. It had been all she could do to keep her hands at her sides, as she had been trained.

Alix reached for one of her parchment books to find once again the comfort she had always found within their pages. She sifted for a while, but she found no solace. Soon, she put it aside and stood up to pace the floor.

She was nervous, she realized. And she was angry. At Robert. At herself. At Severin.

She didn't care.

She never did when the rage came upon her. She never had. It surged with its own life to wash over her like a flooding tide.

Alix had never spoken of this rage except to her priest—she had been too ashamed and too frightened. Even with her confessor she had made light of the fury and taken the fault of it to herself. It was obvious that she suffered the sin of pride, which was, of course, the sin of Lucifer's falling. Her pious priest had agreed with her. Robert had chosen him to do just this.

Many women suffered much in life, he had assured her. A husband who took another woman to his bed was really not such a heavy cross to bear. Especially when one was helped to bear it by the addition of jewels and costly silks. Many women—most women— bore the same burden with less consolation.

He had winked at his young charge as he said this, and had gently patted her hand.

His assurance had done nothing to stop the rages, though. They would come over Alix with tidal force when she least expected them—just as the memory was coming over her now. She would be sitting and thinking and the next minute she would be overcome with hatred. She would hate the maid, or hate the dog. She would hate the way the tapestry hung upon her wall or the way the sunlight hit it. Everything or nothing triggered her silent rages. She could not control them. Her only consolation was that neither did they control her. She had always remembered who she was—the Countess de Mercier, wife of one great peer and daughter of another. She had been raised as a lady. She must just accept her lot. The rages came and she forgot them, methodically, once they had passed.

She never located their origins. She did not do this now.

Instead, she walked through her room. Back and forth, her feet kicking at the dried thyme on its floor.

Severin had left her before morning, just as Robert always had. He had spent the first day of their married life with the duke and his army, not with her. He had told even the Wise Woman that he planned to take his new wife with him into Italy—but he had yet to tell the new wife herself.

Talk to your husband, the Wise Woman had whispered.

But how could she do this? What would she say?

Back and forth. Back and forth tramped the new Lady Brigante.

Waiting for a new husband who promised to be much like the last.

Seventeen

Well, he would have to do it. Severin managed to stay away from his wife for the whole day although he watched her from afar. He had seen her tramp alone back and forth, wearing a path through the greening garden and then go through the wicket and hurry down past the village. He knew she had visited the Wise Woman by the side of the brook. One of his men-at-arms had told him this. Severin was happy to hear it. He trusted few women but he trusted Sophie and he was happy that Alix spent time with her. He thought she might learn interesting things. Certainly the Wise Woman would have told his wife that he planned to take her with him into Italy.

He was less content to know that she had spent time with the dowager and her ladies. Mercier, like all castles, was a hive of gossip. The Knight Brigante had been told what was said.

He rode her well.

Troubadours, true gossips, would already be composing some ditty. Severin hated that Alix had been compelled to listen to such silly twaddle and he wanted to cut the viper tongue right out of the woman who had said it. Alix and her feelings should not be so easily trifled.

Still . . .

She had defended him vigorously. She had not allowed aspersions to his honor. Why she had done this, he would not imagine. During their first night together, she had not touched him. His wife had not once raised her hands from the bed.

The idea that people would gossip that he had slept with a queen, a married woman, was repulsive to him. He would never do such a thing—not after his own lonely childhood and the laughter concerning his runoff mother. He had no desire to do to another child's mother that which had so carelessly been done to his.

Again he caught himself thinking of his mother as he walked the long corridor to his wife's rich chamber. How many years had she been gone now? Why had she left him? These are questions he had run from in the past and still fled now. But the day was coming when he would have to face them.

Once he arrived in Rome.

Once he met the Silver Man.

Once that man told him the truth about the Maltese Star, and about his mother.

Chiara Conti, his mother, remained nothing to him but a blurred memory of fine lace and silk and sweet scents. He did not even know if the memory was true. He could not remember loving his mother, though perhaps he had. There had been flashes of her in all the women he had been with.

Even in Alix. The silks were the same and the lace and the warm scent. Alix could be extravagant and Severin knew it, just as Chiara had been. They were so similar in their tastes and in what they wanted. In some ways they even shared the Maltese Star. But there was a difference and Severin knew this. He could not name the difference nor distinguish it, but he knew it to be essential.

The difference—whatever it was—was the real reason he had married his wife.

His wife. This woman who would not touch him. Who came to him from duty and from nothing more.

Last night he had made love to her for the first time with the candle from her dead husband's shrine twinkling at him through the gloom. She had kept her hands quite at her side; she had not once reached to him or touched him.

For the first time in his life, Severin Brigante, the great *condotierre* of the Gold Company, wished that he were a hard-drinking man.

If only . . .

If only what? he asked himself as his honor guard accompanied him to the chamber of his young bride. They had not even asked his pleasure. They had just assumed that a new bridegroom who had been busy during the day with the needs of his men would now gladly attend to the needs of his wife. Without being told, they passed the room that had been assigned to him by Lancelot de Guigny—that small one with its single cot bed upon which no wife could join him in—and down the narrow stone hallways of Mercier Castle.

As they drew nearer and the torches in the sconces grew few, Severin thought of what lay before him, of how it had been last night and how he wanted it tonight. She had come to him willingly enough, her body had yielded to his knowing fingers. She had cried out when he wanted that response from her and she had moved against him when he wanted that as well. He had done everything right. He had never lost control. Even when she came swiftly against him, almost as though she wanted the whole thing over and done. The thought niggled at him.

She had not enjoyed their lovemaking. She had not enjoyed *him*.

This was the true reason Severin had kept himself busy during the day executing orders that a lieutenant

could easily have performed. The duke had given orders and Severin could easily have given these to someone else. He hadn't. Even his young pages had giggled
at him.

He was Severin Brigante the *condottiere* general of a
great army. And he was afraid of his wife.

It was even harder this time for Alix to act the lady,
harder to keep her hands at her sides when he touched
her, even harder not to moan aloud. But she managed.
She expected that he would say something to her. She
lay beside her husband and listened to his ragged
breath and the beating of his heart as it stilled. Perhaps
he would thank her; occasionally Robert had done just
that. In her depths she wanted to hear that she had
pleased Severin. She wanted to ask why he had gone
from her bed last night. She had tried her best to keep
her body still and to breathe deeply. No man who
thought he had married a lady would want a wanton.

Or would he?

In his sleep, Severin Brigante moved his arm to embrace his wife. She lay beside him, frowning into the
dark.

The once-great chatelaine of the Castle de Mercier
wished she had someone in whom she could confide.
Someone who knew about men and what they wanted.
She desperately needed to know what she was doing
wrong and why she had not pleased either of her hus-
bands. She thought of the dowager duchess or one of
her ladies but immediately put that thought away. They
were *too* knowing. Even a woman of the street might
be shocked at what these great ladies of Burgundy said.
Besides, Alix knew they could hold no secret. They
would blazon her secrets from one end of France to
the other.

She did not want this.

The unexpected thought came that she could talk to Severin about this. They had talked of many things together in the past. They had been friends once, she remembered, when she had given him the reading lessons. When they had been in the forest. When their bodies had not yet touched intimately, but their souls had. But she quickly dismissed this idea. She could never discuss anything so shocking as lovemaking with a man. Even if that man were her husband—*especially* if that man were her husband.

Marriage to Robert had taught her this.

"We go to Rome," Severin said. "I have asked the duke if I might take you with me and he has given his permission."

Alix glanced up from her early morning mending, unsure exactly what she should say.

Talk to him.

It was an astonishing idea.

"I know this," she said finally. "The duke told me already, as did the Wise Woman."

"Indeed," said her husband. He looked relieved.

Alix was not. She had slept little and awakened with a dull ache behind her eyes.

"Why didn't you tell me yourself?" she asked. "Why did I have to hear it from others first?"

For an instant Severin looked genuinely astonished, and in that instant Alix thought he looked quite young. Little older than she herself was.

"It never occurred to me to tell you myself," he said. He walked to the window and stared out at his men before speaking again.

"I thought you would have preferred to receive the news from Burgundy. It seemed like an honor."

Now it was Alix's turn to be astounded.

"You thought I would have preferred to hear this news from someone other than you?"

"Not just *someone,* the duke." Severin turned back to her, his face flushed. "I thought you would be honored."

Alix almost laughed aloud at the notion of this. Despite the fact that he was her liege lord, she had not formed a good impression of the Duke of Burgundy when she had first met him. His visit to Mercier had not changed her opinion.

But she did not say this to Severin now. She had no idea what she had done to offend him, but she had to find out. She could not go back to the rage and the pain that she had lived with throughout her marriage to Robert de Mercier.

This had to be different.

"Now that I am married, I could return to my parents until you claim me," she said. "Or I could wait for you in the convent."

"I will have you with me," he answered. He began to pace the floor in the same way she had paced last night. "I go to Italy and your home is there. Would you not like to see it once again?"

"The duke has invited me to Dijon. The dowager has offered me a place among her women."

"Would you go with her?" Severin stopped in midstride. He looked genuinely horrified.

"No," Alix answered thoughtfully. "I don't think I should like her court."

"Good." Severin did not turn to face her as he pulled on his tunic and studded belt, as he strapped on his sword. "We are wedded now. I will keep my vows to you but I want no white wedding. You are my wife. You stay with me. If the Gold Company returns to Italy then you must return with it."

"Yes, Severin."

Alix wanted to ask him why he wanted her near him when he spent his days away from her and when he had others tell her his plans. She decided against it. They were talking again; at least she had that. The rest could come later.

After all, they had been married but two days' time.

"However . . ."

Severin was looking down at her from his great height. "There are certain things that you must get used to. You are no longer the wife of a grand lord. I am but a simple knight and must work hard to provide for both you and my men. It is my responsibility to see that their needs are met. At the best of times the land required to equip a Knight of Burgundy is almost four thousand acres. Few of my men have resources such as this but in their turn they must pay for their equipment, their squires, and their men-at-arms. I want the Gold Company to be the best—just as it was when your father commanded it. Therefore I must be willing to make up the deficit."

Alix faced her husband squarely. "Neither was my father a wealthy man when he took on the Gold Company. The resources of his family had been destroyed to pay his ransom from the Sultan; his Castle of Belvedere lay in ruins."

"But Oliver Ducci Montaldo had regained that fortune by the time you were born," said Severin. "You have never known want."

He glanced around at the affluence of her rich chamber.

"My life has not been so easy as you might suppose," Alix said. "I did not even meet my father until I was all of five years. Before that I lived alone with my mother. She served as a village Wise Woman—hardly a profitable venture. But you are right on one count.

I would like to see Belvedere again. I would like to see my home."

"Then I would like to take you there," said Severin. An unexpected smile softened his face. He crossed to the door but hesitated there and turned back. "I have another reason for taking you with me to Rome. There is a man there who possesses knowledge about your family, and my own. Probably more than any other living person, he understands the secret of the Maltese Star."

"A man in Rome? But my mother never journeyed south of Tuscany; neither did her mother. As far as I know—as far as my mother told me—my grandmother fled directly from France to seek shelter in the east. They thought her a witch in Lyon. They would have burned her at the stake."

"Yet my own father learned of this amulet in Rome," said Severin, watching her closely. "He was given it by a powerful man. One thought dead for many years now."

"A dark man with a limp," said Alix quietly. She had no idea what had prompted these words, yet she knew them to be true.

Severin nodded. "My father called him the Silver Man."

"But he is dead?"

Again he nodded.

"Who killed the man?"

"My father," Severin said. He opened the door then, and disappeared through it.

Eighteen

Of course she was making comparisons and Severin knew it. How could she not be? *He* was comparing, and in every way he did, Robert de Mercier came out the better man. He had been handsome and wealthy and from a grand lineage. His lands stretched out in all directions, much farther than even the eye could see. Living in his castle day by day, seeing what a cultivated man he had been, had weighed on Severin.

He would be happy to leave this place.

Again he labored diligently through the day and well into the early evening. Work had always been a solution to him for any problem and he embraced it with a vengeance. He issued orders to his men concerning their next day's departure. He listened to petitions, heard hardship pleas, and dispensed money. He decided which knights he could safely leave behind at Mercier and on what pretext.

Severin had no faith in Guigny. He knew the man must be watched.

But for once, he found, work was not enough. It could not completely keep his mind from roaming to the thought of his new wife. He saw her eyes as he ordered the animals packed and made decisions as to what his army would need to carry with them over the Alps. He felt the silk of her skin beneath his fingers whilst ensuring that there were mangonels and giant catapults and seige engines ready for the great battle that his warrior instinct told him was soon to come. He snapped at his men, calling Sergio di Palermo a fool for leaving a sack of nails on the newly constructed barbicans that had been erected for Mercier's defense.

Sergio looked at him with wonder, and then with amusement.

"Love," his men mouthed behind his back with a roll of their eyes and a shrug. Severin was known as a good general—the Gold Company had always been well generaled in its history—and they knew he would come to himself soon.

"But you told me just the opposite not one hour's time back, my lord!"

Severin heard this exclamation more than once during the course of his day's occupations. It didn't matter; each time he heard it he was instantly ashamed. In the past he had been strong in his disapproval of generals who had to shout before they were obeyed. He much preferred a softer discipline.

It didn't help that he knew they laughed at him behind his back. "The new bridegroom." They put it all down to the happiness of his wedded state with the Lady Alix. If they only knew how little happiness his wedded life was actually bringing to him. He loved his wife, but he had sword-won her. Severin was under no illusion that the Lady Alix would have married him had she not been threatened with her husband's murderer in his stead.

Severin strode through the castle's inner curtain. He needed to return to Italy, that was all. Once he was in his own country again he would be able to better understand the drastic step he had taken.

His blood froze and stopped in his tracks.

He had no home, not really. No place to take a new wife, especially one like the Lady Alix—a woman who

had been always spoiled and cosseted and even controlled by expensive gifts and bright and pretty objects.
And he had no things to offer her. She might sweetly
agree when he told her of the knight-costs he paid.
She might mention a childhood where riches had
played no part. But, while still young, the Lady Alix
was hardly a child. Could she possibly understand just
how poor she would be? For years now Severin had
carried his home about with him. It consisted of a
small bed and a few chests—and, of course, his armor
and his weapons and his horse. He doubted his new
wife would consider this an adequate life.

Severin glanced once more at the luxury that surrounded him. Certainly it was a hive of purposeful activity. Foot soldiers scurried to follow his commands,
carrying light arms and swords and armor before them
in wooden bayard wagons. On the castle bulwark, men
scurried to remove the *oriflamme* from the ramparts of
Mercier Castle. The duke had explicitly ordered this.
The sacred banner of St. Denis, a banderole of two
points of red and orange silk, had been attached to a
lance and presented by King Louis the Saint to an illustrious Count de Mercier for his aid in the Second
Crusade. This had been immediately struck and
packed deep away when Burgundy had entered the
castle. Originally the banner had been given by the
hands of the Abbot of St. Denis into the king's own
hands when he had taken the Cross and set out for
Outremer, the Holy Land. The duke wanted no re-
minders that any Mercier had vowed allegiance to any
king of France—though everyone, including peasants,
knew full well that they had been doing just this for
hundreds of years.

But the only thing Duke Jean wanted remembered
was that Robert de Mercier was his vassal and that he
had died in revolt against his liege lord.

Late in the day the duke called for Severin once again. They sat together in the castle's Great Hall with the afternoon sun piercing through the small panes of its windows and the banners of defeated armies fluttering gently over their heads.

"You are ready then?" said Jean of Burgundy.

Severin shrugged. "As ready as can be expected. My men have worked hard and without complaint. 'Tis always an easy chore to go home."

"They will be back soon enough," said the duke. " 'Tis but one week 'til May Month. Henry will leave Britain soon for Calais. That will be his initiating point. The English have held that foothold for a good many years now. You go to Italy now—but you will not remain there. Seek the pope's support and return as soon as you obtain it. I will have need of you, as will King Henry."

A page brought spiced wine but the duke declined it, as did the Knight Brigante.

"See the pope," said the duke once they were again alone. "Gain his approval. You are still determined to keep your wife with you?"

Severin nodded.

"That is well. She will need safekeeping. I offered her hospitality as did my mother, but it is better that the Lady Alix stay with you. You will keep her out of harm's way. Accidents have been known to happen to those who thwart our brother Lancelot." Burgundy paused as though considering this. "He wanted the Lady Alix for himself."

"He wanted the Maltese Star," replied Severin.

The duke sat silently for a moment. The noise of an army breaking camp echoed into them from the castle's outer rings.

"Perhaps in the beginning," replied Burgundy. "And perhaps that is still the most important thing to him. But the lady counts also in this matter. My brother wanted *her.*"

Severin said nothing to this. There was nothing to say.

"I would also keep a keen eye to my own flank if I were you. Lancelot spends a great deal of his time in prayer and fasting. He has become quite the guest at the shrine to St. Bernard. He mentions miracles. His is an unexpected conversion—indeed, coming at this particular moment, it is quite unique. I intend to keep a close eye upon my brother. In fact, it is for that reason that I have sent him to examine the fortifications of my castle at Dijon. I want him kept near where I can keep him under close watch. With war coming, it might behoove me to learn just exactly what it is within my brother that has been so suddenly and profoundly transformed. One can never be too careful where treachery is concerned."

The two men sat a little longer in silence. There was no need to discuss the meaning behind the duke's words.

Never in her life had Alix worked with such diligence. With both the Gold Company and the Duke of Burgundy quitting Mercier Castle on the morrow, all of the maids and the men were occupied with one group or the another. Help had even been brought in from the village. Alix managed to find two girls who, along with Young Sophie, helped her with the packing of all that must now be taken to her new home. The things from Mercier belonged to the castle and its new seneschal. Still, she had her own dowry and though she could not hope for the gold coins that it included, she did not think Lancelot de Guigny would begrudge her what would legally be forfeit to her now. More importantly she had the beaten silver and the pewter, the laced linens and the fox throws, the pottery and the herbs and all the other wealth she had brought with her from Hungary into France. All of this needed packing and crating. She would need to make another castle habitable. She would need to make another place into a home.

Alix had never thought herself one to dress with extravagance and was thus surprised to discover that the packing of her tunics and mantles and pattens took up five enormous chests. Her mother had given her a scrolled steel tub for bathing and, of course, this must be carted and taken as well. Severin had not yet told her where they would settle but she hoped for Belvedere. Her own first home had been much upon her mind lately. She knew there was no bathing tub at Belvedere.

The four women toiled well into the afternoon. Alix opened hemp packets that she had brought with her and had not opened since her arrival. She sorted cloths and linens. She put pieces of the same silver together. Dust whooped up from the packets and covered her apron and the wimple she had wrapped around her head. At first she wiped sweat from her brow with lace-edged linen but she lost it in the confusion that engulfed her chamber and started wiping the sweat from her brow with the back of her hand. She felt it trickle down her spine and into the hollow of her back. The muslin apron clung to her work tunic.

"He could have told me before," she mumbled, even though she knew this was not true. Two days ago they had not even been married. How could he have warned her that she would have to leave for Italy with such short notice? He had not even known himself. Rationally she knew this but emotionally she was still quite angry with her new husband. One morning's conversation had not changed this.

But at least it had done something. Severin had smiled at her once again. She had felt him ease back, if just a little, to the happy times on the rampart when the magic had opened, and they had watched symbols change into words.

Alix missed their reading lessons. She hoped, one day soon, to start them again.

" 'Tis mine the washing water," snapped one of the maids. "If you want more you should go to the well and get it yourself."

"Yours is that mess there, splashed all about on the paving. Go yourself and get more of it. I've gone out to the well five times now."

Alix would have stopped the fighting but she remembered her pigeons.

"We must take them with us," she said wearily to an equally weary Sophie. "They are well trained and they might be useful. We cannot leave them for Lancelot de Guigny."

Alix said this with a shudder. It was the castle's rumor how the Knight de Guigny had stuck a knife into the heart of his prized falcon. No one would want to leave an animal under his dominance. The pigeons were fetched and brought down. Naturally, they needed food for their journey and straw for at least one change in the coops. Alix had no idea how long it took to get to Italy and she did not know the way of her journey. How could she? Her husband had told her nothing. But she had organized herself as well as she could.

She was sure he would preen with pride when he saw all that she had accomplished in the short span of one day.

The pigeons were removed from the rampart and

put into traveling coops. Sophie was pleased to bring
her pet dog from the village. He was a surly cur but
Alix did not have the heart to say no to the request.
Sophie was leaving an ill and tortured mother and had
never gone much beyond the borders of her village.

What harm could one small dog do?

Most of the packing was finished by vespers bell.
Alix—tired, hungry, and grimy with dust and sweat—
looked about her with great satisfaction. She had managed an enormous job. Chests and wooden baskets
filled her large chamber and lay piled everywhere in
the corridor. The two maids, when they were dismissed,
had to shift and wiggle through them in order to get
away.

Alix heard them bumping into packing containers
as they made their way down the corridor.

"By all the blood of St. Eustace!" swore one of the
girls. "That dim bird bit into me."

Alix looked at Sophie and the two women burst out
laughing.

She had taken nothing that belonged to Mercier.
She had even left favorite books that Robert had let
her use. Most of the large things in the room still
remained in it but the smaller things—tapestries, mirrors, pewter candlesticks, spring flowers—had belonged to her and she had packed them. The luxury
of Mercier was so great that she had always thought
she contributed very little to it, but she found that
without her own small things the room became cold
and distant.

She knew—just knew—that Severin would be proud
of what she had accomplished in such a short time.
She thought of bathing and looked to Sophie, thinking
she might send the maid for water. But Sophie was
seated on a trestle stool, her head against the mantel,
sound asleep and softly snoring.

"I have time," said Alix, mumbling aloud. "I will let her sleep a while. There is time before the duke will call us to the evening meal. Besides, when he sees all the good we have accomplished this day I am sure the Knight Brigante will be so pleased with us that he will reward Sophie with a solid half-coin."

"God's tooth, what has happened here!" swore the Knight Brigante. He stubbed his best new boots against a wooden cask. His sleeping wife and her sleeping maid woke instantly and jumped to their feet.

"Is something wrong, my lord?" Alix asked.

Sophie, more knowledgeable about men's anger than was her lady mistress, started to edge toward the chamber door.

"Wrong?" Severin kept his voice even at obvious cost but he could do nothing about the redness of his face. "What has happened to this chamber?"

"Why, we have packed it for Italy," said Alix. "Obviously. But what, my lord, would induce you to ask such an ill-considered question?"

"Ill-considered?" Severin's voice rose higher. It could easily have cracked glass. Alix had the urge to grab at pottery pieces so they would not shatter—but of course these were all packed. She had spent her day packing and she had accomplished a great deal. Perhaps her husband should be made aware of that fact.

"We have finished with the packing and we are ready to accompany you into Italy," she said, seating herself upon the trestle stool with much dignity. "Are you not proud?"

Severin's face changed swiftly from red to white and then to red again. His eyes narrowed. "You may leave us," he said to Sophie, who, indeed, seemed very much intent on doing that very thing.

"No, you may not!" snapped Alix. She turned toward her husband. "Sir, I am sure that my maid would not think of leaving me with a man who is in such choler that he takes the Lord's name in vain."

Sophie, eyes wide, actually looked quite capable of leaving her mistress. Her hand sidled to the door latch.

"My lady," she reminded Alix. "Did you not ask for bathing water?"

"It can wait," snapped the Lady Alix. "First we must hear what has sent the Knight Brigante into a rage."

"I? In a rage?" raged Severin.

"If, indeed, he has a reason," added the Lady Alix, with an equability that was fast ebbing away. "Some men are just choleric by nature, or so I have been told."

"The reason surrounds me. What is in these boxes and crates?"

"In these boxes and chests?" echoed Alix, but she immediately caught herself. "Is that all? Why, they are the things necessary for our trip into Italy."

"For our trip into Italy?" Now it was Severin's turn to sound the echo.

"Of course," replied Alix, much pleased with herself. "Am I not a wonder? I was able to accomplish all of this in one day—with Sophie's aid and that of two girls from the village. We accomplished this all, just the four of us, and will be ready to leave with your army at first light."

"Not that I helped much," added Sophie hastily. She paid more attention to the growing thunder on her lord's face than to the sunshine that still shone on that of her mistress.

"Leave us," Severin repeated.

The door closed with a thud behind Sophie before her mistress could stop her.

"You intend to take all of this along as you accompany a moving army into Italy?" the Knight Brigante asked his new bride. He used the same tone she had always used with him as they did their daily lessons. She recognized it now as the voice of authority.

Alix nodded. She wished Sophie had not seen fit to leave with such great haste.

"May I ask how many chests you've packed?"

"Forty-seven."

"And might I also ask how you intend to carry these chests—these forty-seven chests—through the Haute Savoy and across the mountains?"

"Why, in caravans, of course, and in wagons."

Although her response was prompt enough, Alix wished that her husband were not slowly crossing the room to stand beside her. He grew ever nearer and she did not quite like the look upon his face.

"Forty-seven chests," he repeated.

"And a few cages."

"Oh."

"For my pigeons and for Sophie's dog. Though naturally he will not need it as we move along. He will run beside us. The cage is for his nighttime sleeping. We've brought straw for his bed."

"I see," said Severin. He was quite close to her now. Too close. Alix had to strongly suppress an urge to follow Sophie through the chamber door. It irritated her grossly that she should feel frightened of her own husband and within her own chamber's walls. She decided to have none of this.

"It takes no great genius to 'see' it," she retorted. "The evidence is all about you. I was told nothing as to what to do and yet I managed—and quite well, I might add—to comport myself in the correct manner. Instead of trying to—to terrorize me, you should be proud of what I have done."

"Proud that you've managed to make such a muck?"

Severin's voice shook. It seemed that an eruption might break at any time through its surface. Alix realized that he was very angry. But she was becoming angry, too. She was hot and tired and bothered. Her husband stood quite near to her—he loomed over her—and the new bride realized she probably reeked more of honest sweat than she smelled of sweet rose perfume.

"In what way have I 'mucked,' as you say?" Her voice was pitched dangerously low.

"You cannot possibly carry these things with you into Italy. My lady, we go with an army and this army must move swiftly—we go barely before a war begins. All wagons and caravans will be needed to transport supplies and provisions for my men. Not one of them can be spared for your fripperies. Not one. You will bring what can fit into your palfrey's sumter pack. What little else you need will be bought once we have reached Rome." He turned from her and started toward the door. "It was a mistake to bring you. I should have known it would be. You are no longer the spoiled wife of a wealthy noble. Pigeon cages, indeed!"

"How dare you!" Alix cried.

She gathered her skirts and ran to the door, putting her hand upon it before his hand could unfasten the latch. "You say nothing to me. You leave me here by myself to make decisions, coming only to criticize and make fun of what I've done and call those very decisions into question. I've worked all day and you've no word of thanks for me. You give not even one glance of appreciation."

"Appreciation?" he bellowed. "You want appreciation for this?"

"It would be in order. I did what I thought would please you. You could at least consider that before you raise your voice. You would certainly have done so for the lowest of men within your precious army."

"The lowest of my men would have had the wit to ask me before bringing half the village with him!"

"That is because, my lord, you would have carefully explained his duties to him!" Alix was righteously angry now. "You would have spent time with him. We are but two days married and you have never once come near me except to breed me! You have not even called upon me to help you or to dress your wound."

"Why should I? You would not kiss me at the altar. You've never once touched me in our wedded bed. You would rather tangle your hands within the sheets than lay them on me. You don't touch me. You don't want me. I stayed away from you, lady, because you so obviously preferred it that way!"

Alix was shaking her head. She stared at him, white-faced and wide-eyed.

Severin stopped abruptly. He stared at the look of horror on his wife's face.

"It doesn't matter," he said hastily. Alix looked as though she was on the verge of tears and he could not bear to be the instrument of her crying. He had not married her to make her cry. "Nothing matters. We can reach some understanding about your things."

"But I thought that was what you wanted," Alix whispered. "I thought that was what I was supposed to do and I tried hard to do it. I tried hard to keep my hands at their right place. Robert told me this was my duty. Robert said I must be restrained, that this is what a man wanted from a wife. Robert always told me . . ."

"What Robert told you was wrong."

Now it was Severin's turn to whisper as he reached out to his wife and drew her near.

* * *

It was some time later when the Knight Brigante left his wife's chamber, but he left it with a jaunty step. They had not made love again—this would come later—but much had been said and some sort of order restored. The chests would be left at Mercier; she could purchase what she needed once they reached Rome. Severin found it nice talking once again to Alix, as he had talked to her for the months in which they had been just friends. He remembered now that they had always spoken easily together—at least before he had taken on the responsibility of her as his wife. Maybe the pleasure he had always found in talking to her could continue into their marriage. He had never even considered the possibility of this before.

"But there is this prospect," he said to himself as he hurried to the evening meal in the Great Hall. His wife would follow after her bathing. He had left an honor guard for her that would wait until she was ready, but he needed to hurry to attend Jean of Burgundy. The duke, his employer, left as well tomorrow, but for Dijon.

He was so deeply lost in his own thoughts that he almost hurtled full force into the Knight de Guigny as he rushed down the winding stairway.

Instead, Lancelot de Guigny seemed in no hurry.

"Well, then, you are off to Italy for his gracious lordship," said the duke's half brother.

Severin had not heard Sir Lancelot's approach. Nor had he expected to see him, though Mercier was his, or at least it soon would be. The duke had seen fit to send his brother to Dijon to check on fortifications in his absence. This was the official mandate, but everyone knew that he had sent his brother away in order to avoid further outbursts. There were rumors abroad that the Knight de Guigny had salted the lance with which he had wounded the Knight Brigante. A salted lance inflicted terrible pain and was firmly forbidden by all the rules of chivalry. Jean of Burgundy did not take well to being the object of kitchen gossip, nor did his brother, the Knight de Guigny.

Severin had never fully trusted Guigny. He trusted him even less now.

"When did you get back?"

"Why, this very morning. From Dijon to here is but a short distance. The duke's fortifications were in place, as of course we all knew they would be. But as an excuse to be rid of me, they served as well as anything else could have. His brother was there—*my* brother."

"Philip of Burgundy?"

"Indeed, the very same."

"I've heard his sympathies are with the King of France and not with the duke's cause to bring Henry to the throne of France."

"The duke has no children—his brother Philip is his heir. But Philip has some problems with the fact that Charles of France is technically Burgundy's liege lord. Nor does he want France ruled by an English prince—no matter how legitimate might be that prince's claim to the throne."

"The Plantagenets have much more right to the throne than the Valois," replied Severin. His eyes narrowed just a bit. "We are all united in that thought."

"And Philip of Burgundy will unite with us. He is still young. He will not withstand both his older brother—*brothers*—in this. Nor will he go against his mother. Like all the men of his house, he is quite hotheaded, but he will not remain strong in this opposition."

"He has stood his ground thus far strongly enough," replied Severin. "He says he will fight with Charles of France against the English. And against his brother."

"But he will change his mind. One brother cannot fight against another. This would never do." Guigny's dark eyes lowered as he picked at a piece of nonexistent lint upon the impeccable dark green of his velvet cape. "Now tell me about married life to the lovely ex-Countess de Mercier. I hope you have a care for her."

They talked for a while longer but Severin was not convinced by Guigny's cool banter. Sir Lancelot had never shown himself to be an easy man with forgiveness. One had only to think back at the ferocity with which he had possessed the fortress of Mercier. He was also not a man who would easily surmount a public humiliation, even when the man dealing it to him was a powerful duke. This in itself was odd, thought Severin. Burgundy's company quitted Mercier before terce bell tomorrow with the Gold Company, though once away they would each take to their separate roads. Severin's eyes narrowed as Guigny saluted him and then turned to his half brother. They greeted each other heartily with the usual sparring and gruff laughter. There is a puzzle to this, thought Severin, and then he remembered Guigny's last words.

"Have a care for the Countess de Mercier."

Indeed, the Knight Brigante made up his mind to do just this.

Nineteen

For the rest of her life, Alix would remember her last day at Mercier. She saw it over and over again as what it was—a moment of amber-caught splendor that separated and marked the two halves of her life. More than two hundred knights of the combined armies were there to act as escort from the fortress—those of Burgundy in the red of their liege lord and those of the Gold Company in their black. Their horses pranced about them, colorfully skirted and with their bright plumes dancing in the breeze. The caravans of the duchess and of the bishop flaunted the fine, dark silks of Burgundy. Laughter rang out amid the keen excitement of departure. Mounted beside her husband, Alix called out to the ladies she knew.

Until she looked up onto the ramparts of Mercier and thought of Robert.

Immediately her smile faded and she reined her frisking horse just a little away from Severin's. Even though his back was to her she could see a tensing in his shoulders as she moved away and her laughter stopped.

She could not help herself. Suddenly the whole horror came back to her again, just as fresh and bloody as it had been that night when Lancelot de Guigny had taken possession of her home. She saw again Robert's mutilated body as it lay, cut down where he had been defending Solange. She saw Yvrain's nurse with her dead arms flung wide in supplication.

She felt again the child's arms clinging to her neck.

And the waking hours after that nightmare—hours in which she had had to face Lancelot de Guigny and plead for her husband's body and days and weeks when she had planned how to save the child Yvrain from de Guigny's wrath. Hours, days, weeks when she had felt herself completely and terribly alone.

But had she been?

She turned now to her husband to find his dark, deep gaze upon her.

"I was thinking of Robert," she said to him. "I was thinking of his death, but also I was remembering what it was like for me the first time I entered his castle. I was a fresh bride then and I loved my husband desperately."

Alix blushed now as she said this to her new husband but Severin's expression did not change. He did not turn away from her.

"Desperately. I know that I will never again be able to love a man the way I loved him," she repeated, and she smiled. "But how could I ever love that way again? I am a different person now. Different in that I can accept that my husband never loved me—and that he could never have done so. His heart was plighted to another—he was meant only for Solange. How much heartache and how much death would have been avoided if only the world had realized that fact. Or if only I had done so."

The duchess waved a long furl of lace to beckon her and Alix reined her horse in that direction. Before she moved away she turned back once again to her husband. "This is no longer my home, if ever it were so. And something within me says that I am destined never again to see Mercier in this life. This fortress was always secure in Solange's keeping. She was always its true chatelaine; she was always Robert's true wife. She gave him his true heir. I once loved him. I once built a shrine to him. But I have left it here."

Severin wondered if she really meant it. How could she possibly mean what she had said? Especially about the child, Yvrain. God knew she had more education than he did and so she would know, more than he did, of the bastards who had gone on in life and taken charge. There was England's William the Conquerer himself, the illegitimate offspring of a tanner's daughter and her liege lord. Severin's own ancestors had come over with him from Normandy, landing at Hastings to take possession of England. His father had told him the story over and over again.

"You come from good stock," Guy d'Harnoncourt had whispered, the stink of wine heavy upon his breath.

There was hope for Yvrain. Guigny would know this. And this hope had been planted by the actions of Alix de Mercier, who had saved the heir's life. This was another thing Sir Lancelot would never forgive— or forget. He, too, was bastard-born. Yvrain was helped also by the fact that Robert de Guigny had left no legitimate offspring—someone who would hold Alix's heart and bind her further to Mercier.

Severin imagined he should at least be grateful for this.

He headed his army south, parting from the duke at the gates of Mercier, and soon leaving the castle far, far behind.

He mused on this all day as he went about his duties, leading his men south toward the mountains that led first into the Savoy and then into that vast maze of independent cities and warring communes that was called Italy. He thought of the duke's last words to him and his last quick instructions. Severin shook his head. There would be intrigue enough ahead of him—and surely fair Italy was the place where intrigue always began.

They chose a fine meadow for the encampment. In the distance Alix could already see the low-ranging mountains of the Haute Savoy. The air, which had been hot and dusty for springtime, had taken on the shivery glow of high land. Alix smelled pine on the air.

She had ridden through the day at the rear of Severin's army and just before the colored wagons that brought its supplies. Behind these she noted other wagons, more colorful ones, that held women who followed the army; young men could not afford to leave behind wives.

"And prostitutes," whispered Young Sophie.

"Really?" said Alix, turning behind with a curious eye.

"But don't look," hissed the maid. "They have bleached yellow hair and are marked. By law they are forced to wear their clothing turned wrong side out—though the Knight Brigante does not approve of these laws and does not enforce them. He looks upon the women with a kindly eye. He says he could not fight his battles without them. They act as nurses during the fighting—many times risking their own lives to help his men. I have heard Sir Severin will not have them maligned."

Alix, who had never seen a prostitute before and was straining to do so now, stopped immediately and righted herself primly in the saddle at Sophie's last words. She and her husband had barely arrived at an *entente*. They were speaking, they were smiling; she did not want to ruin this with rash action.

But she was curious about the women all the same. Once they stopped, the Knight Brigante left his army to help his bride from her horse.

"Our tent will be there," he said, pointing to a small space away from the others.

"Is it my duty to settle it?"

Severin smiled when he heard the slight shudder of alarm in her voice.

"That is not necessary, my lady," he said. "There are squires and pages who are tasked for that. You have but to amuse yourself. And there will also be no need for cooking. We have men assigned to that as well."

"Good," replied Alix. Her sigh was heartfelt. " 'Tis all new to me, this being wife to a soldier."

Severin actually laughed.

He laughed with me, thought Alix as she slid deeper into the water. She had gone off with Young Sophie to find a place for bathing and had left the maid to stand guard. She thought how beautiful Severin had looked with the mountains of the Haute Savoy behind him and the sun sinking down in the west. How its rays had turned his wheat-colored hair to strands of gold. She remembered how the light had seemed also to come up from him and well through his eyes. It had warmed her. It warmed her now as she lathered fine, rich-smelling soap upon her body. Her husband had a nice smile. And it was glorious to watch it turn into an actual laugh.

Severin had also talked to her.

"The Knight Brigante talked to me," said Alix as she wiped water from her hair with a flax towel and prepared to take her watching post so that Sophie could enjoy the pool as well. "He told me that we can expect to be in Rome within a week, once we have passed through the Haute Savoy. A week is not a long time in these conditions."

Sophie, who had lived all her life in a small village with a perennial shortage of men, did not see the grace in such a quick parting from the Gold Company. She said this much to Alix, though her mistress did not seem to care. Or even hear her. The Lady Brigante was busy with her own new thoughts.

My husband talked to me. He told me something.

It felt so nice to say the words after all these years of being alone in her chamber with only parchment books and pretty trinkets for company. She felt part of something at last.

It was the first day of May and she'd never been so happy. She looked up to the wide expanse of the sky. It was just dusk; there was the promise of a big, fat moon in the sky.

The evening meal was simple, but Alix doubted that she'd ever eaten such good goat cheese or drunk such good red wine. Even the dark, coarse peasant bread tasted wonderful after the refinements of Mercier. It had been months since she had eaten bread shaped like bread. The chef from Paris, imported by Robert and paid much more than decency explained, had been a frustrated artist as well. He had envisioned himself on the rampart of some new cathedral carving gargoyles or saints or the Virgin herself. Failing this, he had contented himself with sculpting elaborate shapes from innocent bread dough. If she desired bread, Alix always had to find it within a rose or kitten or sometimes even a bird.

But tonight she bit heartily into her plain loaf. She ate her cheese and spring peaches. She grew slightly dozy on the richness of the wine.

"Now, my lady, 'tis best you take to your tent," said the Knight Brigante from her side. There was a certain urgency to his voice. "Tomorrow brings with it another long day's journey and you should be fresh for it."

Alix nodded, but as she looked around she saw that not all the camp was heading to the tenting. Instead she saw them gathering in a field and heard the breaking rhythm of someone practicing on a frame drum.

And then she remembered.

"But why should I leave? There's to be a dancing feast—'tis May Day, after all."

"What do you know of May Day practices?" said Severin. "You were gently bred."

"That does not mean I could not know of May Day," retorted Alix. The drowsiness left her in a flash. "We had celebrations in Hungary and at Belvedere as well. My mother said that all the world follows the Old Religions on May Day."

"At least all of its women do," said Severin. He looked about himself dubiously. Spring's hour ruled the world now and there was still some light about.

"The men profit from their observance," said Alix wickedly. She was enjoying the blushes of the great Knight Brigante. " 'Tis the time for May lovemaking."

"You've taken too much wine. I think it best you sleep off its effects within your bed."

"Only if you come with me," Alix said.

"What a hoyden you've become," retorted her husband but he settled back beside her and held her close.

The happy jangle of tambourines joined the drumming as a strange rhythm filled the air. Women streamed out from the brightly colored wagons that Alix had gazed upon so curiously—women dressed in loose clothing and already swaying to the music's hypnotic beat.

Alix had no intention of leaving now and she said as much to her husband.

"I've seen the May Dancing before. I went once with my parents to the festivals in Hungary. It is but innocent fun."

"This is not innocent," said her husband. "It is—it is *Italian.*"

Alix snorted, wide-awake now. "What under heaven does that mean? *We* are both Italian and we seem no different from the French with whom we have most recently lived."

"But we are," insisted her husband. "And even if we were not—but we *are*—there is no doubt but that this dancing is different."

The more he blushed and faltered, the more perversely innocent his bride became.

"Tell me of this difference."

The frame drums continued softly, but the tambourine rose on the beat. Alix glanced over. Their flowing, brightly colored ribbons caught the wind's flow. But their sound was still low, so low that Alix heard a wolf howling at the full moon in the distance.

Her husband moved nearer toward her around the campfire so that he could be heard. Alix glanced at the people around her. They were mostly still—not laughing. They stopped their swaying. She could almost feel anticipation as it licked the air.

"My men are mainly from the south of Italy—as am I," said Severin. "And this is our native dance. It is called the tarantella."

As if on cue, three women moved into the circle that had cleared around the campfire. The night grew heated.

"It is a dangerous dance," said Severin.

Alix quickly glanced at him and again caught a hint of the warmth welling up. Severin seemed already moved by the dance, heated by it. For the first time, Alix felt there might be more to her soldier-husband than she knew. She felt he might himself be dangerous.

The idea was not wholly unpleasant.

"Dangerous," he repeated. She saw the flicker of a heartbeat at his throat and at the same time blood pulsed in her ear.

Music filled the night—borne on the tambourine and the frame drum.

"It is our dance, but no women are allowed to touch the instruments," said Severin. "Only the men, who are called *tarantati*. Their purpose really is to help the women in the dance. To heal the women."

"To heal them?"

The music grew stronger, vibrating life into the night.

More women moved to the circle's center. A few started to undulate to the music. Alix closed her eyes. Her lips felt dry and she licked them.

"It is a healing dance," continued Severin. "From the old religions, the ones that ruled the earth before the coming of the light. It is a wild dance, meant to cure women from the mystic spider's bite. Hence it is known as the tarantella—the Spider's Dance. The original name of the dance is *pizzica tarantella*. It tells of the bite of love that happens when a woman is filled with desires that are kept hidden and firmly bridled. When, perhaps, they are so hidden she does not even know that they exist."

No longer did Severin seem shy about explaining the dance's meaning to her. Alix felt his breath brush lightly against her cheek. She felt its heat through the light wool of her fresh traveling tunic.

"A woman inflicted by this bite is called *tarantata*," he said. "She must be released."

The beating and the clash of the tambourine grew deeper. More women entered the circle and writhed to its beat. More men reached out to play the wild instruments.

She felt her body sway and it frightened her. The dance was dangerous, overwhelming. She was not sure she could abandon herself to its wild beat.

"Tell me more," she said.

"In Greece, southern Italy, North Africa, and Spain where the 'bite' of the tarantella afflicts women, the only healing comes through music and the dance. The origins of the tarantella come from the ancient Greek and Roman rites in honor of their god Dionysius and Cybele."

Severin's words were low, as hypnotic and compelling as the dance he described. "In ancient times southern Italy was part of Greece and was called Magna Grecia. Here, worship of the Mother Earth Goddess was connected to a strong matriarchal society. The frame drum, the tamburello, is an ancient musical instrument connected to rituals often associated with women, dating back to the ancient Egyptian and Sumerian cultures. In Magna Grecia and the Middle East women used the frame drums for rituals honoring the Moon Goddess."

Now Alix heard the first singing. At times it was rhythmic and at others the voice held long notes while the tambourine either supported it or played its counterpoint.

"The words have a magic, ritualistic origin," whispered Alix's husband. "In the lyrics the men express their desire to climb the mountain, to enter the garden and the woman invites the man to go across the waters, to climb higher in order to be unified in an act of universal love where anguish and fear disappear. The dance was orgiastic from its beginning. It always has been. The dancing is always directed by the women, who reach a state of euphoria as they dance to the rhythm of the tambourine played by their men. Both the dancing and the music are equally needed. Both are equally important. The women cannot dance their way to purification from their *pizzica* without the music of their men."

Blood pulsed in Alix's ear. The music was louder now, its beat hypnotic. Alix swayed to it, just like the other women. Tentatively at first, she let its rhythm overflow her. The web of the mythical spider had held her in thrall for years. It had tangled her and bound her and tied her very soul into a thousand knots.

Now she longed to be free.

She heard the hypnotic rhythm. She felt her blood pound against the Maltese Star at her throat. She closed her eyes.

She got up.

No one saw her. Instinctively she knew all the other eyes were closed. Just as hers were.

"No one is watching," Severin whispered. It was part of the dance's magic and its mystery. In places where women were dressed in dark colors and lived even darker lives, no one gawked as the women whirled to the freeing rhythm.

Alix whirled with them. The music grew louder. It enfolded her in its rhythm. She whirled and moved and danced with the other women, as the tambourine beat louder, echoing into the night. She felt pebbles beneath her bare feet and saw fire on her eyelids. Blood rushed through her veins. Even with her eyes closed she knew that the other women within the circle undulated and moved and grew into the music that

the men played. Just as she did. She sensed that
Severin had a tambourine now and that he played.

Knowledge came from an instinct within her and as
she danced this instinct grew stronger. It pulsated upon
the heavy night air. She knew now that it had been
growing stronger since she had met Severin and her
life had begun its great change.

She trusted this instinct. She trusted her knowing.
Together, they would show her the way.

Alix danced on and on and on—until she felt the
hand of her husband. Until his touch led her away to
the tent that they would share.

Twenty

"Rome is smaller than it should be," said Alix. She sat beside her husband on the crest of the hill. Below them the small city spread out like a beckoning palm.

Severin laughed. "What do you mean, smaller than it should be?"

"For so much power," insisted Alix. She was laughing, too. Happiness bounced from both of them in the sunlight of late May. "You always hear about Rome, even more than you hear of Paris or Buda. The pope is here. It is the center of the Church and of all Christendom."

"I would say more the center of intrigue," replied her husband. "Or have you forgotten that there is another pope at Avignon?"

"He is not our pope," said Alix staunchly. "He is the *French* pope."

"The French pope?" Severin's laughter warmed Alix again. "How quickly you have changed, my lady Brigante. It was but a month ago that you yourself were French."

"Really?" Alix wrinkled her nose. "I cannot recall that time. I cannot recall a life without you."

"Gratifying," Severin said, "but not true. Does not Rome remind you of something, or somewhere, else?"

Alix looked out again, more closely this time. She saw a clustered city of small, low, sienna-roofed buildings that hugged close around a meandering river. She saw vast expanses of rolling green hills.

"Buda," she said finally. "It reminds me of Hungary's capital. Though Buda is much smaller, more compact. Somehow it feels older than Rome, though I know it cannot be."

"The river is the Tiber," replied her husband. "It has stood important since the time of the Roman Republic. Rome has hugged its shores since Romulus and Remus founded the city."

Alix shivered dramatically. "A city founded by men after they had been suckled by a she-wolf. I hardly know what is to be expected here."

"You can expect that I will shortly meet with the pope and with God's grace will complete my mission for the duke. You can expect once again to eat good food and wash in warm water. You can expect to sleep beneath linen sheets and on something more comfortable than a soldier's hard bed. You can expect to love me. And I can expect to love you."

Alix looked her husband straight in the eye.

"Rome sounds enjoyable," she said.

Again her husband laughed.

"Few places are more ancient than Rome," Severin continued. "Most of the roads into it and the bridges you see were built by the Romans more than a thousand years ago. They have been in continual use ever since. See that one there—far, far down the Tiber River? That is the Pontus Milvius. It has linked the two parts of the city for centuries already—and will probably continue to link it for centuries to come."

"Centuries?" asked Alix with a laugh. "What a long view you take of things!"

"Oh, I can take a short one as well," replied Severin as he handed Alix once again into her palfrey's saddle.

"Let me see—it should take but three sand-spans before I can decently take my bride to bed once again."

"Decently?" Alix lifted a coquette's brow. "Or indecently?"

Severin held a hand to his heart in mock horror. "Is this my lady bride who speaks? The same cool woman who would rather dig her hands into the linen of her sheets than into me? What has changed you, lady?"

"You have changed me, my lord husband. Now let us hurry to our lodging place—and to its bed."

Rome had seemed both peaceful and sleepy as Alix viewed it from the northern hills. However, as she and Severin passed through the Salerian gate, she soon discovered it was neither.

"What a hive," Alix said. She had almost to shout to make her words heard, though they rode not two feet apart. "Not even Paris holds this much activity. And the vendors! We are but a tree's length inside the city and already I have been offered gold ribboning, and honey cream for my face, and a true bargain in verifiable Etruscan earrings."

"I would be wary of verifiable Etruscan earrings if I were you," replied Severin. "They were probably manufactured not five minutes ago in someone's silversmithing warren. The Romans are great merchants. They could sell heaven to St. Peter himself if given but the chance."

Alix laughed. "I will be careful and strong and not allow myself to be seduced by mendicant mercers. I know I am the wife of a simple soldier now and must learn to watch my half-coins and livres."

"You are in Italy now and not France. Here you must watch florins, not livres. But the concept is the same." Abruptly Severin stopped laughing to turn a scrutinizing eye upon his wife. "Though you could do with some spending."

Alix turned from politely returning a length of green silk that a spry woman had thrust into her hand. "I could do with spending? Is this my husband speaking—the general of an army that he must house, feed, and supply? The stern man who once strongly reminded me how many acres of producing Burgundy soil it took to outfit just one of his knights for battle?"

"Your gown looks awful," said her husband bluntly.

"Indeed, it does not," replied Alix. But then she glanced down at her dusty wool tunic and the lace gloves she had mended even before they crossed the Haute Savoy. "It is only that I have got dirty and patched up along the road."

"I did not say *you* looked bad, my sweet" replied Severin as he skillfully wended his horse through the narrow, cobbled streets. "I said that your gown did."

Alix sighed with relief. "Oh, that can be skillfully rectified. I will clean it once we have reached our destination. It will become good as new again."

"Cleaning will not change its color," said Severin. He swiveled in his saddle to face her. "It will always be mourning black."

"But I am widowed," she said quickly. "By Church law I must hold to public grieving for three years time."

A mischievous light twinkled just beneath the surface of Severin's dark eyes.

"I've never known you to be the great conformist, my lady Alix. In your own quiet manner, you have yet managed to go against every dictate and expectation that has been prescribed for you. But, of course, it is your decision to make," said Severin. Will you be widowed—or will you be wifed?"

Alix wrinkled her brow in mock concentration. "I imagine being wifed would mean that I must leave my grief clothes behind me?"

Severin nodded.

"Then spend many weary hours at the mercer's stalls buying bright, new cloths?"

He nodded again.

"And after that, just as many more being cosseted and patterned by a premiere member of the dressmaker's guild?"

"Indeed, that would be part of the bargain."

Alix raised her head nobly into the sunlight. "I am prepared to sacrifice myself," she said.

Severin looked most thoughtfully stricken.

"What have I wrought!" he exclaimed.

It was well past the midday prayer bells before they reached their destination. The day had grown warm and Alix felt stifled in her wool tunic. Her stomach also roiled slightly. She decided that the goat's milk they had shared for morning meal had not quite agreed with her. She had noticed this sickness in the last few days, though she had said nothing to Severin. It would pass, she decided, as soon as they were once again within the walls of a true dwelling.

She hoped that they would find a small cottage somewhere, quiet and peaceful—though the hustle of Rome did not bode well for wishes that included silence or peace. Severin had instructed her once on the strictures of her changed circumstances; they had argued about this. She had no intention of ever arguing with her husband again. But she thought she could safely hope for a small house with a garden. June was full upon them and the Lady Brigante dreamed of bright flowers. As her husband had said, she had little enough experience with budget and costs. Still she thought hers a modest enough dream.

"Violets," she whispered as they joggled along through the stench-filled streets of bustling Rome. "And perhaps roses as well."

"I have left the army outside the city gates," Severin said. "But you will stay in Rome, with friends. I will join you often—every night if I can. Count Urbano Massimo offered us hospitality when I sent word ahead that we would sojourn in Rome for a few weeks. Count Urbano is himself a *condottiero* in service to the Tuscan league but his family owns vast holdings in the south of Italy. Much of his time is spent there. The Massimi trace their lineage to one of the ruling families in the Roman Republic. Urbano has a lovely wife. I think you will like the Countess Barbara. I hope she is in residence at Rome. I have much to do with my commission and it might be nice for you to have such a friend. Someone who is lively and interesting."

He paused, as though considering. It sometimes remained difficult for him to talk with her about sensitive matters—just as it remained difficult for her to speak about them with him. But they were both trying.

Talk to your husband, the Wise Woman had whispered.

This was still difficult; she was still wounded. But with all of her heart, Alix wanted to try.

"Lively and interesting," Severin repeated.

"Mercier was lonely," Alix agreed.

Her husband nodded. "Quite frankly, it always struck me as cold. I am different from many of my countrymen because of my light hair, but I am a true child of the south. I like the warmth of its people. And the Massimi are basically southerners. Despite her high position, I think you will find the Countess Massimo to be a kind friend. Their palazzo is near Castel Sant'Angelo, which is surrounded only by great green fields. You can see the castle from the windows of the Massimo palazzo. There is nothing to obstruct the view. I think we will be happy there."

In a shy way, Severin seemed proud that he could put his wife in such company. Alix could imagine exactly why he should be proud. He had started life as a pauper knight's page and had risen from that low point to command one of the greatest armies in all of Christendom. One day soon he would face his powerful uncle as equal, knowing all that he had achieved had been achieved on his own.

"I am so pleased that you are my husband," she whispered so low that she was sure he could not possibly have heard her. But he beamed over at her as though he had.

The Louvre might have been larger than the Palazzo Massimo, but Alix doubted that even the Parisian royal palace was as well outfitted as this Roman noble house. Nor could Queen Isabeau hold a beauty's candle to the lovely Countess Barbara.

"Welcome to Rome," she said, wrapping a solicitous arm around Alix. "And to our house. We are, indeed, honored to have you as our guests."

She was dark-haired and dark-eyed—just like Robert and Solange, thought the fair Alix, but with none of the cold brittleness these two had displayed. The woman who welcomed her gave the impression of actually enjoying good food and fine things. She was not what one would describe as thin; in fact, she was slightly rounded. Neither her eyebrows nor the richness of her hairline had been fashionably plucked. Indeed, her abundant hair fell in a smooth wave well past the curving of her waist.

Barbara laughed as she caught Alix staring at it.

"I can't stand strictures," she said, plucking sweet grapes from an enormous silver bowl. "Here, have some of these. You will find them delicious. They are grown on our own lands outside Rome. The emperors made wine from the Massimo grapes. Are they not fine? Now, what was I saying? Ah, yes. I cannot stand strictures. I cannot stand pretensions. But I do enjoy the simple pleasant things of life—good food, fine wines, warm bathing water. You will find all of these things in abundance during your stay. What you will not find are marzipan lovebirds. I *hate* the idea of eating into an elaborate confection, don't you?"

Alix, who had eaten into a great many of these in her life as the Countess de Mercier, nodded enthusiastically as she followed her hostess through the elegant marble hallways of the Palazzo Massimo.

"I hate them," she agreed. "And replumed partridges!"

"Ugh! They forced that upon me once in Paris. I had to leave the table or become sick. Did you ever have to eat cakes formed into the semblance of your castle?"

"Tens of them!" exclaimed Alix. "It is the latest cooking fashion from Paris. Few visitors came to Mercier but those who did inevitably brought their high-bought chefs along with them so that we could be favored with this gastronomic nightmare!"

"Beautiful to look upon, but horrific on the intestines. All of that strange gluing and icing and sprinkling on of sugar—you know it cannot come naturally. One never really knows what goes on in the kitchens. I always thought the chefs sly enough to use sheep glue to keep the whole pottage together. Especially if he were lucky enough to have a cushioned job within a noble house."

Alix grew thoughtful at having her own secret suspicions confirmed. "Indeed, I've often thought this myself. Sometimes the marzipan has even tasted of lambing, though I dared not say this aloud."

"To the Duke of Burgundy or the Count de Mercier?" exclaimed Barbara Massimo. "You were wise not to. Urbano was once offered a position with the duke but I begged him not to take it. Such food! Such mannerisms! I would have had to part with half my body weight to feel comfortably established."

"But you are beautiful," said Alix. She felt shy, but was starting to enjoy this woman immensely.

"Because I stay at home," said the Countess Massimo. She led the way up a broad expanse of marble stairs that led to the noble floor. All around them pert, well-fed maids peeked curiously from the numerous chambers. "My looks fit well with all the life around me. They would never have fitted well in Burgundy or in the land of Charles of France."

"I am starting to think that perhaps I'll never fit in as well," said Alix. "And that Mercier, and all that surrounded it, was never my home."

Barbara Massimo paused for a moment and smiled at Alix with her lips and with her warm, dark eyes.

"Well, that life is over," she said, reaching to a basket. "May I offer you a ripe peach?"

Severin had been whisked away immediately by Urbano Massimo. Alix caught only a quick glimpse of him but found him to be quite intense. Short, energetic, and elegant, he seemed the match to his vivacious wife. He was graciousness itself—inquiring as to the voyage, making plans for an excursion to some property he possessed outside the Roman walls—but Alix had the odd sensation that he studied her closely.

"My husband has been quite eagerly awaiting your husband's arrival," said Barbara, bustling through the

large chamber on the noble floor that had been assigned to the Knight Brigante. "Although Italy is not
directly involved in the conflict between France and England, Rome is always *indirectly* involved. If you know
my meaning."

"Because of the Church?" asked Alix. She had been
staring across an expanse of green field to the Castel
Sant'Angelo, the residence of the pope. Now she
turned back.

"Oh, the Church," said Barbara with a shrug. "And
the Lombard bankers."

"But what have they to say about the political battles?"

"Everything," replied Barbara. She reached into a
housekeeping chest and pulled out white linen edged
in heavy cream lace. Alix, used to the splendors of
Mercier, had nevertheless never seen anything this
fine. "They are the catalysts for this battle."

"Important as the knights?"

"Important as the kings," Barbara assured her. She
handed the linen to a maid who, in turn, carefully laid
it on the samite-covered bed. "What with war and battles and famine and pestilence, the kings find no way
to keep their coffers brimming. They cannot make
money unless they wrest land from another sovereign;
they cannot wrest land without battle and they cannot
wage battle without monies. It is a vicious cycle in
which the bankers are most eager to assist—for a
price."

"A price?"

"Since it is now forbidden that the Jews lend money
at interest, the bankers of Italy have taken their place
at it. This war will not be waged without them and they
have become extremely powerful. It is not at all a co-
incidence that your husband is here on mission from
the Duke of Burgundy and that Gian Galeazzo Visconti

has also made his way south from Milan at the very same time."

Alix drew nearer. "But Gian Galeazzo Visconti is hardly a banker. He is noble enough to have married his daughter to the younger brother of the King of France."

"But not noble enough to have stopped that same brother—Louis d'Orleans—when he wanted to be rid of his bride so that he could be more attentive to his mistress, the queen."

"I didn't know this." Alix's voice was breathless.

"You may leave us," Barbara motioned to the maid. She waited until the door had firmly closed before she continued. "Indeed, he certainly did this. The Duc d'Orleans arranged an annulment of his marriage through the pope at Avignon and packed his legitimate wife off into a convent—of course, retaining for himself the gold from her dowry."

"And there was nothing Gian Galeazzo could do."

"There was nothing he chose to do then. He is in the money lending business, which is why he was able to make such a fortuitous match for his daughter. He could not afford to anger either the king, though he was in and out of spells of madness, or his more lucid brother. He bowed outwardly to his daughter's disgrace."

"Outwardly?"

"In appearance." Barbara lifted an elegant eyebrow. "Underneath, he seethed. As you will see, Gian Galeazzo is a taciturn man, much given—or so they say—to astrology and all manner of superstitious arts. He is contained, and perhaps even fearful. In a time when a man is measured by his prowess in battle, the Visconti ruler disdains warfare and has yet to be blooded. He is not thought of as loving, yet it is widely known that he thought the earth moved around his daughter, Valentina. When she was convented, he said nothing but he made copious inquiries. What he found out is that the Duke of Burgundy, for his own purposes, urged his cousin to the annulment. Burgundy wished to place a wedge between the throne of France and its finances. Orleans, a hothead, for once took the advice of his cousin because it so closely wove in with his own inclinations in the matter. But Visconti was distraught at what had befallen his favorite child and it is assumed—at least here in Italy—that he wrought a most horrible vengeance. One in which your father was involved."

The two women had moved to the bed and sat comfortably upon it.

"You are speaking of the Battle of Nicopolis," said Alix.

Barbara nodded. "Where the French fought in crusade against the Sultan Bayezid and were decimated by the Turks. Thousands and thousands of Frenchmen were killed. It is widely rumored that Gian Galeazzo, who helped to finance the crusade for France, also fed information to the Sultan."

"But did not the Duke of Burgundy lead that crusade?" asked Alix.

"Indeed, he did," replied Barbara.

"And yet the duke seeks aid from him in this new venture?"

" 'Beseeches' might seem the better term," said Alix's new friend. Her eyes grew serious. "The forces of France are strong, those of England considerably weaker. I hope you do not think it an imposition on my part, Lady Alix, or that I am in any way being presumptuous. But I have no trust in the Visconti. Gian Galeazzo may not be content to avenge himself only once against the French. In this battle, he is allied with the French and with Burgundy. This seems legitimate enough. But he has played Duke Jean false once already. If he has allied himself with someone . . ."

". . . Someone who might also be playing a double game . . ."

". . . just like the game that was played once before." Alix paused. "But you mentioned that I might meet him."

"Tonight," said Lady Barbara. "He is staying at Castel Sant'Angelo. He lends money to the pope as well as to lesser mortals. He sent word to us of his sojourn in Rome and I have invited him for the evening meal—which, of course, I was meant to do. He inquired about the presence of the Knight Brigante—and most specifically about his wife, the Lady Alix."

"He inquired about me?" asked Alix, puzzled.

"More than once in the space of an eight-line parchment note," said Barbara. "I thought you should know that—I don't know why, I just thought you should."

"Thank you," said Alix. "I will remember what you said and I will be wary. Though I've no idea what someone as powerful as the Visconti might want with my husband—or with me."

"You seem an intelligent woman," replied Barbara. "I gauged this of you immediately, which is why I allowed myself to be so frank at our first meeting. Though, I'm sure my husband would never credit it of me. I'm sure he thinks I've closeted you talking about the best mercer stall for buying blue cloth, or some such nonsense."

Alix eyed her shrewdly. "I've an idea Count Urbano knows exactly what we have discussed this bright morning."

"Mayhap." Barbara Massimo's eyes glittered with mischief "My dear Lady Alix, what an interesting amulet you wear."

* * *

"We can't kiss now, my lord. 'Twill cause a scandal!"

"What scandal?" whispered Severin, easing Alix against a tapestried wall and nuzzling the words into the delicate skin at her throat. "We are in Italy. 'Tis mightily difficult to cause scandal here."

He cupped his wife's breast with his hand and eased his body close to hers. In the near distance Alix heard laughter and the sound of a lone flute playing. The evening meal was due to begin soon. But, like Severin, she thought it could wait.

"Your honor guard, what will they think?" Alix kissed the words into his mouth. She rasped them against his tongue, whispered them into his throat.

Severin groaned, though very softly. "They have already rounded the corner. If they take time to think of me at all—which I doubt they will, considering the state of their inebriation—they will think their stern general is taking time to console himself before facing the staid strictures of a boring evening meal. Or else, that he is preparing himself for the long night of lovemaking that he hopes will soon follow it."

"Noble pursuits," whispered Alix, just before Severin's kiss cut her words short.

"My dear Lady Alix," said Gian Galeazzo Visconti. "What fine, high coloring you have. Have you always had such a bright complexion or do you find the air below the Haute Savoy to be beneficial in this respect?"

"Thank you for your compliment, sir," replied a demure Alix. "I find Italy's air to be particularly beneficial to me."

"So I am told. I have never gone above the mountains myself. Though I have been called many times to Paris on business, I have yet to go. I saw no interest in it. Not when one can live and eat so well in one's own land and can experience the company of so fine a chatelaine as the Lady Barbara. I am a simple man."

Alix doubted this. When Visconti turned to the Lady Barbara in order to emphasize his fine words with his attention, she used the opportunity to study him. He was by far the most simply dressed man at the table: his tunic, though of fine wool, was plainer even than the one worn by Severin. Its darkness suited Visconti's fine-boned, shrunken figure. He seemed determined to blend in with his surroundings but while she studied him, and while he seemed to concentrate upon his conversation with the Lady Barbara, Alix saw his eyes dart continually. He missed nothing. He knew she watched him.

"You plan to remain long in Rome, my lady?" he asked.

Alix shrugged. "This depends upon my husband," she said. "He is in service with the Duke of Burgundy. He has been sent on mission to Rome and when this is finished we will return to France."

"But not forever, I trust," said Visconti. He tried a smile that did not quite touch his eyes. "You would not want to be long away from your homeland."

"I have been away from it for many years now."

"Since you were five years old," said Visconti equitably. "Now perhaps you should come home again. There are those who have missed you and others who might seek your acquaintance. One person in particular. He has been awaiting you for quite some time. You will enjoy his company, of that I am sure. But we will discuss that later."

Visconti smiled, disclosing small yellow teeth. For no reason, Alix felt a shudder of dread. She looked toward

Severin but his head was bent low in deep conversation
with Count Urbano. She felt the heat of Visconti's
gaze.

"Perhaps, my lord," she said. "It would be an honor
to meet with you again but we have limited time in
Rome. Once my husband . . ."

"Your husband," repeated the Lord Visconti, "will
most probably have his days full in contacting the pope
and securing his support. He will be glad that you are
protected and entertained."

Again Visconti smiled. "He will thank me for it."

Twenty-one

Alix woke screaming. She fought against the hands that reached out to her, clawed against them as she struggled back from deep darkness and reached for the light.

"Alix, what is it? What's happened?"

But she was still screaming, screaming. She couldn't stop, even though she realized it was Severin's voice calling to her and that it was he whom she sought.

"Oh, God, it was awful. He was all burned, Severin. Completely burned!"

He held her close and gradually Alix's sobs quieted. She held tight to him.

"Terrible."

But her words grew clearer now, her breath steadier. She let her husband hold her while reality again took hold of her mind. She remembered that she was in the grand Massimo Palazzo in Rome. She heard birds chattering outside the window. She felt morning light against her eyelids.

"You dreamed badly," whispered Severin, stroking her hair. "It was only a vision and it is over now."

"It seemed so real," she insisted. "He was burning and he wanted me. He said that I was his."

"Only a dream," repeated Severin. He kissed her cheek. He held her close. "No one wants you but me.

No one can have you but me. We are wedded now, forever and forever."

Alix nodded, gulping air, wanting so hard to believe him.

But she couldn't.

"Is anything wrong, my dear?" asked the Lady Barbara. "You are not eating and these figs are delicious. They are the very first ones of the season. Do you know the Italian custom of the wish? Of course you do. You are Italian. It is your heritage as well. But just in case . . . When one eats a fruit for the first time in its season, one makes a wish and that wish . . ."

Alix was grateful for the chatter. She felt nauseous and sick to her stomach—a byproduct of her nightmare, she decided—and was glad to hide herself within a curtain of the Countess Massimo's incessant chatter. She nodded, smiled, and allowed her thoughts to drift.

It had started out pleasantly enough. Alix walked through a meadow, much like the one that edged Mercier Forest and in which she had made that last, fateful promise to Robert. Except this time she was not at its edges; she walked through it, looking straight ahead, knowing she would see someone and therefore not surprised when she did.

The figure beckoned to her from the forest's edge, but it was dark. Alix could not clearly see, especially now that the bright afternoon sun was quickly fading to gloaming. She squinted into the dimness.

"Severin?" she said, and then, "Robert?"

She hesitated. She did not want to see Robert again. She did not want to have him near or follow where he would lead her. That part of her life was finished, over and done with. She had Severin now. He loved her and she loved him.

"No, Robert," she whispered. But it was not Robert who beckoned and she knew this.

Then it must be Severin.

She hesitated, not absolutely certain, but sure enough in the end to continue on her way. The grass beneath her feet grew wet and sodden. The sky above her head turned gray and chill. In the distance came the roll of thunder. Her eyes had been fixed upon the forest but as she walked she saw that now there were other people in the meadow. Some she did not recognize, but others she knew. Her mother, Padre Gasca, a bloodied knight loaded down with amulets, a handsome man with a hand cupped lovingly around a wine tankard.

A blond woman who slowly shook her head no.

They said nothing to her; it was the beckoning man who softly whispered her name.

"Alix."

This was not Severin's voice. Alix felt the first, faint stirrings of unease but she was also—intrigued. The air grew taut, the thunder nearer. The gray sky seemed to reach down and kiss the beckoning man with silver. She remembered the freedom of dancing the *tarantella* and she sensed that same freedom all about her now. She felt a force scintillate upon the air. Though she could not clearly see him—she was still too far away from that—she sensed the beckoning man beam upon her. He glowed as he—not she—drew close.

But . . .

The corner of her eye caught movement. Alix turned to it, breaking one spell but moving into a deeper one. From just beyond the forest's rim she heard the sounds of steel clanging against steel and men cry out and once again the sound of nearing thunder. She heard an animal scream in pain. It turned dark suddenly and rain cascaded all around her. She felt it upon her face. It weighted her clothes.

* * *

"Alix!" A harsh whisper. A command. She had forgotten the beckoning man—though he had not forgotten her. He was nearer now. Almost upon her. No longer did the tarantella dance around and through her. Fear took its place.

"Severin!" she called. But how could he hear her over the din that echoed from the forest? How would he find her in the night?

The man was almost upon her now. And she was so frightened, so very frightened. As Alix stared, transfixed, one lone arrow shot from the forest, its tip tarred and flaming, aimed straight for the man who beckoned to her.

It whooshed to life against his dark clothing. But the man did not stop. He beckoned to her with his charred hands.

"We shall meet again at Agincourt," he whispered. "You will see me there and you will wear the Maltese Star and you will choose."

". . . and these are the best figs of all." Barbara's words seemed to come from a great distance but Alix forced herself to focus upon them as the spell of the nightmare faded away.

"They are grown on Massimo land from seed and you will never find better."

Alix forced herself to concentrate on the words, forced herself to smile, forced her heart to stop pounding in her chest.

Just a dream. Just a dream.

She took solace from Severin's words. She had almost managed to believe them when the door to the Lady Barbara's chamber flew open and a page hurled his way in.

"I bring word from the Knight Brigante," he said,

cheeks aglow with the importance of his news. "Henry of England has just landed in France at Calais! He has brought the Sire of Harnoncourt with him and joined forces with the Duke of Burgundy. Together they move to take Paris and the king."

Conquest

Twenty-two

Alix awoke with a start. She could not quite remember the nightmare but she knew it had been dreadful. Frightening. She felt her fingernails digging into her clenched hands as they gripped the lacework covering. She thought immediately of Severin and tried to sense danger on him. She did this often now, though she could not remember when she had started. Or when this sense of *knowing* had begun. But whatever had frightened her did not concern Severin, at least not as yet. What frightened her was nearer. For the first time in a very long time she thought of Yvrain and wondered if the duke had removed him from the sanctuary of Haute Fleur, and if he were safe. Alix shivered, though her chamber was hot and still.

The dream was still there, so close that she could almost see into it. So close that she could almost remember. For an instant she saw a figure forming, someone or something shrouded in a dull silver light. The figure tantalized her from a distance and then moved slowly away.

The carillon outside her window chimed sexte—the first bell of daylight—though Alix could see that it was still quite dark outside. But she was restless and her stomach churned with nausea. She rose from her bed and draped a linen robe about her shoulders. She pulled open the door to her chamber and peered out into the hallway. The heat was oppressive. It was early, she reasoned, and the few people left to swelter in Rome would still be abed. She decided that perhaps she could walk back and forth through the courtyard. At least there might be a breath of air there, as well as marble statues. They would be cool to the touch and Alix longed to rest her hands and her forehead against their coolness. She did not want to stay in her deserted chamber; she was still a little frightened by the remnants of her dream.

"I miss Severin," she thought as her silk slippers beat a pattern against the cold marble floors. Then she remembered and quickly added, "But of course he is head of the Gold Company and has his army to tend."

The words sounded hollow, even forsaken, just as they had always sounded at Mercier. She had been thinking quite a bit of Mercier since Severin had left her at Palazzo Massimo. Worse yet, she had been feeling as she had felt there.

" 'Tis this wretched nausea," she said aloud. " 'Twill pass."

It had been three weeks since the Duke of Burgundy had sent word of King Henry's arrival at Calais. Severin had left immediately, the next morning, for Bari in order to raise men and money for his army.

"Belden of Harnoncourt is coming,"

Alix's husband had glowed with excitement as he picked her up in his strong arms and whirled her about in the air. She had been breathless when finally he had righted her but not so dizzy that she could not mark the brightness in his clear, dark eyes. Alix remembered how haunted he had looked when first they had met as he had stepped out from Lancelot de Guigny's shadow on the night of Robert's death.

It seemed an age ago. It *was* an age ago. Severin had changed since then and perhaps she had as well.

"Severin," she said, laughing and catching at breaths.

But he interrupted her. "Almost finished." The words were practically a song. "Belden of Harnoncourt is coming and he will find me at the head of the army that he founded. I will lead his men to victory over the French and that moment will be the culmination of my life."

"Severin."

"Later," he whispered as he brought his lips to hers.

And maybe she was wrong. She *might* be wrong.

Alix thought this as she watched his horse prance away toward the stretch of green that surrounded Castel Sant'Angelo. After all, she had never been with child before. Severin was so tantalizingly close to his goal and she loved him so much. How could she tell him something that might distract him when he needed all his wits about him in order to accomplish his mission?

As yet the pope had not promised his support to the Burgundian cause. Secretly he might favor Henry V and England but few men, either lay or priestly, would dare run the risk of alienating Charles VI and mighty France. This meant that Severin still had his mission and he was driven by it once the first flush of his excitement had passed. Just as he had been driven by it for the whole of their short time in Rome. No longer did he find time to squeeze in reading lessons; no longer did he play the drum so that she could dance the tarantella for them beneath the full moon.

At night he came to bed late after endless meetings with the duke's latest emissary or with Urbano Massimo or with Gian Galeazzo Visconti. He spoke often of the Lombardian lord and Alix smiled when he did so, although she did not like the head of the powerful Visconti family.

Alix hugged her secret closely, waiting for her husband's return. She did not even tell Barbara Massimo, although the two of them had grown close.

"You should come with me to Ostia," Barbara had said as she wiped milk from the face of the youngest of her four children. "No one stays in Rome in August. It is much too warm."

Alix stopped fanning herself long enough to lift another child. "I promised Severin to wait for him here—that is, if you don't mind."

"Of course I do not mind," said Barbara. "But you can just as easily await his missive at the sea where it is cooler. Urbano is with him and he will know to have any message forwarded to our house at Ostia if it comes from my lord Severin."

They had all taken to giving him the noble appellation which they were certain the Duke of Burgundy would grant to the Knight Brigante once the battle against France had been set and won.

Indeed the Roman air was stifling. Alix walked to the window and stared out at the haze before speaking. "I know you must take your children to the sea and it is kind of you to include me, but I think I will await my husband here."

She did not add that she felt compelled to wait for Severin in Rome, nor did she add that she was certain something, or someone, waited with her. Barbara would not understand these things; Alix was not sure she understood them herself.

"It will be quiet here," she added.

The Countess Massimo laughed. "Quiet is something that most surely will be missing at the sea—at least once I've arrived there with my brood. Still, I am worried about you staying on with only the servants for company." Then she brightened. "But there is always the lord Visconti. He has promised to return and perhaps he will prove amiable company. He says that he finds you—interesting. Yes, that is the word he used."

"I am sure the lord Visconti will be too busy with his own interests to concern himself with me," replied Alix, a little too quickly. "There is still much to do in preparation for this war, and especially in its financing. Really, I do not mind spending my time alone."

Again Barbara laughed. She hugged her baby close and gently rocked him. " 'Tis true, Alix, that you were once destined to a life of solitude—first at Mercier and then in the convent—but much has changed since then. You might find you now miss the companionship you have grown used to. Promise you will send word to Ostia should you tire of your own company and I will immediately dispatch someone to fetch you. There is nothing but plague and disease in the city during the hot summer months."

That had been ten days ago. Now it was so still within the palazzo that when the man emerged from the shadows and spoke to her, Alix had to stifle a short scream.

"Lord Visconti," she said. She made him a slight reverence and pulled the linen robe closer.

"My Lady Brigante." There was no hint of the day's heat upon Gian Galeazzo. With his beard freshly trimmed he looked rested and dapper. Indeed, he acted as though he had been expecting her. The Visconti lord did not make the obvious remark about her early rising. Instead he fell into step beside her as though they always spent their mornings in this manner.

"You are about early this morning, my lord," she said.

"The Lady Barbara was kind enough to extend me hospitality should I again find myself in Rome," he answered. "I have just returned."

"From Bari?" asked Alix, thinking of Severin.

Visconti stretched his thin lips into a smile. "No, my lady. I bring no word from your husband. I have been in Milan attending to urgent business in my own state. Someone has accompanied me to Rome."

But Alix had lost interest since it was evident he brought no news of Severin. The remnant of the dream still clouded her morning.

"I hope your stay will be pleasant," she said and made a slight reverence in preparation to take her leave.

But Visconti cut her short. "My friend—the man who came with me from Milan—knew your mother well . . ."

Alix stopped. "My mother?"

". . . And your grandmother. He was—how shall I phrase this—an intimate friend to both."

Now they had both stopped. Gray light slatted through a narrow window and outside, in the courtyard, a lone bird began to sing into the absolute silence. Alix stared closely at the man before her and she felt the chill as his blue eyes studied her as well.

"Julian Madrigal, your mother," said Visconti finally, "and Aalyne de Lione, your grandmother. She was the last true Magdalene, and perhaps the greatest. The last to rightly wear the Maltese Star."

This was the man from her nightmare. Alix realized this immediately as soon as the door had closed her inside and alone with him. She knew this though the room was dim and she could barely make out the figure sitting huddled in a chair in its darkest corner.

"He is a friend." Visconti had laughed when she pressed him. "Someone who was once quite powerful but is now completely forgotten by the world."

Alix doubted this. She stopped, closed her eyes, and sensed no hint of bitterness or resignation or frustration on the still air of this small room. Instead, she sensed the crackle of an active power.

"They have forgotten me because they think me dead," said the man, reading her mind. His chuckle rustled the air. "But you, my dear, may draw nearer. You have no need to fear me. In a sense we are related."

"Through my mother and my grandmother? Is that how you know of them?" Alix kept her place at the door.

Again the dry chuckle. "Oh, no. I have no link of parentage with them. We were merely friends, nothing more. I am related to your husband. But we will come to that by and by. Now would you not like to join me?"

His voice was low, as though air rasped against flint in his throat. Alix noticed that he paused occasionally and wheezed, as though he pulled the words out and they hurt him. The man pointed to a low stool close to his own seat and Alix took it. A servant entered with a pitcher filled with water on which floated lemon slices and fresh mint. She left these on a silver tray between two beaten-work goblets. As the woman left, Alix took the time to examine her host.

On this hot and muggy day he sat huddled on his high-backed chair, swaddled top to toe in what appeared to be porous black linen. His head hung low, huddled against his dark garment, and Alix could not make out his facial features. She could not see his eyes though she was sure they missed nothing. A slight odor seemed to emanate from the man, some strange incense that Alix could not quite identify.

"You are related to my husband?" She allowed doubt to lace her voice once the servant had left them alone once again.

"I see you wear the Maltese Star," said the man, ignoring her question. "As your mother did before you and her mother did before that. It becomes you. I feel its power."

He paused and drew breath. "Indeed, I feel it. You have the potential to become a great Magdalene, perhaps the greatest of them all. More powerful even than your grandmother—who ended badly. Or did your mother not tell you that?"

"My mother told me nothing of this amulet," said Alix. For an instant the urge to run away from this man surged through her. She actually rose on her stool before the hypnotism of his voice—and curiosity—stayed her.

"A pity. Hers was a misguided attempt at protection. In this wicked world the only way you will be safe is to know who you are—and use it."

"And who am I?" Alix spoke very quietly.

"The Magdalene," replied the man in the same tone of voice one might reply about the weather. "The warlock's witch. You are the Templar Knight's revenge upon those who would destroy the Order."

"I know nothing of witchcraft." Alix laughed outright but this did not break the spell of the man's words. She felt them web about her.

"You know more than you believe," he said. "And eventually you will know yet more—infinitely more. Once you choose the path that has been laid for you. Once you take back what has been stolen."

"Sir, you speak in riddles. The Templar Knights are long destroyed." The air around Alix grew oppressive.

She realized suddenly that she did not even know this man's name.

"I will speak of myself later," he said, again answering an unasked question. "When I speak of your husband and ask for what I have come to beg of you. Because I have come to seek a favor from the Wise Woman, just as all must ask her aid in the end. I will tell you what I know of your history and you will then decide if what I tell you is worth the price I will ask."

Alix nodded, fascinated by this man and his story, already lightly gathered in his web.

"You know, of course of the Knights Templar and what happened to them at the end?"

"They were disbanded and burned by King Philip the Fair of France and Clement V, the first of the Avignon popes," replied Alix, who had read parchments of this history and knew it well. "But that was at least a century ago."

"But do you know of their beginnings?" prompted the man who sat before her.

Alix shook her head.

"That is the story that is always lost." The man settled into his garment again, as though preparing himself for a long tale. Alix, keen for knowledge, forgot the heat and the stillness and even her initial misgivings as she leaned closer. "But it is the part that is the most important and it alone explains what happened and why the cult of the Magdalene was formed."

A breeze fluttered at the small window bringing momentary life to the drapings that hung there.

"I hear you have taught the Knight Brigante to read," said the man.

Alix nodded.

"Still now there are many knights without knowledge of their letters," he continued. "But in the past there were many more. Learning was left to the monks and a few—a very few—of the priests. The warriors were kept busy with their battles and their crusades. This was their mission, and war the drug that kept them ignorant of their own peril. Severin is wise to realize the peril one faces when one leaves knowledge entirely in others' hands. Hugh of Payns, who founded the Knights Templar, did not realize just how exposed he would leave his Order when he insisted that their mission was to fight for Christendom and not seek to understand its intricacies.

"He came originally from a small village in Burgundy, a place within the demesne of the Counts of Mercier, in fact. He enthusiastically heeded Bernard of Clairvaux's call to take the Cross and made his way to Jerusalem to liberate the sacred places from Saracen hands—at least this was his intent. He thought himself involved with holy men sent by God on holy mission. Instead, once in Jerusalem, he found his world turned upside down. The French, who had established the Kingdom of Jerusalem, turned out to be more corrupt than the 'infidels' who surrounded them. They had taken on eastern habits without the moderation that marked the eastern way of life. And not only that. The crusaders, crying out God's name, raped women and killed young children. Mothers frightened their children into obedience with the threat of Christ's name. The atmosphere sickened the simple Burgundian and he sought to do something about this. This was a time of great monastic growth in Europe. The same St. Bernard, who had called so passionately for crusade, had himself established more than a hundred cells scattered throughout all of Christendom who looked toward the great Cistercian monastery of Clairvaux as their source."

"Including the monastery at Haute Fleur," said Alix, thinking once again of Yvrain.

"Indeed, including Haute Fleur." The man coughed his dry, ragged cough. Alix heard him moan softly and reached to pour water for him from the pitcher. He reached across to take it and she noticed that his hands were hidden by knitted gloves.

"Haute Fleur," he repeated, once he could speak again. "The most beautiful monastery of them all. Hugh of Payns had grown up near it and had loved its order and the peace of its life. He thought the holy monks to be worthy models. It was the remembrance of Haute Fleur that eventually sparked his imagination. This gave him the idea of creating a warrior Order that would be grounded upon the virtues of chastity and obedience that so permeated the great Benedictine and Cistercian Orders that dotted Europe with their monasteries.

"He called his Order the Knights of the Temple and quickly established the first Temple at the holy city of Jerusalem. The idea of an Order of warrior-monks caught fire immediately and soon others imitated his initiative. The Knights of St. John Hospital followed, as did the Teutonic Knights. But the Templars were, from the very beginning, considered to be the elite. Hundreds of knights, including many younger sons from the noblest families in Christendom, flocked to kiss the Cross and take up the defense of Christendom. The knight-monks dressed in white, as befitted their chaste status, and soon were granted permission to wear the blood-red Cross of Christ upon their scapulars as well."

"I have seen pictures of them, painted on miniatures in some of the manuscripts in the library at Mercier," said Alix.

"Indeed, they were well welcomed throughout Christendom even after it proved impossible to retain the kingdom that had been established in the east.

When they were expelled by the Saracens they found many a king willing to make a home for them upon European soil, including the rulers of France, who had dynastic interests in the east and had looked to the Knights Templar to defend these."

Alix's brow wrinkled. "But with no Crusade and no battle, how did the Templars continue to justify their existence?"

"They took on a new mission." Again the man made the low, painful sound that served him as a laugh. "You know of course that all men who took up the Cross of Crusade were given indulgence and forgiveness of past sins?"

Alix nodded.

"This was especially true of the Templar Knights. Except theirs was not just a metaphysical indulgence. The grateful kings of Europe showered them with earthly benefits as well."

"They were not required to pay tax," said Alix.

The dark figure before her nodded. "And more importantly—or infamously—once the Jews were forbidden to lend money at interest, the Knights Templar eagerly took up this task. They had been greatly endowed with large fortunes left them both by the kings and by other nobles interested in placating God and ensuring his good graces for the way they blithely had spent their lives within the devil's keeping."

"So they became money lenders."

"And wealthy, powerful ones at that. Once they quitted Jerusalem they established their main Temple at Paris right beneath the noses and protection of the Kings of France. In short order the Order of the Temple was rumored to be wealthier than the state of France itself. The last of the Order's Grand Masters, Jacques de Molay, had grown so powerful that he was named godfather of Philip the Fair's only daughter."

"This was Queen Isabel who married Edward II of England and merged the royal Capetian blood of France with the Plantagenet blood of England," said Alix.

"Though she was hated and feared in both countries," the man continued. "She was Jacques de Molay's goddaughter, after all, and he and his Order had been accused by King Philip and Pope Clement of magic, sodomy, sorcery, and witchcraft. Many found it convenient to attach these labels to his goddaughter as well. The Order had been disbanded in 1307 and Jacques de Molay and his followers thrown into dungeons and cruelly tortured, all so that the king could right the listing ship of his royal finances with the gold he thought hidden within their Temple vaults."

"Was the gold found?"

"Never." The man shook his head. "Many say there was no gold, that only greed stoked the rumors of it. They say the king and pope both sold their souls to the devil for nothing. Naturally, these two paid lip service to God's justice. They evoked courts of law and called in learned Inquisitors to man them. The trouble was that the Templars themselves were not educated. Jacques de Molay was called upon to defend both himself and his Order before scholars from the universities at Oxford and Bologna and Paris. He was an old man by then and had been brutally tortured. He ranted and raved before the men who tried him but it was of no use. He had been trained as a warrior and though he was Grand Master he could neither read nor write. As he himself said, 'I am a knight, unlettered and poor.' He could convince his accusers of nothing."

Again a hot breeze rustled at the window drapings.

"But there was one man who could."

Alix waited, now deeply caught in the web of this man's tale and wanting to know its ending.

"And only one. His name was Peter of Bologna and he was that rare being—a learned priest within the Templar Order. He mounted a spirited defense of his brothers—so spirited, indeed, that the charges against them appeared more and more ludicrous. Indeed, it seemed he might even have persuaded the Inquisition to his thinking had he not disappeared."

"He was killed by Philip of France?"

"He was deemed dead." The man laughed, "Just as I was."

"But he escaped."

"It was the only thing he could do," the dark man insisted. Alix, glancing up, caught a shadow of silver light surround him, just as she had seen it do in her dream. "That and plot revenge. He was Italian, as I am, and from the same small town from outside of Bologna. We are expert at vendetta and his was fitting indeed. The Templars had been accused of sorcery and witchcraft. They had been accused of necromancy with Mary of Magdala and of worshipping her ghost. Well, he would make the charges true. He would gather the remnant of his Order and nurture it; together they would work to wreak the havoc that Jacques de Molay, as he sizzled upon the pyre, called down upon the king and his bought pope."

"They were both dead within the year," Alix recalled from the tales the Dowager Duchess of Burgundy had told at Mercier. "And the Capetian dynasty ended as Philip the Fair's three hale sons perished one after the other as they ascended the throne."

"But it wasn't enough for what we had suffered." The man's voice had grown vehement; it sounded ancient. "Not for what they had taken from us. Philip of Bologna knew this as well. He studied the ancient texts. He grew strong in secrets and in power and his hidden men grew strong with him. They had the knowledge, you see—and they also had the funds."

The man chuckled. "They had the funds. You see, Philip of Bologna took the Templar treasure into hiding with him. With all his torture and his threats and his killings, Philip was never able to lay hands upon the object of his greed. The hidden remnant of the Templars had all they needed to recapture their strength and position in the world. Only one thing was missing."

"Their Magdalene," said Alix.

"The warlock's witch. But they found her soon enough. She was a young girl working as the Wise Woman in a village in Provence. A great beauty, they tell me, and I believe this as I look at you."

"This was my grandmother?"

"It was your grandmother's grandmother. But hers also was a tale drenched in martyrs' blood. She was a Cathar, a member of the heretical sect that the Inquisition and Simon de Montfort had first thrown upon the martyrs' fire. She was a simple woman but she had heard stories. She, too, craved vengeance and sought to right past wrongs. Promises were made, secrets spoken. She became more than happy to consecrate her progeny to the meeting of our needs. As I say, she was a simple woman and poor. There had been many times when she would gladly have sold her soul for a loaf of maggot bread—and we offered her much more."

"We?"

"I, too, have faced injustices that needed righting." The man paused. "I have worn the Maltese Star since I was forced into the seminary and it has served me well."

Ah, so he was a priest.

Alix edged closer.

"Why are you telling me this?" she whispered. The spell was broken. She felt her own nausea untangling its web. "What is it that you want?"

He had a ready answer. It seemed he had thought this out for some time—perhaps for ages and ages of time.

"You," he said simply. "And your unborn child."

"For witchcraft?" she asked, incredulous. Without thinking, she wrapped her arms protectively around her womb. "For revenge?"

"I prefer to see it as righting past wrongs." He was quite close to her now and the scent of his strange incense grew strong. "Besides, you cannot escape your power. It is part of you, just as the Maltese Star is part of you as well. And you have called upon it. You called upon it the first time, quite unthinkingly, when you needed guidance to save the child Yvrain. And then you called upon it quite consciously to guide the lance of Severin Brigante when he jousted against Lancelot de Guigny for your hand."

"Severin won without assistance! He bested the Knight de Guigny at the lists!"

"Did he?" The man's voice rustled.

Alix, caught, remembered the power that surged through her, the jolt it had caused and how Severin had suddenly turned to her, startled, just before Lancelot de Guigny fell from his horse.

"Or did you help him?"

Within the shroud of linen, old shoulders rose and then lowered. The man held wide his gloved hands.

"Severin Brigante could never have won without assistance. He had been blooded with a salted lance. Without your healing touch he would never have raised his weapon; the pain would have been excruciating. But you used your will and your power. You healed that pain. And when you did that, both you and your unborn daughter became mine. You became the Magdalene. You must feel that. You must know that."

"But my mother?"

He shook his head. "Julian Madrigal never used her power. She was tempted once, when your father left her for another woman. But she did not use it. She let him go. Instead she sought protection for you by never telling you of your heritage. She thought that by keeping the story from you she could make the Maltese Star go away. It didn't. It never does."

He chortled.

Alix felt nausea well up within her, strong enough to break this man's spell. "I don't believe you. I used no power."

"It does not matter what you believe. What matters is what you have done and the power you have used. It makes you ours. It makes you mine."

Alix jumped up. "Who *are* you?"

The man did not seem at all frightened by her anger.

"I am Archangelo Conti," he said. "Cardinal Archangelo Conti."

Alix stopped and shook her head as a memory teased the corner of her mind.

"But you are dead," she said finally. "You were killed by Belden of Harnoncourt more than twenty years ago."

"Not by Belden," said Conti, rising slowly but still holding to the shadows that surrounded his face, "but by his brother, Guy. He thought himself finally the champion of his superior brother. He pulled together his sotted self to best me and then left me to perish in the flames. After that he married my ward, Chiara Conti."

"Severin's mother."

"My daughter."

Once again he let out a rattle of laughter. "The Harnoncourts thought themselves done with me. But as you see, I have come back."

Twenty-three

During the months of their short marriage, Alix had grown so used to talking to Severin that she found it difficult not to talk to him now. But she didn't. She did not dare. She could not even tell him of their child. Not with what the man had threatened.

"You are ours," he had said. *"Not his. Once you use the power you cannot turn back. I have waited patient years to claim you and I will not be gainsaid of my victory. No one will take the Magdalene away again. I will not allow it."*

She felt the silence of her isolation even as she watched her husband dismount from his charger and hurry to her through the courtyard of the Palazzo Massimo. She felt it choke back the words in her mouth. She was more alone within the confines of this bright palazzo than she had ever been in the grand and elaborate solitude of Mercier.

Severin rushed into the chamber and lifted his wife high into the air.

"Henry has landed," he said breathlessly. "He sailed from Southampton and has already seized the French fortress at Harfleur."

Alix counted herself lucky that Severin was so filled with his own news.

So excited that he could not wait for her answer, he continued on with the tales he had brought. "I've raised both men and money in Bari. Not as much as

I wanted—stories still abound about the invincibility of the French. But we've enough. We shall leave in these next days for Burgundy. I'll be pleased to get you out of the city and into the Haute Savoy once again. The air is filled with pestilence. There's even mention of a breaking of the plague once again. Oh, I'd quite forgotten."

He shouted for a page and then searched carefully through the sumter that was brought to him.

"I've brought this," he said, very attentively pulling a flax-wrapped parcel from the pack. "I could not wait to show it to you."

"It" was an old manuscript, very fragile and beautiful, that Severin laid upon a trestle with great care.

" 'Tis a treatise on falconry—a manuscript entitled *De Arte Venandi*. The Emperor Frederick II wrote the preface two hundred years ago in Bari when he ruled there. When I saw it, I knew I must have it. Once this war is finished and I've met with the Sire of Harnoncourt, we will read it together. Won't that be nice? 'Twas actually falconry that brought us together. If my hunter had not brought down your message pigeon we would never have had the reading lessons—and the reading lessons were the beginning of it all."

Alix listened to her husband and let his excitement cue her. It was easy enough to exclaim over Henry of England's determination and to gingerly leaf through the pages of the beautiful manuscript he had brought. She felt genuine tears in her eyes when, shyly, he brought forth a length of blue samite that he had purchased for her, and a pair of soft, green kid gloves. Severin had started life as a beggar knight and she knew how careful he still remained with his coins; that he had thought to take time from his business to purchase these gifts touched her.

"And we will go to Belvedere when this is over," he

said as he bathed and Alix lathered his back with fine lavender soap. "I know you must want to visit your castle—your very own home. I promise just as soon as Henry has won and I have fulfilled my pledge to my father, I will take you there."

Alix nodded as he said this because she knew he expected this of her; she smiled at all the appropriate stories he told her and praised King Henry's resourcefulness at Hanfleur because she knew this was expected of her as well. But in her heart she was still with Archangelo Conti. She still heard herself being called a witch and a Magdalene. She still heard the words *the choice has already been made.*

But had she really? Had she sent the power that enabled Severin to win her hand in the lists? The only one she could ask this of was Severin himself and this she dared not do. She would have to tell him everything then. About his father, about the killing of Cardinal Conti. Above all, she would have to tell him that his wife was a witch—not a Wise Woman but a true witch.

And she realized that, indeed, she was one. She had only to remember her hatred of Yvrain to know that this was so. Would a true woman—a good woman—so hate an innocent child?

Again she realized as she toweled her husband with linen sheeting and then wrapped her arms around him and reached up to meet his fine lips with her own that she had never, never felt so alone and isolated in her life.

Something was wrong and Severin knew it. He sensed it in the way Alix kissed him, as though willing him to be satisfied with her body and leave her soul alone. She had been like this in the beginning. But

then, starting with their argument about her packing
at Mercier and then especially after she had danced
the tarantella to his drumming at Mayfest, she had
seemed different. Open and warm and loving. Once
again she had been the girl he had glimpsed in Paris
so very long ago.

Now she had changed. She was hiding,

He knew this as surely as he knew his own name
and his mission. Something had happened during the
fortnight he had spent in Bari and she would not tell
him of it. Nor could he puzzle it together by himself.
At first he tried coaxing her into talking with simple
questions about whom she had seen and what she had
done while he was away.

Alix had seen no one. She had gone nowhere.

"But Urbano told me that the lord Visconti was staying at the palazzo," he asked her. "Did you not see
him? Have you dined each night alone?"

She had indeed, she assured him, dined by herself
in her chamber since the Lady Barbara had taken the
children to the sea.

Strange, that.

Severin decided not to insist. It was better that she
had stayed close to the palazzo and had not strayed
into the dangerous Roman streets. Besides the pestilence of summer and the brigands that traditionally
roamed the byways of any large city, there was also the
added danger of war. This time the pot might be sim-
mering in France but, as had so often happened in
the past, one of the sparks that ignited it had been
struck in Rome.

"Lancelot de Guigny has disappeared again," he
told Alix that night as they lay close together in their
bed. "The Duke of Burgundy has sent word."

He felt her stiffen, but when she spoke her voice
was low, contained.

"Is Yvrain safe?"

"I've heard nothing to the contrary. I think the Knight de Guigny may have other interests now, well beyond those of Mercier."

"You think he plans treason?"

"The duke thinks this. He has sent parties in search of his half-brother. No one has found him. The monks at the shrine to St. Bernard have not seen him in months. He is an astute warrior. Undoubtedly the king offered more of a position and Lancelot de Guigny has defected. It would not surprise me."

"I remember the first time I looked upon him," said Alix softly. "It was the night of Robert's death, the night Lancelot de Guigny murdered him. I did not feel this at the time, I was too distraught. Too hurting. But I have thought of it many times since and I remember how the Knight de Guigny talked of his brother. He was wistful when he mentioned him. Hurt. Almost as though he could not fathom why the duke, who had so much, could not spare him the freehold he had so richly deserved."

"If, indeed, he has joined the king's forces, Lancelot de Guigny is a traitor to his brother and to all of Burgundy. There is no polite way around knowing that."

"Yet, I cannot help thinking," replied Alix, "that if only . . . but of course it is silly to think of such things. You sleep now. We still have tomorrow to discuss these matters."

She was starting to sound again like the Alix he knew and Severin smiled, relieved.

"Yes, tomorrow," he said with a satisfied yawn. "And tomorrow and tomorrow after that."

Alix waited until Severin's breath slowed before she asked him.

"What do you know of Archangelo Conti?"

He had been almost, but not quite, sleeping. His voice was muffled as he spoke. "He was a Cardinal in Rome—let me recollect—almost thirty years ago. I've heard he was crippled and perhaps unattractive. Supposedly his family made him take priestly vows to keep him from the clutches of an unsuitable marriage. He worked his way diligently through the intricacies of the Vatican, rising to the rank of Cardinal and amassing quite a following among the common people. Many thought of him as a saint. In the end, he became like Cola di Rienzo and allowed himself to be controlled by a power he had once controlled."

"Do you know how he died?" she whispered.

"He was killed by Belden of Harnoncourt." Severin was awake now and leaning toward her. "In fact, it happened quite near here. Conti was a wealthy man and owned one of the largest of the palazzi on the Clelian hill. Why do you ask?"

Alix answered his question with another of her own. "Did he have connections with the lord Visconti?"

"They had been friends. Gian Galeazzo was rumored to be a supporter of Archangelo Conti, though no one seemed to know why. The Visconti are nothing if not aristocrats and Conti gained his power through the plebeian poor. Still, when none of the Contis came forth, it was Gian Galeazzo who identified the body of the Cardinal and arranged its proper burial. He had been sworded by Belden but his body was horribly disfigured, burned apparently beyond recognition, in an accidental fire that destroyed a vast portion of his property. There was nothing anyone could do. My father said it was most natural that Visconti would help him. Gian Galeazzo has always been implacable against his enemies but the embodiment of loyalty to his friends. He considered Archangelo Conti a friend."

"Then how could the lord Visconti recognize him?"

"Through jewelry, I imagine," replied Severin. "Yes, that's it—he recognized his body through something that he wore. It was probably the ring of his bishopric or perhaps some holy sign or other."

Or perhaps it was the Maltese Star.

Alix shivered. "Are you sure that he died there? Are you certain it was Belden of Harnoncourt who killed him?"

"Oh, yes, quite certain," said Severin, kissing her forehead. "My father told me the story himself when I was a boy."

She wasn't sure, and the lingering doubt again forced her from bed before daybreak. She wanted to think that the man she had met, the man who called himself Archangelo Conti, was an impostor. She thought of the Knight de Guigny and the threats he had made both to her and to Severin. It was not impossible that Sir Lancelot was behind this.

But the man she had talked to had known too much about her. She doubted that even a man as cunning and astute as Guigny would have woven story-pieces and tale-fragments into whole cloth as easily as that strange, silver-illumined man had done. He had known the flash of power that went through her on the list field. He had known it was her mother who had given her the Maltese Star.

Other things—tales of a grandmother and great grandmother—might have been fiction, but there was a ring to what he had told her—a ring of truth that she heard knell deep inside her heart. Alix remembered half-heard words from her childhood. She remembered whispering and pointing as she walked through the streets of Hungary with her mother. A few people had even lowered their fingers in the ancient sign against the Evil Eye. Could it be true what the man had told her? Was she a witch? Was she his Magdalene?

But the single most troubling thought that whirled through her mind was that the man knew about her child. Not even Severin knew about their child. And if what the man had told her was true, then their child was in danger. Alix shivered when she thought of this and paused on the long marble staircase that led to the deserted courtyard. For an instant she thought she heard something behind her, perhaps a brush of something against the stone. Curious, she turned but there was nothing there. Only the gray shadows of night growing silvery and vague.

"I must tell Severin," she thought. "Even though I am not certain and his mind is filled with what is happening in France, I must tell him. He must know."

Of course she must tell her husband.

The thought was so clear and perfect in her mind that for a second she wondered why she had not considered it before. All the excuses she had made, all the reasons she had given were just that—excuses and reasons. Echoes from the life she had been expected to live at Mercier, but which had nothing to do with the life that she lived now.

She had to talk to Severin. She had to tell him what had happened and ask his advice.

Alix had started turning to do just that when the first blow came and she felt herself falling, falling into the dark.

Twenty-four

Yvrain was crying. Alix was sure of it. He needed her and she must get to him. There was her mission, after all—the promise she had made to Robert. She heard her name called and again the sobbing as she whirled about in the silvery mist, trying to position the sound.

"Yvrain!"

Frantically she searched, trying to locate him, trying to do her duty—and then she saw the light.

"Yvrain!"

She ran toward it and it looked so peaceful. She heard music and laughter and a tinkling sound of water—but above all she sensed its peace. Everything would be over once she reached it. She would not have to face the things she somehow knew crouched in the silver mist behind her. Demons that wore the Maltese Star and wanted to destroy her and all that she loved.

If Yvrain is there, he will not need rescuing. Alix thought this as her feet pattered forward. *If Yvrain is there he will be . . .*

Instead it was Robert de Mercier who stepped out before her. Robert de Mercier who blocked her path.

"No, Alix," he said, shaking his head but smiling at her with great affection. "You do not want to come here. It is not your time. You still have much to do where you are now."

"Oh, no," she said, shaking her head. "You don't understand. They tried to kill me. They killed my . . ."

"Don't think of that now," replied Robert de Mercier. He waved his hand and Alix felt the mist invade her mind and drive out the thought that had troubled it. "Time enough to think about that later when you are safely back with the man you love."

Alix turned to him and smiled shyly, as though they shared a secret. "I don't love you anymore?" she asked.

"You never loved me," said Robert, and he too was smiling. "Not the way you love him. How fortunate you are, my little Alix. You have someone who loves you at last."

"I am fortunate," she agreed. "I love him so much."

"You must tell him that," urged Robert. Alix noticed that he had moved away from her and stood, once again, at the edge of a vast forest, just as he had long ago when she had dreamed of him at Mercier. "You must tell your husband that you love him. You must be strong—stronger than you have ever been in the past. You must tell your husband that you love him. And you must remember how that love grew and when it began. This is so important for you, Alix. It is with this knowledge that you can change your world."

Alix nodded.

"But Yvrain!" she called.

"Yvrain is safe," said Robert. He was so distant now that she could barely hear his words. "And because of you, he will be blessed. Now be brave, Alix, and turn back—back, indeed, to the demon that awaits you at Mercier. But back to the love that awaits you there as well."

Alix strained hard to see her lost husband, but he had disappeared, covered by the fog that surrounded

the far-forest. Even his last words came to her as a
mere sigh upon the breeze.

Adieu! Yvrain will be blessed, and for this I thank you!

The fog ebbed, and sometimes Alix found she could
peek through it. Sometimes she saw Barbara bending
over her, sometimes a strange, apple-faced woman in
a white wimple, and sometimes a kindly man. They
smiled at her.

But the crying continued.

Once Alix opened her eyes and thought she saw
Severin beside her, his head in his hands. She tried to
reach out to him yet she wasn't sure that she touched
him. She was just so weak and tired. She drifted away
again, certain she would never find the strength to
speak the true words:

Severin loves me. And I love him.

"Ah, we never thought you'd make it, lady," said
the apple-faced woman, "though you had us on our
knees from morn to night."

She tucked light linen coverings over Alix and held
a pewter tankard with lemon water for her to drink.

"My husband," said Alix, once she could speak.
"Has he gone away into France?"

"Into France?" snorted the woman. "It was all we
could do to get him into a resting bed and a change
of garments—and that is with the Lady Barbara coaxing and Doctor Moscato as well. He would not be
parted from you until this very morning when he was
assured that the fever had left you. Indeed, he has only
gone into the next chamber to right himself because
Lady Barbara convinced him that the sight of his hag-
gard face might undo all the good of Dr. Moscato's

ministrations and, in the end, frighten you from this world into the next."

The woman sighed as she set about fluffing Alix's pillows and righting the crisp linen that covered her. " 'Tis gratifying to see a man so in love with his wife," she said. "It restores my trust in human nature."

"You are sure he's not gone off to France?" said Alix, struggling to a sitting position. "Henry of England has landed at Calais with Belden of Harnoncourt. Severin will want to be there for the battle. It is the moment for which he has worked his whole life."

"Tut, tut," said the woman. "I know nothing of this war and the goings-on in France. I am Italian and the Good Lord knows that we have enough rascals and business to mind in our own land without taking on the troubles of others. The French must see to themselves. And obviously they must manage this without the aid of the Lord Brigante—because he has remained here and not gone there."

Alix was no longer listening to the nurse's cheery talk. There was a movement at the door of her chamber and she turned to it. Tall, dressed in black, his bright hair catching the sunlight, Severin stood in her doorway.

He was looking at her from the depths of his deep, dark eyes. She saw no love upon his face.

"You've not gone to France," whispered Alix.

Severin did not answer her. Instead he nodded to the nurse and then waited, before venturing further, until she had shut the door behind her.

"You are looking better," he said. He pulled a stool close to her bed and settled on it with the air of one who was doing only what was expected of him. "I—we were quite worried."

"Why are you still here and not in France? Has

something happened? Is that not your place?" Alix struggled higher in her bed.

Severin reached out to her and then abruptly pulled his helping hand back.

"My place is where I choose to make it," he snapped and then softened. "Duke John sent word that the Gold Company should join him at Dijon and not unite with the English on the coast. Since the early victories, things have not gone well with King Henry. Word has been sent that his army languishes and is full of disease. My lord of Burgundy is taking no chances. He has plighted himself to a traitor's troth and thrown his country into civil war. In the end, should Charles of France triumph, the duke might find himself in the delicate position of an insurgent. It is he who pays for the protection of the Gold Company and it is he who has decided to use that power to ensure the safety of Burgundy and not to further the English cause."

"But what of Belden of Harnoncourt?" cried Alix. "What of all you have worked toward?"

"And what of my child?"

His voice was low and dangerous. Alix heard every word.

"I've lost my baby," she said. The words were a statement, not a question. They were part of the reason she had not wanted to turn back. They had been there, she realized, as part of the demon behind her in the mist. "My baby isn't living in me anymore.

"*My* baby, too," rasped Severin. "Or perhaps you had forgotten that. Certainly you had forgotten to tell me of its existence. I imagine you did not think me worthy enough to be its father, *Countess* Alix. I have worked well to better myself but I am still a simple knight. Largely unschooled and without the grace of a great lord such as Robert de Mercier. It must have been a great comedown to you to think you bear a child to me rather than to a great lord. It must have surely compromised any plans you had to have our farce of a marriage annulled once you were safely freed from the clutches of Lancelot de Guigny."

Alix shook her head. "We don't have a farce of a marriage," she said.

"What would you call it then?" The words exploded from him like thunder. "I wake up one fine morning to find my wife lying lifeless at the bottom of a stairwell covered in . . ."

Severin controlled himself with visible effort.

"Covered in blood," he continued. "I picked you up and carried you here and sent immediately for Ya-copo Moscato. I would not leave you, even though I thought you dead. Instead it was our child who had died."

He stopped again, pulled himself together. "Every-one was so kind. Barbara Massimo came as soon as she heard and there was the doctor, his nurse, this house full of strangers. They commiserated with me. They assured me that you—that you had not been damaged by your fall. You are still young, said Doctor Moscato, there will be other children. Yet, I had not even known about this first."

"I wanted to tell you," said Alix quietly. "In fact, I remember turning back to do that very thing when . . . When what happened, happened. I wanted to tell you, Severin. But only when I was certain. I thought you might be angry with me. You had worked so hard. You had come so far. You talked only of meeting with Belden of Harnoncourt and avenging your father. I thought you would think the child a burden and me an inconvenience with it. It was selfish of me; I know that now. But after all my years at Mercier, I just couldn't bear to be an inconvenience yet again. I thought you had married me as a kindness to save me

from Lancelot de Guigny. I could not imagine that you
would want our child."

He stopped and looked at her; for Alix, the world
stopped with him. She saw his eyes narrow with focus,
she saw through the brightness of a new morning's
light right into the depths of his soul. And she found
herself there.

"Is that true?" Severin asked quietly and Alix nodded. He broke down then and the tears that flowed
out of him were filled with years and years of pain.
She felt them wet through the light linen of her night
tunic as he gathered her close, but by then she could
not tell which tears belonged to her and which were
his. They mingled softly against her skin.

"Oh, Alix, you've no idea how wrong you are about
me," whispered her husband. "You've no idea how
much I've wanted you and how much I've longed for
our child. The only thing I've ever *really* wanted, in all
my years of searching, was the family that I've never
had."

They cried and grieved their loss and left Rome together in two weeks' time when Alix was deemed well
enough again to travel. She had told him of the push
she had felt upon the stairs and so the Knight Brigante
refused to leave for France without his wife.

The Duke of Burgundy was understanding. The
Gold Company had already settled in at his fortress of
Dijon and he felt himself safe.

"Leave your men with me—I will general them,"
read his missive, "and go yourself directly to King
Henry at Calais. He is in grave danger and has asked
for you. Go to him! And may God have mercy upon
both your souls!"

Twenty-five

"I am happy indeed that you made it through the lines," said Henry of England to Severin Brigante as soon as the latter had finished with his brief reverence, "but they tell me you have brought your wife as well. I hope 'tis not true. This is neither the time nor the place for a gentlewoman. Even most of the camp followers have left us to the ravages of dysentery and this infernal rain. She would find nothing of convenience here."

"I requested hospitality for Alix at Agincourt Castle, which stands nearby," replied the Knight Brigante. "She insisted. Rumor had already reached us of the troubles that you faced and she did not want to oblige me to have to care for her."

"Agincourt? Is she not chatelaine of Mercier?" Henry raised an eyebrow in his handsome face. "But was there not some dispute about that castle and did not this dispute involve your wife?"

"I, not my wife, was involved in dispute with the Knight de Guigny," replied Severin. He had never felt so weary and sank gratefully into the simple chair indicated by the king. "But he is no longer at Mercier. He deserted to the French king, a move it seems his half-brother Burgundy had long suspected. The castle has once again devolved to the Lady Alix and the duke has named me as her champion."

"Then it is good you brought her to Agincourt if that turn-rabbit Guigny is still afoot."

"Rest assured, your majesty, that I did not leave her even there without a struggle. She was adamant to return to Mercier. She said that should the war veer in that direction she would best serve her people by remaining by their side. The duke has sent a large contingent from the Gold Company to defend the fortress and to block Guigny from any eventual return." Severin paused. "Not that I think Sir Lancelot the man to take Mercier other than by trickery. He is counting on having played well at traitor's dice and that Charles of France will gift him with much more than Mercier once he has won and the battle lines are cleared."

"Charles will not win," said Henry. "And if you believe he will, you can well take your place beside Lancelot de Guigny."

Severin looked levelly at him. He slowly took in Henry's face, his keen eyes, his simple crown and jewels. Many said that Henry, a thorn in his father's side for years, now boasted the exaggerated piety of the reformed rake. But Severin thought he saw something different in him, something deeper.

"Had I wanted to join with Charles of France I might well have done so," he said finally. "I traveled through enough of his territory to reach you."

"Well said!" exclaimed the king, bringing his hand down with a thump upon the trestle. "Your uncle said you would be like this—outspoken and sure. I must tell him how right he was about you!"

"Belden of Harnoncourt is here?"

But of course he was; Severin had known this all along.

"He is always either right beside me or fighting off the Scots from my borders to the north. The Sire of Harnoncourt is a man of fixed habits," said Henry. He shook his head and laughed softly. "When I proposed this excursion he dropped everything at Harnoncourt Hall to accompany me. Brought his two eldest sons with him, one of whom—William, if I am not mistaken—is due to receive the golden spurs of his knighthood upon tomorrow's battlefield."

Severin wanted to ask his uncle's whereabouts. He found himself eager to hear more about his two cousins as well. But now, so close both to them and to the confrontation of which he had so long dreamed, he found himself shy. After the death of his child and the near-death of his wife, he found that he could no longer find the hatred that had so long sustained him.

"I hope Alix is safe." Severin only realized he spoke the words aloud as he heard them. "I hope my wife is well."

"I've heard she was ill in Rome," said the king. He walked to the flap of his tent and held it wide. "And that this is the reason the Duke of Burgundy called the Gold Company to his fortress and left you free to join me. I am saddened, of course, for your wife's illness but I am glad that fate has reserved you to me for the great battle to be fought upon the morrow. Belden of Harnoncourt tells me that you are one of the greatest warriors in Christendom."

"My uncle knows of me?"

"Indeed," said Henry of England. "In truth, to find you was the reason that he came."

In the distance they could see the French campfires stretched out like an infinity of stars into the night.

" 'Tis a wonder they find dry wood for kindling," said Henry with a grumble. "There has been nothing but rain for weeks now. The ground is so sodden that a horse cannot find sure footing upon it."

"This will work for you and not for France," said Severin, the general in him gauging out the land. "The French still fight strictly in the old-fashioned way of formation."

"My spies tell me that they have ten men for each of mine," said Henry. "But I would not have it otherwise. I would not have a single man more. If God gives me victory then it is plain that we owe it to His goodness. If He does not, then the fewer we have will be the less loss to England. My men will fight with their usual courage and God and the justice of our cause shall protect us!"

Severin heard Henry repeat these words over and over again as he walked among his men exhorting them, talking to them, being their leader and their king. Only a half-mile of drenched ground separated this small army from the French; the noise of shouting, murmuring, and bursts of merriment carried toward them on the wind. It contrasted oddly with the disciplined quiet of the English camp where well-trained soldiers saw to their weapons, confessed, and were shriven. No one said a word in discouragement but Severin knew that each man was chastened by the fact that he might well die upon the morrow. Certainly he thought this. He had already called upon the Duke of Burgundy to champion Alix should he die.

King Henry took little rest. He continued to walk quietly among his men.

"The lord of Harnoncourt is a brilliant spy," he said once, turning toward Severin with a chuckle. "I have sent him with his sons out on reconnaissance but I hope they find their way back here before the battle begins!"

At three o'clock the moon rose and the whole army began to prepare itself for the day's battle. To keep their hearts cheerful, the king ordered the trumpets, drums, and fifes to play familiar tunes as the new day dawned.

"St. Crispin's Day," said one of the English bowmen, a grizzled figure whose voice held the strong ring of the lowlands. 25 October."

It had stopped raining, but the sky was gray and water-laden as the men began to be deployed by their marshals into battle formation.

Severin, the veteran of many warrings, looked at them with the eyes of a general. They were no longer the tidy, brightly dressed band that had set sail with Henry two months ago from Southampton. Their tarnished and dented armor gave them a workaday aura. No longer did bright plumes fly jauntily from the headpieces of the knights; the sleeves of rich cloth that had once adorned their armor now hung in faded tatters. Over and over again, Severin found his glance catching on the English archers. For the most part they were bare-chested, without the protective covering of chain mail. Many of them were barefoot, even in the cold rain. Some wore caps of boiled leather and others of wicker-work crossed over with bars of iron. They stood apart from the knights and with their commanders.

They looked determined, Severin thought. He found himself thinking:

Perhaps. Just perhaps.

The king heard three Masses held at various parts of the camp so that all could take part. He was clad in his armor but without his helm and emblazoned surcoat. After the last Mass, Severin stood with the other nobles near him as these were brought to him. On the helm was a crown of gold studded with pearls, sapphires, and rubies. Henry's surcoat was resplendent with the leopards of England and the fleur-de-lys of France. Just as he mounted his gray palfrey, another armor-clad warrior galloped up and saluted him. The two exchanged words that Severin Brigante was too far away to hear. It didn't matter. He had recognized the great knight's gold-and-black banner. Recognized it because it flew from his own standard as well.

"Belden of Harnoncourt," he whispered. He swallowed and found his mouth had gone quite dry. But then the king was riding down the line of troops, calling out words of encouragement as he received their cheers.

"For God!" he called. "For England!"

The clash of battle had begun.

Alix waited quietly for the man all morning and well into the bleak afternoon. She had prepared herself, knowing that he would prefer to sneak up on her. He had done that once before, when he pushed her down the stairwell and claimed her baby's life. Indeed, she was surprised when she heard his approaching footfalls quite clearly, heard them even above the din of the battle that played out in the midst of the forest below.

"Mine," said Archangelo Conti. "My Magdalene."

She turned to face him upon the parapet of Agincourt Castle. Below her someone cried out, a lone voice that Alix heard distinctly and that chilled her. But she could not let herself think of that now. She could not let herself think of Severin and what could be happening. If she wanted to save him—if she wanted to save *them*—then she had to forget what might be happening below and face the demon that confronted her now.

"Not yours," said Alix. "Never yours."

Though her hands had grown quite cold with terror there was no tremble of fear in her voice. She noted with some satisfaction that she had never sounded stronger. For both the first and last time in her life, she felt the cold Maltese Star at her throat glow warm.

"Indeed, you are mine," said the hooded figure. "You were promised to me more than a century ago. You are mine to give and mine to take."

"Because of this?" she wrenched the amulet from her neck and held it high.

Conti gasped.

"You cannot take off the Maltese Star." Conti's words were imperative but his voice had grown soft and wheedling. Alix sensed fear lace it as well. "You have already accepted it. You cannot now undo its power."

"Tell me why you killed my child." whispered Alix.

"To show you that I could do it." Conti giggled and Alix knew that this man's hatred had long ago driven him mad. "Guy of Harnoncourt tried to kill me. I could not allow my Magdalene to bear his son's child."

"But Guy of Harnoncourt's son is your blood grandson. How could you kill something that was part of you and part of the woman that you claimed to love?"

For an instant she could almost feel the turmoil of Conti's confusion but then he laughed again.

"Severin Brigante is a Harnoncourt. 'Tis but a cruel fate-twist that he married you and that the child you carried would have been his. I could not have that. Eventually, after Severin dies today, you must marry again. You must bring forth a daughter who will continue on the tradition that you have already claimed. You remember when you claimed it, don't you, Lady Alix? You remember when you sent the power forth to stay Sir Lancelot's hand?"

"I remember," said Alix. The rain had started to trickle down again and she felt its cool wetness as a benediction. "I remember it well."

"You sealed your fate with that decision." He moved

to reach out for her. "You chose to use the power. Now hurry along—we have a far distance to go before the morrow. You have no idea how long I've waited for you, how many weary roads I've traveled. Your mother . . ."

"My mother?" Alix prompted. She moved the Maltese Star just slightly with her fingers so that it caught the day's light.

Below them the battle played out amid sharp cries and steel-strokes. Alix thought that perhaps this wicked man might refuse to answer her question, but then he spoke up.

"Your mother refused to acknowledge her power," said Archangelo Conti. "Still, try as she might, she could not keep them from you."

"But *I* can keep them," said Alix very quietly. "I can keep them because you killed my baby. You made me the last of my line."

"You chose," said Conti. Again he grew impatient. "You cannot now unchoose just because it suits your whim. There will be other babies. Not Harnoncourt babies, because that whelp Harnoncourt will be dead. But others. Many others. You can have whatever it is that you want."

"What I want," repeated Alix thoughtfully. "I have thought much since first you came to me. I have thought much and so remembered something of great importance. My life had started changing long before that day when Severin bested Lancelot de Guigny on the list fields of Mercier. The change in me started to grow on the ramparts when Severin came to me for reading lessons. It grew more when he helped me to find succor for the child Yvrain and when he taught me to feed deer with my bare hands. In the end this change and newness surged out of me when Severin Brigante Harnoncourt stood in unfair danger from Sir

Lancelot. It is *love* that defeated Lancelot de Guigny and not the curse of this Maltese Star."

"Are you sure?" said Conti quickly, sensing her purpose. "He fights now and the Duke of Burgundy's half brother fights against him. Would you not save him? Would you not use every bit of your power to do so?"

"My mother used no power but love in life's living," replied Alix. "She trusted love alone to protect her and to save her and in the end it—alone—did just that."

"No!" gasped Conti. He lunged toward Alix but he was too late. She held the Maltese Star aloft and in that swift instant the amulet seemed to take in all the gray silver color of a clouded day. It shimmered with life and with power and purpose. Alix had never seen it look so beautiful. But it shone that way for only an instant, because then it was falling, hurled across the ramparts and into the churning chaos of the forest below.

"Fool!" cried Conti. The hood of his cape fell away, revealing the scarred remnants of a disfigured face and eyes that sparkled with evil. "You cannot turn away from your destiny. It will haunt you until it kills you!"

Without another word he leaped up onto the great stone walls of the parapet.

"Don't!" cried Alix, reaching toward him, but it was too late. The man who had once been the great Cardinal Archangelo Conti followed the deadly pathway of the Maltese Star as it led him slowly, slowly to the ground.

For an instant Severin felt himself surrounded by silence. He looked up toward the high hill and saw the Castle of Agincourt bathed in bright light.

Alix.

He had only an instant to think of her, to cherish her, before the din of battle reached up to cover him again. But that instant of loving his wife had been enough. He knew that within its warm confines everything had changed.

The great army of the French floundered in the mud, weighted down by their bright armor, as volley after volley of expertly aimed English arrows punished them to the ground.

"Harnoncourt," said a soft voice beside him.

And without thinking, Severin heard himself saying, "Guigny."

They could have been alone on a list field rather than on this crowded battlefield. They could have had all the time in the world.

Thrust, parry. Thrust, parry. The two knights moved as gracefully as though they were being orchestrated. Thrust, parry. Thrust, parry. While all about them men cried out and the sky grew black beneath a shower of arrows.

" 'Tis over, Lancelot," Severin shouted. "The English are winning against the French. Call retreat and throw yourself upon the mercy of your brother. You saved Burgundy's life at Nicopolis. He will be bound to give you yours now in return!"

Lancelot de Guigny's mouth twisted into a grimace. "My actions never mattered to my brother. 'Tis but my low birth that carried through to him. I have done murders aplenty to further the House of Burgundy, and rapings and pillagings. Before this day ends I will face hellfire for my actions. But I'll not face hell in the solitude with which I have faced life. I'll not die alone. No, not alone. I'll take you with me, Severin of Harnoncourt, if it is the last thing that I do."

What happened next would always be clouded in mystery. Severin felt himself slip in the mud, fall back—and look up.

High above his head he saw a small daystar. He saw it arch closer and closer as Lancelot de Guigny raised his great sword for the kill. Severin felt the earth draw breath, grow still.

And then it was over.

He was being raised by a strong hand and held close within strong arms.

"Did you see that?" said a man's gruff voice. "Did you see heaven's own arrow come down to save you? The same thing happened to me long ago, except it was your father's hand that rescued me. Your father, Guy, who was my brother dear."

The knight's helm was off now and Severin found himself staring into tear-filled, ember-dark eyes that were the exact color of his own.

"I am your uncle, Belden of Harnoncourt," he said. There was great emotion in his voice and there was love. "My sons—your cousins—and I have searched a lifetime to find you. We have come to France to bring you home."

The battle was over.

Henry of England sent for Mountjoy, a French herald who had been sent by King Charles for permission to bury the dead. Henry Plantagenet stood surrounded by his nobles with Severin Brigante, now truly Harnoncourt, squeezed between his uncle and his cousins, Will and Richard.

"We will talk later," Belden had told him. "I will tell you truthfully what happened, long ago, between your father and me. I will tell you, and then you can choose the path you will take."

Choose?

In his heart Severin knew that he had already chosen. On the ramparts of Mercier, with the deer at Haute Fleur, in the safety of his marriage bed.

Each time he held Alix to him, he chose love anew.

And he knew that he would continue to make this same choice instant by instant, hour by hour, day by day—until his path was through.

"To whom belongs this victory?" Severin heard Henry shout to the herald Mountjoy.

"To you, sire!" came the prompt reply.

"And what castle is that which we can perceive in the distance?"

" 'Tis called the Castle of Agincourt, sire."

"Then this be called the Battle of Agincourt!" called out Henry.

His troops cheered and jostled as Severin Harnoncourt looked upward to the high walls that crowned the hillside and smiled.

Belvedere

Twenty-six

It was so right that their first child should be born at home, at Belvedere, but it was even more right that he should burst forth heralding a great surprise.

"This wee one's brought his brother with him," said the Wise Woman as she held the bright-faced babies up for their young father to see. "What a fortunate man you are, my lord Severin, to have such a full family ready-made."

Family.

This is the word that warmed Severin as he held his babies up for the world to see. And what a splendid world it was, filled with the fresh Tuscan sunshine bringing live greening to the far hills—and with his family. Severin watched them all as they crowded close around the castle courtyard to proudly coo and cluck over his young sons.

"They've the light eyes of the Ducci Montaldo," said Lord Olivier, their grandfather, as he ran a rough warrior's finger along one of their chins.

"Indeed, they have not!" cried an indignant Sire Belden of Harnoncourt, their great uncle. "They're dark-eyed like their father and all the Harnoncourt men. Just look yonder at my youngest boys, Godfrey and Robin. Eyes as dark as midnight—just like their brothers, Will and Richard, and their cousin Severin."

"You old fool," scoffed Olivier, growing quite indignant. "Why, a blind man could see . . ."

". . . that this child is related to your sister, Francesca," said his wife, Julian Madrigal, lightly. "They've been birthed barely an hour and already sun spreckles are starting to do the bridge of their nose!"

"Indeed, that is not possible," cried the Lady Francesca, the Wise Woman, as she bent over to inspect her young nephews. "But even if it were, I have been working away in my laboratory and have *finally* come upon the remedy of all remedies . . ."

The others roared with good-natured laughter. Her sun-spreckles had always been the one, true bane of the Lady Francesca's life and she had searched for their remedy with the diligence that other alchemists had applied to a search for the Philosopher's Stone.

"Really," cried Francesca indignantly. "Really and truly this time."

"Ah, Franni," said Belden as he scooped his loved wife in his arms.

From behind their embrace, Julian Madrigal smiled and winked at her son-in-law and then motioned him toward her daughter's room.

Family, thought Severin Harnoncourt as he took the stairs three at a time.

And home.

Because they were all people who had loved Belvedere and, for better or for worse, had called it home.

He thought briefly of Alix's mother, the wise and beautiful Julian Madrigal, who had been the first to say no to the Maltese Star's strong pull. And Alix's father, Olivier Ducci Montaldo, who had traveled back to Belvedere so many years before—and once at Belvedere had begun his journey back to life.

But mostly Severin's mind was filled with Alix, just

as it had been from the first day he'd seen her and just as he knew it would always be.

"Thank you," he said simply, kissing the bright gold of her hair.

"Aren't they beautiful?" Alix said. "We've not had boys born in our family for generations. My mother said they have broken the spell."

"Of the Maltese Star?" whispered her husband. He climbed into the bed beside her so that he could hold his wife close.

Alix nodded.

"It was already broken," said her husband. "First by your mother, Julian Madrigal, and then by you. Bad spells and mischief always break whenever someone takes a stand for love."

"I think so," replied Alix. "And it is so strange but it was Robert who reminded me of that."

"Do you believe that Cardinal Conti was real—or do you think you dreamed him? Belden of Harnoncourt led the search but no one ever found his body."

"He was real," Alix said with conviction. "Real enough to do grave harm had he realized his plans. My mother felt it when he died, she told me. And the Lady Francesca did as well. What was it she said? Ah, yes—it was like the lifting of an oppression."

"There were rumors," said Severin, "of a man kept hidden by the lord Visconti in Pavia. A man gravely disfigured—and insane."

"And now gone forever from all of our lives. Have you picked names for the babies?" Alix asked him.

Severin laughed. "I thought you might have some preference in that."

She looked at him shyly.

"We might name one of them Guy and one of them Belden. I thought in this way we could bring peace to your family at last."

Guy and Belden.

Severin could almost feel his father's benediction shining down upon him and he nodded, too filled with happiness to speak.

But Alix spoke for him.

"Did you know that Belvedere is haunted?" she asked him, settling up high in her birth-bed. "Indeed it is—don't laugh at me. I've seen the ghosts myself. Once when I was a young girl and we were leaving the castle and just recently, now, when we returned. It is the ghosts of my warrior grandfather and his three knight-sons who linger. They stand upon the ramparts of Belvedere. I have seen them. I have heard them."

"And what is it they say?" Severin's voice sparkled with laughter.

Alix turned with bright eyes to face him and to kiss his loved face.

Welcome to Belvedere.

Welcome home.

Embrace the Romances of
Shannon Drake

__Come the Morning $6.99US/$8.99CAN
   0-8217-6471-3

__Blue Heaven, Black Night $6.50US/$8.00CAN
   0-8217-5982-5

__Conquer the Night $6.99US/$8.99CAN
   0-8217-6639-2

__The King's Pleasure $6.50US/$8.00CAN
   0-8217-5857-8

__Lie Down in Roses $5.99US/$6.99CAN
   0-8217-4749-0

__Tomorrow the Glory $5.99US/$6.99CAN
   0-7860-0021-4

DO YOU HAVE THE
HOHL COLLECTION?